"ADMIT THAT YOU FEEL SOMETHING FOR ME."

"Of course I do," she said, deliberately sidestepping the answer she knew he wanted. "You're Cal's brother."

He went terrifyingly still. In a cold, precise voice, he said, "Don't ever set him up as some example for me."

Eden shrank back.

He gripped her shoulders. "And don't back away from me like I'm not fit to wipe his boots."

"Nick . . . " She started to deny any such intent when he plunged his hands into her hair and lowered his head.

"Open your mouth."

Defiantly, she seamed her mouth closed.

"Call it a welcome home kiss if that will ease your conscience."

"My conscience is clear, thank you very much. And yours?"

"I don't have one."

Then he kissed her.

Other Contemporary Romances by
Dee Holmes
from Avon Books

JONATHAN'S WIFE

When Nick Returns

Dee Holmes

AVON BOOKS NEW YORK

This is a work of fiction. Names, characters, places, and incidents either are the product of the author's imagination or are used fictitiously. Any resemblance to actual events, locales, organizations, or persons, living or dead, is entirely coincidental and beyond the intent of either the author or the publisher.

AVON BOOKS
A division of
The Hearst Corporation
1350 Avenue of the Americas
New York, New York 10019

Published by arrangement with the author
Visit our website at **http://AvonBooks.com**
Library of Congress Catalog Card Number: 96-95486
ISBN: 0-380-79161-7

First Avon Books Printing: August 1997

Printed in the U.S.A.

WCD 10 9 8 7 6 5 4 3 2 1

In memory of my father,
Dr. Richard C. Harwood.

Summer and winter and springtime and harvest;
in the Beloved, accepted and free.

Prologue

Boston, 1984

FEBRUARY'S COLD MORNING LIGHT SLIPPED through the slanted blinds and across the satiny white quilt on the floor. Her dress and his slacks lay carelessly on an upholstered chair where they'd been flung the previous night. Her gold hoop earrings lay on the nightstand beside the empty condom box.

Eden Parrish awakened and rolled to the side, reaching for him to hold her, to reassure her, to give her the peace that should follow pleasure.

Instead Nick sat on the bed's edge, leaning forward, stretching out his leg, working his palm on the knee in a massaging motion across the four-week-old surgery scar. He'd been Boston University's most promising hockey star, headed for the pros after graduation, until his knee was crushed in a practice game. Surgery followed, but not even the best doctors could give him back what he'd lost forever—a career in pro hockey. Nick's anger and frustration had led to self-destructive distancing from the other parts of his life. He dropped out of college, ignored his friends and wanted to end his relationship with Eden. Since the accident, Eden knew she'd been the one holding on, refusing to give him up, determined to show him that they could get through this together.

Last night had been her idea, from borrowing a friend's apartment, to dinner at Nick's favorite Italian restaurant in Boston's North End. Her best hope was that their relationship would resume; her worst fear turned out to be the reality.

Carefully he rose, pulling on his briefs. He moved away from her without glancing back. The dim light caught the tallness, the leanness, the muscles that were still impeccably toned to athletic promise.

He walked to the triple windows, snapped the blinds closed and then turned to leave the room.

"Nick, wait."

"It's early. Go back to sleep."

"Come back to bed."

He didn't answer nor did he accept her invitation. Instead, he lifted his slacks from the chair and then picked up her white satin teddy. He concentrated on the filmy material in the same way she'd seen him examine the blade sharpness of his hockey skates.

When he laid it aside, Eden scrambled across the bed, reaching for his blue oxford shirt at the same time he did. Both holding the garment, she kneeling on the bed, he standing beside it, their eyes met. The shirt was stretched as taut as the tension between them. Eden felt her heart beat harder and harder the longer Nick stared at her. His gray eyes were cold and remote and angry. Fury at himself, no doubt, for giving in to her plea to see him one more time before he went home, for wanting to hold on to him when he no longer wanted her.

"I didn't want to say good-bye on the phone," she whispered, praying he cared enough about her to at least understand that.

"This made it harder."

Some scrap of hope within her found life. "I'm glad."

But he gave no quarter. "What do you want from me? Telling you the sex was great? Okay, it was great. It's been great since we started six months ago. But it hasn't made my leg okay. It hasn't given me back my chance to play pro hockey." He paused. "I don't want to hurt you any more than I already have. You need to get a life. Mine's finished."

"It's not finished!"

"Eden, give it up."

She released the shirt, which in some weird way meant releasing him. Giving him up, getting on with the business of finishing her own education, starting her career, moving on . . .

"I left my bag in the other room. Could you get it for me?"

Nick had pulled on his slacks and shrugged into the shirt, the wrinkles numerous, the buttoning process ignored. He left the room and then returned with the nylon pack into which she'd shoved morning-after essentials.

He was careful not to touch her, and it annoyed her. No, on second thought, it infuriated her. Wrapping the quilt around her, she left the bed and grabbed his arm before he could escape.

"I don't like being treated like this, Nick."

"Last night was not my idea."

"I didn't see you objecting. In fact you couldn't get enough."

"And neither could you. So let's just leave it at that."

"I don't want to leave it at that. We have or had a relationship that we both enjoyed. Now you suddenly don't want it, and I'm supposed to smile, wish you luck and disappear."

"For godsake, grow up. Any luck I had ran out when I wrecked my knee. It's no good between us because it's no good for me. Nothing is. It's not going to get good, and in a few years you aren't going to remember what all this was about."

"Not remember! I've been sleeping with you since last September. You think that's going to fade away like a spoiled picnic on a rainy day? Okay, last night wasn't your idea. I wanted to see you and I wanted to be with you. And I'd waited for you to call me, but with typical Nick Scanlon stubbornness, you didn't."

Those gray eyes bored into her. "And this argument is why." Then he sighed, lowering his head and shaking it. "Eden, let it go. Let us go, okay?"

He didn't wait for her to agree or argue some more; he simply left the room.

She hated that she was so angry, that she was deeply crushed by a relationship that she'd known from the beginning would end with Nick's graduation. Admittedly she'd gotten involved with few illusions. Nick Scanlon had been on his way to hockey greatness; he'd had little time for love or for commitments to anything or anyone else.

But for a while he'd wanted her. And he'd gone after her with the same drive and relentless energy he displayed on the ice. There had been no such thing as no; all there had been was the length of her resistance.

And now she was furious that she hadn't resisted, that she'd stupidly fallen in love with him.

She hated even more that the fun they'd had together, the memories of silly times, of serious talks about who they were and what they wanted, were all just past events. Loving him with her body and her heart hadn't been enough.

She showered and dressed in jeans, a turtleneck and a huge BU sweatshirt that hung almost to her knees. She'd forgotten her hair dryer, so she towel-dried her hair, combed it out and pinned it with a big red barrette. She looked all of her twenty-one years. The woman of the night before in the white satin teddy and the green dress with buttons Nick had undone one at a time—that woman had slipped away like a broken fantasy.

With her clothes stuffed into her nylon sack, Eden walked into the kitchen. A jar of instant coffee stood open, granules splattered from jar to mug. Steam coated the window over the sink where Nick had run the water to get it hot.

He put the mug under the faucet, then sipped and grimaced before he looked up. "Want some?"

"No."

He shrugged.

They stood still, each wary despite the four feet separating them. His shirt remained unbuttoned, and she hated that it took all her concentration not to walk to him and slide her hands around him. She resented her volatile emotions that were so raw, so ready to take from him anything he offered. But he offered nothing. His hair was messy, his face divested of anything close to the singular passion they'd shared just hours ago.

The end had come, and yet she didn't move. He didn't either. He wouldn't change his mind, and the longer she lingered over false hopes, the less respect she would have for herself.

Finally he put the mug down and moved toward her. Her eyes widened, and her pulse began to jump.

He slid his hands into her hair, being careful not to dislodge the barrette. Her knapsack was slung over one shoulder, and he didn't disturb that either.

To her horror, her eyes filled with tears. She swept her lashes down, squeezing them shut.

"You're going to make some man happy, Eden."

"I wanted it to be you."

"You made me happy."

"No . . . You wouldn't be sending me away . . . You . . ."

He lowered his mouth and kissed her, his tongue slipping in so easily that Eden felt the fine edge of desire cut into her thoughts. She made herself stand stiff, but she couldn't resist returning the kiss. It wasn't harsh or hurried; it was gentle but not a promise. Their last kiss, the kiss to remember, this final touch of softness from him nearly undid her.

Then, when she realized how vulnerable she was, how much she was going to hate herself when he stepped back, eased her away, instead of waiting for him, she shoved him, stepping back and rubbing her fist across her mouth. Her anger bubbled up and spilled.

"Damn you. I'm glad we're finished. I'm glad I won't have to see you again."

He gave her a long studied look, then nodded as if finally getting the reaction from her that he'd wanted. He moved past her, and she watched while he gathered up his stuff and shrugged into a leather jacket. No hesitation, no second thoughts, no tiny maybes that she could cling to.

He simply walked out the door and out of her life.

Chapter 1

Thirteen years later

ON A WINTRY AFTERNOON IN MID-JANUARY, Eden Parrish was running late. Lonsdale High School had dismissed over an hour ago, and most of the teachers were gone, leaving the halls a hollow echo. Eden had stayed to finish the presentation that she would be giving later that evening to the school board. As the head of the guidance department, this was her first major project since coming to Lonsdale High the previous year. The project was ambitious and risky and very exciting. She already had preliminary approval; tonight would be the final okay.

She made sure that all the pages were in order and that her recent marginal notes were legible before tucking the sheaf of papers into her briefcase.

"No rest for the wicked, I see."

Eden jumped, her head coming up. Seeing who it was, she sagged back in the chair, a smile lighting up her eyes. "You scared me, Cal."

"I can see that," he said, grinning back.

Cal Scanlon was tall and handsome and impeccably dressed. The cashmere overcoat looked as if it had been tailored for him.

"Why are you still here?"

"Just finishing up some things. I didn't expect to see you until later." She closed her briefcase, pushed her chair back and went to the closet for her coat.

"Thought I'd see if I could talk you into dinner. The board will be at my house around nine, so we'll have plenty of time."

"Oh, Cal, I'd love to, but I can't."

She laid her leather gloves and red angora hat on the desk while Cal helped her on with her coat. He bent down and kissed the side of her neck. Eden shivered, his caress sending a languishing feeling of satisfaction and happiness through her. Life was the best, she'd decided in these past few weeks. Her friends, her work and her relationship with Cal all melded together with a rhythm and a substance for which she was grateful.

"Can't is not in my vocabulary when it comes to you," he said, nipping her ear lightly. "I want to turn all your cannots into cans."

"What a sweet thing to say."

"We could skip dinner," he murmured, turning her, kissing one side of her mouth, then the other, before slipping his tongue in. Eden closed her eyes, sliding her hands inside his open coat.

"Hmm," she whispered, kissing him again.

"Is that a yes?"

"That's a You take my breath away and make me not want to think."

"As good as a yes."

"On any other night, but not tonight." She gave him a disappointed look. "I'm sorry."

He drew back, then grimaced. "Don't tell me. The hockey game."

"All the teachers are going. I promised. We're all sitting together, and I really do want to see the game."

"Guess I can thank my little brother for making you into such a hockey fan," he said with a bite of sarcasm. But it was soon gone. He sighed and lifted his hands in futility. "I know, I know, it's the Lonsdale mantra. All-out support for the hometown team."

"You understand and you love to hear about the wins. I've heard you brag to Scanlon customers about what talent the players have."

"I suppose," he muttered.

"In fact, you could come with me."

"No thanks. I know I'm in the minority, but freezing my ass at one hockey game every three years is plenty for me."

Cal would definitely be in the minority. Most of Lonsdale would be at the game. The Wolves were having their worst season, and while that worried fans, they were true hockey lovers. They were there to cheer at the wins and be supportive after the losses.

Eden liked hockey; to say she loved it would be a bit of a stretch. Her memories of Nick playing and getting hurt had killed a lot of her onetime enthusiasm. Still, when she sat in the stands and watched the passion, the power and the obsession of the players, she remembered her college days, recalled her pounding excitement when Nick skated onto the ice. And she had never forgotten her icy terror that day he was hurt. God, it was so long ago, and yet even now, when she stepped into a hockey rink and got caught up in the rough and tumble of high sticking and hard checking, memories of Nick slipped back as clearly as if it had been yesterday.

She buttoned her coat, settled the red angora hat at a jaunty angle, lifted her briefcase and took Cal's arm.

"Okay, so dinner is out. How about a cup of coffee?"

"You're on. And maybe even a quick burger."

Just before she flipped off the lights, she remembered her gloves.

Later that night, the buzz down at Bubba's Sports Bar wasn't about the bruising cold that had gripped Rhode Island for the past two weeks. Nor was it about the game that night and the fourth straight loss for the high school hockey team. And it wasn't about Eden Parrish's new guidance program dealing with teenage pregnancy awareness.

Nick Scanlon had come home after a five-year absence, and that caused winter doldrums in Lonsdale to disappear like ice after a sixty degree thaw.

A few miles from Bubba's, in the rink parking lot, two teenage boys, with their hockey equipment bags slung over their shoulders, ignored the girls trying to coax them into dates for Saturday night.

"Hey, bet that Explorer is his," George commented to Eddie.

"Yeah, ain't seen it before."

"Hear he was a big deal hockey player for a while. A Lonsdale star. Bigger even than you, Metcalf."

Eddie Metcalf shrugged. He was the current "big deal" and high scorer for the Lonsdale Wolves. Eddie liked the limelight. He couldn't get enough of the praise he received when his name was mentioned. His best-on-the-ice status was beyond the reach of any challenger, and being reminded that he still hadn't broken Scanlon's record bugged him. It wasn't like the guy had really gone to the pros.

"He's nothing now, and him comin' in the side door proves it. Shows you he knows he ain't no big star, just some has-been. Ain't like Bobby Orr beamed in from Boston."

"No one since Scanlon has scored six goals in one game."

Eddie scoffed. "Yesterday's news."

"Ain't seen you break his record, Metcalf."

"I'm waitin' on the right game."

"Yeah, yeah." George reflected, "Gotta be cool to just take off and not have no one hasslin' you 'bout nothin'."

"Yeah, cool."

"A kick back kinda life. No parents yellin', no stupid homework, beer when you want it."

"Girls."

"Sex."

The boys elbowed each other and walked toward a white van with a cocky strut.

The girls, shivering, and not interested in nostalgia about Nick Scanlon, had climbed into the van and started the engine, turning the heat to high. The horn blared and a window was rolled down. A perky blonde with lipstick that shone like red chrome yelled, "If you guys don't hurry up, we're leaving without you."

The van's engine rumbled, white exhaust pouring from its tailpipe. The two boys shoved their equipment bags in through the van's rear doors. They climbed in and crawled forward onto the seats.

Eddie Metcalf lifted Liza, the perky blonde, onto his lap, unzipped her jacket and slid his cold hands under her sweater. Her yowl was quickly followed by giggles and a long sigh when he kissed her.

Within a few minutes, the van's headlights came on, and it slipped and slid out of the icy parking lot.

Inside the building, Howard "Poppy" Malone, the rink's full-time manager stepped away from the window where he'd been watching the last of the boys leave the rink.

His office, with its nicotine-yellow walls, had been called the annex to the town dump. Malone could lay his hands on any item in ten seconds, from old Bruins ticket stubs to the game-strategy plans marked up by the Lonsdale coaches.

A single bed covered by a faded patchwork quilt his late wife had stitched hugged one wall. Since Aggie's death, Poppy didn't much like going home to an empty house. Here he had his back issues of *Reader's Digest*, his coffeepot and a TV for the hockey games in winter and baseball in the summer. On the wall, beside a calendar from Essex's Used Cars and Trucks, was an autographed World War II pinup of Betty Grable.

Near the door, a golden retriever lay at the feet of Poppy's unexpected but welcome visitor.

Nick Scanlon had waited until the game had finished and most of the crowd had exited before he'd come into the rink via a side door. Now he was sprawled low in a barrel-backed chair. Lean and dark-haired, Nick looked as though he'd lived his three and half decades twice and found them worse the second time. He had gray eyes, and when he stared, you had a sense he was expecting more than you had any intention of giving.

Expectation, he realized, was like a tough habit to break. Driving back into town, coming here to the rink that had once been his second home, had filled him with anticipation. This was where he'd had hope, where he once shone. His emotions now were a mixture of pensiveness and anxiety. He wasn't sure what to expect, but he was very sure this was where he wanted to be.

He no longer moved with the loose, limber strides that came of full confidence in his abilities. His last hockey game had been played thirteen years ago at Boston University. It was a game he could recall in chilling detail. In fact, it wasn't a game. It was *the* game.

Tonight, however, he'd come to see Poppy, and he'd come because he couldn't stay away. He itched to skate, but not while anyone was watching. Wouldn't do to have the original Beast of the East fall on his ass in front of a crowd.

Poppy poured coffee and handed a chipped Bruins mug to Nick.

"Sure is good to have you back, Nick."

"Good to be home," he responded with genuineness.

Poppy, never one to let a question he wanted answered lie like ungutted road kill, asked, "You been a long time hidin' out to brood about life, you know. You coulda been doin' life instead of thinkin' about what might have been."

Poppy's heavier-than-lead-philosophy was one of the reasons Nick liked him. "You make it sound like I've been in a funk for thirteen years."

"In and out. You been away from here for five, and I'll wager you ain't been practicin' your slap shots."

Nick winced. "Went to a few games in Detroit."

"Sober?"

Nick shook his head, amused. "Poppy, I always could count on you to cut the bull and draw some blood."

"You're still golden, son."

"Not golden. Just a new face."

Poppy poked a finger at him. "It's a good face despite that boneyard of self-pity you're carryin' around. So most people don't know you, so you got messed up, but you're home now. Once word is out that you're workin' here with me and the old stories about you make the rounds—well, a lot of the kids will want some pointers from you."

"Now wait a minute," Nick said, suddenly alarmed at the direction Poppy was taking. "I'm the last one who should be giving advice to anyone."

Poppy's gray-webbed eyebrows came together into a single straight shelf of a scowl before he glanced at Nick's leg. "You got a bad knee, but you're still walkin'. You can still skate, too, if you put your mind to it."

Nick straightened. "Maybe."

"Forget maybe. Try yes."

"You're not going to let me feel sorry for myself, are you?"

"You done too damn much of that already."

"Thanks, pal," Nick grumbled. Poppy was right, but that didn't mean Nick had to admit it.

"None of you guys ever gets too old to hear the truth." Poppy shuffled over to pour more coffee, then reached into a low cabinet and brought out a bottle of whiskey. After adding a generous amount to his mug, he offered the bottle to Nick.

"Better not," Nick said.

Poppy merely nodded and put the bottle away before taking his seat behind the desk. He took a full swallow of the liquid, then closed his eyes to savor it.

"So how's the high school team doing?" Nick asked. "From the few comments I overheard, they played sloppy tonight."

"Tonight? Hell, they've been sloppy most of the season. Coach is doin' double duty with the Squirts, so the big guys aren't gettin' the finer points. And they're all a bunch of horny toads. Too much time figurin' how they're gonna get into some girl's panties instead of concentratin' on the game."

Nick chuckled. The retriever at his feet lifted his head, tipped it a little to one side, his gaze on Poppy's office door.

"Quite a dog you got there. Real pretty. What's his name?"

"Bobby."

"Ah." Poppy grinned. "Like in Orr?"

"Yeah."

"Should have known right off."

The retriever got to his feet and wandered to the door, where he stood for a few seconds, and then ambled back to sit beside Nick, who reached into his jacket pocket and took out a biscuit.

"He don't look like no stray," Poppy said.

"Nope. Won him in a poker game." Bobby lay down, crunching the biscuit.

"Yeah? Kind of a weird bet."

"The guy gave me a choice. Bobby here or sleeping with his wife."

Poppy made a disgusted sound. "Generous bastard. Or was he?"

Nick shrugged.

"Well? Was he being generous or was his wife a dog?" Then he laughed when Bobby whined. "Oops, no offense there, Bobby."

"She was redheaded and stacked."

"And you took the dog?"

"I'd already been to bed with his wife."

Poppy's eyes widened, and then he roared with laughter.

Nick leaned forward and set his mug on the desk. He reached down to scratch the retriever behind the ears. "Besides, Bobby looked like he wanted to move on. Didn't you, boy?" The dog wagged his tail in response. Nick glanced up at Poppy, who now had a scowl on his face. "What is it?"

"The guy know you'd diddled his wife?"

"Not unless she told him."

"He never wondered why you took the dog?"

"Sure. I told him I don't mess with married women."

Poppy guffawed again. "You still got some piss and ginger in you, Nickie."

"Hope so."

Poppy took off the dirty, stained Bruins cap he'd been wearing since Boston won the Stanley Cup in 1972. Scratching his fingers deep into his thick gray hair, permanently dented by the cap, he said, "Sure am lookin' forward to gettin' all caught up with you. Bet you got some stories to tell."

"Not a lot of good ones, Poppy," Nick said in a low, hollow tone. "Some bad stuff you don't want to know about."

Poppy peered at him. "You always were a mystery, you know. Never will forget when you was a kid and you quit the baseball team at two homers away from breakin' a record."

"Did I do that? Don't really remember." But Nick did remember; he remembered too well.

"Your brother didn't quit, and Lord knows he should have. Had to give the kid credit, though. Cal never could play worth a shit."

"Yeah, well, that's ancient history. Who cares now who played and who quit. Besides, you're probably the only one in Lonsdale who remembers." Nick smoothly changed the subject. "I haven't seen Cal yet, but I hear he's doing great.

Running the family business, school board chairman, built that house out on Foxtail Drive, dating the head of the guidance department. Pretty successful. The old man would be proud."

"Yup. Cal's done okay. What are you goin' to do?"

"I just got home."

"You gonna need a job."

Nick peered at him. "You offering me one?"

"Not mine. No way. But we got a lotta parents who're sendin' their kids to that hockey school upstate. Bet they'd love it if they only had to drive them here to the rink."

"You want me to start a hockey school?" Nick asked, incredulous.

"Not right away," Poppy said quickly. "Maybe later on. In the meantime, I was thinkin' like you could give some private lessons. Good money in private lessons."

It was something to think about, Nick realized. He had some money put away, but that wouldn't last forever. Besides, since he was home to get himself back together, a regular job was necessary.

His silence encouraged Poppy. "Let me know, and I'll put the word out."

"Could be no one will be interested."

Poppy scowled. "Then they'd all be a bunch of damn fools."

Nick grinned. "With you in my corner, how could I miss?"

Headlights swung across the window, and Poppy lumbered over to peer out. "Someone forgot something. Happens after every game.

These kids don't take care of their stuff. Parents replace it too quick, too. Had one of them boom boxes here for a month. I mean, how could anyone forget one of them noise crankers. They make enough racket to crack the ice. Kid didn't know where he left it, so his old lady bought him a new one. Then the kid remembered." Poppy rolled his eyes and jerked his cap on low. "Mighty convenient, if you ask me."

The dog got to his feet and wandered to the door, his head cocked to the side.

Nick whispered, "Just one of the kids, Bobby. It's okay."

The dog took that to mean he could hone his greeting techniques. He lumbered out and disappeared into the darkness of the rink.

Poppy started forward, then gripped the edge of the desk.

Nick immediately got to his feet. "You okay?"

The older man winced, pressing his hand to the calf of one leg. "Damn cramps," he muttered. "The doc says I need to cut back on the coffee." He winced again.

Nick knew about cramps. His own knee became unreliable if he sat in one place for too long. He lifted and lowered his leg, stretching it, massaging it with his palm—a ritual he could perform drunk, sober, or stoned. "Why don't you sit. Bobby and I can take care of this."

The dimly lit rink with its unrelenting cold was a stark contrast to Poppy's office. The pathway between the boards that enclosed the ice and the building's walls made for uneven and sometimes slippery walking. The floor creaked and heaved as Nick made his way in the dark.

Bobby had raced toward the main exit door, which led to a sheltered entrance way. The double doors helped to maintain the low temperature inside the rink.

Nick looked around for the lights. The rink had been upgraded a number of times, and the bank of lights had been moved since he was last here five years ago. He was about to go and ask Poppy when Bobby woofed, a deep, cutting sound that usually meant he'd found something he wanted. Nick squinted into the darkness.

Then he heard a thud followed by a woman's scream.

He moved instantly.

"Bobby!" he called sharply. With no lights, he had to go by the scuffle of noise near the door.

"Get off me, dammit!" a female yelled.

"Oh God," Nick muttered, when he found the retriever sitting with his rump planted square on the skirt of the woman's coat.

She was struggling to get to her feet and severely hampered by Bobby's eighty-pound weight. The dog's tail swished back and forth, while his grin said, "see what I found."

A red angora hat dangled from his mouth.

Nick grabbed Bobby's collar and yanked him away. "I don't think she liked your greeting."

The dog slunk back and lay down a few feet away. Nick reached to help the woman. She allowed it, but only until she was standing. Then she pulled away and began brushing at her clothes. Nick's eyes had grown more accustomed to the darkness, but this particular area was deeply shadowed.

Nick asked, "He didn't hurt you, did he?"

"Oh, no," she snapped sarcastically. "It's always been my fantasy to be roughed up by a dog."

Roughed up was a little strong, but he doubted she wanted to hear that. "Look, I'll be glad to pay for any damage to your clothes."

"Of course you will. But unfortunately you can't manage that in the next ten minutes."

He reached for her arm. "Come on into Poppy's office and we'll have a look."

She sidestepped his hand, brushing at her coat, obviously frustrated and annoyed. "No, thanks. There's a mirror in the hot room. I'll make the repairs. Just what I needed," she muttered, "one more thing to make this day entirely too memorable."

"Let me do something," Nick said, feeling useless and trying to calm her. All he needed was some broad filing charges against him for being mauled by his dog. As far as he was concerned, she was overdoing the outrage.

"I have a thought," she said. "Why don't you try turning on some lights." Then, as if he was too dimwitted to understand English, she said, "Oh, never mind." She turned and marched to the hot room, jerked open the door, flipped on the room's interior light and slammed the door closed behind her.

Nick caught sight of her back, the red coat and her black boots. She had brown hair, cut in one of those short flippy styles that must have been covered by the hat Bobby still held clenched between his teeth.

He glanced at the retriever, now settled in with the red hat.

"She's royally pissed, Bobby. And she's gonna be ranting big time when she discovers you have that."

Bobby grinned and tucked the hat tightly between his paws.

"Explaining you have a red fetish isn't gonna cut it. Then again," he said with some amusement, "she sure won't want it back covered with your slimy spit."

Bobby wormed his muzzle deep into the soft wool fabric.

Good God, he'd been home less than twenty-four hours and already he had a problem. "You know, if I'd taken the redhead instead of you, none of this would have happened." The dog whined. "Okay, we're still pals. But listen up, you're going to pay for the hat out of your biscuit allowance."

At that moment, the sidelights came on—the lights Nick couldn't find—and he turned to see her standing near the switch. He stared, and she stared back.

For more than a few moments the silence froze between them. Forgotten was the dog, the hat, the chill of the rink and her outrage. Nick's gut twisted and his mouth felt as dry as sand. Desire tore through him with a sharpness that fascinated him with its power and scared him with its need.

"Jesus, it's you," he whispered, stunned all over again by his intense reaction.

Her blue eyes were wide, her face pale, her voice suddenly husky. "Nick?"

"Eden . . . My God, I can't believe it."

The distance between them was about six feet, but it might as well have been a hundred and six. She was all sophistication and elegance, with a cool maturity that in that instant of longing he found her daunting, sexy and challenging.

She didn't move except to anchor her shoulder bag. Suddenly he recalled that moment before he kissed her good-bye thirteen years ago—the nylon pack, the red barrette, her eager mouth—and he wondered what she would do if he simply tugged her into his arms and kissed her right now. He took a step closer, then halted. Good God, had he lost his mind?

She backed away as if she'd read his thoughts. "I heard you were home. Your mother called and told me."

Nick rested against one of the rink's beams. His knee was raging with a sudden pain, but he'd be damned if he was going to let her know it. "She mentioned that you and she have become good friends."

"Yes, we have."

He couldn't mistake the distancing edge to her voice. Maybe she felt the tension, too, although she looked as if she wanted to run away from him rather than toward him. Once again Nick started forward, but she swung away, grabbing at her handbag when the shoulder strap slipped. He felt the agitation roll off her. Had to be his imagination or a fluke of the night. How in hell could they feel more than a vague curiosity about each other? But curiosity could never burn through his gut like lava. He took a guess that Eden felt the same unwanted heat.

"You're nervous."

"What?"

"Nervous, uneasy, tense. As if you want to run like a scalded cat."

"Run from you? Don't flatter yourself."

But she was on the defensive and they both knew it.

Nick wanted to touch her, to feel her skin and see her reaction. "Just caught you by surprise, is that it?"

"Actually, it was your dog, remember?" She glanced at the bleachers that stretched along the side of the rink. "I was here for the game and forgot my gloves. I came back for them."

"Must be my lucky night," he murmured, watching her, thinking that the path his thoughts were traveling meant major trouble and he didn't give a shit. Seconds beat between them before he said, "Why don't you tell me where you were sitting, and I'll take a look." At her hesitation, he added, "Come on. Given that Bobby and I are not on your random act of kindness list . . ."

That brought a tug of a grin. Not much, but at least the anger had cooled. "Sixth bench. There in the corner under the third heater."

"I should have known. You always liked the heaters." In college, when he'd skated onto the ice for a game, he'd automatically glanced up at the heated area, where she sat for all the home games. When she was there, he always played better.

He found the gloves where she said they'd be.

They were hand-stitched and made of soft black leather.

Nick handed them to her, careful not to touch her. His thoughts tumbled back to when they'd been lovers in college.

Eden had never been overtly sexy, but when he'd seen her walk across the campus those first days of the fall semester, he'd wanted her. He'd flirted and chased and charmed his way into her life with the tenacity only a determined college jock could display.

He quickly learned that she was no bubble-brained coed.

She was on the Dean's list, a member of one of the best sororities, but what worked for Nick was finding out she collected music boxes. To bribe her into a date, he'd blown money on a music box that he'd intended for new skates.

And when they had sex, she liked being on top and he hated being on the bottom. Mostly he won.

Hell, he thought now, their attraction had worked and life had been incredibly simple. Thirteen years ago, and enough shit had gone down since for him to have forgotten even her name. Yet in these few moments, ne had a recollection overload that stunned him.

In an even voice, he said, "Mom told me you head up the guidance department at the high school. You'll have to fill me in on how all that came about."

"Didn't she tell you?" She was obviously surprised Mary Scanlon hadn't given him the details.

"Only that my brother helped you get the

job." The moment he spoke, he knew he'd screwed it. Well, hell, so what. The niceties of conversation had never been his thing as they had been his brother's.

She drew herself up. "Cal recommended me by writing a letter to the school board and being supportive. However, I wouldn't have been hired if I hadn't been qualified."

"Right," he murmured.

"Are you insinuating it was Cal, not my resume?"

He held his hands up and took a step away. "No, ma'am."

She pulled on the gloves, and Nick watched as she eased each finger into its snug sleeve. All put back together now, she looked at Bobby asleep on her hat. "I intend to hold you to a new hat. Exactly like that one." She named a store in Providence that didn't use price tags.

"I'll rush right up there first thing in the morning."

"You do that."

She turned and started for the door.

"Eden?"

"What?"

"I heard you and Cal are dating."

"We are and we're very serious."

He'd heard that, too, but coming from Eden it had more impact. He didn't say anything, letting the implications of her having a sexual relationship with his brother take hold. Something deep and primal licked at his ego and taunted him.

On the one hand, he didn't give a shit who Cal slept with, but Christ, of all the women in the state, did he have to choose his old lover?

His long silence hadn't eased the tension, and she quickly moved toward the exit. Nick let her pass him, still without touching her, but just before she pulled open the door, he said, "I hope my big brother knows how lucky he is."

She hesitated, her gloved hand on the big handle, then slowly turned and looked at him. "No, Nick, I'm the one who is lucky and I couldn't be happier."

He watched her leave, waited a few minutes, then walked over to the boards and looked out at the expanse of empty ice. Bobby, the red hat still in his mouth, came over to sit beside him.

Nick absentmindedly scratched the animal's ears. "Well, Bobby, guess the next thing to do is see if I can still skate."

Bobby whined.

"Then we buy her a new hat."

Bobby woofed.

"Yeah, yeah, yeah, then I pay a visit to Cal. You're worse than my conscience, you know that?" He glanced toward the door. "Since I had her once and broke it off with her, none of this sex shit matters, does it?"

Bobby woofed.

"Glad we agree. Let's say good night to Poppy and go home. Tomorrow we skate and start being civilized."

Chapter 2

EDEN PUSHED OPEN THE DOOR AND STEPPED into the front hall of Cal's roomy two-story colonial house. A maple staircase was directly to her right, and to her left, a wood-paneled study opened into a huge living room.

From there, voices carried out to her, and she glanced at her watch. The school board was here and probably wondering why she wasn't. Promptness mattered to her, and given that tonight was so important, the fact that she was twenty minutes late when she should have been ten minutes early irked her.

She carefully closed the door, hoping to slip unnoticed upstairs and do some hasty repair work before she saw Cal and the others.

Just as she had her foot on the first stair, Cal came around the corner. Eden set down her briefcase and reached for his hand.

He clasped it and said, "I thought I heard your car. Everyone else is here and anxious to get started."

"I know I'm late. Are they annoyed?"

"Of course not. I told them you were going to the game. Was there an overtime?"

"No. No overtime."

He drew her closer and Eden absorbed all his stability and graciousness. What had begun as a friendship after she moved to Lonsdale a year ago had grown into a satisfying and intimate partnership. Tall and distinguished, Cal Scanlon was strikingly handsome. His hair had been recently cut and waved endearingly over his forehead, softening his sophisticated demeanor. He wore a dark-gray suit complimented by a white shirt and a hand-painted paisley tie that fitted him so well that it might have been custom-tailored.

Now his blue eyes studied her with concern. She wanted to burrow into him and forget those moments with Nick.

"Okay, sweetheart, this is more than you just being a little late."

She took a deep breath. "If you'll just give me a few minutes to freshen my makeup and take a few deep breaths, I'll be right in."

He slid his hands under her coat collar, his thumbs brushing lightly beneath her chin. His touch reassured her, but more than that, the man himself steadied her; she was able to gather her emotions back from the dangerous cliff where they teetered.

"Not before you tell me what happened."

The concern in his voice brought a raspy lump to her throat. Cal continued to stroke her chin, pressing his mouth to her forehead. She closed her eyes at the pleasure and began to relax.

He continued, his voice soothing, "Now that I think about it, you were distracted when we spoke this afternoon."

"That call from Dad was unnerving as well as unexpected."

"And you've probably been dwelling on it most of the day."

She nodded. "I don't know how I'm going to handle that."

"The way that's best for you and Jennifer," he said with the authority that made worry a wasted emotion. "The call distracted you and what else?"

"Karen Sims dropping out of school today because she's pregnant and hates the father, who she refuses to identify." Eden shook her head in frustration, and Cal's hands fell away. She added, "Maybe a complicated day does account for me being so scatterbrained. Anyway, I left my gloves at the rink, and since I had an extra ten minutes, I decided to go back for them. Poppy's good about collecting stuff that's left behind, but the gloves were expensive and I wanted to make sure I got them and . . ."

"Sweetheart, get to the point."

"Yes, yes. The main rink lights weren't on, and I was trying to feel my way toward the switch when this huge dog came out of nowhere. I was so startled, I slipped or he unbalanced me. . . ." She shuddered. "I don't even remember. But he wanted my hat, at least I think that's what he was after, because once he got it in his mouth, he plunked himself down on my coat like a prizewinner preening himself on his victory. He wouldn't move and I couldn't get up—" She took a breath, astonished at how fast her heart was beating. "Then your brother was there."

"Nick?" Cal sounded genuinely startled. "Was he at the game?"

"I don't know. I didn't see him if he was." But she knew he hadn't been there. Nick was an icon, permanently carved in Lonsdale's hockey history; his presence would have been noted by those who remembered him and applauded. "In fact, I almost didn't recognize him."

"I heard he looks like he spent the past five years at hard labor in hell."

"I take it you haven't seen him."

"Not yet. But we've got plenty of time to catch up."

They were both silent a moment, then Cal said, "So he got the dog away from you?"

"His dog, not just any dog."

"Really. I hadn't heard about a dog." He drew her against him, whispering, "Forget about Nick and his mutt. Do you want me to tell the committee you're not up to this meeting? I can send them home, add some more wood to the fire and we can relax."

"Oh, Cal, that sounds wonderful."

"Consider it done." He kissed her deeply, his tongue taking possession of her mouth.

She kissed back, wanting to do as he'd suggested; she wanted to curl up in his arms and pretend this entire day hadn't happened.

"You go on upstairs. I'll tell them the meeting is canceled."

He let her go, but she grabbed his arm, responsibilities overcoming her romantic urges. "No, wait. We can't do that. They'll be furious and I wouldn't blame them. They were good enough to come, and I am all prepared. Let me have a few minutes and I'll be right in."

He dipped his head and kissed her again, and Eden slid her arms around his waist under his suit coat. She gripped him against her and felt him stir to life.

He lifted his mouth, murmuring, "You're too tempting, you know that?"

"Am I going to be able to tempt you later?"

"I was counting on you staying."

Eden shivered, welcoming her own arousal. "You'll be the perfect end to an otherwise horrendous day."

He winked. "Then let's get this meeting over with so we can start on the perfect part."

Minutes later, upstairs in the master bathroom, Eden leaned over the sink and shuddered. "Dear God, this is crazy. Shaky over an ex-lover. I haven't seen Nick in thirteen years—it's ridiculous." But even as she sought to dismiss her reaction, the overload of sensations, which Cal's arms had only temporarily quelled, worked their way through her.

From astonishment to incredulity to anger and—most disturbing—an edge of fearful uncertainty. Nick Scanlon had come out of nowhere and she had reacted like a defensive female. By contrast, he was cool-headed, apologetic and so controlled that he made her twice as angry.

Then, as if he'd known that, he baited her by having the effrontery to ask if she was nervous, when she'd been showing him just how nervous she was by being sarcastic and bitchy.

She had an excuse, of course. His dog.

She scowled at her reflection as though the

mirror would reveal the source of her turmoil. Okay, it wasn't just the animal knocking her down, it wasn't just her embarrassment, it was confronting Nick himself. *Face it,* she said to herself, *you expected to run into him eventually. What you didn't expect was to have it happen when you weren't prepared.*

Prepared and controlled and at her best, not caught off-guard. And most certainly she hadn't expected to meet him in a dark ice rink and have him sweeping through her mind like some dangerous erotic phantom.

Erotic phantom, indeed. Nick was merely a man with a painful past who had at last come home. His mother had never sounded happier than when she called Eden. No doubt Cal and he would have plenty to catch up about. As for herself, the best approach was just to be natural. *My God,* she thought, *thirteen years is long enough to heal from a personal tragedy. It's surely more than enough time to forget an old lover.*

She straightened now, lifted her chin, blinked her eyes as if she'd just awakened from a long sleep and threaded her fingers through her hair. She carefully searched for any smudges or dirt marks on her face, then washed her hands. Finally she took makeup and a brush from the drawer of the double-sink vanity and began her repair work.

Ten minutes later, she stepped back and took one last look. She wore a double-breasted black silk suit over a champagne-colored blouse accented by a botanical print gold and yellow scarf. Professional but accessible. None of the frazzled nervousness she'd felt earlier was visible. The encounter with Nick receded as if her erotic phantom had more fertile minds to tease.

She flipped off the vanity lights, left her purse and coat on Cal's bed, and with just her briefcase, descended the stairs and walked toward the living room.

Her presentation to the Lonsdale school board and her time later with Cal were important, she decided. Not an erotic phantom and his dog.

"Good evening, ladies and gentlemen," Eden said as she entered the living room.

The men rose, a courtly gesture that Eden knew came from Cal's influence. Civility and good manners, Cal believed, went a long way toward the betterment of society. The two women nodded and smiled. Cal indicated a chair and fixed her a cup of coffee.

Eden set her briefcase down. "I do apologize. I had a unexpected encounter with an overly friendly dog."

They all made solicitous comments, and Eden gave a shortened explanation, hoping to stave off a discussion of Nick. "I know you all want to get started."

She opened her briefcase when Julie Gallo said, "I heard he'd come home. You and your mother must be pleased, Cal."

Julie was single, a bit flighty and tonight looked as if she'd stepped from the pages of a Victorian ghost story. She wore a white ruffly blouse piped in ebony and tucked into a full black skirt. She sat sideways on a blue tufted couch, her legs folded close to her body and hidden beneath the skirt's folds. She was the newest school committee member and along with Cal, one of Eden's strongest supporters.

"Mom's already fixing all of Nick's favorite dishes," Cal commented, and Eden noted that he'd deftly avoided any mention of how he felt about his brother's return.

Seated next to Julie was Delphine Maxwell. She was in her sixties, short and compact, with gray hair tightly curled and close-cropped to her head like springy Astroturf. She was a grandmother, the organist at the Calvary Methodist Church and had been the school board's highest vote-getter until Cal topped her numbers in the last election.

"My goodness," Delphine said, "I remember Nick at about fifteen when my husband was coaching hockey. He was so impressed with your brother's natural ability."

Cal nodded. "He was once pretty good."

"Good! Come on, Cal, he was one of the best in New England." This endorsement came from Claude Newman, a local lawyer, who had done a great deal of *pro bono* work in Lonsdale. He was married, charming and well respected, despite a recurring rumor that he had a mistress down in Newport whom he visited on Mondays.

Don Tucker, the fourth board member, shook his head sadly. "Too damn bad he got injured. The NHL would have had another Gretzky. Can you imagine the hoopla in town if Nick had come home as an NHL star? Gotta be tough on the guy, knowing he missed that opportunity. A has-been when he never even saw the big time." Tucker was a contractor who built cookie-cutter houses that were ugly but affordable starter homes for young families. Don knew about families. He had six children. The two boys were avid hockey players.

Eden sipped her coffee, listening, but saying nothing.

Cal said, "If we're all done ruminating about Nick, I think it would be a good idea if we got started."

Eden threw him a grateful look, and the exchange between them hummed with promise for later on.

Cal cleared his throat. "Just to make sure we're all up to speed here, Eden is proposing a program to revitalize pregnancy awareness and hopefully raise the prevention rate for our young people." Cal reiterated Eden's past experience in Providence and in her hometown, Chicago, her coming to Lonsdale High after the guidance department head retired and her winning the position because she had fresh ideas. "Basically, we wanted to broaden guidance beyond assisting students in choosing the right college or tech school. With the mushrooming pregnancy rate, this was an apt area to try and inject some answers—"

Delphine interrupted, "I heard that Karen Sims dropped out of school today. Is that true, Eden?"

Eden nodded. "She's three months pregnant and hates the father. The latter being the reason why she quit school."

"Why would she get pregnant by a guy she hates?" Don Tucker asked.

"Obviously she didn't hate him when she had

sex with him." Cal's succinctness told Eden he wasn't pleased by yet another side issue.

This time Eden didn't agree. Karen Sims and her pregnancy were the issue. This was exactly the kind of problem she hoped could be prevented by her program. "From what Karen tells me, the father, whom she won't identify, isn't interested in being the father-to-be and told Karen she should, quote, get cool and get rid of it, unquote."

"Nice and supportive, isn't he?" Cal muttered.

"Abortion would be a terrible choice," Delphine said. "I hope you discouraged her, Eden."

"It's not Eden's job to encourage or discourage. She just presents the choices. And that choice is Karen's." Claude walked over and poured himself more coffee. "You're too rigid, Delphine."

Eden and Cal glanced at each other. Both were aware of the divergent views of Claude and Delphine on a number of topics. Whether the board members' opinions added insight or stirred controversy, the end result was always spirited debate. Lonsdale voters, too, had differing ideas and they consistently made clear in election after election that they wanted a diverse school board.

Now Delphine leaned forward, taking off her glasses and holding them like a tool to keep her hands still. "And you'd know all about not being too rigid about right and wrong, wouldn't you?"

Claude narrowed his eyes. "And what in hell is that supposed to mean?"

"Don't play us for fools by pretending ignorance," she snapped back. "Everyone knows you're carrying on some clandestine affair."

"Well, everyone is wrong!" Claude set his cup down, the rattle on the china saucer very loud.

"We're getting off the topic here," Cal said, holding up a hand. Claude glared at Delphine, and she sat back, putting on her glasses with an ease of motion that said she'd won the round.

Unable to resist a final comment, Delphine added, "You have a patient and long-suffering wife, Claude, that's all I have to say."

His neck reddened and he lifted his suit jacket from a nearby chair. "I don't have to listen to this crap."

Cal intercepted Claude at the door.

"Forget about her." Cal said in a low voice. "She's just blowing smoke."

"My life and my marriage and what I do and don't do with them is none of her goddamn business."

"Exactly. And if you leave, you're as much as admitting she's right."

Claude scowled, then nodded.

The two men returned, and Cal immediately began speaking. "Karen leaving school begs us to find some solutions to an entrenched problem. Solutions that will work. Eden, why don't you lay out what you have, and then we can ask questions."

Eden took a sheaf of pages from her briefcase. "What I've tried to do is keep this presentation simple, with the emphasis on one or two changes rather than a dozen. One of the recurring links to teenage pregnancy is not enough information."

"Eden, may I just add something?" Delphine asked.

"Delphine," Cal said, clearly irritated by her, "why don't you wait until Eden is finished."

"It's okay," Eden said.

"When there was very little information and not the availability of condoms, safe sex pamphlets, abortion clinics and counseling centers, there weren't these problems. Shame kept young women pure, and it worked better than this current blizzard of information."

"It was a different time. There were more factors than just girls fearing being shamed and ostracized. Boys were less aggressive, families more traditional and divorce was the exception. Life seemed simpler, but what's going on today went on years ago. We just didn't hear about it."

"Because people were ashamed to talk about it and young girls were sent away to have their babies and those children were given up for adoption."

Eden swallowed, keeping her eyes wide, careful to show little reaction. Cal caught her eye and stepped between Eden and Delphine. "Let me get you more coffee, Delphine."

Don Tucker said, "Look, this is all very interesting, but I promised my wife I'd be home early. Let's listen to Eden and forget the side issues none of us are going to agree about."

"Don's right," Julie said. "Though I respect your view, Delphine, information should always be as full and complete as we can get. If Eden can get the attention of these kids and make them think about the consequences of their behavior, that's not a negative."

Both Don and Claude agreed. "Afraid, you're outvoted, Delphine," Cal said. "Eden?"

"These are the two principles I want to emphasize. Information is the best protection, but abstinence is the guaranteed protection." She went on to explain her view that the guidance department should work in conjunction with the parents to find solutions rather than taking them from a special interest group or a department in Washington. "I want to bring in students with babies and let them tell what it's like to have a child when you're still a child. And I want the kids to realize they can accomplish incredible things by their lives and their influence if they don't get trapped by the temporary pleasure of sex. Once they have a child, their life will never be the same."

"Pretty ambitious, Eden," Claude said. "You're working in a culture seeped in sexual activity."

"But kids are kids. They want to be loved, they want to be popular, and they're struggling with moral choices." Despite a few skeptical looks, Eden emphasized that most kids crave discipline and structure and that they weren't much different from the boys or girls of Delphine's day. "Karen left school because she hates the father, who's saying he doesn't want her. That's nothing but rejection. Karen is embarrassed and ashamed, and so she's hiding to avoid being unwanted and unloved."

"Makes sense."

"I want to be tactful with this, so if you're all

agreed I'll start with the parents. From the calls I've had in the last month, the majority want some changes implemented."

By the time Eden finished her presentation, she had answered many of the board's questions. Don excused himself, as did Delphine. Claude and Cal had their heads together on a local political issue.

Julie put her empty coffee cup on a brass-colored tray, then stacked the others. "I'm so impressed, Eden. This project has real potential."

"I hope so."

Eden carried the tray to the kitchen and Julie followed with the coffee carafe.

"Can you believe Delphine accused Claude of infidelity? If Cal hadn't intervened . . ." Julie grinned, her eyes mischievous. "But it might have been interesting."

"It's all gossip."

"Where there's smoke."

"You said that about Cal and me."

"And I was right—about the smoke, I mean. It didn't take long to find the fire. I've seen the way you two look at each other. You obviously adore each other, and I have to say you make a dynamite couple." Julie rinsed out the cups and put them in the dishwasher.

Eden smiled, finishing up in the kitchen and turning off the lights. She hadn't given even a passing thought to Nick since she'd come downstairs. And she knew why. It wasn't complicated or mysterious or elusive. It was very simple. She loved Cal.

To Julie she said, "Cal and I do make a great couple, don't we."

It was not a question that needed to be affirmed.

Chapter 3

"God, I thought they'd never leave." Cal loosened his tie and took off his suit jacket, tossing it on the back of the executive desk chair in the den. Just minutes ago, he'd added logs to the fire while Eden said good-bye to Julie.

Eden curled into the corner of the sienna leather couch, and kicked off her shoes. She pushed her fingers through her hair and took a deep breath. "I thought the presentation went well."

Cal poured two snifters of brandy and handed her one. "I never had any doubts. They're all so impressed with you that you could have given it to them in French and they would have bought it." He sat down beside her and stretched out his legs. "For hours, I've been looking forward to this"—he sipped from his glass, savoring the brandy, then murmured—"and being alone with you." He slid one hand along her thigh.

She raised her own glass, her face taking on a thoughtful frown Cal had seen often. It usually predicted a discussion of some sort about her job at the high school. He grimaced. Tonight he'd talked all he wanted about school plans and problems.

He moved his hand higher. "You're tense. Relax."

"You make the goals I presented sound like snake oil."

Cal groaned inwardly. He knew that tone, an artful combination of defensiveness and irritation. Most of the time he backed off. "You have to admit, sweetheart, it is very ambitious."

"Of course it is. I wasn't hired for wimpy and cautious ideas."

"I was making an observation, not a criticism," he said, soothing her and damning himself for his careless choice of words. "I just don't want you to be disappointed if it doesn't work."

"Wait a minute." She straightened, pulling away from him just when his hand slid between her legs. "You assured me this could be done. Now you sound as if you're expecting some roadblock or even worse. You have no confidence in me."

Cal lifted his hand away and sat forward. He was unsettled by the wideness of her eyes, which always meant questions and quizzing which he neither wanted nor interested him tonight. Trying to head her off, he said, "I have all the confidence in the world in you. But the parents and the kids may not be cooperative. Hell, there are a thousand divergent opinions out there. You saw a bit of that tonight. The moralist versus the liberal. I want you to succeed, but I also want you to be realistic."

Eden sighed. "I'm sorry. I'm being ungrateful and egotistical."

"You're enthusiastic and believe in what you're doing. God knows that in itself should get you an accommodation. If more guidance counselors cared as much as you do . . ."

"I know," she said with a grin, expanding on his compliment by adding, "the world would be better and safer, and crime would drop thirty percent."

Cal chuckled. "Hmm, we've had this conversation before, haven't we?"

"A few times. I wasn't being fair. You have been and are very supportive."

"I want to be." He watched her. "In more ways than just backing you in your plans to keep Johnny from screwing Janie and Janie from lifting her skirts and inviting it."

She raised her eyes and looked at him over the rim of the snifter. "You mean supportive about the phone call I had this afternoon from my dad."

"That you've been thinking and worrying about ever since."

"Only because I have to call back and give him an answer and I don't know what to say."

Cal stood, slid his hands into his trouser pockets and walked to the twin windows that looked out on the frosty night. The grandfather clock in the front hall boomed eleven o'clock. His own opinion in this particular matter was so strong and so clear-cut that it escaped him why Eden, who rarely dithered about anything, couldn't see it from the same standpoint.

Glancing back at her, he hoped his own impatience wasn't showing. "Tell him to call Jennifer's parents and say no."

"It's not that simple." She ran her finger around the rim of the snifter. "Maybe it is that simple. Maybe if I'd just said no in the first place . . ."

Firmly Cal said, "It would be moot and if you had realized that earlier, you wouldn't have forgotten your gloves at the rink and tangled with Nick's mutt."

She nodded, placing the snifter on the table. She perched on the edge of the couch, arms folded across her knees.

He sat down beside her. "Come here."

She leaned against him, but clearly not to cuddle.

"Cal, what am I going to do?"

"About Nick? Nothing. Given his tendency to come and go at will, he'll be gone in a few weeks, if not days."

Cal took a long swallow of brandy. She touched his jaw where the muscle tensed.

"I wasn't talking about Nick. I was talking about calling Dad back. Never mind." She paused when he scowled as if she knew he didn't have the answer about Jennifer. Only she did. Touching his cheek, she drew her finger across his mouth. "You're upset about Nick, aren't you?" He knew she was searching his expression for something more complex than a returning brother that most of the time Cal viewed as a wandering has-been. Long ago, Cal had concluded that Nick was a master of disrupting the family with his selfish attitude and complaints about past failures.

"Want me to be honest? Then, yes, I'm upset. He arrives, causing havoc and getting up everyone's hopes that he'll stick around for longer than five minutes. Then he disappears again. This time won't be any different. Of course, Mom is planning a welcome home party to honor the prodigal son, who will then disappoint her again by leaving and starting the cycle all over again. In the meantime, we'll all have to listen to the usual rehash of poor Nick and his failed hockey career and on and on."

"Cal, that's not quite fair," Eden said rushing to Nick's defense. "He was hurt and unable to play. That's not the same as failure because he couldn't cut it. After the surgery on his knee and being told he'd never play professional hockey—my God, I've never seen anyone so devastated. You were there. You saw how torn up he was."

"That was thirteen years ago, for godsake. What has he done since? Drink? Prowl around? Sleep around? Make everyone in the family crazy? Now he's back and . . ." He let his voice trail off, getting a grip on his emotions. "Look, he's my brother, I love him, but I also know him better than anyone else. I could name a dozen things he's quit on. Even the family business. I worked at Scanlons for years when Nick was too busy chasing a hockey puck. Then Mom asked him to come in and help after Dad died. I'd lost Betsy and Nick knew how torn up I was."

"Are you saying that Nick refused to help?"

Cal heard the astonishment in her tone. His father's fatal heart attack and his wife being killed by a drunk driver had happened in the same year. Cal had been so devastated that for months he could barely function.

"He didn't refuse. He worked, but only for a

short time. We had a disagreement about who had put the most time into Scanlons over the years. It was silly and stupid, but he got all pissed, packed his things and left town. That was five years ago. Now he's back, and we're supposed to roll over in awe or sympathetic understanding. I'm never sure which."

"A sibling disagreement seems like a minor reason for a five-year absence."

"With Nick, any excuse works." He waved away any further analysis she was contemplating. "I realize you had a fling with Nick when you two were in college, but I know him better than you do," he said flatly.

"I wasn't questioning you."

"Thank you, God." He addressed the ceiling before slipping his hand around the back of her neck, drawing her toward him and kissing her. "Besides," he murmured, nuzzling her throat, "I don't want to talk about Nick. I want to get you naked."

She pulled back a little. "I have to ask you this."

"Unless it's about whether we make love down here or upstairs, the answer is no."

"You don't know the question."

He sighed. "Let me guess. You want to know if I'm frothing with jealousy because my kid brother and you were once lovers."

"It would be perfectly understandable if you felt awkward."

"Me? Awkward?" He laughed. "What about awkward for him? He's the one who walked away from you. Oh, pardon me. Limped away from you."

She looked a little stunned at his sarcasm, but then she had rarely discussed Nick with Cal except in the most general terms. Cal preferred it that way.

"I apologize," he said with an exasperated sigh, but a moment later added, "Dammit, I'm not sorry. I've watched him worry my mother and infuriate my father. For years Dad cajoled and begged Nick to pull himself together. His going to the NHL was history, and the sooner he accepted that and got on with life, the better it would be for everyone. Has he done that? No. Does it matter to anyone? No. You heard them tonight. Poor Nick. I heard it at the store today. And you, sweetheart, you come here all flustered because of him and his mutt. I mean, the guy's a loser, and all of Lonsdale treats him like some long-lost hero because one time he was scouted by the NHL and set a scoring record in high school hockey."

Eden searched his face. "You're really angry with him, aren't you?"

Cal framed her face and kissed her deeply and thoroughly until she relaxed against him. In a softer voice he said, "I'm weary of his rebellion and his self-centeredness. He never fitted in and instead of trying to, he looked for ways to point out how different he was. I'm not angry as much as annoyed. And he's going to annoy me even more if he keeps intruding on us."

"He can't intrude on us."

"Good. Now can we quit talking about him for at least twenty minutes?"

"You mean it's going to take that long?" she said in an amused voice as she unbuttoned his shirt and fanned her hands over his chest. "There is a definite advantage to sleeping with the school board chairman."

"Hmm, you know just what to do to get my vote."

"And what exactly is that, Mr. Scanlon," she asked, slipping her hand over the bulge in his trousers.

"That's it," Cal whispered, closing his eyes at the pound of pleasure.

A few minutes later they were kissing their way up the stairs and tumbling onto his king-sized bed. Clothes were discarded, breathing accelerated, groans of desire were the only sounds in the room. Cal lifted her astride him and cupped her breasts while she tossed back her head.

"You feel so good," he murmured, "so right."

"Make me come," she whispered, and for an instant Cal was sure he saw a flash of desperation. Odd, he thought, for she was obviously aroused and always honest when she wasn't. But then her knees pressed into him and made his own craving border on pain.

Joined deeply, Cal gripped her hips, moving her into a riding rhythm that sent him soaring.

He felt her climax, knew the arch and the pant followed by quick puffs of breathing, and then his own culmination drenched him.

She lay replete atop him. Their breathing evened out, and Cal felt settled, satisfied and content. It just didn't get any better, he decided, his thoughts musing on how fortunate he was to have Eden.

Unlike his brother, he'd never cruised through

bedrooms; his discernment when it came to women had never been in question, not when he dated in college or when he married Betsy Gordon, a Brown graduate and a member of its faculty. Even after her untimely death, Cal waited over a year before he began dating. Even then his enthusiasm for another relationship wavered. He had his community work, the management of Scanlons and his friends at the country club.

Eden's arrival and work at the high school had brought them together first as colleagues and friends. But to his surprise and delight, his respect grew into fascination, and he began to court her. They saw each other a number of times before becoming intimate. The fact that she was once his brother's lover wasn't an issue as much as a curiosity. His taste in women and Nick's were as dissimilar as their views on success and responsibility.

Now, as Eden kissed his chest, his neck, his mouth, lingering a few seconds, then slid off and curled up next to him, Cal realized that Nick was definitely the big loser when it came to Eden.

Cal cradled her, brushing his mouth across the top of her head. "You were incredible," he whispered.

"So were you."

Better than Nick? The question jumped to life in his consciousness and hovered like an old bitterness. Of course he was better. He'd always been better. All anyone had to do was look at their lives. Cal's was successful and Nick's was a mess. And what better proof did he have than the presence of the lady he'd just made love to.

"Stay with me tonight," he murmured, feeling his arousal come to life again.

"Oh, Cal, I can't. It wouldn't set a good example. Head of the guidance department shacked up with the head of the school board."

"Spending one night together isn't living together. Besides, everyone in town knows we're lovers."

"I don't want to flaunt it. Especially with the pregnancy awareness program still in its early stages."

"Ah, discretion."

She played with the hair on his chest. "And you agree with me."

"My cock doesn't."

She grinned, glanced at the bedside digital clock. "Once more."

Once became twice, and by the time Cal stood by the front door kissing her good night, Nick was the furthest thing from his mind.

Toward the end of the week, Nick's homecoming dominated the chatter in the halls of Lonsdale High School. Words such as *star*, *stud*, *sexy* and *tragic* were bandied about, as though everyone had a piece of Nick's personality and wanted to show everyone else what they knew. Nostalgic recollections of the days when Nick ruled the ice at the Lonsdale arena predominated.

Eden stayed at a distance from the talk, thinking that Cal did have a point about Nick breezing in and whipping the town into a frenzy.

She hadn't encountered him since her collision with his dog, and she told herself she was glad. That shock of recognition followed by her instant burst of old desire had unnerved her. But that had now passed, and she was quite sure her emotions wouldn't be rattled again. Scowling, she recollected that he hadn't kept his promise to replace her red hat. She sighed, telling herself it didn't matter. Nor did Nick. If there ever was someone she'd put firmly in her past, it was Nick Scanlon.

That afternoon, like the past three, she'd concentrated on scheduling informal sessions with parents who wanted their sons and daughters participating in the pregnancy awareness program. Eden had been adamant about keeping the word *pregnant* in the forefront—even for the guys. The condition involved the boy as well as the girl and to put all the burden on one side sent a subtle message that only the girl had the problem.

She had one appointment before going home, and she quickly cleared her desk and closed up her file drawers and was about to get a cold soda when Karen Sims' mother arrived.

"I'm just so upset about all of this," Linda Sims said, clearly trying to hold her emotions in check. She was tall and gangly and hunched over. She wore a loose-sleeved coat, which she'd unbuttoned to reveal a waitress's uniform. Obviously she taken time from work.

"I'm glad you came in," Eden said, indicating a chair. Karen's mother perched on the edge. "I promise not to keep you too long."

"It doesn't matter." She shifted in the chair as if she wanted to avoid the whole issue and knew she could not. "Pregnant, quitting school, refusing to have anything to do with the father, not wanting to tell who he is—I just don't understand it. It's like my daughter has become some weeping stranger and no matter what I do or say, she just won't come out of it."

Eden took a deep breath. She was supposed to sympathize and she did, but she also knew that being too understanding and solicitous delayed what had to be said.

"Mrs. Sims, Karen is dealing with some huge changes and she's going through a period of self-pity. And what better place to find comfort than you?"

"I want to help her," Linda said. "What with having to work, worrying about bills, and not being home as much as I should be, I feel like I've failed her. I've tried to teach her right from wrong."

"And you taught her well. Karen knows right from wrong. She's a sweet girl with a great deal of potential."

"I so hoped she'd go to college and be—" She shrugged. "What does it matter now?"

"And be what?"

"She wanted to be a nurse, which made me real happy. That was what I wanted to be. Once. But then I met Tony and nothing else was important. I was seventeen and thought I was in love. Hah! What a fool I was! Later, when I got pregnant with Karen, the real Tony came out. He resented that he didn't get all the attention, and after Karen was born, he hated being stuck with a kid." Her voice rose and fell, breaking occasionally. "Eventually we divorced, and I vowed that Karen would never feel like she'd missed out on having a father. I could be both parents. I thought I was doing a good job."

"You were doing a good job and you still are."

"Then why did this happen?" Linda asked, her voice rising to a high pitch. "I warned her enough about sex and boys and what they wanted."

"She thought she was in love," Eden said evenly, feeling as if nothing she said was going to reassure Linda Sims.

"Love?" she spat. "At fifteen? I thought I was in love, too. Lord save us. Like mother, like daughter." When Eden said nothing, Linda leaned forward and narrowed her eyes. "That's what you're thinking, aren't you?"

"Actually I was thinking how little things have changed. A teenage girl in love is a universal. I, too, was madly in love in my mid-teens. So are all Karen's girlfriends. What we adults view as silly crushes are serious relationships when you're young and thinking about love and honor and one special boy who will make all your dreams come true."

Linda scoffed. "What a joke. Nothing changes, does it?"

"But that means that we need to explore solutions."

"So why did you call me in here?"

"Karen needs your help, but not your worry and self-blame. That will keep her from taking control of the situation and moving forward."

Linda scowled, confused. "You're saying I shouldn't be a supportive mother?"

"I'm saying that real support isn't just sympathy." Eden paused, then plunged in. "I don't want to mince words, Mrs. Sims. Karen is distraught because of her own choices, ones she made with no thought of the future beyond her own fantasies. First she chose to have sex—"

"Now wait a minute! You're wrong! Karen told me he seduced her into going all the way."

Eden shook her head. "He told her that if she really loved him, she'd make love with him."

"He seduced her," Linda said adamantly, clearly determined to make her daughter the victim.

Eden said emphatically, "He lied to her to get what he wanted and she believed him. With the same trust, she honestly believed she and her baby's father would build a life with their baby. Now she knows that was all baloney and she's feeling hurt and victimized."

"The bastard tricked her," Linda snapped with enough vehemence for Eden to guess that this was what had happened between Linda and Karen's father. Then she glared at Eden, spilling her anger and frustration. "Don't look so all-knowing. You don't know what it's like to love someone and have them dump you."

Now Eden was very sure the subject was Tony and Linda rather than Karen and the nameless father of her child. "Look, Mrs. Sims, maybe it would be better if we continue this discussion at another time."

Linda stood, closing her coat in an overlapping motion, clearly agitated. "You're blaming Karen, and I won't stand for that. Why aren't you looking for the kid who did this to her? He's going to walk away like Tony did. Just walk away like all he's leaving is yesterday's garbage."

Her face was red, the pulse in her neck jumping.

Eden was getting concerned. "Please calm down."

"Well, isn't that what's going to happen?"

"I don't know. Of course, it's possible. Karen isn't helping by keeping his name a secret. She's made a series of choices. She chose to have sex because she thought she was in love, when the boy was only scoring. Then she expected the boy to respond with the love and commitment she'd pictured, because she'd proved she loved him. She believed he'd be responsible, as young couples are in idealized love stories. Since the boy messed up the picture, she's made other choices to quit school to pay him back, to salve her crushed pride, to worry you and finally to weep and wail because no one understands her."

Linda Sims had sat down again, her body rock-still except for her hands twisting her purse strap, her mouth set in a grim line. In that moment, Eden realized that in laying out Karen's choices, she'd struck at the choices and the emotions that Linda Sims had experienced with Tony. "That's all I was to him," she said in a monotone. "Just yesterday's garbage."

Eden rose and came around the desk, wanting to say something comforting. But before she could fashion some encouraging words, Linda Sims came out of the chair, tears streaming down her face.

Eden reached for her hand to try and calm

her, but her eyes were wild. She shoved Eden away. "My daughter isn't yesterday's garbage! She's good and sweet and that boy has to pay for what he's done to her!"

Alarmed now, Eden started for the door.

"Dammit, you think I'm crazy, don't you?" Linda shouted.

"No. I think you were badly hurt and you don't want that to happen to Karen."

"And it won't!" Her voice rose to a shriek. "I won't let it!"

The noise had attracted attention. Eden's office door burst open. Paul Bagshaw, the principal, followed by Evan Corrigan, a senior, hurried in.

"What's going on?" Paul asked.

Linda had turned away, her face buried in her hands.

"It's okay, Paul. Linda and I just got a little emotional. Evan," she said to the senior, "will you go and get us two cans of Coke?" She handed him some money.

"Eden, this is very troubling. Perhaps we should call someone."

She shook her head adamantly. "We're fine. She was upset, but it's going to be okay."

By the time Evan returned with the Cokes, Linda had sagged into a disconsolate lump in the chair. Eden urged the others out.

"I'll be right outside if you need me, Eden."

Eden nodded and closed the door. She popped the tops on the cans, urging one into Linda's reluctant hand. "Drink some." Linda did, swallowing and then rubbing the cold can on her cheek. Her voice was husky, her anger gone. "Why didn't you throw me out?"

"Because you love your daughter and when you love someone and don't know how to help, you get frustrated and angry. No one can blame you for that." Eden sat on the edge of her desk, her manner open, her voice soft. "I care about you and Karen and her baby. I care that all of this turns out in the best possible way for all of you."

"The best possible way," she repeated dully. "Is there such a thing now?"

Eden leaned down and patted her hand. "Yes, there is. I promise you there is."

"And what about the father?"

"I'm going to continue trying to find out who it is."

"And if you can't?"

"Let's focus on that when and if we get to it."

Linda Sims got to her feet, gathering the folds of her coat around her. "Maybe I can get Karen to tell me. I'll try."

After Linda had gone, Eden sagged into the vacated chair. Her heart was pounding and her neck ached from the built-up tension.

Paul stopped in, briefcase in hand. "You okay?"

"Just exhausted. Paul, is there some way to know when you've stepped into a hornet's nest?"

Paul chuckled. "You mean, before you get stung? Dealing with parents does occasionally bring the unexpected. I have total confidence in you. Cal and I were playing racquetball the other evening, and he bragged about you and the board's enthusiasm. The Sims woman is probably an aberration."

"I hope so. Otherwise I'll be an emotional mess before the school year ends."

Chapter 4

SINCE THE PREVIOUS SPRING, EDEN HAD lived on Winesap Road in a sandalwood shingled cottage with gray-blue trim. She'd made an offer to buy when she saw the generous backyard and the park across the street. The former owner had showcased the front yard with tulips, daffodils, hyacinths and stately purple lupines. Eden had little doubt she'd been beguiled; she probably would have been more objective if the season had been midwinter. The house was small and had none of the spaciousness and grace of Cal's, but she liked its snugness and its proximity to the high school.

At four in the afternoon, darkness was already descending. Eden had just made herself a mug of hot tea and was sitting down to examine a new music box Aunt Josette had sent her. She'd begun collecting music boxes more by accident than by design after her mother died of pneumonia-related complications. Eden was only seven. Her father had brought her a music box that featured a song her mother had often played on the piano. He had been only minimally successful in cheering her, but the box remained one of her favorites. Her Aunt Josette, who had helped raise Eden, had found this one, according to the enclosed note, at a close-out sale down in Chicago's Loop. Eden needed to call and thank her, which in turn reminded her that she also had to call her father.

While speaking with him a few days ago, Eden had explained that she needed some time to make a decision about Jennifer. He hadn't argued—she was well aware of her dad's feelings. Hers were in question, too, sliding between anxiety and curiosity. Yet this limbo of indecision allowed her a grace period.

She wound the key at the side of the box. Tiny glass kittens chased a mouse to the strains of "Some Enchanted Evening." Either the song was a spoof on what cats think when they chase mice or the maker made an error in selection. Eden studied the details as the kittens slowly circled the mouse. She was about to check and see if she had any music boxes by this particular maker when the doorbell rang.

As she set the box on her desk, Killer, her three-year old husky-shepherd, wandered in from the kitchen.

At the second ring she opened her front door to a blast of cold air that made her shiver. Her dog tried to nose his way past her.

Sitting on her doormat, ears drooping and tail swishing, was a golden retriever. Dangling from the dog's mouth were white cords attached to a lavender gift bag.

Eden chuckled while Killer sniffed.

"Hmm, let me guess. Since I don't know any goldens who work for a delivery service, you must be my hat thief." She could hardly hold a grudge against such a winsome dog. "Not only are you bringing a gift, but you managed to reach one paw up and push the doorbell. Quite a feat, I'd say."

By this time Killer's tail was wagging and his ears were laid back in welcome. The retriever tipped his head, wiggled and swished his tail faster, clearly wanting to be relieved of the lavender sack. The dog deflected the resistance Eden would have made at seeing Nick standing there.

"I'll make a bargain with you. You can come in for a cookie if you promise not to bite when I take the bag."

The dog sprang to his feet. Eden took the sack, while the two animals strolled into the house like long-lost pals.

She took a step outside and peered around the doorjamb. "Very clever."

Nick straightened from where he was leaning against the decorative molding around the front door. Despite a heavy jacket with its collar turned up, he looked cold. His grin, however, was far too devastating for a man she'd been happily avoiding.

"I was afraid you'd slam the door if you saw it was me. Bobby's more charming, and since he was the hat thief, I figured this was his responsibility." He took a step closer to her.

"Well, I guess it worked, since Bobby's inside and you're still out here."

"I could be persuaded to accept a cookie, too."

She folded her arms, refusing to smile, although she knew her eyes gave her away. "You're far too engaging, Nick Scanlon."

"And I only bite on special occasions."

"I'll try to avoid any of those."

Dusk descended. Two footsteps separated them. At six feet, he loomed over her five foot five. Yet in those intimate college days so long ago, they'd fitted together like a study of sensual grace. Eden firmly erased the remembrance, reminding herself that old fantasies bring new trouble.

He stood patiently, as if making any move would be suspect. For her, doing the natural thing and inviting him inside wouldn't be natural at all. Their past precluded spontaneous invitations and risked coded ones. In just these few moments, electricity sparked. Nick wasn't just an old lover; he was Cal's brother, and Eden was as aware of that as she was of Nick himself.

Just Mary's son. If she could just keep him in that context . . .

And after all, he had come for a reason. And he'd brought Bobby to apologize. And it would be horribly rude to say thanks and send him and his dog away. And, and, and . . . Just the same, she wouldn't be that rude and crass to anyone.

She stepped back, holding the door open and then closing it once he was inside.

He began to unzip his jacket and then hesitated, as if he expected her to tell him not to bother because he wouldn't be staying long. Which, of course, is what she should have been saying.

"Would you like a drink?"

"What are you having?"

"Earl Grey tea."

He frowned.

"I have scotch or bourbon or—" But before she could finish, he shook his head.

"The tea is fine."

In the kitchen, she handed out biscuits to the two dogs, fixed the tea and then grabbed a bag of Oreos before returning to the living room. Nick sat in a chintz chair opposite the couch, looking at the Queen Anne cabinet that housed her collection of music boxes, including the Cinderella one he'd given her when they were in college. She wondered if he would ask about why she kept the music box he'd given her and then hoped he wouldn't; there had been too many memories to deal with in these past few days.

"You still have it," he commented, as if reading her mind.

"Of course. Why wouldn't I?"

He shrugged, the why, obviously, of no consequence to him. "I think I hunted through every antique dump in Boston to find that. It was very embarrassing. Your dad told me you'd been wanting a Cinderella music box, but finding it wasn't half as hard as putting up with the Here comes the prince jokes."

"You never told me that." She managed to hold back a smile.

"Not cool to have the girl you're trying to score with find out you're the joke of the week with the guys."

As hard as she tried, Eden couldn't imagine Nick being the recipient of ribbings. But even harder to understand was why he put up with it. "You could have bought something else."

"Nope. Had to be that. When you unwrapped it and your eyes got big and your hands trembled, it was worth all of the jokes."

Eden felt a warmth spread through her just as it had that September afternoon when he picked her up after class, drove off campus, stopped at a burger place and then, like a kid who couldn't wait any longer, handed her the package. She'd been beguiled, charmed and totally smitten by his thoughtfulness and obvious nervousness.

Now she shook away the nostalgia; she knew better than to allow those fonder memories of Nick to captivate her.

Looking at him now, she noticed how the years had hardened him. He wore a dark-blue chamois shirt, old jeans and boots that looked as if they each weighed about twenty pounds. He could have used a haircut, a shave and some hint of recent pleasure in his life. She had the definite impression that vices she hadn't heard of he had known intimately and already forgotten. Still, she could detect some of the Nick she'd once adored. The nervousness when he'd given her the music box, but also the quips, the recklessness that was fun rather than dangerous. And of course the unexpected charm. Like today.

"Not homemade?" he asked, taking the Oreos and the tea.

"I don't bake."

He popped a cookie into his mouth. "Too bad."

Eden mused about how unlike Cal Nick was in a simple exchange of conversation. There was little predictability, and those short sentences seemed overly loaded—or was she just reading too much into them? But then, she was different with Nick, too—guarded, and yet engaging in banter with a bite that carried implications and complications.

In a cool, snappy retort, she said, "I have a whole new box of dog biscuits if you'd prefer those."

"I'm trying to quit," he said, as if he'd been lying in wait for the comment.

"Then say thank you and eat the Oreos."

His grin was deadly. "Yes, ma'am. Thank you, ma'am."

Eden sat down, hiding her smile at such an idiotic conversation and yet finding herself drawn in. He was just too quick, too savvy. And his laid-back coolness—just what, she wondered, would rattle him?

She took up the gift sack and was about to remove the tissue when the phone rang. Picking it up, she felt a slight jolt on hearing Cal's voice.

"Are you okay?" he asked, his concern obvious.

Confused, she glanced up at Nick. Was it possible Cal knew Nick was here and that prompted the call?

"Eden? Are you there?"

"Yes, uh, I'm here. And I'm fine."

"You sound odd. Maybe I should come over."

No, you can't! The thought slipped around in her mind like mercury. But she said, "No, Cal, that isn't necessary."

"Now you sound like yourself. Paul stopped

at the store and told me what happened with Linda Sims."

"Oh." Relief seeped through her.

"Oh? That's all you can say? Sweetheart, the woman sounds like a nutcase. Paul said she was screeching so loud she could be heard in the halls."

"Paul was exaggerating. Linda was upset about Karen. It was partially my fault and—"

"No, it wasn't," he interrupted firmly. "I don't want to hear you blaming yourself for this. This is a serious matter. If this is the kind of reception the program is going to get, then perhaps we better do some rethinking."

"No!"

Silence filled the line. She guessed Cal was trying to think of a way not to interfere while at the same time making sure there would be no repetition of what had happened earlier that afternoon.

Eden didn't want that either, but these had to be her decisions. She was accustomed to Cal's support occasionally crossing over into protectiveness, and usually she let it pass. This time she felt smothered. She told herself the feeling had nothing to do with Nick sitting three feet away.

She stood, walked to the desk and kept her back turned and her voice low. "Cal, you have to let me work the program in the way best for the parents and the students. Linda and I understand each other. For you to make an issue of what happened would be a disaster."

"Paul was concerned and frankly, sweetheart, so am I."

"It'll be all right. I promise."

They finished the conversation by confirming a dinner for the coming weekend. By the time Eden punched the "off" button, she felt as if she'd picked her way barefoot through broken glass.

When she turned, Nick had moved into the kitchen, where he was petting her dog.

He glanced up. "What's his name?"

"Killer. But I call him Pupper."

Nick grinned. "Killer to cover up his pussycat personality."

"Actually, yes. He's big and does a respectable-sounding growl when necessary, so I figured Killer would scare any intruders and give him confidence."

"I think deep down he has the heart of a fearless protector."

"He is that." She slowly relaxed. "I got him when I worked in Providence. A little kid was giving away puppies near Brown, and I couldn't resist."

They returned to the living room, where Nick once again took the chair opposite the couch. After Eden was settled, she took up the lavender sack.

"How did you train Bobby to sit holding this?"

"We've been practicing."

"Then practice does indeed make perfect."

"Yeah, he wanted to impress you, surprise you and apologize."

"Well, he's accomplished all three things."

"Good," he said so softly that she almost didn't hear him. He lifted his tea, drank and then set it down. "I wanted to tell you the other night . . . You look wonderful, Eden."

She glanced up, the unexpected compliment singing through her like a chord run on a perfectly tuned piano. His expression was open and, as far as she could tell, honest. "Thank you. Cal and I are very happy, and I love my work."

She noted he didn't follow up, but allowed a too-obvious silence to spread between them. Eden once again concentrated on the lavender sack. Frowning at the embossed lettering that she'd just noticed, she said, "This isn't from Davols. You went to Boston?"

"Looks that way," he said matter-of-factly.

"But why?"

"I promised you a new hat. Davols was sold out. I'm lousy at a lot of things, but I do keep promises."

"But if Davols didn't have it, you could have gone to your brother. Cal deals with a lot of the same suppliers. He could have special-ordered it. I certainly never intended for you to drive to Boston." She paused, then in case he thought she'd kept their collision a secret, she added, "I told Cal about Bobby taking the hat."

He shrugged. And she waited for a comeback, even a gotcha. She expected him to say, "But you didn't tell him just now that I was here." And when he said nothing, her confusion about him deepened.

She fiddled with the sack, saying casually, "Have you and Cal gotten together yet?"

"Yeah."

She waited for more, but he didn't offer anything else.

"He hasn't mentioned it."

"I'm not surprised." Nick sat forward, his tone lightening. "Hey, are you going to open that sack or rub it till the color comes off."

Eden took out the lavender tissue and then reached in and lifted out a duplicate of her red angora hat. She held it up, about to thank him, when Bobby came bounding toward her.

Eden yelped. "Not again!"

"Bobby, no!"

The moments that followed were a melee of fur and bodies. Killer thought Eden was being attacked and charged Bobby. Nick leaped between Eden and the animals, crushing sack, tissue and the red hat.

When it was all over, Bobby was whining in the corner, Killer was glaring at the retriever. Eden found herself snug between the couch cushions beneath her and Nick above.

The feel of him from the solidness of his chest to the muscle of his thighs burst through her body with a significance that astonished her. Thirteen years disappeared in a heartbeat.

"You are indeed too clever by half," she said, annoyed by the memory overload. Inwardly she cursed herself that she'd been fascinated and forgiving enough to invite him into the house. She'd mused earlier about his unpredictability, but this?

The devastating smile and the charming quip never came. He stared at her. "You think I planned this?"

"Get off me."

"Not until you answer me."

"I don't have to answer you. The evidence is

sprawled on top of me. The last time it was your dog, this time it's you."

"You believe I'm so hard up for a woman that I'd go through all this hassle to get one under me?"

"Are you?" The two-word question spilled out so fast, so automatically, that Eden was astonished at her own audacity.

His gray eyes darkened to pewter. "As a matter of fact, I climbed out of a woman's bed to come over here. You can relax. I can't get it up enough to do you."

"Bastard," she spat, effrontery giving way to anger.

He held her chin and lowered his mouth. "But I can do this."

The kiss was raw and carnal. Eden tried to push him away, but he was unrelenting. She felt herself sink into it and pushed at him harder, fighting the haze that looped around her like warm syrup.

Finally he pulled back. "You're out of practice," he murmured, devastating her pride. "Or doesn't my brother even know how to kiss you?"

Spots of primal fury pricked at her eyes. "Goddamn you, Nick Scanlon."

"He already has." Rising to his feet, he reached for his jacket and shrugged himself into it. Then he gave a low whistle. "Come on, Bobby, time to move on." He reached down and petted Killer, who snuggled into his hand as if to say, Come back anytime.

Eden lay still for a long time after she heard his Explorer start up and drive away. Her body felt drained, exhausted and hot like a runner's after finishing a marathon. Her mind spun in crazy spirals, as if it had been pushed into an unknown orbit.

She wanted to assure herself that the most unexpected thing that had happened today was the encounter with Linda Sims.

Not the one with Cal's brother.

Chapter 5

"PUMP THOSE LEGS! HEADS DOWN! STICKS on the ice where the puck is. This is hockey, not baseball. Good God, you guys skate like someone poured lead over your feet." Nick shouted all this from the penalty box where he was standing, stopwatch in hand. Bobby sat on the bench beside him, a kerchief in the school's colors—red and black—hung around his neck.

It was six-thirty on a Saturday morning, nine days after Nick and Bobby's visit to Eden. Nick had made sure he stayed clear of her after that. Kissing her had stunned him in ways he'd long forgotten and didn't want to remember. He would have preferred being amused, because Cal deserved to have his sanctimonious possession of Eden shaken up. But never mind, Nick reminded himself, he was home to get his life going again, not get bogged down in old resentments and new problems.

Nick scowled at the sluggishness of the players. "Hey! Do I have to bring in Sharon Stone to liven you guys up? Move, for godsake!"

Only half the team had shown up and of those, most weren't quite awake or fully sober from Friday night. The grumbles since they'd trooped in, suited up and laced their skates had been unrelenting. Nick had ignored the grousing and sent them onto the ice to do stop and goes, fast-paced skating that built up endurance and speed.

The rink was nearly empty. The only people to be seen were Poppy in his chair near the boards, nursing a mug of decaffeinated coffee and complaining that the stuff was tasteless, a few kids from the Squirt team, who'd come to watch the practice, and Don Tucker, a school board member and father of two of the players.

Nick had run into Don earlier in the week at Bubba's Sports Bar, not exactly by accident, as Nick learned when Don launched into his woes about the listless players and the beleaguered team.

On that afternoon, Don had literally begged him to work with the team and suggest some improvements. Nick had already taken on three players for private lessons. The boys' fathers had spoken with Nick after Poppy made his pitch about "learning skills not taught in the upstate hockey school." It was amazing how quickly word had spread. Nick had a pocketful of messages from other fathers. A few more, and he'd have a hockey school whether he wanted one or not. Talk of getting into actual coaching, however, had made him wary.

He didn't want to denigrate the current coach's abilities or step on his turf, but privately he thought Buck Cranston had done a half-assed job. The team was lazy, careless and focused on individual stardom and record breaking rather than team effort.

Nick and Don had sat at the bar, discussing the team's potential. Don had a beer, Nick was drinking ginger ale.

Don said, "I'll talk to Buck. He's not going to raise a stink. Hell, he wants a winning team as much as the rest of us. Besides, the kids are so awed by you they'll probably turn back flips if you take this on."

"I'm already giving lessons, thanks to Poppy being my biggest cheerleader."

"Think of this as an extension. I don't see why we can't capitalize on the enthusiasm I'm seeing in the players."

Nick tossed a handful of peanuts into his mouth, his attention on the big-screen television. The Bruins were up by two goals. "Let me think about it."

"At least you're not saying no. When I talked to Poppy, he said you were adamant about not getting overly involved."

"That's true."

"Got to tell you, Nick, that puzzled me."

"Yeah, that's me. Just one big box of puzzle pieces."

With no serious reason or refusal forthcoming, Don ventured a possibility. "You saw how lousy our guys played and figured why waste your time, right?"

Nick lifted his glass. Wasting his time. He almost chuckled. At the obligatory visit that he'd made to Cal's, his brother had snapped that Nick had refined wasting time to a science.

To Don, Nick said, "It's a fact they play lousy.

But not because they're lousy players. They're lazy and sloppy when they could be blowin' the doors off the rest of the league."

"Dammit, I knew you'd seen past the mistakes!" Don grinned as though someone had given him a free season pass to the Bruins games. "How about this? Give it some thought, and I'll call you tomorrow."

"I'm moving to my own place in a few days, but I'll be around the rink."

"You'll be just the jolt the team needs."

"I haven't said yes yet."

"You will, Nick. I can see it in your eyes."

Don had been right.

Now, watching the skating, the puck passing, the checking and the work the kids still needed, Nick had, in fact, said yes the moment Don suggested it. Thinking about what he wanted to do never took time. It was the things he didn't want to do that made his head hurt.

Like wanting Eden.

But specialized coaching for the team? No sweat. He wanted to do it, wanted to prove he could do it. For the kids, but also for himself.

Like coming home.

That had been for himself when he found the bottom of hell in a motel room somewhere in the midwest in bed with a woman he didn't recognize. Five years of soggy days after nights of drinking, of drifting, of dragging himself from one nameless town or job to the next. Discipline had been as scarce as his once promising hockey career. Self-pity ate at him like a leprosy.

On that numbingly blank morning, he'd witnessed his personal abyss. He was wasted, wanton and going down faster than a weighted body buried at sea. Darkness—even his, he decided—contained a few dried seeds of enlightenment. Something weird happened in the motel that morning. A dawn broke within him and whispered, "I'll deal with you where you are and I'll take you where you need to go."

Where he was, was in hell and where he needed to go was home.

The miracle, of course, was that he had been sober enough to get the message. Simple. No confusion. All neat and straight and scary.

Home was supposed to mean hearth and happiness. Instead he'd learned that Eden was sleeping with his brother, and like a gun's cocked trigger dead-aimed at his darker side, Nick knew the bullet would explode all his good intentions.

Of course, he knew what Scanlon family tradition demanded: he should back away, step aside, tell himself it didn't matter. Hell, he'd done that since he was three. He'd been told by the old man that his brother was the example to follow and Nick had dutifully obeyed.

Cal had been his hero. He was the oldest. He set the pace. He led and Nick followed gladly, until he realized he was denying himself his own achievements.

Stepping aside to make sure Cal did the shine, sparkle and successful stuff had become an ingrained habit, a knee-jerk reaction by his early teens. Nick had kept his own talents reserved or hidden until he started playing hockey. Then something odd happened. Accidentally or by some fateful design, Nick had found his place, his circle of excellence. Cal couldn't even stand up on ice skates. Nick mastered the blades immediately.

All his years of compressed energy poured into hockey. He broke long-standing rink records at Lonsdale, got scouted by the NHL and won a hockey scholarship to Boston University.

Ah, those glory days when hockey was his life and life was hockey! Everything changed in those fractional seconds when his kneecap was shattered. Glory days vanished into endless empty nights and lost, barren years.

That was then, he assured himself now with a relieved shudder. He was home and sober and intended to stay.

Nick blew the whistle. "Okay. Puck shots at goal. Metcalf, wake up. I want them so fast I can't see them."

To Nick's surprise, the players managed to show some enthusiasm and for the next fifteen minutes he began to think that they might get it together.

By eight o'clock, they were dragging. Nick called them to the sidelines.

"Come on, you guys have played in games easier than this practice."

"Not on Saturday morning before the FM station cranks up."

Nick grinned. "It's a tough life. Okay, new rules. No drinking and no sex the night before a game or the night before a practice."

They grumbled and they scowled, as if he'd suggested abstinence for life.

"Clear heads, guys, and I want the energy you expend in the sack out here on the ice."

"Jesus, sounds like you been talkin' to Ms. Parrish. She's big into all that no sex stuff."

"Yeah, the two of us are conspiring against all of you. Just think you can win hockey games and not knock anyone up. You'll all be heroes."

"Sounds boring as hell."

"Builds character. See you guys tomorrow morning same time."

The groans made him smile again. That grin held while he watched them skate off the ice, nod to Don Tucker, give the customary salute to Poppy and tromp past Cal.

"Looks like we got company, Bobby."

The retriever woofed.

"And he's too dressed up for a morning at the rink. Topcoat looks like cashmere. Probably stopped by to remind me he's on his way to a real job."

Moments later, the two brothers shook hands.

"So what brings you over here?" Nick asked.

"Mom asked me to remind you about the party tonight."

"Haven't forgotten."

"And I wanted to apologize for being so short-tempered the morning you stopped by. I was running late, because I overslept. I'd had a meeting the previous night with the school board, which ran later than I anticipated—" He cut off what he had intended to say, adding instead, "Anyway, I was rude and I wanted to tell you."

Nick scowled. His brother's graciousness was usually reserved for everyone but Nick. Yet maybe he did mean it. Coming here to apologize was about two miles out of his way, and frankly

Nick couldn't find any suspicious barbs.

"I should have called. Bobby and I went out for a walk and I just decided to stop by."

Cal took a step closer, then leaned down to pet Bobby. "Heard about you, boy." Bobby whined with pleasure at all the attention. Cal straightened. "Listen, Nick, we should get together. Maybe for lunch, or you might like to get a date. Julie Gallo, one of the school board members, has asked about you. Maybe the four of us could go to dinner. Let bygones be bygones. We're both adults. We've both been through a lot. Losing Dad. Betsy's death. Your difficulties. But from what I saw, with you handling the kids and Don's bubbling enthusiasm, you seem to be back in your element. It's time we both just got on with being brothers."

Nick listened and for a few lucid moments he believed Cal might be on the level. It all sounded good and grown-up—and too practiced. "What's the catch?"

"Catch? I don't know what you're talking about."

"This make-nice stuff wouldn't be because Eden once occupied my bed."

To his credit, Cal didn't flinch. In fact, he lowered his head as if embarrassed. "Don't you think we're both a little old to be jealous of past relationships?"

"No."

"Then you're the jealous one."

"Yeah. I'm not gifted with superhuman qualities, like you."

Cal looked pained, and for the first time, Nick knew he'd crossed the line. It was time to grow up or at least act that way. Besides, what in hell was he trying to prove? That he hadn't lost his ability to act like a jerk? "That last crack was unfair."

Cal nodded. "I meant what I said, Nick, about letting go of our past differences." He glanced at his watch. "Now I have to get to the store. I'll see you tonight. Oh, and I know you don't like being told what to do, but I suggest that you might want to wear a suit for the party."

Nick grinned. "Translated to mean wear it or else."

Amused, Cal said, "Just trying to give you a heads up. Stop by, if you want a new one."

"I might do that."

Cooperation. Getting along. Being a brother instead of a jerk. Nick jammed his hands into his pockets, aware suddenly that this was what his coming home was all about. New beginnings or at the very least putting the past into the history books instead of revisiting it with every word and gesture.

Cal strolled away, waving good-bye to Poppy and Don Tucker.

Nick absently scratched Bobby behind the ears.

A new suit. Christ, he hadn't worn one since his old man's funeral.

Chapter 6

An hour before Nick's homecoming party, Cal arrived to pick up Eden. With his topcoat unbuttoned, hands in his pockets, he leaned against the doorjamb just inside her bedroom. She was putting on the emerald and diamond studs that Cal had given to her the previous Christmas. Having grown up the daughter of a bar owner, she had been accustomed to practical and sometimes whimsical presents, but not expensive ones. When she'd opened the small package, she'd been astonished by his generosity and touched by his thoughtfulness.

"I'm almost ready," she said, giving her hair a final touch-up. She sat at a white faux French Provincial dressing table she'd found at a yard sale last autumn. The three-paneled mirror reflected four discarded outfits tossed across the bed.

"I thought you were going to wear that red dress," Cal said, his tone one of disappointment. Coming into the room, he lifted the dress and studied it carefully, looking for a stain. Seeing none, he laid it down. "How come? You look so sensational in it."

"I don't look sensational in this one?" Eden asked, arching her brows, pretending offense. The green velvet halter dress had a satin collar and sash. The full skirt skimmed her legs just at the knee. It was dressier than she'd planned to wear, but it was one of her favorites. After two encounters with Bobby and his penchant for red, Eden concluded that wearing anything even accented with that color was asking for trouble. And no doubt Nick's dog would be at the party.

Cal came up behind her, leaned down and kissed the back of her neck. Eden shivered.

"I like you in red," he murmured.

"I know."

"Hmm, I like you in bed, too."

"I like you, too, but I can't say the same for your poetic effort. It's terrible."

"And here I'd been practicing all afternoon."

She chuckled. "I don't think practice is making you perfect."

They both laughed.

Cal slid his hand under the halter, brushing her breast. "If this party wasn't for my kid brother, I'd say let's stay here and have our own."

She sighed. "And I'd say you'd be disappointed."

Sliding her stool back, she stood, then playfully danced away from his attempt to pull her into his arms. She stepped into green pumps and took a small beaded purse from the closet.

"Disappointed? Why?" he asked.

"I got my period today."

"Damn. I had things all planned for later."

"I'm sorry, but we'd both be a lot sorrier if I missed it."

He nodded. "You're right. I want to be married to you first."

Eden took a last look in the mirror and then put the portable phone, which had been tossed onto the bed, back into its charger.

"Speaking of which . . ." Cal began in a serious tone.

His pause sent her mind rushing ahead. "Marriage? Cal, you promised we wouldn't discuss it until after the school year is finished."

He shook his head. "Not that. Have you called your father back?"

Eden bristled instinctively. "Did anyone ever tell you that you have a one-track mind? That's the fourth time in the past few days that you've asked me."

"Because you keep putting it off."

"Let me worry about it, please."

"That's the point, sweetheart. If you'd get it done, then neither of us would have to worry."

Eden turned away from him, holding in check her rising irritation with his nagging.

Tonight, after the day she'd had, she didn't need this pressure. She'd visited with Karen Sims that morning at the apartment she shared with her mother. It was their third meeting since Eden had spoken with Linda Sims. Finally Karen had agreed to return to school, but Eden knew the decision was fragile and until she saw the teenager in the halls, she wasn't counting on anything. Also, she'd had a routine appointment with Eddie Metcalf, one of Lonsdale's hockey stars, but she was having difficulty getting his parents in at the same time, so little had been accomplished. Gliches always appeared insignificant, but added up over the day, they became huge barriers.

Added to these issues was her indecision about returning her father's phone call. All day she'd waffled, decided and undecided and decided again, but in the end she was still in a quandary. How she wished some omniscient being would grace her with the wisdom of a firm decision.

In retrospect, confiding in Cal about the initial phone call had been a mistake. She'd wanted support, someone with whom she could discuss her feelings, her fears and her angst, someone who would let her whine and wail and wring her hands with some old-fashioned guilt.

Instead, Cal wanted the whole problem tied up and discarded. It irritated her, and tonight she seriously considered saying, "Yes, I called and I did what you told me, too," just to end the discussion.

Instead, she murmured the truth. "No, I haven't."

"What are you waiting for?"

She hung up the other dresses, keeping her voice even. "I haven't decided what I'm going to tell him to say."

"Eden, really. I told you what to do."

"It is not your business to tell me or not to tell me." She enunciated the words as though they'd been clipped with sharp scissors.

"Okay, I advised you. Advise him," he said with an emphasis that was disconcerting. He sounded as if he was giving an order, not making a suggestion. "Advise him to call Jennifer's parents and say no. It's out of the question."

"It is not out of the question. You don't understand the implications of this."

"Sweetheart," he said gently, "I know this isn't easy, but you're stalling, and the longer you stall, the harder it's going to be."

"What's hard is you browbeating me about it," she said tightly.

Hands low on his hips, he frowned. "Is that what you think I'm doing?"

Ignoring his question, she said flatly, "We're going to be late. Your mom called and wanted us to pick up two more bottles of champagne. She's afraid she doesn't have enough."

"Answer me, Eden. Is that what you think I'm doing?"

She gave him a direct look. "Yes. This is my decision, and I'll make it when I'm ready. I promise you'll be the first to know. Now, don't ask me about it again."

His expression wasn't conciliatory. He wasn't, or chose not to be, intuitive enough to know that she'd reached her limit. Perhaps she expected too much from him. He probably felt threatened, and she'd become so snarled in her own emotional turmoil that she'd misjudged his. But good God, how difficult was this? He didn't have to do anything except understand. Instead he'd treated the problem as a pesky incident that she was too namby-pamby to face.

Then, as if he'd heard nothing of what she'd just said, or chose to ignore her request to let go of the issue, he took her arm and turned her to face him. "You're counseling students to make difficult decisions because those are the right ones and the responsible ones. Here you are, the head of the guidance department as well as a crackerjack counselor, with a decision that is perfectly straightforward and simple, and you're dithering as if it involved sending troops into battle."

She shook free of him, swinging away. Her rein on her temper gave way. "Dithering? Simple? Dammit, it might be a lot of things, but it is not simple! It's excruciatingly hard, and I resent you comparing a decision by a teenager on whether or not to have sex with my decision to give my daughter up for adoption."

He stared at her as if unknowingly he'd detonated a bomb and wasn't sure whether to exit or stay and try to survive it.

Eden crossed to the bedside table. The drawer was partially ajar.

Tucked inside were her only tangible memories of Jennifer: a pair of booties, a small journal she'd kept while she was pregnant, and a music box nestled in a miniature cradle that rocked and played Brahms's "Lullaby."

She'd seen it in a pawn shop and talked the owner into keeping it aside until she'd saved enough of her allowance. Finally, a month before Jennifer was born, she'd bought it. Eden had wanted her daughter to love and cherish music as her grandmother had, as Eden did.

At sixteen, Eden had grand plans to keep and raise her baby daughter. But her Aunt Josette had pointed out the reality and the consequences of raising a child with no husband and no father. With only a high school education,

Eden would have a very small choice of job prospects.

Loving and wanting her baby was maternal and honorable, but listening to Aunt Josette's reasoning stirred deeply within Eden; she'd realized that as worthy as her intentions and her love were, it took money and maturity and most of all, doing what was best for her baby instead of what was best for herself.

In the end, she made the heart-wrenching decision to give her baby to David and Laura Maynard through a private adoption.

Once the determination was made, the papers signed and her daughter on her way with the Maynards, Eden forced herself to move her life forward. She'd chosen Boston University simply because it was so far from home and Jennifer.

Distance, however, couldn't provide closure in her heart. She'd had emotional bursts of regret, pangs of uncertainty and the inevitable second guessing. Time and college life blunted the immediate pain, but her choice of a career in teenage counseling had been the most effective. It was taking her experience, not in a maudlin or self-delusional way, but using it to give her the rare privilege of insight and experience while remaining objective.

Yet the detachment she scrupulously applied to students had little effect against the lively expectation that had swirled within her since her father's phone call.

Jennifer wanted to meet her "real" mother.

Eden's indecisiveness was more complex than simple procrastination. It was a true wrestling within her on whether to step through the door to see Jennifer or close it forever.

But in that indecisive limbo, her heart-tugging questions refused to go away.

What did Jennifer look like?

How did she smile and what did her laugh sound like?

Was there any resemblance between them?

All the questions carried deeper impact than just learning the answers.

And therein lay the crux of her dilemma.

Now Eden firmly shut the drawer, rounded the bed and walked past Cal out of the bedroom to the hall closet, where she retrieved her coat.

Killer lay sprawled in the hall, watching. She leaned down and patted his head. "Keep the burglars out, Pupper." He wagged his tail.

At the front door, Cal helped her on with her coat. Brushing his mouth across her forehead, he whispered, "I love you."

She nodded. As if her acceptance of his words gave him permission to reopen the issue, he added, "I was talking about the decision you have to make now, not the difficult one you made years ago. Believe me, I wasn't making a comparison. Sweetheart, I know your personal experience and how it has affected you is what has made you so good and so dedicated to the awareness program you've created here."

She deliberately waited until they were in his car and on their way before she answered. "Please don't patronize me, Cal."

"I wasn't. I was just pointing out—"

"Stop it!" She pressed her gloved hands to her ears. Then in a ragged voice she said, "Giving

Jennifer up for adoption wasn't even close to an experience, as you put it. It was a devastating life-changing decision and the hardest thing I've ever done. I'd been rejected by the father, who had the spine of a worm when it came to taking some responsibility. In turn, I believed I was making my baby pay for my stupid mistake. Jennifer may want to see me out of curiosity, or she may want to know the whole truth, spit in my face for what she thinks was abandonment, ask about her biological father—God knows what. At least, give her parents credit for trying to prepare me instead of acting as if you wish it had never happened."

She braced herself. If he said he did indeed wish it had never happened, she'd break off their relationship. A tiny voice within her whispered that she was overreacting, going to extremes, but this was fundamental. Maybe it wasn't a lack of sensitivity but something deeper—a selfishness that resented anything that interfered with her attention to him.

His silence unnerved her.

He lifted his hands from the wheel in a you win gesture. "Okay, whatever you say."

Eden let out the breath she didn't know she'd been holding. "And you won't ask again? Promise me?"

"Jesus."

"Cal, I mean it."

"All right. I promise."

She slid over next to him and brushed her hand down his leg.

Cal stopped for the champagne. By the time

they got to the party, her mood had lightened and she was looking forward to the evening.

Mary Scanlon's house bulged with friends, relatives and neighbors. Cold platters and hot food in covered dishes had been catered with the exception of a huge pan of barbecued spareribs. Mary had cooked those because Nick loved them and insisted no one could make them better. A fully stocked bar set up in the dining room was doing brisk business. Cal's colleagues from the school board and their families had come, neighbors—who included two of Nick's former girlfriends, now happily married, and some Scanlon cousins, who had driven down from Vermont. Most of those Nick hadn't seen since he graduated from high school.

"Curiosity about the family has-been," he commented without rancor when the last of the cousins strolled in.

"Nonsense, and I don't want to hear any more of that talk," Mary Scanlon warned. "No more indulging in self-pity."

Nick winced. "You're too quick and truthful."

"I have to be to keep up with you and your brother. But your outlook is better than when you came home."

"It's the jacket," Nick said blandly. The blue-gray worsted sport coat had come from Scanlons. Top of the line, Cal had assured him, adding a blue cotton shirt and a tie that, to Nick, resembled a soft rag spattered with spilled paint. But he'd acquiesced, and he had to admit he liked the look. It was almost respectable.

"The coat, yes, of course. And a decent haircut

and a shave that doesn't leave behind more than it takes off."

"That reek of respectability, Mom." He winked. "Just can't get enough of it. By the way, the ribs are great." He picked a meaty rib from a foil-lined pan as his mother moved efficiently about the kitchen.

She peered over her shoulder. "It's not a death sentence, you know."

"Your cooking?" he asked between bites.

"You know what I mean. Being respectable."

"Like Cal."

"Not like Cal, like Nick," she said, addressing him as she'd often done when he was a kid and complained that the old man wanted him polished and polite like his older brother.

"It's not that simple," Nick said, wiping rib sauce off his mouth. "Following social rules bores me."

"Rules are not what I'm talking about. I'm talking about the real Nick, the Nick I know, who, despite his sarcasm and rebellion, is a fine man with a depth of honor that he refuses to acknowledge."

"I think you're prejudiced."

"I'm also right."

Unexpectedly rattled by her unflinching support, Nick laid down the partially eaten rib. His appetite disappeared, replaced by a bitter realization that the man his mother insisted he was existed only in her mind.

Watching her reinforced what he'd known for years—that she was a remarkable woman. She wasn't tall and imposing, and yet the impression she gave was one of commanding elegance. Her hair was golden brown and very long; Nick couldn't remember the last time he'd seen it unbraided. She wore it up and wound into a figure eight, held with strategically placed pins. Her clothes looked fashionable because she wore them with style.

She was the quintessential mother in the traditional sense, and once her sons were grown, she became a subtle reminder of what she'd attempted to teach them: manners and grace peppered with a bite of occasional judgment. She had no illusions about her boys; neither Cal's striving for perfection nor Nick's penchant for rebellion. She'd told them years ago that sibling rivalry was just selfishness. Getting along, she insisted, was nothing more than a series of small sacrifices.

Wearing the sport coat, Nick realized, could be pegged as a minor sacrifice if obliging his mother was the only issue. But his trip to Scanlons earlier that day had proved to him that the discord between him and Cal would take more than a few small sacrifices to displace.

When Nick had walked into the upscale men's store, Cal had been talking to two customers. He'd glanced up, but instead of signaling that Nick should look around until he was free, Cal arched his eyebrows and indulged in a too familiar, too superior smile that zigzagged through Nick with all the subtlety of a rusted straight razor. Images from their thorny past punctured Nick's consciousness with nightmarish precision.

Old memories of his father's hidebound rule that Cal set the example and Nick was to follow.

Old resentments of blunting his own skills, especially in sports, so that Cal could look good.

Old anger that no matter what he did right, if any praise was forthcoming, it was first given to Cal as the shining example of what success was all about.

And so, as he roamed about Scanlons, something inside Nick let go—one of those demons from his days of living in hell, he decided, but it lunged forth with more power than the fragile benefit of the doubt that he had been willing to give Cal after their talk that morning at the rink.

When the customers had left and they were alone, Nick made his move. He had chosen the coat he wanted, slipped it on, liked the fit and then asked Cal, "Are you sleeping with Eden because she used to sleep with me?"

The question slid out in such a low-voltage manner that for a few seconds Cal stood slack-jawed and unresponsive.

Then his face darkened to a ripe magenta. "Christ, where do you get off asking me that?"

"Seems like a reasonable question."

His composure limped back. "Then here's the reasonable answer. I'm sleeping with her because I love her. What was your excuse?"

"I wanted her, I went after her and I got her."

"A real gentleman," Cal said sourly.

Nick shrugged. "My flaws are many, but lying isn't one of them."

"What in hell is your point?"

"I'm trying to convince myself I should behave." Nick turned, held up the tie Cal had picked as a good match to the coat, studied his reflection and decided he might just get used to civilization. By the time a cotton shirt and slacks were added and the outfit had been assembled in one of Scanlons trademark black and gold boxes, Cal's color was back.

"Don't be a bastard, Nick. You and I will get along fine as long as you don't try anything."

"Like getting Eden out of your bed and into mine again?"

Cal stepped closer, his eyes glittering with intensity and a know-it-all reasonableness that was vintage Cal. "You had your chance with Eden and blew it. Blew it big time . . ." He hesitated, and when Nick said nothing, continued, "So if you're thinking of making a move to bust us up and break Eden's heart again, you're wrong, little brother."

Little brother. The two words chilled Nick.

Nick shifted the box and started toward the street. Two women were coming in, and he waited until they were through the door.

"Nick?" Cal came up close so that he wouldn't be overheard. He was an inch or two taller than Nick, and the contrast of styles—the rough scrapper in denim, the smooth sophisticate in finely tailored wool—had never been more evident.

"What?" Nick asked wearily.

"I don't want to have to say this more than once."

The statement tossed Nick back to when his father would recite the very same words when dealing with some undisciplined action on his part. Nick shoved the door open.

Cal's last sentence dogged him. "Stay the hell away from Eden."

If ever there was a line that threw down the gauntlet, that was it. His brother deserved to lose Eden. And if he could find a way to make that happen, then all the better.

Nick had reached that conclusion before his mother's probe about honor and manners and him being a fine man.

The two sides of Nick Scanlon, he decided. The side that intended to get along with Cal and start his life afresh and the darker side, which couldn't give up the sweet revenge that would be his if he won Eden back into his bed.

Now he glanced up at the sound of a car.

Mary peeked out the window. "At last. I was beginning to wonder what had happened to Cal and Eden. They're usually so punctual."

With his mother's back to him, Nick tried to ease out of the kitchen. No such luck.

"Are you avoiding them or is this just a case of bad manners?"

"I'm going to wash my hands. I don't think Cal would appreciate barbecue sauce on his fingers." At his mother's frown, he added, "When we shake hands. You know—that old custom that shows one doesn't have bad manners."

"We have soap and running water here in the kitchen," she said sagely, obviously not taken in by his excuse. "But go ahead."

Once he had finished in the bathroom and was on his way to greet his brother, he got waylaid by his Uncle Al Scanlon and his wife Flossie.

Al and Flossie had driven from Hartford, where Al, Jack Scanlon's younger brother, owned a hardware store. Before Nick was born,

Al had sold to Jack his percentage of Scanlons. "I ain't the high-priced clothing type," Al had said. "Give me some boots and chinos and some cheap cigars and I'm happy."

Jack Scanlon had been only too happy to oblige. He'd made no secret that he believed his brother had no taste, whether he was putting catsup on prime rib or marrying Flossie the Floozy, as Jack called her. Flossie's clothes were usually out of season and out of style. She'd never been impressed by the Scanlon name. She played poker with a deftness and a stony strategy that had made Jack so furious that he told his friends she was a professional gambler in drag.

"Your daddy really didn't know what to do with me," Flossie was telling Nick.

"Yeah, well, guess we're in the same club. He didn't know what to do with me, either."

Flossie towered over most of the women, and tonight, quite true to form, her outfit caused more than a few of them to look twice. In the mint-green dress with puffs of extra material at the shoulders, she reminded Nick of a six-foot, long-eared rabbit outfitted far too early for the St. Patrick's Day parade.

Nevertheless, he liked her. She didn't care what anyone thought and seemed oblivious to criticism.

"Your brother certainly looks happy now that he has Eden," Flossie said, nodding toward Cal, who had Eden glued to his side. Al had gone to get a beer. "You dated her when you were in college, didn't you?"

"Yeah." Nick stared at Flossie, unsure

whether the kick in his gut was because she belonged to Cal and Cal didn't deserve her or whether it was a lucid reminder that once he had her and he didn't now.

"Quite a coincidence," she mused.

"It is that," Nick said easily.

"And what about you, Nick?" Flossie asked.

"Me?"

"No steady girl?"

"Uh, I'm working on it," he said vaguely. He was about to excuse himself when Al returned.

"By the trapped look on your face, Nick, I'd say she's got her nose stuck in your love life." Al grinned and tipped his beer to his mouth. Nick relaxed. Flossie's curiosity wasn't anything to break a sweat over. "Big crowd here, Nick. Didn't know you knew so many people."

"I didn't, either."

One of his cousins tapped his shoulder. "Your mom asked me to come and get you. It seems Bobby has a guy cornered in the den."

Nick rolled his eyes and excused himself.

At the same time that Nick walked into the pine-paneled room, Eden appeared also. He waited for her to go ahead of him, his hand lightly on her back. She didn't flinch or pull away, but he noted a slight stiffening.

Over her shoulder, she whispered, "One of the guests was wearing a red tie."

So that was the problem. "Bobby was in the mud room. How did he get into the house?"

"Cal felt sorry for him."

"You said you told him about your red hat."

"I did. I even said I thought that might be why you didn't want him in the house."

"So he ignored all that. A little payback, no doubt."

"Payback?"

"Never mind."

"I told him he should check with you."

"Oh, I bet he loved that suggestion," Nick muttered.

He crossed over to where Bobby was sprawled at the feet of a man who now wore no tie. Bobby had the tie wound between his paws.

Hands low on his hips, Nick scowled. "Your fixation is costing me serious money, buddy."

Eric Fogerty, a neighbor who belonged to the same bridge group as Mary, stood to shake Nick's hand. With a good-sport attitude, he said, "I decided it was easier to let him have it than have him sit in my lap and chew."

"I'll replace it."

"Forget it, Nick. I've got a ton of ties and this one wasn't expensive. But I'm curious as to why he has such an obsession with red."

"He's had it since I got him. Have no idea why, but he tends to indulge it at the worst possible times." Nick and Eric continued to discuss the quirky habits of dogs while Eden, now accompanied by Mary, walked back into the living room.

Eden could still feel the light imprint of Nick's fingers against her back. The gesture had been polite and natural, and yet she was uncomfortable about it. Not because she didn't like it, but because she did.

As they circulated among guests, Mary said to Eden, "I haven't had a chance to talk to you since Nick came home."

"I've been meaning to stop by, but what with getting the program off the ground, I've been just swamped."

"I thought maybe you were afraid you'd run into Nick."

Eden started to deny this, but then nodded. "Probably."

"He hasn't said anything about you beyond the incident at the rink."

"There's no reason why he should."

"Has Cal said anything?" Then Mary held up her hand and shook her head as they moved into the kitchen. "That was out of line, Eden, I'm sorry."

"Of course it wasn't out of line. We're friends." Eden sighed. "Actually we only discussed Nick once. It was fine. I think Cal views Nick as too reckless and somewhat of a drifter who feels sorry for himself."

"For the most part Cal is right. Nick has indulged in a lot of self-pity since that knee injury. Oh, I don't mean the whole time. For a while he was doing okay, but I know Nick has never gotten over losing his chance to go to the NHL. It's as if his dream collapsed and he went with it."

Eden shuddered. She'd been at the Boston University game when Nick's knee was shattered. Those moments of watching him collapse on the ice and being struck with the horror that he might be gravely injured seemed as long as a lifetime. His injury wasn't fatal, but it was serious.

Surgery followed and then therapy, but the ugly truth didn't change. His knee was too damaged; he'd never play professional hockey. In fact, the doctors doubted that he'd ever skate again.

To Mary she said, "He seems to have been on the right track since he came home. I understand he's giving private lessons to some of the players and recently started doing some coaching."

Mary nodded. "Yes, thank God. My worst fear was that his homecoming would only be temporary. But I really think this time it's permanent." She glanced around the kitchen, her eyes thoughtful. "But now I have to make sure the champagne gets poured and find Cal. He's going to do the welcome home toast to Nick. You coming?"

"Yes, I'll be right in."

Mary left the kitchen, and Eden poured herself a glass of wine. She slipped her shoes off and was deciding whether to just leave them off when Nick appeared with Bobby.

Grinning at the animal's woebegone expression, she said, "Banished back to the mud room, aren't you, boy?"

Bobby whined.

"Don't look to her for any reprieve, buddy."

Bobby slunk along looking dejected.

Eden leaned down and rubbed him behind the ears. "Tell you what. I have an old red sweater and the next time you come to visit Killer, I'll let you have it."

"Sounds like a pretty good deal," Nick said to the dog.

Bobby grinned, ears back, tail wagging.

Eden looked up at Nick. "Do you think he really understood me?"

"He's a brilliant dog." He held Eden's gaze. "You serious about the visit?"

"Sure. He and Killer got along great. It was you and me that had the confrontation," she said lightly, if for no other reason than to let him know she wasn't worried about mentioning it.

Nick stared at her like he was debating on saying something, then led Bobby back into the mud room. Eden found that her heart was racing. If she was going to exit the kitchen, now was the time to do it. She had just slipped one foot into a shoe when he returned.

"You look gorgeous even with your shoes off."

She was holding her glass of wine in one hand and balancing herself with the other while she tried to work her foot into the second shoe. She tipped her head in acknowledgement of the compliment. "Notice I avoided red."

"I noticed," he said softly. "I like you in green." He hunched down, taking her shoe and slipping it onto her foot. His fingers were light on her ankle and made a soft pressure on the arch of her foot—a butterfly touch that fluttered all the way up her thigh. She wanted to pull away, and yet to do so would be allowing Nick to presume she was affected by him.

He folded his hand around her ankle, his thumb feathering across the bones. Eden flinched and she knew he'd felt her reaction.

"But then I have a sweet memory of you in green."

"A sweet memory? I don't recall . . ."

Then she felt heat rise in her cheeks, a giveaway blush that rushed all the way to her toes.

She'd worn green that last night they were together.

"Not when I broke up with you," he said, as if following her thoughts. "The other time."

Eden lowered her head. She recalled the other time and she couldn't believe he would so cavalierly bring it up. Then she glanced down at her dress, a favorite, too dressy for this party, but she'd worn it just the same. Oh, God! Was it possible that she'd worn green tonight with some subconscious memory of that afternoon in her dorm room? That time she'd done sexual things with Nick she'd never done with anyone else? Conversation drifted in from the other rooms, but with the bar and food not in the kitchen no one came. Dammit, where was Cal?

"I think we should rejoin your guests, Nick," she said, wanting to leave before he listed all the details of that afternoon.

He straightened, and leaning against the counter edge, arms casually folded, made no move to leave. "You really don't remember?"

She took a swallow of wine and it sizzled down her throat. "Uh, no, I don't. Listen, I promised Julie Gallo we'd catch up and—"

Nick shifted his body so that he was closer to her. She instinctively took a step back.

"You forgot that time when I couldn't figure out how to get you out of that green leotard or whatever it was?"

She took a deep breath, her face warm, her eyes too wide and her mind feverishly wondering how to stop where he was going with this. Distraction hadn't worked.

"Nick, this isn't a good idea."

His face was thoughtful, too much so. He didn't touch her, didn't try to trap her in any physical way, but she couldn't deny the sexual pull that was so strong it made her dizzy.

"Hmm. Since you don't remember, let me see if I recall the details."

She closed her eyes and ground her teeth together.

"You'd been working out after spending three days hunched over a desk, finishing a sociology paper. You were wrung out, and I suggested we cancel our date—"

"Nick, don't." She felt a panic grip her and she tried to step around him.

But he moved and stopped her, continuing to talk in a low, conversational tone. "You wanted to see me, begged me to come."

He paused, watching her, and she suddenly had the urge to slug him for the obvious double meaning. How could she ever have forgotten how targeted and lethal his words had always been on her emotions?

"And unless I have a terribly bad memory, it turned out to be some of the best sex we'd ever had."

Don't sweat this, she told herself. *Don't panic. And for godsake, don't let him know your own recall is more vivid than his.* "It was a long time ago."

"And you haven't forgotten, have you?"

Her mouth was so dry that she couldn't form words. He moved again, crowding her. To her annoyance, her body hummed in anticipation as though welcoming the arrival of a long-lost soul mate. Then he touched her halter strap.

"Have you, babe?"

She shook off the floaty feeling and reminded herself that they were adults, not a couple of horny college kids. This whole scene was infantile.

"No, I haven't forgotten and you know I haven't, but none of that matters," she said firmly, her control and good sense limping back. "I don't want to flirt, Nick, and you're not going to seduce me."

He brushed his knuckles down her halter strap. Not touching her skin acted on her like a withheld promise begging for more. "And here I was going to ask you to ignore all those sanctimonious excuses you're clinging to and come to bed with me."

Eden felt a double jolt of energy. One part of her wanted to say, "When?" but that, of course, was out of the question. So she applied the second choice.

Sliding beyond his reach, she set the wine glass on the counter and gave him a direct look. "You're acting just like the jock you were in college. All filled with sexual ego and thinking I'm some besotted coed intrigued by your roughness, your sexy talk, and willing to turn on a dime for a chance to be in your bed. Grow up, Nick. We're not in college anymore, nor do we have any kind of relationship that warrants your come-on behavior. Furthermore, I don't appreciate being treated as a means of staking your unrestrained appetites."

Feeling better and not wanting to lose any of her momentum, she moved around him and walked out of the kitchen without looking back.

Chapter 7

FIFTEEN MINUTES LATER, MARY WAS CHECKING to make sure everyone had a glass of champagne.

Eden took the last one from a tray and eased through the crowd that had assembled for the toast. Cal, glass in hand, took his place in the living room near the fireplace, where all the guests could see him. His grin was a little too magnanimous, Eden noted, not drunk, but not entirely sober. Many of the guests shared the same happy state. Mary had already started a big urn of coffee.

"Where's my homecoming brother?" Cal asked, scanning the expectant faces. Eden had a sinking feeling that Nick might have walked out, but just as she was about to start feeling responsible and thinking she could have handled the episode in the kitchen with more grace and humor, he strode in.

He made a mock bow. "Sorry, folks, I was filling up on Mom's ribs."

Cal laughed. "We thought you might have taken off again."

"And miss this?"

"You'd have been running true to form, little brother."

It was the kind of comment Cal never would have made fully sober. A few of the guests laughed self-consciously, while others muttered about typical brotherly "gotcha."

Eden found it horribly tactless.

In a low voice, Mary said, "Really, Cal, that was uncalled for."

"Mom, it's okay," Nick said from behind her. "Cal says what he thinks."

"He's also had too much to drink."

Nick squeezed her hand. "Then let's do the toast before this stuff goes flat." Nick reached for the last two glasses on the tray and handed one to his mother. They stood side by side a few steps from Cal. Eden was just behind them.

"Okay, is everyone ready?"

"We've been ready, Cal. We're waiting on you."

"Yeah, get on with it. My bubbles are shrinking."

"Make it short."

Cal scowled. "Hey, you wanna come up here and do it?"

Mary stepped close to him. "For heaven's sake, you're turning this into an embarrassment. Nick's going to wish he had left."

He gave Nick a smug grin. "Okay by me," he said a little too loud.

Mary glared at him.

Undaunted, he raised his glass. "A toast to my little brother, who most of the time lives up to all our expectations."

"Christ," Nick muttered, lowering his head in obvious annoyance.

Cal swung the glass sideways as if the room was so huge that those to his left and right might otherwise miss the toasting ritual. Liquid sloshed precariously. "Now he's home and working and coaching and well, hell, we're hoping he's finally gotten it all together. Here's to Nick." He lifted his glass a little too high. "Welcome home, little brother."

Everyone shouted, "Hear, hear," and drank. All except Eden, who stared appalled at Cal. Never had she witnessed this petty, mean-spirited side of him. Nick obviously wasn't as stunned as she was, but he was clearly not expecting what he got. He never drank the champagne, but instead set his glass down, accepted some claps on the back and then walked forward and extended his hand to Cal. The two clasped palms, with Cal laughing heartily and Nick's light smile revealing nothing. Eden gaped at Cal, her astonishment at his behavior turning to vexation. The toast had been condescending and more worthy of a snub from Nick instead of his stepping forward as if he'd had years of experience of saving his brother from deserved criticism. It was such a switch—the usually gracious Cal being an ass and I-don't-give-a-damn Nick being the gentleman—that Eden wondered if she was the only one who had noticed.

She made her way through the crowd toward Cal. Setting down her still-untouched glass on a tray of empties, she overheard Nick say something about taking Bobby outside. He glanced in her direction, and her eyes searched his, wanting to convey some sympathy for what she had just witnessed. Instead she became aware of a starkness in his face etched in his iron will. It plainly revealed that none of what had just occurred was a surprise but rather an ingrained sibling habit, and both brothers knew it.

Eden started forward to speak to him, but the expression vanished, and he turned to speak to another guest.

Cal was talking to Don Tucker.

Eden touched Don's arm. "Would you excuse Cal for just a moment?" Don nodded and moved away.

Cal slipped an arm around her waist. "Hi, sweetheart."

Eden's smile was empty. She said, "I want to talk to you privately."

"I'd rather do other things in private." Cal leaned down, his eyebrows bouncing.

"Like get drunker?"

Immediately he drew back. "Uh, oh, I'm in trouble."

"It's not funny."

"Lighten up. This is supposed to be a party."

"To honor your brother."

"That's what someone said." He smiled, as if he'd said something clever, but not getting any response out of her, he shrugged. "You want private. Private you'll have. Lead the way."

The bedrooms were at the farthest end of the house, all of them filled with overnight bags belonging to the Scanlon relatives. Eden chose the one room where they'd be guaranteed no interruptions: Mary's bedroom.

It was decorated in yellow chintz. The scent of potpourri lingered in the air. A crucifix hung on one wall near a double bed with a wedding ring quilt and pillows enclosed in lacy shams. Framed pictures of Mary's two sons from babyhood through college were proudly displayed on a mahogany dresser. One large photo was of Cal and Betsy on their wedding day.

Cal loosened his tie and swept a hand through his hair before pushing his suit jacket back and sliding his hands into his trouser pockets. Grinning at her now, he looked sexy and amused and, she had to admit, handsomely endearing.

It wasn't as if she hadn't seen him slightly tipsy before. He tended to be boyish and playful, showing a funny side rather than the familiar sophistication. However, she'd never seen him as he'd been to Nick—deliberately hurtful. Something was off-kilter, and she hoped his behavior was more the effect of alcohol than the real Cal.

Eden closed the door on the noise, standing with her back against the knob, shaking her head when Cal held out his hand. When she didn't move, he shrugged. "Guess we aren't gonna make out, huh?"

She shook her head. "You've had too much to drink."

"Probably. Hey, it's a party. I promise to let you drive. Come and kiss me."

She didn't move. "How could you have toasted your brother the way you did?"

For a moment he looked as though she'd taken him aside under false pretenses. "What are you talking about?"

"Please. Don't look as if you don't know what I'm talking about. You as much as called yourself a success and Nick a failure."

"Ah, Jesus, another plea for poor Nick. Maybe someone should take up a collection for him."

Eden wasn't about to be sidetracked by Cal's sarcasm. "And to make it worse, you implied he was still a failure and probably always would be. I wasn't the only one who was uncomfortable with your remarks. They were tacky and insulting."

He stared at her, his eyes leery, and she realized suddenly that he wasn't as tipsy as he was pretending to be. He walked a few steps as if giving himself time to figure out the best spin. "You're exaggerating, but if it will make you feel better, I'll tell him I'm sorry the first chance I get."

"No, you won't," she said instantly.

"Okay, I won't," he said flatly.

This was going nowhere. Eden tried a different approach. "Cal, what's wrong between you and Nick? You were horribly insulting to him. We both know that. But why did he just take it? It was an astonishing few moments. And the handshake! My God, I don't understand why."

He shrugged, turning away. "Maybe he's a sucker. I just said what everyone thinks—the truth."

Eden walked around him so as to face him. "Fine. Tell him privately, if you think it's so relevant, but to say that in front of a whole roomful of people . . . I mean, put yourself in Nick's place."

"Not in this lifetime. That's the last place I

ever want to be." He dropped an arm around her. "Come on, Eden, you're getting worked up over nothing. Nick and I understand each other. There isn't a helluva lot of love lost between us. If he was so hurt and insulted, how come he's not bellyaching? Even you're wondering that." When she didn't answer, he answered for her. "Because he knows I'm right and frankly he probably doesn't give a shit what I say about him." He glanced toward the door. "Lots of partying going on out there. No one's wringing their hands or walking out because of some irrelevant toast. You're the only one who's all worked up about it."

Eden had to admit Cal had a point. The two of them had shaken hands, and Nick had seemed more embarrassed for his mother than for himself. But still, she'd felt the tension, seen Nick's stark expression, and she couldn't shake the feeling there was a level of raw unease between the brothers.

Cal gave her a light squeeze, his voice low and curious. "But I'm fascinated by your defense of him."

"I've never found public humiliation a sport."

He remained silent and she wondered if she'd hit a nerve. But then he blandly said, "Look, Nick might have everyone else tripping over themselves to tell him what an icon he is, but I grew up with him. He's had lots of chances and walked away from all of them. One was an opportunity to use his partial ownership of Scanlons as a foothold after the accident. Did he take that as a second chance? No, he snubbed his nose at it when Dad suggested it. Look what he did to you after he got hurt. Was he grateful for the girlfriend who cried over his injury and sat with him in the hospital? Sure as hell couldn't tell by his actions. He left college, left you and came home to sulk and feel sorry for himself. You were lovers and he didn't give a damn once his hockey career was gone. Nick cares about Nick. Always has, always will, and if anything bugs him, it's that he knows I know it."

Some of what Cal was saying was probably true. God knows Nick had his faults. Still, the picture of selfishness Cal had painted was too skewed, too one-sided and too obviously framed in the view of a very biased brother. Eden knew Nick, too. She'd known laughter and teasing and a joy in their relationship that was still lodged in her memory. She'd known how devastated he'd been when his hockey dreams were shattered. And God, she knew about broken dreams. She'd given away a daughter. That single decision had changed forever how she viewed herself.

Cal cupped her chin and tipped up her face. His voice was warm and affectionate. "The dumbest thing he ever did was let go of you."

"We were kids, Cal."

"You once told me you loved him and now you're defending his rejection of you?"

"I'm putting it in context. We weren't all that serious about each other." What a half-truth that was. She'd been more than serious.

"So you slept with other guys you weren't serious about?"

"No, of course not."

"Can't have it both ways."

"I'm just saying I knew Nick wasn't into forever after. He loved hockey. That was more important than anything."

Looking pleased, as if she'd just destroyed her own argument, he said, "As far as Nick is concerned, I rest my case. But you. You let him use you."

Eden glanced at the green folds of her dress, the scene in the kitchen rushing back. Nick reminding her of his memories of her in green. His voice floated through her thoughts. *It was some of the best sex we ever had.*

"Maybe I used him," she replied softly.

"You? Not a chance. You once loved him."

How had they gotten onto this topic? "I'm not sure that at twenty-one I knew what love was. We had fun together, but my world didn't fall apart when he ended the relationship." But it had for a few months; she'd been sad and weepy and had felt terribly alone.

"Nor did his world, since it was already in the tank." Cal drew her into his arms, his hands brushing across her back. "I love you."

She relaxed against him, resting her cheek against his shirt. He felt welcoming and strong and very sober. She wasn't angry anymore, but she was still unsettled. Obviously Nick wasn't disturbed, and Cal acted as if it was all much ado about nothing. She sighed, tipped her head back, went up on tiptoes and kissed him. "Perhaps I blew things out of proportion."

"You're aware of feelings, and that's not a crime. That empathy is what makes you such a good guidance counselor."

They left the bedroom, their arms around each

other, and when they reached the living room, Cal said, "See? Nick's over there surrounded by all his old girlfriends. Plus Julie, who'd probably like to be one of his new ones. And if I'm not mistaken, he doesn't look like he's having a lousy time. Does he?"

"No, I guess not."

Cal gave her a perfunctory squeeze, then walked toward the bar. Eden remained where she was. At that moment, Nick laughed, as did the women sitting with him. He turned slightly, and their eyes caught and held.

Eden couldn't pull her gaze away, nor could she prevent a sense of wild catapulting. In those seconds, she saw no one else, was aware of nothing but the pounding in her chest. What did it all mean? This ricochet of feelings? Nostalgia seemed too simplistic and besides, he'd offered that in the kitchen and she'd been furious with him. A new relationship wasn't an option; she'd moved on years ago. And even if she hadn't, there was no hint that Nick wanted more than to rachet up the sexual tension between them. She felt caught in a trap more divisive in her own mind than in reality.

She sighed, once more concentrating on her surroundings. Guests moved from group to group, their laughter proving this was indeed a real party. Cal was getting a fresh drink and chatting amicably with a cluster of men. Nick had turned back to the women and now rose to shake hands with a late arrival.

It seemed suddenly surreal. Eden began to wonder if she'd imagined Cal's spitefulness and

Nick's bland response. She glanced down at her green dress; she hadn't imagined the encounter with Nick. That had been far too real for comfort.

Chapter 8

By midnight, guests were finding coats, complimenting Mary on a great party and slowly making their way out the front door and into the chilly night. Al and Flossie had gone off to bed, as had the cousins from Vermont.

Earlier the kitchen had been straightened, and the dishwasher was now humming through its final load. Mary had been shooed out of the way while Eden, Flossie and three other guests worked. Plates of leftover food had been wrapped and put away. Bobby was happily munching on a bowl of scraps.

Now the house was quiet as Eden shelved the last of the glasses and tied up the trash to go out to the cans. She was about to go in search of Cal and her coat when Nick appeared.

"Mom wants me to drive Cal home," he said from the doorway. "She'd insist on him staying here, but with all the guests, she's out of room. Call me nasty, but I'm not giving him my bed. After I get him home, I'll drop you off."

"That's not necessary, Nick. I can drive him. Then I'll just take his car."

"He's drunk."

"I know he's tipsy."

"Not tipsy. Drunk," he said flatly. "You'd never get him into the house."

At that moment, Mary entered the kitchen. She was shaking her head, both annoyance and concern clearly evident. "Nick's right, Eden. I'll worry about you if you go alone with him."

Eden had seen Cal have at least two more drinks since their confrontation in Mary's bedroom, but she hadn't been counting the refills. Then again, she shouldn't have to monitor him as if she was the alcohol police.

"Where is he?" she asked.

"In the den."

Eden slipped past Nick and Mary and entered the den, where she found Cal slumped in a chair.

"Oh God," she muttered, staring at him in some astonishment. His jacket was gone, his tie knot loosened and yanked sideways to his shoulder. The tie looked as if he'd tried to take it off and had been frustrated by the intricacy of the knot. His hair was mussed, his eyes bloodshot and his lower lip was swollen as if he'd been pulling on it. His wrinkled shirt collar had a lipstick smear on it. Cal, like Nick, had gotten lots of hugs and more than few kisses, but the mark summed up his unkempt appearance.

One arm gripped the chair; it seemed that he'd tried to rise and had failed. The other dangled over the arm. His dishevelment was so out of sync with the Cal she knew that Eden half expected him to morph back to real life and tell her the drunk act was all a bad joke.

"Cal?"

When he didn't immediately respond, she moved closer.

"Cal, come on, we have to leave."

His eyes swam into focus and he sucked in his lip, as if that was the key to getting to his feet. When that effort failed, he tried to straighten up by bending first one knee, then the other, but his balance was off. His attempt to lunge to his feet failed, and he collapsed even lower in the chair.

Disgusted, Eden moved closer still. "Take my hand. I'll pull while you come forward." But instead of cooperating, he yanked her to him, ensnaring her in arms that felt like eight instead of two, and held her in an octopus squeeze. She landed on the arm of the chair and across his lap. His breath spewed across her in a belch of fumes. She shuddered. If she'd struck a match, she'd have had a human blowtorch. She tried to scramble away when one of his hands fumbled under her skirt and the other shoved her halter aside to snag at her breast.

"Cal, stop it." She pushed one hand away only to find the other more aggressive.

"Wanna play in Eden's garden." The words were so slurred that it took her a second to understand what he said.

"Wanna pick the flowers." Then, playfully groping, his fingers forged ahead, climbing over her knee, up her thigh, until he found the edge of her panties.

Fumbling under the folds of her dress, she grabbed his hand and jerked it away from her. "You don't need to play, you need to sleep it off."

"You sleep with me, then I can play." His grin was sloppy, his bloodshot eyes triumphant, as if he'd invented cleverness.

"Then you have to let me go, get on your feet and come with me," she said with childlike precision. If she played along, maybe that would get him moving. When he scowled, she repeated what she had said, but still he made no response.

Nick came in, shook his head, assessing the scene before him as more stupid than difficult, then crossed quickly to the chair.

Cal sobered enough to glare at his brother. "Little brother Nickie isn't gonna play in my garden."

"Party's over, Cal. Let go of her."

But he held her even tighter. "No. She's mine. All mine."

"Yeah, yeah, I can see that."

Eden scowled impatiently when Nick didn't move. Irritated by Cal's groping and Nick's inaction, she snapped, "If it's not too much trouble, could you do something to untangle me?"

Nick yanked her skirt down as she tried vainly to push Cal's roving hand away from her breast.

"What the hell were you trying to do," Nick fired at Eden.

She narrowed her eyes, frustration and fury racing through her at his deliberate obtuseness. "Why, I just climbed right into his arms, hoping to get some satisfaction from Nickie's elder brother," she said in a high syrupy drawl, and took some pleasure from his surprise at her mockery. "What in hell do you think I'm doing?

Are you here to ask stupid questions or help me?"

"Always willing to help, ma'am," he drawled back at her, "You want me to do you now or after I get rid of him?"

Glowering at him, she muttered, "You don't miss a beat, do you?"

"Practice, babe. I've had thirteen goddamn years to practice."

Then his hands gripped her waist, and he jerked her up and out of Cal's grip as if she were a sack of feathers.

"Thank you," she said succinctly, straightening her clothes.

Cal flailed his arms. "Never gonna let her go. She's mine. Aren't you, Eden? You're not his, you're mine."

Nick wrestled Cal to his feet. Cal swayed toward him, so that Nick had to take a step sideways to keep his own balance.

Nick sagged a bit under Cal's weight, and Eden said, "Be careful. Your knee."

"You can kiss it later and make it all better. Come on, Cal, try and carry some of your weight."

"No kisses," he slurred. "She's not yours, she's mine."

Nick ignored him and said to Eden, "Can you still drive a stick?"

She gave him a pointed look.

A glimmer of amusement flitted across his face. "You have a dirty mind."

"I had the consummate teacher."

Nick chuckled. "My offer in the kitchen still stands."

Eden folded her arms, as if the gesture would block the sizzling current jumping between them. "Offering to drive Cal home? I definitely accept."

"Yeah, I figured you would. See if you can fish my keys out of my pocket." When she didn't move, he scowled. "Either that, or you hold him up so that I can free one of my hands."

Resigned, she came forward and slid her hand into his pants pocket. She encountered change, a very solid and warm thigh through the fabric and finally the keys. By the time she got them out, her fingers felt singed.

Nick started to walk a stumbling Cal out of the den. To Eden he said, "You drive the Explorer and follow me. I'll take Cal in his car. Then once we get him settled, I'll take you home."

She wasn't about to protest after watching Nick struggle with his brother. No way could she wrestle Cal into his car, never mind up the stairs to his bedroom.

The next ten minutes were spent shrugging into coats, getting a very wobbly Cal into the car, saying good-bye to Mary—Eden promising to come for a visit the following week. Finally Eden settled behind the wheel of Nick's Explorer.

She'd driven a neighbor's sports utility vehicle last December, when she borrowed it to transport some students to an out-of-town hockey game. But Nick's felt different. Or maybe it was because it was his and the scent of him swirled through the interior. The leather driver's seat held the imprint of his body and seemed to fondle hers as if she was in his lap. She shook away the the images she was conjuring in her head and wiggled in an attempt to dissuade her body from thinking about his.

She had turned on the dash lights and was looking for the heat switch when she noticed the console tray. It overflowed with loose change, dog biscuits, a few stray lottery tickets, a hockey puck. Just barely visible under the puck was what looked like a photo.

Not your business, she told herself and then picked it up anyway. It couldn't be too private or it wouldn't be lying here. She held it under the strongest of the dash lights.

Her pulse jumped. "Oh my God!"

There was no mistaking the place: outside the hockey arena at Boston University.

There was no mistaking the couple: she and Nick.

And there was no mistaking the fact that she'd never seen this picture and had no idea who had taken it or why Nick had it on the console.

But she clearly remembered the circumstances sealed in time by the photo. It had been taken at the height of their relationship, when they'd laughed and done silly things such as snowball fights in front of her sorority house and serious things such as visiting an old professor in a nursing home. It had been a time of high intensity and higher ideals that in any reasonable world couldn't last, but while it had, Eden had never been happier. The sexual tension added a deeper layer and often erupted so automatically that containing it until they had privacy had given rise to a whole new set of jokes and teasing.

Eden smiled wistfully in the darkened vehicle. Where had all the wonder gone? What had happened to the dreams of a lifetime, the lover she'd once believed would be hers forever?

Before the photo had been taken, Nick had scored the winning goal in a game against Michigan State. She'd waited outside for him, as she did after every game.

When he'd sauntered out of the rink, so sure of himself and his abilities, so sure of her, sure that she'd be waiting for him, Eden had raced forward. In jubilation, she'd leaped into his arms. Her legs wrapped around his waist, her fingers wound into his thick hair, she was kissing him as if she couldn't get enough. That night they'd made love three times.

She wriggled again now, too aware of the way he'd once made her feel, but also too damn aware of how she'd felt tonight. Arousing memories, that's all, she assured herself, not lost love or even forgotten love suddenly revisited. She and Nick had been kids. Yes, it had been wonderful, but Nick had ended it—hardly proof of even the weakest feelings of love.

Sure, she'd loved him and she'd suffered a few months of pain when it was over. But she hadn't pined away, missing him, wanting him in some misguided, overheated belief he was the one man she'd always love. She'd had other boyfriends after Nick. One relationship, with Michael Hartshorne, a commodities trader at the Chicago Mercantile Exchange, had lasted two years. They broke it off by mutual agreement.

Eden had wanted to return to New England and he didn't want to leave Chicago.

At Lonsdale High, she and Cal formed a friendship out of their relationship as colleagues, and then began dating. Eden's intimacy with Cal showed that she had moved beyond Nick, beyond the past.

Yet her relationship with Nick, illustrated by the photo, predictably brought a memorable rush of those freedom-filled college days. And the feelings.

Would it be as good between them now? They were older. He had an edge that made her furious but also fascinated her. That kiss at her house astonished her by its power to frighten her while at the same time it exposed her willingness, albeit reluctant, to venture further.

Sex. Flirting with sex, letting emotions leap unchecked. Playing at the dangerous edges of seduction and pretending nothing was going on.

She sighed. The pretense baffled her. Not only did it show her the hypocrisy of her own denial, but made her wonder why she was caught between wanting nothing to do with Nick and terrifying desire for him.

Cal would be appalled, and the more her practical, rational side thought about it, the more she was, too.

Now she looked at the photo again. Why had it been lying on the console like it had meaning for him? If she'd been into Machiavellian theories, she might have believed he was sending some message. But even Nick couldn't have predicted she'd be seated in his Explorer tonight.

The interior lights came on when he opened the driver's door.

She dropped the photo as if it was hot.

"You ready?"

"Yes, I'm all set." He nodded and was starting to close the door when she said, "Nick, do you know why Cal got so drunk? That's not like him."

"Beats me. I haven't been around for five years, remember?"

"Aren't you curious?"

"About getting drunk? Nope. Been there. Done that."

"Not drunk in general. I was appalled by his toast and told him so. Obviously I didn't change anything. Did you and he have an argument earlier about something?"

The darkness shadowed his face, but she had a sense that if she asked the right question, he'd answer it, and she wouldn't like the answer.

"Cal and I could argue about which FM station to listen to," Nick said lightly, and then just before closing the door, added, "See you at his house."

"Wait." She took a breath, the question suddenly obvious. "Did you and he argue about me?"

Either he didn't hear her or chose not to.

Fifteen minutes later, she parked the Explorer in Cal's drive. Nick had already pulled into the garage, and once Eden had walked in, he hit the automatic door closure switch. From the garage a door opened into the kitchen.

"How can I help?" Eden asked, feeling as if she was doing more shivering from the cold than anything. The trip hadn't been long enough to get the car's temperature beyond frigid.

"I'll get him out and on his feet. You steady him on one side and I'll take the other."

The walk from the garage to the kitchen snailed along in wobbly, lumbering steps.

Eden flipped on the kitchen lights, blinking at the brightness. Cal was barely conscious and Nick was literally holding him upright.

"Through here and up the stairs." She shed her coat, then came back to Nick, and they worked their way to the front hall. She turned on the lights.

Nick peered at the staircase. "I can take most of his weight, but not all of it. Can you balance the other side?"

"I think so."

Cal suddenly straightened, almost knocking Eden aside. He muttered something about another drink.

Nick glowered in disgust. "Let's get this done before he pukes or passes out."

Eden and Nick struggled up the stairs with Cal, a laborious process that drained them both.

"Bedroom is to the left," Eden said, her breathing strained, her side aching from trying to balance.

In the spacious bedroom, while Nick held Cal, she turned on the bedside lamp and pulled back the covers. Nick unceremoniously dumped Cal on the blue-striped sheets. Then he retreated a few steps and bent at the waist, taking deep, slow breaths and bracing his hands just above his knees.

"How's your knee?"

He raised his head. "Feeling cranky at the moment."

"There's some aspirin in the medicine cabinet."

"Yeah, good idea." He straightened and walked toward the bathroom. Eden went to work taking off Cal's shoes and socks. Next, she began to wrestle him out of his trousers. She glanced up to find Nick standing in the arch of shadows coming from the partly open bathroom door. He was taking the stopper from a bottle of perfume.

"You could help," she said, ignoring what he was doing.

He glanced up, the open bottle in his hand. He gestured. "Yours?"

She considered lying. "Yes."

He brought the container up and passed it under his nose. watching her, his voice was low. "Very nice. Intriguing. Erotic."

Eden swallowed. "Could you come over here and help me with the rest of his clothes?"

He tipped the bottle against his forefinger. The motion was slow and deliberate. Eden straightened, the thump of her heart ringing in her ears.

"Come here."

Dammit, he was not going to do this to her.

Instead of arguing or pretending she had no idea what he had in mind, she finished up with Cal, pulling the covers over him, and then closed in on Nick. "I warned you in your mother's kitchen," she whispered.

"Right. I need to get rid of my unrestrained appetites." He touched just the edge of his finger to the pulse in her throat. "But right there in bed is the drunk with all his appetites in total control. So much for the good guys."

Eden glanced back at the sleeping Cal, then took Nick's arm and led him out into the hall. She pulled the door slightly closed. Nick's expression was amused and she gritted her teeth. To him this was all a joke.

In a tight voice, she said, "I'm not going to go to bed with you."

His eyes shuddered down as if he was about to apologize. Just when she'd begun to think she'd unnerved him for a change, he said, "You told me that twenty minutes before I made you come on our third date."

Color flared in her cheeks and she stepped back. Angry, embarrassed and ignoring the shot of desire, she snapped, "You are a bastard."

"And an overgrown jock. Don't forget that." He tipped the bottle against his forefinger again, never taking his gaze from hers. She shuddered despite herself, and when he dragged his finger down to the halter's vee, Eden snagged his wrist.

"Please, don't do this."

"I want you."

"Because I'm with Cal. It's just ordinary sibling rivalry coupled with a naughty kind of lust that wouldn't exist if you and I hadn't once been involved."

"You don't know what you're talking about."

"I know you're not making things easy for me."

"Admit you feel something for me."

"Of course I do," she said, deliberately sidestepping the answer she knew he wanted. "You're Cal's brother."

He went terrifyingly still, then methodically he capped the perfume bottle and put it on the floor. Straightening, he said in a cold, precise voice, "Don't ever set him up as some example for me."

Eden shrank back, not because she was afraid, but because of the vitriolic undertone. "I—I wasn't."

He gripped her shoulders. "And don't back away from me like I'm not fit to wipe his boots."

"Nick—" She started to deny any such intent when he plunged his hands into her hair and lowered his head.

"Open your mouth."

Defiantly she pressed her mouth closed. There was something obscene about doing this with Cal a room away.

"You can't—not here—"

He raised one eyebrow, as if she'd offered a challenge, but more staggering was how hauntingly he reminded her of the Nick who had pursued her so relentlessly in college. Eden shoved the image away.

"Call it a welcome home kiss if that will ease your conscience."

"My conscience is clear, thank you very much."

"Good."

"And yours?"

"I don't have one."

Then he kissed her.

What astonished her was that his mouth

wasn't harsh and plundering, as it was that afternoon on her couch. She almost wished it was, but his tongue drifted through the kiss as though time was meaningless and her relationship with his brother was outside the bond that couldn't touch what they were now feeling.

Eden felt herself softening, sliding away from token protests. Her arms were trapped between their bodies, but Nick's hands were relaxed, coming around to frame her face, to brush his thumbs just under her earlobes.

He shifted slightly, not breaking the kiss, but riding against her thighs until she, too, moved enough for his leg to insinuate itself between hers. Somehow Nick had turned her so that her back was against the wall and he flat against her.

Her desire to push him away and worse, her resistance, to push him back ebbed away.

"Let's go some place," he murmured, his mouth against her throat, his fingers opening the catch of her halter. She felt his tongue on her skin and the halter dropping. Her breasts swelled, his hands folded over them and her nipples snuggled into his palms.

Feeling powerless against her own desire while at the same time hating that she was so easily seduced by him filled her with frustration and disillusionment. Pushing him away, she sagged against the wall, lowered her head and folded her arms across her breasts.

"Eden?"

She squeezed her eyes closed hard to stop the tears.

He cupped her chin, lifting it, shaking her a little. "What's wrong with you?"

"It's what's wrong with us, Nick. Your brother is a few feet away, and we're out here in the hall engaged in the early stages of copulation."

"You make it sound like a terminal disease."

She turned aside, refusing to look at him. "I'm disappointed in myself and in you."

Silence crept between them, and she waited for Nick to swear or make some quick comeback. The soft snoring of Cal in the distance punctuated the quiet, and Eden listened for the one-two breathing pattern as if it represented steadiness when her volatile emotions were in disarray.

She jumped when Nick brushed his mouth across her bare shoulder. Then, without saying anything, without touching her skin again, he lifted the straps of the halter and carefully rehooked them at the back of her neck. He stepped back from her, giving her every opportunity to leave. His expression was void of anger or insistence or argument.

She reached for his hand. "I'm not blaming you, Nick."

But he eluded her fingers, backing away. "I'll wait downstairs for you."

Eden stood very still, listening for his descending steps and hearing only the empty stillness of the night. Her body felt anesthetized, her heart porous and vulnerable, her thoughts of Nick unstable and upsetting.

Slowly she reentered the bedroom, crossed to the bed and pulled the quilt up over Cal, her knuckles skimming across the stubble on his cheeks. "Are we going to be okay, Cal?" When her only answer was another snore, she straightened and said sadly, "I don't know anymore."

Chapter 9

WITHIN A WEEK OF THE PARTY, NICK HAD relieved his mother of his company and Bobby's shed hair by moving into one half of a duplex on Waterview Road—never mind that the closest water to view was a lake fifteen miles west of Lonsdale. The street was known for its transient renters, and the landlord was willing to sign a six-month lease. Dogs were allowed on payment of an extra security deposit.

A backyard the size of a hockey penalty box was the single drawback; Bobby had no room to run. Nick compensated him by taking him for walks and so discovered that the duplex was just two blocks from Eden's house and Barrington Park.

"Guaranteed my brother will see this as a plot for seduction," Nick muttered to Bobby as they wandered through the park across the street from Eden's neatly maintained house.

Bobby woofed softly.

"She'll see it that way, too."

Another woof.

"How about you?"

That rated two woofs.

Nick scratched Bobby behind the ears. "This time I'm innocent."

Bobby tipped his head, his watery brown eyes soulful.

"Yeah, yeah, I know innocence is a foreign concept for me, but stumbling over it by accident does occasionally happen."

If ever Nick needed an excuse to leave town, the past few weeks had provided a myriad possibilities. Eden headed the list.

Given that he had never been an organizer when it came to his motives or his pursuits, he was struck with how dauntingly simple it was to focus when the one thing he wanted he didn't have.

Eden.

In the days following his welcome home party, he'd kept his distance from her. His need to prove to his brother that getting her back hadn't troubled him. Cal was a big boy. He sure as hell knew that barking an order to stay away from Eden presented Nick with an irresistible challenge. What Nick hadn't figured into his plan was Eden's resistance.

It had been a long time since he'd been so totally rejected. Among the seamy shadows of the past five years, he could recall few turndowns. His encounters with women who wanted sex—numerous in comparison with the look-but-don't-touch recreational virgins—came with a price. Nick had grown jaded and too sure of himself. Even the occasional rebuff usually came disguised as coy flirtation.

Yet in his mother's kitchen, Eden hadn't been subtle or coy. Calling him a man of unrestrained appetites and a jock who needed to grow up had all the appeal for him of an outdoor shower in January.

His suggestion that she come to bed with him had been intentional, though a bit crass.

He winced now at his bravado. Hell, when you lead with your chin, then you better damn well expect a couple of jolting counterpunches.

The fact that he'd backed off to lick his wounds provided him with a discomfiting insight. What if she had fallen into bed with him? Then what? He had no plans to walk down any long-term roads here. Christ, he hadn't a clue if he was even on the right road now. What he did know was that he was home, he was working, he was sober and he was horny. The first two were laudable, the second two were definite danger zones. The prospect of falling back to old habits of getting drunk or cruising to score rattled the hell out of him.

He had, however, bought a bottle of Johnnie Walker, which sat unopened on his kitchen counter. It was a vivid reminder of what his life had been: too many years of excess and desperation. Also, in a twisted way, the liquor was reassurance that since waking up in the motel room, he had acquired or discovered some core to his character.

He whistled for Bobby, about to start for home, when he halted in sudden recognition. Barrington Park. Good God, he should have remembered instantly. And if he wasn't mistaken, that old tree was near the Winesap Road entrance.

Bobby trotted along beside him as he got his

bearings. Benches, empty and snow-covered, were scattered about, and a winding path toured the park's interior. Ice patches made for slippery walking, but after examining three trees, Nick found the carved heart. Time had scarred and darkened it, the tree's natural growth sinking the engraving deeper into the bark.

The heart was crude, the initials cut as though done by a blind man with a dull knife, but then he hadn't been too sober that spring day thirteen years ago. His hockey career was a failure, his knee therapy still required a weekly visit, his mood was despondent, his drinking the prelude to those years of stumbling through the bowels of hell.

In those days, there had been little remaining of the Nick who had so avidly pursued Eden Parrish. Then he had returned home to take that tiny ember of devotion and put it in some place safe, and innocent and permanent. Initials in a heart carved in the bark of a tree had been the gravestone of their relationship—a marker for life of what once was and would never be again.

N.S. loves E.P.

What he found curious was that from this tree he could see her house. Coincidence, of course, that she bought a house across the street from this park, this tree. To his knowledge, Eden knew nothing about the carved heart and the initials. Yet standing here, he felt as if he possessed some new rights to their past, present and future. He was bound to her, because this tree had held on for all those years when he had been falling apart. She belonged to him in an everlasting way because of her choice to live across the street. Sure.

Just how in hell had he gotten so spiritual and melancholy? He needed a dose of reality. Yet deep within him, something took hold, and it had more to do with who he wanted to be today and tomorrow than who he was yesterday.

The wind made little progress shaking the leafless branches. Snow nestled in the crevices. Nick took out his pocket knife, scraping away the time and dirt so that the initials were clearer but the bark was left undisturbed. *What a sentimental idiot you are,* he mused, a grin tugging at his mouth. Finding the heart reassured him when his optimism about any relationship with Eden was abysmally low.

Bobby barked, and Nick swung around in time to see some poor squirrel take off, with Bobby in pursuit.

He whistled, and Bobby lumbered back to him. Together they walked back to his place.

When he turned the corner onto Waterview, he saw an old red Firebird parked behind his Explorer. It was running, and as he drew closer, a figure climbed out.

Dressed in boots, cords, a heavy gray jacket with the collar turned up, Eddie Metcalf waited for him. His uneasiness or nervousness—Nick wasn't sure which—twitched around him.

"Hi," the teenager said, following with a short laugh.

"How ya doin' Eddie?"

"Not so good."

Nick sighed. He imagined the kid was here to beg for a second chance. According to the stats

Nick had seen, the seventeen-year-old had been Lonsdale's highest hockey scorer this season. Nick had heard of his deftness on the ice from the other players and Coach Buck Cranston. But from what Nick had witnessed at the practices, the kid was mediocre. Two nights ago, he suspected, despite his rule of no drinking and no sex, Eddie had done one or the other or both. Just that afternoon he'd pulled him for fighting and for messing up a play even the sloppiest player could have done with ease.

Lonsdale had a game tonight, and Nick was responsible for making up the roster for the coach. So far, he hadn't decided whether to let Eddie play.

Now the teenager shivered and folded his arms together against the cold wind. "I gotta talk to you."

"I haven't finished the player setups for tonight. But from what you've shown me at practices, I'm not impressed." Nick took his house keys from his pocket.

Eddie didn't move; his hips were slung back against the Firebird's rear fender. He watched Bobby instead of looking at Nick.

Finally he said, "Look, I know I haven't done too good."

"Lousy."

"I got things on my mind."

"So do the other guys."

"This is different."

"Booze and sex? How's that different from every other jock in the state?"

"No! I ain't been drinkin'."

"Sex."

"Not lately."

Nick almost grinned. He knew that feeling.

Eddie shoved his hands into his jacket pockets. A patch emblazoned with a wolf and two crossed hockey sticks showed on the right sleeve. "Look, I know I ain't got no business expectin' you to help me, and when you first came, I wasn't too, you know, hot to know about you. I mean, almost getting to the NHL ain't no big deal. But all the guys really like you, and Poppy told me you were cool—" For the first time he looked at Nick and his eyes were filled with desperation. "Ah, shit, I don't know, but I gotta tell somebody and I figured like maybe you'd be okay about this and—" His voice choked.

Warning bells clanged in Nick's head. "I'm not a counselor, Eddie. You probably should talk to Ms. Parrish or maybe one of your teachers."

"They don't know nothin' except what some textbook tells them. I'm talkin' my whole life here. You know, big time serious? You gotta listen. You don't know how hard it was just drivin' here."

Nick studied him. Yeah, he knew about hangin' tough when you wanted to puke and be done with it. Gesturing, he said, "Come on inside."

The duplex was furnished with sturdy but uninspiring pieces. The working fireplace in the living room, a decent enough shower and Bobby's claim to a red rug in the bedroom had sold him on renting the place.

Once inside, Bobby headed for his water dish. On the small dining table were the game plans for tonight and the unfinished roster. There was also a stack of videotapes of games that Johnston High School, their opponent tonight, had played. Nick had been through them all, looking for weaknesses and strengths as well the strategies their coach used.

Eddie nodded toward the tapes. "They're the best in the league."

"More hustle than skill."

"Their center is a ball-buster."

"Buck tells me you are, too. The problem is I haven't seen any evidence of it." Nick watched Eddie move about, then stop again by the dining table. He picked up a hockey puck, hefting it and turning it, keeping his hands busy.

"So is he full of bullshit?" Nick asked.

"I'm good. I'm damn good."

Nick shrugged.

"I am! I just got things that are distractin' me."

"Look, kid, I told you I'm not a counselor. You got problems with anything other than puttin' the puck in the net and hustlin' your ass on the ice, I'm out of my league." Nick looked at his watch. "I gotta finish up here and get over to the rink."

For a moment Nick thought the kid was gonna split. Then he dropped the puck onto the table. Releasing it seemed to give him courage. Words spilled in a rush.

"There's this girl . . . I swear I'm a victim here. It wasn't like I made any moves first—well, maybe I did sorta look her over, but that's all. She wanted me first. You know? She wanted it bad, chasin' me and hangin' around at the rink, rubbin' up against me. I mean shit, what was I suppose to do?"

Give her what she wanted, Nick thought, but a flash of Eden's face kept him silent. For sure, she'd freak if it got back to her that he was peddling sexual advice. He could hear her now: Was that out of your Unrestrained Appetite manual?

"You tell me." Nick was already pretty sure of the answer.

Eddie looked at him like he'd just stepped out of a monastery. "What do you think? I did her. I did her a lot."

"And it was always consensual?"

"Huh?"

"You didn't force her? She was willing?"

"Yeah, yeah, but that ain't the problem."

Then Nick knew. Sweet Christ, but he knew.

"She's, uh, well, gonna have a kid."

"Yours, I presume."

"She said it was." Then Eddie brightened like he'd been handed an unexpected sliver to escape. "Maybe she's lyin', you know, tryin' to trap me."

"Hope springs eternal."

"Huh?"

"You're looking for a way out."

"Well, hell, sure, wouldn't you?"

Nick ignored the question. "If you had legitimate doubts, you wouldn't be shaking like a wet puppy."

Eddie shuddered, then dropped into the lounge chair, slumped forward, hands dangling between his legs, looking suddenly like a small lost boy. "I don't know what to do. My old man'll kill me. My mother'll flap around about being mortified when she'd warned me about sex and staying pure, as she calls it. Man, I'm gonna get my ass fried big time."

"What about the girl?" At Eddie's blank look, Nick explained, "You're telling me about you and your family. What about her? Her family?"

"She's the problem, man."

Nick took a deep breath. "The pregnancy is also your problem."

"Yeah, well, I thought she was, you know, gonna get rid of it. That's what I told her to do. She even dropped out of school. I figured, hey, she's an okay kid. You know, not tryin' to saddle me, what with me havin' college and hockey fillin' up my future. But last Monday she was back in school and comin' at me with what I gotta do. Then yesterday the little bitch goes and spills her guts to Ms. Parrish. She called me into the office and now she wants to talk to my parents. She kept saying stuff about me facing up to my part in it and being responsible. . . ." He ran out of breath.

"Sounds like Eden," Nick muttered.

"She screwed this up by buggin' Karen when she quit school."

"Wait a minute. You screwed up by getting the girl pregnant in the first place. Now that it hasn't turned out the way you planned, you're blaming Ms. Parrish."

"She wants to tell my folks. We were all supposed to meet with her. I knew that was comin', but I thought it was about this program she's doin' and she's wantin' to mix it up with the parents. But when I saw Karen back in school and perkin' around like someone gave her a get Eddie pep pill, I pretended I was sick and got a pass to go home. Now the meeting's set for to-morrow and you gotta help me."

Nick raised an eyebrow. "First off, I don't have to help you. The truth is you've messed up and now you have to deal with it."

"It wasn't my fault!"

"I get it. Your cock just took off all by itself while you were home watching PBS."

"PBS?"

"Never mind. You screwed around and you got careless and you got caught. It didn't hap-pen by magic and it won't go away that way either."

Eddie barely nodded. Reality was finally sink-ing in. "You know Ms. Parrish. I thought, you know, maybe you could talk to her."

"That's why you came to tell me all this? Not for advice, but to ask me to talk to Ms. Parrish?"

"Yeah."

"What makes you think I know her well enough to say anything?"

"I heard she used to be your girlfriend. At the rink, a couple of the guys were saying how cool you were 'cuz she's makin' it with your brother and you aren't, you know, freaked about it. I thought it was weird."

Nick absorbed that like an unexpected body shot. Gossip that gave him the benefit of the doubt? Then again, why not? Growing up as Cal's kid brother had ingrained in Nick the habit of always stepping back and letting Cal lead. Now he was getting credit for being cool—translated, that meant being a good guy who didn't cruise into Cal's sexual territory—but clearly Eddie thought his restraint wasn't normal; a fact Nick had known and lived with for years.

"You got any brothers, Eddie?"

"Yeah. And a sister."

"What if your brother was dating one of your ex-girlfriends?"

"Huh?"

"Would you be cool or would you freak?"

"Depends on why she was an ex. You know, was she a jerk or was I the jerk for lettin' her go."

"And if you were the jerk?"

"No way, man. I'd clue my brother so he knew he only got lucky because she couldn't have me." Eddie shrugged. "So you gonna talk to Ms. Parrish?"

Nick almost laughed at that potential scenario. Eden was about as likely to take advice from him as she was to put credence in initials carved thirteen years ago in an old tree.

"I don't think that's the answer, Eddie. Why don't you talk to her before you tell your parents?"

"Hell, man, you don't get it. I don't want to tell them. I just want it to all go away."

It was an appropriate time to give a pep talk on responsibility, but Nick and responsibility weren't on good enough terms yet for him to be giving sage guidance to others.

"Eddie, look, you came here and spilled your gut. To some that's probably a first step because you're doing something. I'm flattered that you think I have some ribbon-tied solution, but I don't."

"You ain't gonna help me."

"Best advice I have is that you talk to Ms. Parrish before she talks to your folks. If she knows you're willing to be a stand-up guy about this instead of a coward, she'll help you." Nick wasn't sure where that pearl of wisdom had come from. The truth was he didn't know any such thing, but he knew Eden.

The kid got to his feet, sniffled and dragged his sleeve across his eyes. Nick felt a slash of sympathy, not because Eddie's attitude had magically matured, but because he was young and foolishly naive despite the swagger and the tough talk.

Eddie started for the door. Bobby lay on his stomach, head resting between his front paws, staring at Nick as if to say, "Do something."

Nick raised an eyebrow at Bobby. "You're a pain in the ass, you know that? Next poker game when I'm losing my shirt, I'm gonna lay you out as the bet."

Bobby grinned, tail swishing like a motorized fan.

Eddie was about to close the door when Nick called to him.

"Okay, kid. I'll talk to Ms. Parrish first and give her your side of this—about the girl."

"Yeah? You mean it?"

"If your side is bullshit—"

"No way, man. I mean, you can ask around. She came after me like I had everything in my jeans she ever wanted to make life work."

"Yeah, well, it worked, all right," Nick muttered. "There's a condition to this."

Leery, he asked, "What?"

"I want two hundred and fifty percent on the ice tonight. Got it?"

Eddie grinned, his eyes lighting up as if he'd found a miracle. "I'll blow their doors off."

"And melt the hinges."

"You got it."

Chapter 10

EDDIE DIDN'T DISAPPOINT.

The Lonsdale Wolves and Eddie Metcalf played with the precision and power of a division-winning team. Johnston seemed flummoxed, and as a result, their usually powerful defense men wielded their sticks like crutches rather than puck movers. Nick was astonished at how, when Eddie was on his game, his enthusiasm worked the entire team into a pumped frenzy.

The stands were packed and the boards lined with fans who couldn't find seats. Among those who had arrived halfway into the first period were Cal and Eden. Cal had positioned Eden in front of him, his head occasionally dipping when he'd said something. Nick wasn't close enough to make out facial expressions, but Cal's body language was clearly possessive and confident.

Nick scowled. His brother was obviously flaunting the relationship and coming onto Nick's turf to do it. Nick knew it and Cal knew it. Yet to any casual observer, Cal and Eden were just two attractive people who cared for each other and weren't shy about showing a natural affection that was neither overdone nor offensive.

"Very cool," Nick muttered, folding his arms and wishing like hell he didn't give a damn. But he did, and it occurred to him that he felt not resentment but something more insidious and more dangerous. Unlike resentment, born at the bone, straightforward, cold and calculated, jealousy licked deep and viperous.

Envy lurked like a rusted key that he'd cleaned and oiled and used to unlock too many of his vulnerabilities. Odd, that the optimism he'd discovered in the carved heart, came, too, from mucking through his messed-up life. Jesus, coming home was supposed to be for getting himself together, not wrestling with some inner catharsis.

The final period proved Johnston wasn't going to give up a win easily. They poured on the muscle and power, but Lonsdale, thanks to a Johnston penalty in the last minute, scored a 4-2 win. Screams and shouts of victory shook the rafters, sounds Nick remembered well from his own glory days. This win might be vicarious, but it sure was sweet.

As the players made the traditional line pass of "good game" sportsmanship, Nick gathered his clipboard and his jacket and made his way along the boards.

Buck Cranston, who had handed over coaching duties to Nick for this game, walked along with him. Fleshy faced, barrel-shaped and bald by choice, his brutish approach to coaching bothered Nick because it had nothing to do with sharp skills and deadly grace. Cranston relied on brawn and a take-no-prisoners policy that could work but was a disaster for the slightly built player. Hockey was a tough game, but Nick knew from experience that muscle too often gets the player into the penalty box rather than goals onto the scoreboard.

"You set up some dicey plays, Scanlon. Had me holding my breath."

"The kids played like pros."

"Or they were lucky Johnston didn't expect them to. And that final period penalty didn't hurt."

"All those early-morning practices worked. They learned that well-executed puck passing wins the game."

"Fine. You're giving private lessons. You got the time. Some of us have other jobs."

Nick didn't dislike Buck Cranston, but his whining and need for ego massages had gotten tiresome. The coach viewed Nick as some hotshot who'd blown in claiming to be an expert. Cranston had been skeptical that a has-been could produce results, so the jabs were not a surprise. Mostly Nick ignored them. Tonight Cranston pissed him off.

Nick asked, "You looking for a reason to resign from coaching?"

"Why? So you can take the job?"

"Might consider it. But I don't come cheap."

"Now, wait a minute, Scanlon. I coached this team to first place in the league two years ago. You come swaggering in like you got all the answers. Just because I let you coach one game doesn't mean I'm gonna let you roll over me."

Nick shrugged. "Considering tonight's win, I guess I do have all the answers. Rolling over is kid's stuff. Try something grown-up, like watch and learn."

Cranston sputtered, "You're nothing but a has-been trying to get your act together and steal my job!"

"You know what, Cranston? You're absolutely right."

"Goddammit, first Don Tucker and then your brother—"

Nick halted, looking closely at Buck. "What about Cal?"

"He called and asked me to give you a chance, and now you're lookin' to screw me."

Nick was silent, but his belly was doing flip-flops. Cal asking a favor for him? Nick doubted that. Had to be a catch.

But the coach was right. He was being ornery and pushy. Eden coming to the game with Cal irritated him; in fact, anything Eden did with Cal soured his disposition. But that wasn't Buck's problem. Hell, he didn't want Cranston's job. He liked teaching, working with the team and seeing their potential become reality, but making an enemy of Buck wasn't and never had been his goal. All in all, Cranston had done a good job.

"You're right, Buck."

"Huh?"

"Has-been is right."

Buck actually looked embarrassed. "Hey, look, that was outta line. Shouldn't have said that."

"I've heard it all before." Nick glanced over

to where Cal and Eden were standing like a couple who belonged together, not, as he had wanted to believe, a man and a woman struggling to define their relationship.

With new insight, Nick realized he'd been buffaloed by his own hormones and old memories. Adding Cal to that mix had made Eden into a trophy Nick wanted to win. That's what all his irritation, bad manners and jealousy were about—not vulnerabilities or some deep sense of hope and meaning behind a heart carved in a tree. This was about nothing more complicated than trophy sex.

The scene before him now showed clearly that he'd lost. Cal was the winner, and the winner gets the girl. Maybe, Nick mused, he'd come to the place of acceptance.

He clapped Buck on the shoulder, suddenly feeling relieved and energized. "I am trying to get my act together, but not at the expense of stealing your job."

Cranston looked puzzled by the about-face, but slowly nodded. "Look, maybe I let off too much steam. The kids played great tonight. I'd like you to coach more often. I want to see that kind of enthusiasm for the rest of the season."

"They keep focused and hustle and there's no reason why they can't win the division."

A number of fans approached and congratulated Buck and Nick.

"Great game, Nick."

"Whatever you did, we need you to do it again."

"Buck's a good coach and laid the groundwork for the results in tonight's game," Nick heard himself saying, and wondered why he suddenly was shoring up Buck Cranston's ego. Because it was the appropriate response for a coach who volunteered and made an effort. And it gave him an easy exit when Buck's chest swelled and he announced, basking in the attention, "Actually, Nick worked from my strategy. . . ."

Across the rink, Nick saw Eden talking to a group of people. Cal stood beside her, arms at his sides, listening.

"Buck will fill you all in," Nick said to the ones gathered to hear the details. "I want to catch my brother before he splits." Nick moved through more congratulations, walking briskly as slaps on the back and shouts of "great game" followed him.

Before he got to Cal, a man stopped him, his smile almost splitting his face.

"Man, I gotta tell you, I ain't seen my boy play like that in weeks." He thrust out his hand to Nick. "I'm Ben Metcalf."

"Eddie played a great game."

"So you gonna coach the rest of the season? Christ, we'll win the division and Eddie will have that shot at the NHL. Once I wanted to play in the pros myself, but, well, it didn't work out. You know about that route, doncha? Now my boy is gonna do it." He studied Nick, wanting some reassurance. "After his shots on goal tonight, there ain't no question is there?"

"Mr. Metcalf, I'm not in the NHL and I don't scout for any of the teams, so I couldn't tell you." Nick knew the kid was good, damn good. But he also knew that to support Metcalf's assumptions would send his expectations into the stratosphere. And then there was Eddie's other problem.

He glanced up and saw that Cal had moved toward the door, chatting with Don Tucker. Eden was walking toward Cal.

"Uh, I've got to catch some people before they leave." Before Metcalf could say anything more, Nick excused himself and skirted a group of giggling girls, headed Eden off a few yards from Cal.

She glanced up, her eyes wide, her mouth slightly parted.

Nick halted before he was within touching distance. "Hi."

"Nick, hello." She shoved her hands into her coat pockets, her smile fixed and uncertain. To his astonishment, he felt totally responsible for her wariness. He wanted to reassure her, to make her understand he didn't intend to move on her.

"Kids played great, didn't they?"

"Terrific. Cal said you'd been working with them."

"Yeah. How have you been?"

"Busy with school and the pregnancy awareness program. I've talked to a lot of parents, and so far the response has been enthusiastic."

"I'd like to hear about it," he said, thinking of Eddie's problem.

"You would?"

"Actually, I was accused of being in cahoots with you when I told the players no sex the night before a practice and a game."

"So it was you." She grinned, her face opening up and relaxing. "Some of the girls said their boyfriends weren't pushing them for sex because the coach had made new rules. I'm impressed by your influence."

"It's one of my old Do as I say, not as I do rules."

"Hmm. Now that you mention it, it wasn't a rule you followed when I knew you."

"Because you were too irresistible. Never had that reaction until I got tangled up with you. The first two dates I had with you had me climbing the walls."

Her silence filled in a thousand blanks.

And I still am, he realized, and just as quickly understood that the likelihood of her admitting that she was aroused by him, never mind acting upon it, was slim to none.

Then suddenly she glanced away, turning one way and then the other, as if she had inadvertently stepped into a cage and trapped herself.

In a flat voice she said, "Nick, we shouldn't be talking about this."

"Eden, look, you and I have a past," he said, feeling like he was balancing a dozen crystal glasses on a tightrope. "It was wild and fun. Pretending it doesn't exist gives it more meaning than treating it as it was." He shifted slightly, more succinct words hovering in his thoughts. He pushed them aside for what needed to be said. There better be some reward for being a good guy. So far all he'd gotten was a frustrated hard-on. "I owe you an apology for being such an ass. You deserve better and you obviously have that in Cal."

She swallowed, looking at him and then looking away. Then, as if his confession spawned hers, she said, "I shouldn't say this—and I don't want you to take it to mean anything—but you haven't done anything that at some level I probably encouraged. That night at Cal's, I wanted you to kiss me."

Nick felt his whole body heat up. What kind of twisted fate was this? "Jesus, Eden, now you tell me."

"I wasn't going to, but we're both adults, and I learned a long time ago that facing the most difficult part of any problem makes the rest look easy. It's a lesson I keep having to relearn."

To Nick it sounded like doublespeak. He wanted to talk about kissing her. "Why did you want me to kiss you?"

"To find out if my feelings for you were just nostalgia, or if I was flattered that Nick Scanlon still found me desirable, or if there was anything real between us." She laughed. "For the past few days, I've reminded myself that women, young like the girls I counsel as well as those who should know better, like me, are too often caught up in the belief that if a guy wants sex it means more. Even when we know better, we always include love in the equation. I know that's a false assumption and one where women get hurt and disappointed."

"Guys offer love to get sex. Women give sex to get love."

"Exactly."

"But I didn't offer love and you didn't give me sex. So where does that leave us?"

"Friends who happen to have a past."

"Have you considered the possibility of testing this so-called friendship in case it might be more?" He asked the question so flawlessly, so easily, he wondered if he was hearing things.

Eden glanced at him with an astonished intensity, as if he'd barged into her most secret thoughts and discovered all kinds of musings about him that she'd never intended to reveal.

He stepped closer so that there was no chance anyone would overhear. "You have, haven't you? Thought about us. Thought about us making love."

"Not seriously," she said lamely.

"A fantasy. Just the two of us somewhere far from here where pleasure and satisfaction are all that matters."

She looked away, clearly unnerved, undoubtedly wishing she hadn't revealed so much. For Nick, there was no way he would back off. This wasn't finished.

Nick felt as though he'd stepped onto a precarious and fragile shelf where the tiniest wrong move would be disastrous. In that instant, Cal might as well have been on another planet.

In a low voice, his words carefully chosen, he said, "Fantasies are for fun, Eden. That doesn't make you kinky or naughty. It's just the way it is."

"It can't be that way, don't you understand? I love, Cal. I do, Nick."

"Do you?"

"Yes! We've talked about getting married eventually, having a family, having a normal and wonderful life. You being here and reminding me . . . It's silly that it makes me uneasy, and it shouldn't."

"But it does."

And like some new twist, their past was suddenly as important as the present.

Cal grinned as he approached, sliding his arm around Eden when she stepped close to him. "Hey, I was looking for you," he said fondly to Eden. To Nick, "A helluva game. That Metcalf kid reminds me of the way you played in high school. I take back all my low expectations. You're a born teacher of skills, Nick. I already talked to Poppy, and he said he wanted you to help him with managing the rink. Going to need an okay from the school board but that shouldn't be a problem." He smiled authoritatively. "With you working here giving private lessons and helping Buck with the team, Lonsdale ought to win big this year."

Cal chattered on, spreading the flattery and the compliments to a point at which Nick began to believe he was sincere. Eden was silent, giving an occasional nod when Cal squeezed her lightly. She looked like a windup doll that had run down.

"Hey, why don't you join us?"

Nick glanced up. "Join you?"

"We got a crowd going to The Windmill."

"Nick probably isn't interested," Eden said quickly.

"Of course he's interested. Or he should be. He's home and part of the community. Besides, a social life wouldn't hurt you any, Nick. Time you found out there's more in life than this ice rink. I even invited Julie Gallo along. Remember her? You met her at the party. She's single and pretty and very interested in you."

"You're fixing me up?" *You have Eden, so I get some flake with a stale come-on.* "No thanks."

"It's not a date. It's being sociable with good company. What you and Julie do on your own time is your business."

What about what I want to do with Eden? Is that her and my business? Nevertheless, Nick sighed and pushed away his more salacious thoughts. "Hell, why not? I'll find Julie and meet you there."

Chapter 11

ARCHITECTURALLY THE WINDMILL, WAS IN no danger of starting a trend. In the 1950s, an old barn with a windmill attached had been reinforced and converted into a restaurant by a Boston businessman. High prices coupled with an elitist attitude when referring to locals as not sophisticated enough to be employees rankled with Lonsdale natives. They, in turn, demonstrated their disdain by refusing to patronize the establishment.

A few in town took their bruised egos a step farther and torched the restaurant one November night. The fire damage wasn't catastrophic, but the owner cashed the insurance check and returned to Boston. The burned-out buildings stood for years as a charred reminder, and a source of "torch" stories about what happens to snobby outsiders.

Near the end of the 1970s, a wealthy Dutch immigrant, John Knoop, bought the abandoned restaurant and the land around it. Instead of stiffing the locals, Knoop hired them to do everything from reconstruction to calligraphy on the menus. He moved his family to Lonsdale and became part of the community. In particular, his wife became good friends with Mary Scanlon.

Knoop landscaped the area with thousands of tulips imported from Holland. That made it a popular place for Lonsdale brides to hold spring wedding receptions. Cal and Betsy had toasted their future on the flagstone patio flanked by acres of blooming tulips.

Nick had gotten drunk there three months after his hockey career ended, and had driven his car through the middle of the flowers. Eden and Mary Scanlon had lunch there often. Mary believed The Windmill served the best lobster salad in southern New England.

Tonight the local patrons were enjoying good cheer and a roaring fire when Cal and Eden stepped into the noisy central greeting area. They checked their coats and moved toward the dining room, where the overflow bar crowd had congregated.

Eden commented, "Looks like we're going to have to wait."

"How many of us are there?"

"Don and Suzanne Tucker, Julie, Nick, us and whoever else you invited."

"Paul and Claude. Their wives are off together on some shopping spree." Cal signaled to a middle-aged woman with a Mary Kay cosmetics complexion and poised smile. He held up eight fingers and she nodded.

"Is there anyone you don't have influence with?" Eden asked, bemused. Her father owned a tavern where getting a stool on a crowded night could only be done if some guy drank too much and fell on the floor. "Getting a table for eight doesn't look doable."

"Sure it is. Especially since I gave her son a job at Scanlons."

"Ah."

Cal shrugged. "Kid's a good worker and wanted something more challenging than flipping burgers."

"So his mom is grateful."

He grinned. "She damn well better be. We'll see how much when she gets us a table."

Cal went to the bar and when he returned with drinks, they moved to a bench that had just become free.

Eden sipped her screwdriver, glancing toward the entrance. "What happened to the others?"

"The Tuckers were going to stop and check on their kids. As to Nick and Julie, maybe they decided to get acquainted privately."

Eden felt a jolt of irritation at that implication. "Nick didn't look too interested in even being with Julie."

"Julie will warm him up. She's been into the store a number of times, dropping hints about me setting her up with him."

"Sounds like high school crush stuff," she muttered.

"Beats me. Girls always did like Nick. That rebel looking for no causes swagger appeals to certain types."

"Like me?" she asked, knowing that she sounded as if she was spoiling for an argument.

"Certainly not like you," he said adamantly, as if the idea was inconceivable. He took a generous swallow of his gin and tonic. "Julie, despite her ladylike demeanor and her school board shyness, isn't all that restrained when it comes to getting what she wants. At least, that's the rumor at the club. I'm just surprised she hasn't been hot on Nick sooner."

"Hmm," Eden murmured, raising her glass to her mouth and concluding it was safer to make no comment.

Her reactive attitude about Nick was nuts. Risking Cal turning on her with the perfectly logical question, Why do you care what Nick and Julie do? was asking for tension she didn't need.

Truthfully, she didn't care whom Julie was hot for. Knowing that the young woman could so easily and instantly capture Nick, however, left her with a hollow feeling, much as if Julie had stolen him when she wasn't looking.

How odd, she thought, and weirdly nasty. She herself couldn't have him, or rather, she didn't want to have him, and yet she resented Julie laying a claim. Eden knew she was being territorial, possessive and most of all disgustingly catty. Hardly the traits of a self-confident woman who loves another man.

"Who knows?" she said breezily. "Maybe she and Nick will really get serious."

"Or Nick will take what he can get and move on in a few weeks."

Eden didn't comment. The safest attitude was to think of Nick only as Cal's kid brother. Already that kiss the night Cal was drunk had resonated within her with frightening stamina. It licked at her commitment to Cal, teased her with explicit details of memories with Nick and posed the insidious question, What if . . . ?

She shuddered. No question but that she'd been lax and careless to have allowed him this deep invisible hold on her. But Nick was Nick, and he'd always had a kind of cut-close-to-the edge charm that beguiled her.

Face it, she concluded brutally, *he makes you think too much about sex.* Never mind all the rational arguments. Some deep primal need for him beckoned her. To erase or at least blur that fascination, she'd tried to be ruthlessly truthful by squarely addressing her disturbing sexual thoughts, believing that carnality would be less tantalizing under the glare of honesty and reality—namely, her love for Cal.

That strategy worked as long as she wasn't around Nick. But tonight—whatever had possessed her to be that honest with him? Talk about throwing out bait! Some perverse streak within her had needed to prick and poke until she got a reaction. Or she wanted him and, unlike Julie, didn't have the guts to just act.

One thing was clear: she didn't like knowing that Nick could so nonchalantly waltz off to Julie's bed when she herself was wrestling with her conscience. But then, Nick claimed to have no conscience.

Tonight her feelings were edgy and raw, far too similar to her emotions in those college days when she was sleeping with Nick while all the time hoping—not believing, but hoping—that she meant more to him than a good lay.

She hadn't.

He'd turned on a dime and ended their relationship after his accident as if she had been only a pleasant but expendable distraction.

And she realized suddenly that he would do it again if she let him. He'd sleep with her, slake himself with her, destroy her relationship with Cal and then he'd walk away. And she'd be left with her heart crumbled into an unrecognizable blob.

No way, Nick Scanlon. No damn way.

Sipping her drink, while Cal scowled at the crowded dining room, she said, "I'm surprised Claude is joining us. With his wife away, I would think he'd have cleaned out the condom counter at CVS and hustled down to Newport to be with his girlfriend."

Cal frowned. "That sounds more like Delphine than you. You're not usually so sharp and prudish."

"In some things I'm very prudish," she said, sounding prissy and not really caring. "I've seen too many kids who have a who cares attitude to all those old-fashioned values like faithfulness and trust and integrity. They don't learn that in a vacuum. They learn it at home."

"And from TV and their friends and the movies and music."

"Don't forget a culture populated by many lawmakers and influence peddlers who worship the bottom line. And we all know sex is a valuable commodity."

"Whoa. I think I uncovered a nest of cobras."

"Sorry. I didn't mean to sound rabid or as if I know it all. It's just that most of the time I feel I'm saying obvious things but I'm being looked at as though I have two heads. Just getting the name of the baby's father from Karen Sims took many, many talks with her."

"Who is it?"

"I can't tell you. His parents don't know yet."

"You don't trust me to keep it confidential?"

"It isn't that."

"Then what?"

"I promised Karen. And at this stage it's very important that she trust me."

"Trust is crucial in any relationship. You're absolutely right."

Eden glanced up at Cal, hearing his words, agreeing and nodding automatically. And yet a small place inside her squirmed uncomfortably at Cal's ease with words. Oftentimes his comments spilled too handily like he had the appropriate lines spit-polished into a benediction. She was never quite sure if he was being sincere or simply ending a discussion by flattering her.

The hostess signaled to Cal that they would have to wait a few more minutes for their table.

Cal stood. "I'm going to get another drink. Want one?"

"Who's driving tonight?"

He grinned, leaning close, his mouth brushing her temple, whispering, "I'll drive on the condition you come home with me."

"I can't," she said, disappointed. "I have an early appointment tomorrow."

"I've missed you. It's been more than a few nights since we've made love."

"I've been so busy with school." And working on not thinking about Nick. "We could go out to the car," she teased, nipping his ear. "The back seat is nice and roomy."

"No, thanks," he said with a disdainful shudder. "We'd freeze our butts. Horny teenagers we're not."

"I think I'm insulted. I offer a quickie and you refuse."

"He looked as if he was unsure whether she was kidding or serious. "Darling, why would I take a quickie now when I know if I'm a bit more patient I'll have you for a lot of hours in a nice comfy bed. Patience does have its rewards when it comes to being with you."

Eden frowned. There it was again. One of those flattering comments he was so adept at. "So did we decide who's driving?"

"Planning to get a little sloshed?"

"No, I just want to make sure you aren't."

"Nope."

Nevertheless, he got himself a fresh drink at the bar. Eden felt a headache coming. Going home and falling into bed suddenly held great appeal.

Cal returned and asked, "So what did you and Nick have your heads together about?"

"Just the game and the program at school," she said lightly.

"Looked pretty intense to me."

"You know Nick when it comes to hockey."

"I also know Nick when it comes to you."

Eden went very still. "I don't know what you mean."

"You didn't want him to come tonight."

"I—" Her mind went blank.

"It's okay, I understand."

"You do?"

"He makes you uneasy."

What if she just confessed her feelings? Cal might even understand. He and Nick appeared to be getting along, and Cal could offer advice if she explained that she needed to be clear of this before they considered marriage. Maybe all these secret thoughts were more dangerous because they were swirling with no anchor. "Oh, Cal, we do need to talk about this. It's more than just feeling uneasy. It's—"

But he didn't appear to be listening. Standing above her, he massaged her shoulder like he'd had some insight from above. "I know you don't welcome his attention. That college jock mentality wears thin when you're supposed to be an adult."

For a moment Eden was puzzled. College jock? Adult? That sounded too familiar. Then she recalled her fury at Mary's. She also recalled the sexual tension and Nick deliberately touching her when he helped her slip on her shoes. Jesus, had Cal been eavesdropping? And if so, why hadn't he mentioned it when she was so angry about his toast?

"Well, I guess all men like to believe their jock days are never quite over," she said casually. Must be the drink—God, she couldn't tell him. This was her problem and she had to work it out.

Cal tipped his glass to his mouth in a deliberate posture of delay as if he'd been privy to some private tidbit and wanted to milk the drama.

Eden waited. Had he overheard or not?

"I'm proud of you, Eden."

Now she was really confused. "For what?"

"Your dealing with Nick, of course."

Was he setting her up in some way? Playing a cat and mouse game? Or was she more paranoid about the issue than normal? Keeping her voice even, she asked, "And what exactly about dealing with Nick?"

"You put him in his place. Actually, I wasn't aware of it until the following day. One of the guests told me he overheard you call Nick a man of unrestrained appetites and tell him that he should grow up. And you're exactly right. I'm glad you made your feelings known to him."

Eden closed her eyes in relief. Made her feelings known to him—she'd sure done that at the rink when she admitted she'd wanted to kiss him. It was crazy, this three-way triangle of emotions was nuts.

She shuddered at the thought of anyone overhearing that conversation at the rink. Just the same, and in both instances, this was definite evidence of how ridiculously dangerous it was to be alone with Nick. Now that she thought about it, every time they ended up embroiled in conflict and tension about their past.

To Cal she said, "Why didn't you say anything before?"

"No need," he said dismissively. "Nick obviously got your message. You haven't seen him since that night, have you?"

"Just at the rink tonight." Thank God that was the truth.

"See? You made your feelings toward him clear. To his credit, he's respected them." He cupped her chin and lifted her face. Leaning down, he kissed her lightly. "Forgive me if I've shown any tendency to act as if I feel threatened."

"Your edginess around Nick right after he came home—were you worried I was still interested in him?"

"Not really. But I don't trust him. I warned him to stay away from you. Given what I said and what you said, he's come to his senses and concluded he won't make any moves on you." Cal straightened, glancing toward the crowded dining room. "It's about time."

The hostess approached, smile in place. "Mr. Scanlon, I have a table for your party."

Cal slipped her a twenty-dollar bill. "I really do appreciate this, Debbie." To Eden he said, "Go ahead with Debbie. I just saw Paul and I think that's the Tuckers behind him."

Eden followed Debbie to a circular booth that looked like a deserted island at the edge of a traffic jam.

She slid into the cushioned seat and was quickly joined by the others. Drinks were ordered along with platters of nachos and cheese. Missing were Claude—gone to Newport, after all—and Nick and Julie.

Obviously Nick and Jule had done what Cal had surmised and decided to have their own private party. Eden tried to convince herself it didn't matter.

". . . and so it's been a helluva hassle with no end in sight," Don Tucker was saying. "Never mind the terrible strain on Suzanne's sister and her husband. As the adoptive parents, Sherry and Kirk resent the late arrival of the mother's conscience and her dubious maternal instinct."

Eden, previously sleepy, came to attention and immediately focused her eyes on Don and Suzanne Tucker.

"So what are they going to do?" Cal asked.

"Their goddamndest to stop this little twit from taking their baby."

Suzanne's cheeks were flushed and her softly styled blond hair looked mussed as if she'd pushed her hand through it too many times. She lit a cigarette, pulling the smoke deep. In a low, monotone voice, she said, "It will probably end up in court."

A lull followed. Eden's sudden interest brought a scowl to Cal's face. He glanced at his watch, a signal he was ready to leave, not wade into Suzanne's sister's problems.

Nearly an hour had passed with still no sign of Nick of Julie. The five at the round booth had talked of the Lonsdale win, and Paul and Eden had filled the others in on the progress of her pregnancy awareness program. Eden had gone to the powder room and blinked at her reflection. Her eyes showed the exhaustion she was feeling both mentally and physically. She needed to go home and go to bed.

On her return trip to the table, she asked the waitress for coffee. Eden had been concentrating on the coffee rather than the conversation—that is, until she heard the words "adoptive parents."

Cal said, "It's getting late and it looks as if my brother is a no-show." He put a handful of bills on the table, then started to slide from the booth. "Let's go, Eden."

Eden didn't follow. Instead, she asked Suzanne, "Does the mother want the child back?"

"Yes," Don Tucker said. "It seems she and the baby's father—"

"He's not the father!" Suzanne said shakily, grinding her cigarette into the overflowing ashtray. "He pumped sperm into her. Period."

Don snapped, "Knock it off, Suzanne. You sound like some barnyard harpy."

"She's the barnyard harpy!"

Don rolled his eyes.

Eden said softly, "Maybe she's genuinely remorseful about giving the baby away."

Silence fell on the table. Eden knew instantly that she wasn't supposed to feel any sympathy for the birth mother. No benefit of the doubt allowed. The woman had been pronounced irresponsible and her intrusion into her child's life was inexcusable.

Finally Paul said, "It sounds as if she could have used Eden's awareness program before she made her decision. Maybe she didn't want to give the baby away and wasn't getting any adult support for her side."

Cal tried to divert the topic from Eden. "Have Sherry and Kirk tried to find some middle ground?"

"You mean something fair like cutting the baby in half and giving each side their piece?"

"For crissake, Suzanne, Cal's not suggesting anything extreme."

"What's being done to my sister is extreme," Suzanne said in a choked voice.

Cal leaned back. He had opened a beehive. "Jesus."

"Suzanne has a point," Eden said. "It's too emotional for objectivity. Look at how hard it is for us to discuss it calmly. For your sister to find middle ground, someone has to give in. And in the end, no matter how this works out, there will be hard feelings and regrets and a lot of second guessing."

In a calmer voice and with a more open expression, Suzanne said to Eden. "A moment ago you commented that the birth mother might be remorseful. She might use that to try and get the baby back."

"And it could work," Eden said quietly, bracing for Suzanne's fury at the mere suggestion.

Instead, she nodded. "And that's inhuman."

Eden took a deep breath. She wished she could offer hope to Suzanne. "In an ideal world the well-being and emotional security of the baby would be paramount."

Suzanne called the birth mother a tramp, and Don pressed his lips together, shaking his head, saying nothing.

Paul jumped in with, "Isn't that a little strong?"

"It's not strong enough." Suzanne cited the young woman's promiscuity, her careless behavior and tenuous grip on responsibility. "What kind of upbringing can she provide a child when her own life is a badly written soap opera?" She leaned toward Eden. "You defending her sounds like you believe she's a poor misguided soul we should feel sorry for. I'm telling you, she's not."

"Wait a minute," Eden said, her voice sharpening. "You're misunderstanding me. I'm not defending her or advocating her side. I'm just saying that she may genuinely regret a decision she made because she had no other choice. All of us have regrets about things in the past."

"Then she can have another baby. My sister can't."

Cal said, "I think we should call it a night. We're obviously not going to solve this." He stood, reaching for Eden's arm to draw her up beside him.

"I'm beat, too," Paul said, looking relieved to escape the topic. He added cash to Cal's, and he, too, got to his feet.

Oblivious to these moves, Don put his arm around his wife, whispering something, and Suzanne nodded. Instead of following Cal's lead, Eden slid closer to Suzanne.

Before she could reason through why she needed to speak, she said, "There's good justification why I feel something for the birth mother's dilemma."

Cal's eyes widened. "Christ Almighty, Eden! You're not going to go into that, are you?"

Even without meeting his eyes, she felt his fury. Nevertheless, she ignored him and said to Suzanne, "I gave up my baby daughter for adoption when I was sixteen."

The sudden motionlessness of all at the table was like a freeze frame.

Suzanne's eyes widened.

Don's mouth dropped open.

Paul's gaze darted around as if she'd said something obscene too loudly.

Cal's anger spilled over. "What in hell are you doing?" he hissed in outrage. "You sound like you're doing a Ricky Lake confessional."

"Really. And why is that?" Eden asked, her own anger at his embarrassment spewing about like hot lava inside her. "Because it makes you uncomfortable?"

"Because it's no one's business and for goddamn sure it's not table conversation."

"It's my business, Cal." She jerked away when he tried to take her arm. "Whether you like it or not, it's a huge part of my past. And by the way, who designates table conversation? You? I don't think so. Suzanne is terrified her sister will lose her baby. For me to sit here and spout opinions without saying why I have them would be disingenuous at best. I want Suzanne to know. Not because I'm looking for sympathy or humiliation," she said pointedly. "It was the hardest and the most heart-wrenching decision I've ever made. And if Suzanne hears a birth mother's viewpoint, she can tell Sherry and Kirk how to maneuver through what's sure to be a minefield of decisions."

"Fine. When you're finished, I'll be at the bar," he said coldly. "Come on, Paul."

Paul looked decidedly uncomfortable. "I probably should be getting home."

Cal cajoled, "Oh, come on. You're not going to make me drink alone. The show here at the table will probably last a while."

For the first time since she'd smacked Joey Grubb when she was eight because he'd said she wasn't good enough to be friends with his sister, Eden wanted to claw that holier-than-thou look from Cal's face. She fisted her hands and watched the pulse jump in her wrists.

Suzanne's eyes filled. "Oh, Eden, I'm so sorry. I had no idea—Don has been warning me I'm overwrought about this—and now I've blurted out a lot of pompous opinions and, oh God, I feel like such a jerk."

"No," Eden interrupted. "In a way you've reinforced my confidence that I made the right decision. I've never tried to contact my daughter or the adoptive parents, although more than a few times after I gave her up, I came very close to changing my mind. Once, at a particularly low time around her first birthday, I thought about kidnapping her."

Suzanne clutched Eden's fisted hands. "I shouldn't admit this, but I suggested to my sister that they disappear."

Eden curled her lips inward, relaxing slightly, trying to shake off her fury at Cal. "I even wished that the adoptive parents would die and my daughter would be returned to me. None of this was rational or reasonable and certainly it wasn't looking out for the best interests of my child. It was a kind of remorse, a sadness within me that I'd given away a part of myself. As a result, I'm instinctively still looking for ways to fill that vacuum." She talked of her career choice being the result of giving up her baby. "I believed that decision would give me a better frame of reference than just textbook theory. But that's beside the point here. When I had Jennifer, my dad and my Aunt Josette were tremendously supportive. This birth mother you're speaking of may have no support system and no one to help her understand that what she wants she can't always have. Believe me, I wanted to keep my daughter, but when I stopped looking at her with only my maternal instincts—and I might add, very immature maternal instincts, and faced the questionable future I could give her . . ." She stopped and cleared her throat. "She needed two parents, stability and a family capable of raising her. At sixteen, I had little to offer."

"Have you ever tried to contact her?"

"No."

"Do you think she knows she's adopted?"

"Yes." At Eden's blunt answer, Suzanne looked quizzical. "It was a private adoption and I know who the family is. My father has had some contact with them."

"Don't you ever wonder what she's like? Wonder if she ever thinks about you?"

Eden smiled wanly. "Do I detect some softening toward the birth mother's side?"

Suzanne's face colored. "Oh God," she said, pressing her hand over her mouth. Then she shook her head. "This is different. I know you. And you were certainly not like this little twit."

Eden said, "But this little twit isn't all bad."

"Oh, please, you don't know her."

"You don't either, Suzanne. Your sister and her husband must get an attorney and let him build a strong case."

Don and Suzanne both reluctantly nodded.

Suzanne said, "Thanks for your honesty. You didn't have to say anything, but I'm glad you did. At least it has put some perspective on this. Do you mind if I tell Sherry? Believe it or not, she's even more hysterical about this than me."

"Of course, tell her. If she wants to talk to me, that's fine, too."

Suzanne pressed her fingers into Eden's arm. "Thanks so much. I'll tell her." She paused, then said, "Uh, you didn't say, and it's none of our business, but, uh, what happened to the father?"

"His parents were rich and my father owned a bar. I went to them, hoping they would deal with their son, who was avoiding me. They called me a tramp and a nobody, not fit to breathe the same air as their precious son. Todd Wynnstock . . ." She realized she hadn't uttered his name in years. "I thought I loved him. My prince," she said distastefully. "He turned out to be worse than a frog. He was a cowardly cockroach. I have no idea where he is. The last time I saw him, he was hiding behind his mother while she blamed me for seducing her precious son."

The three of them were silent.

Eden had the strangest sense of inevitability. Telling her story to Suzanne and Don had been a catharsis for her, a purging that she needed in order to take the step she'd been avoiding—calling her father.

Don put money with the other bills and all three of them stood.

He went to get their coats, and Suzanne said, "I hope this hasn't spoiled things for you with Cal. He wasn't pleased. Does he view your past as a threat?"

"Actually, you know more than he does. It's not one of his favorite topics, as you saw this evening. Cal would like me to put it from my mind and never mention it again."

"Probably most people would do that."

"Then I guess I'm not like most."

"No. And you know what? I'm very glad you're not."

Don returned with their coats. "Nick and Julie just came in. They went on into the bar."

Suzanne extended her hand to Eden and then withdrew it. "What am I doing? You deserve a huge hug."

Good nights were said, and Eden went to get her own coat. Sliding it on, she went to a pay phone to call a taxi. Then she sat down on the bench where she and Cal had sat earlier.

Nick came out of the bar, laughing, his arm flung around Julie, who looked up at him as if he was the last single man in Rhode Island.

"Hey, Eden, we were wondering where you were." Julie giggled, adoring eyes on Nick.

"How come you got your coat?" Nick asked.

"I'm going home."

"But Cal's in the bar."

"I called a cab."

"Does Cal know you're leaving?"

She stood when she saw headlights sweep across the front entrance. "You tell him for me."

Nick untangled himself from Julie. "Eden, wait a minute."

But she sidestepped his attempt to touch her. *God, please, just let me get out of here. Please.*

She pulled the door open and stepped outside. Nick, however, was too quick. His hand curled around her forearm, turning her so that he could see her.

The light spilled across him. His cheeks were whiskery, his mouth unsmiling. His eyes were all serious, all concern, the gray softness of the past reflecting her memories, her longings.

She ducked her head, willing herself not to fall apart.

"Come on, babe, what's wrong?"

The endearment swept through her self-control like a sudden gust of wind. She clutched her coat to her body. "I'm tired and I want to go home. Please let go of me."

She pushed against him to free herself and he suddenly released her. As if she were Cinderella dashing down the steps to the carriage, she hurried into the taxi and closed the door. When the cabby circled the parking area to the exit, she caught sight of Nick.

He stood watching, unmoving, a man left behind.

Chapter 12

"EDEN? IT'S AFTER ONE YOUR TIME. NOBODY makes phone calls at this hour unless someone croaked or ran away."

She sighed with relief when she heard his voice. "I'm not dead, but disappearing, that sounds plausible." She dabbed at her eyes. "I was afraid you might still be at work."

"Curly works the bar on Thursday nights. You know that."

"Oh, yes." How could she have forgotten? Curly Janas had worked for her father since she was thirteen.

"What's going on?" Frank Parrish asked, his concern evident.

Eden was seated in the middle of her bed, a mixture of anger, moroseness and self-blame pressing down on her.

She'd come home from The Windmill and let Killer out to run and while she waited for him to water the neighbors' bushes, she'd poured herself a glass of wine. After he had lumbered in, begged for a cookie and sprawled out on his old quilt, she'd showered, washed her hair, which was still wrapped in a towel, and put on her favorite flannel nightgown. She then took the booties, the journal and the music box out of the bedside drawer. She wound the key, listened to the lullaby twice, and then she called her father.

"I should have phoned weeks ago," she said.

"Me and Josette, we been wonderin' what happened. I wanted to check, but she said I shouldn't rush you."

"Bless Aunt Josette. She always did have good radar when it came to me."

"So? You got an answer?" Her father's peppery to-the-point gruffness was both familiar and endearing.

"The reason I took so long is because I didn't know what to tell you."

"Seems pretty clear to me. It's either yes, you want to meet her or no, you don't."

"One answer automatically eliminates the other," she said, hearing her own defensiveness. "Before you called me, this was settled, or at least as much as it could ever be. Now it's all boiling around as if my heart and my brain are in a pressure cooker."

"Tough decisions aren't made by gutless idiots."

She sniffled, sipped her wine and rewound the music box for the third time. "I know."

"You know?" he bellowed. "You know what?" When his patience gave way to bluster, Eden learned long ago to brace herself. "It's a tough decision you gotta make? Or that you're a gutless idiot? Bullshit to both. Get a hold of yourself, girl. No daughter of mine wrings her hands so I have to say poor baby."

A shudder pitched through her. *Poor baby* was her father's derisive term for anyone who complained about life giving them a hosing. He'd been raised near the Chicago stockyards. He fought in Korea, watched his own father die of lung cancer and his mother from Alzheimer's. He married a piano teacher, Lucy Conant from Diversey, and within a year Eden was born. Frank bartended his way up to manager, then when the owner retired, he bought the corner tavern, working eighty hours a week for years to turn a profit and put money away for Eden's college expenses. For him life was comprised of hard work and hard choices. Frank Parrish never made excuses; he made decisions.

Eden sighed. She adored her father, despite his verbal hatchet-wielding. Sentimentality didn't get in the way of his opinion, nor did he worry about offending her pride. To him hurt feelings were as useless as unpaid bar tabs in a bank deposit.

Despite his brusqueness, his annoyance was directed at her angst and fence-straddling, not at her ultimate decision. Once her decision was made, he'd stand by her, whether or not he agreed. Cal, on the other hand, not only didn't want her to see Jennifer, he objected furiously when she even talked about her daughter.

"Oh, Pops, I sound like a wuss, I know. But I can't decide what to do." She hesitated, wincing inwardly at her claim of indecision. It wasn't true. "No, I do know," she added flatly. "I do know and I don't want to do it."

"Now we're getting someplace," Frank muttered.

"It's all such a mess. I wish the Maynards had never called you."

"Yeah, well, I wish money flew into the cash register without me working for it. Wishes are about as useful as walking through skunk piss in the woods on a hot night."

She laughed, his crassly delivered and often insightful expressions made her love him even more. Without considering her words, she said, "Nick would say something like that."

"Who's Nick?"

"Nick Scanlon. Remember I dated him in college?" She quickly filled the gap in her father's memory, emphasizing the hockey angle and asking herself whatever possessed her to mention Nick's name.

"Yeah, yeah. He's the one who bought you a music box."

"Yes. He's Cal's younger brother."

"You datin' them both?" Frank sounded shocked.

"No," she said quickly.

"Well, which is it?"

"Cal. I'm involved with Cal." She cleared her throat. "Nick and I are just friends."

He guffawed. "And I sold a cold one to the Pope."

"If he were in town, I bet you could," she quipped, deliberately dodging his meaning. She did not intend to get into a discussion about Nick. That was even more complicated than her situation with Jennifer. She wound the music box again. The sound was scratchy and tinny but the lullaby brought a dampness to her eyes.

Her father didn't say anything for a few seconds, then, "You remember after your mama died and you were so unhappy?"

"You tried to do all kinds of things to cheer me up."

"And nothin' worked."

"The music box did a little. It played "When You're Smiling," but not as well as Mama played it on the piano."

He was silent again and she heard him clear his throat. "You started collecting them."

She touched the one in her lap. "Yes, I did."

"I figured that was a good idea—to get your mind off losin' your mama."

Eden sipped her wine, wondering what he was driving at. "It helped."

"Until you bought that one for the baby."

"My baby," Eden corrected. "Then she was my baby."

"It was a mistake you buyin' it, but keepin' it like some rosy memory lane trip to take whenever you're feelin' blue was a lousy idea."

Eden clutched the music box. "How can you say that? You wanted the music box you gave me to make me remember all the good things about Mama."

"Not the same," he said, not at all deflected by her argument. "Some memories you keep, some you let go. Josette and I wanted you to give it to the Maynards."

"Give it to the Maynards! For godsake, Pops, I gave them my daughter!" Eden's chest constricted; her heart felt squeezed in a vise. "All I had left of her was the music box and—"

"Eden!" Frank shouted.

She pressed her hand over her mouth to silence herself.

"Listen to yourself. One in the friggin' morning you call me, not with a decision, but to groan about feelin' sorry for yourself. And I bet you're mucking through all that stuff you saved. It's the past. It's over, and here you are keepin' yourself tied to it as if it's the last novena you'll ever say."

"You don't understand. I've been torn between what I should do and what I want to do. Tonight I was with some friends and I bragged about how understanding you've always been, and now you're being mean and critical."

"Oh, for crissake, stop that blubbery whine! I taught you better than that." Then his voice softened. "Honey, listen to me. Do you think this was easy for me? I wanted to tell the Maynards to go to hell. You think I even wanted to call you? I didn't. I knew you'd chew and re-chew this. And I was right. Weeks have passed, and here you are, Eden, stuck, stubborn and more weak-willed than when you gave Jennifer up in the first place."

She squeezed her eyes closed. God, he was blunt, crude and so damn right. She was vacillating, still looking for some pink-winged angel to flutter down with a heart-saving answer. She wanted it both ways and she wanted to know the outcome before she made the decision. She sighed, about to agree with him, when the doorbell rang.

She jumped, so that the music box almost fell off her lap. Killer growled softly, got to his feet and moved toward the front door.

"Pops, someone's at the door."

"At this hour?"

"It's probably Cal. We had—never mind. Can I call you back?"

"Yeah. Christ, I'm not goin' get any sleep with this hangin' anyway."

She hung up and scrambled off the bed, patting Killer as she went. Cal, no doubt, would be self-deprecating and apologetic, which was the least she deserved after his boorish behavior in front of the Tuckers and Paul. Her forgiveness wasn't going to flow immediately; she intended to make him work damn hard for it.

Killer sat at the front door, head cocked.

"Who is it?" she called, not about to let Cal think she was expecting him.

"Nick."

Nick? Her insides rose and fell into a full throttle tumble. This was followed by annoyance that the visitor wasn't Cal. Apparently he'd gone home and decided he'd done nothing warranting an apology. Not even a phone call. The fact she'd been in the shower and then speaking with her father was no excuse. If Nick could find his way to her door, Cal could have, too. Pride and her own self-esteem were at stake, and, dammit, she could be stubborn also.

"Eden?"

She pressed her hand to her chest. Now, if she were the vengeful, spiteful type . . . of course, she wasn't, and yet . . . It would serve Cal right if she invited Nick in and . . . God, what was she doing? Thinking and considering and . . . *Get a grip.*

In a cool detached voice, she said, "What do you want?"

"What a leading question. How about I'm selling crotchless panties on the door-to-door midnight shift."

"I already have a drawerful. Go away."

She heard his chuckle even through two doors.

"Come on, Eden, open the door. It's freezing out here."

"Then go home where it's warm."

"Cut me some slack, huh? This is important."

"Go talk to Julie."

"About Eddie Metcalf? I don't think so."

Eden blinked. Eddie? She had an appointment with him and his parents. Had something happened to him? An accident? If so, then how did Nick . . . ? Speculating was ridiculous and doing it through a closed door was moronic.

She threw the dead bolt and opened the door, then unlatched the storm door.

He was huddled against the protected side of her house, out of the worst wind. His collar was turned up, hair ruffled, cheeks red from the cold. From what she could discern, he wore the same clothes as earlier. He also looked dark, heart-menacing and too damn sexy for either his good or hers.

"Ah, Eddie Metcalf are the magic words." He straightened and took a step forward.

She held up her hand in a halting gesture. "What about him?"

"I told him I'd talk to you and get you off his ass."

"Then we have nothing to say. I'm not about

to get off his ass." She started to pull the outside door closed, but he quickly blocked her.

He moved inside, and the stormer clanged shut behind him. "There's his side to the story."

"And he's perfectly capable of telling me himself."

"He thinks you're on Karen's side."

"I'm on both sides. That's my job."

"He's freaked out."

"He should be. He—" She stopped herself. She was doing what she'd just said she had no intention of doing: explaining her position. And her father was waiting for her to call back. "Look, tell him I'm open to what he has to say and I promise not to throw him any curves when we meet with his parents."

"Karen told him she was getting an abortion."

"What? He told you that? No way. She wants this baby. As far as she's concerned, the problem is his refusal to acknowledge he's the father."

Nick shrugged. "Not the way Eddie tells it."

She wrapped her arms around herself to ward off the cold. Nick seemed unaffected by it now that he was inside. Behind him, the glass in the storm door steamed.

"Eddie says she's trying to jerk him around, force him into something permanent."

"You mean like standing up like a big boy and saying I did it?" she asked sarcastically. "Admitting it's his baby, too, instead of acting like a total sleaze? He's been ignoring Karen and dating Lisa Krause, and I just hope she doesn't show up pregnant, too. If you really wanted to help Eddie out, a crash course on responsibility wouldn't hurt."

Nick gave her an arch look. "Me? The jock with unrestrained appetites giving tips on responsibility? Not anytime soon. I'll leave the duty and dependability speech to the master. My big brother can trip through it without notes."

She narrowed her eyes, suspicions building. Obviously Eddie was more ruse than reason for this visit. "If you're here because Cal and I had a fight and you think you can lure me into bed because I'm furious with him—"

"Now, that's an interesting segue from Eddie and responsibility to me luring you into bed. Dare I think the latter is more on your mind than the former?"

"Oh, shut up," she said wearily, distressed that he always seemed to know what she was thinking; that sex with him was on her mind and that she was tempted to let it happen. "If you've said all you're going to say about Eddie, then let's say good night."

As if she hadn't spoken, he went on, "And you're furious with Cal. Hmm. And here I thought you were mad because I was with Julie. That cold brush-off you gave me at The Windmill had me believing you might be jealous."

"In your dreams, Nick Scanlon."

He gave a gentle yank to the towel wrapped around her hair. "As to luring you into bed? A turban and flannel down to your ankles makes me think I'd be bedding my landlady. Only thing you're missing is pink sponge curlers. Or are you going to surprise me by proving you're wearing crotchless panties?" He reached for her again, but this time she sidestepped him, which didn't deter him a bit.

He circled her, his body mere inches from hers. Eden closed her eyes, her breath trapped and dizzy in her lungs.

"Christ, you smell good," he murmured. Warmth radiated from his body, and she had to make herself lean away him. Her teeth were beginning to chatter. No wonder. She was standing here with the main door open to a twenty degree night.

"I must be nuts allowing you within five feet of me." She stepped back. She was leery and too vulnerable and too fascinated by this drumbeat of desire she felt for him.

"Yes, ma'am." He moved closer.

Another step back. "I don't trust you for one single second." But worse, she didn't trust herself.

And another forward. "Yes, ma'am."

They were so close that she could smell him and feel the brush of his clothing against her nightgown. "I know all about that devastating charm you so casually toss about."

"Yes, ma'am."

"Will you stop saying that?"

"Yes, ma'am."

Eden sighed with frustration. Her own jumpiness was one thing, but she also didn't trust him. He was too charming by half. She should tell him to go to hell and stay away from her, but she'd done both and neither had worked. Here he was and here she was, and if he came any closer they'd be breast to chest, thigh to thigh and tucked and gloved and . . . Oh God, kissing would be only the beginning.

She tried to tell herself she was too tired and too preoccupied with the issue of Jennifer to work herself into a frenzy of denial about Cal's brother.

Nick ruffled Killer's fur, stroking him behind his ears. The dog lapped up the attention as if he never got any. "Yeah, I know, Pupper. Bobby wants to come and play, too. There was mention of a red sweater, and he's been licking his chops ever since."

He gave Eden a sideways glance. She shook her head in defeat, took his arm and pulled him inside. "I have to return a phone call. Then I'll give you the sweater and then, dammit, you're leaving."

He grinned. "Yes, ma'am."

She rolled her eyes, then marched past him and returned to the bedroom, where she caught sight of her reflection in the dresser mirror. No makeup, wet hair wrapped in a towel, a humongous nightgown hiding prim cotton panties, floppy socks and red-rimmed eyes. "Too gorgeous for words," she muttered grimly, returning to the bed and calling back her father.

" 'Bout time."

"Sorry, Pops." She took a deep breath. Eddie Metcalf's name was indeed the magic words if only to shake her out of her self-pity and bring her back to the reality of her life today. Her father's shaft of conviction earlier had finally hit its mark. Jennifer was her past. Eighteen years of yesterdays. Moving forward had been her goal since she'd left Chicago for college in Boston. While she'd never totally put Jennifer from her heart, these last weeks her mind had been a battleground of circling and pondering instead of acting.

Sighing heavily, she turned from the music box, the booties and her journal. They were things, things to keep, yes, but not to—what was it Pops had said?—muck through? He was right, as usual.

"Pops, tell the Maynards it's best if we leave things as they are. Tell them I can't meet with Jennifer. Tell them . . . t-tell them . . . no." She squeezed her eyes closed and clamped her teeth together so as to not snag back her words.

Decision made.

Finally and forever.

It was done. It was for the best. It was over.

Behind her, moments later, Eden felt the bed dip and turned to find Nick stretched out, hands clasped behind his head as if lying down next to her was an every night occurrence.

She covered the phone. "Just what do you think you're doing?"

"Waiting for you to get off the phone."

"There's a long empty couch in the other room."

"But you're in here."

"You're pushing it, Nick."

He closed his eyes. "Yep. Figure I don't have anything to lose. You already don't trust me."

"Nor are you doing anything to change that."

"Nope."

Her father was talking, and already she'd missed more than a few sentences. She turned her back to Nick.

". . . and all I can say is thank God," her father was saying with obvious relief.

"It's the right decision. Actually, I think I made it earlier tonight. I just needed you to shake me up a little."

"You're gonna be fine, applecheeks," Frank said, using an old childhood endearment that meant approval and pride.

"I love you. Talk to you again soon. Good night."

She replaced the cordless phone on its stand and began putting her Jennifer memories away.

Nick reached over and picked up the music box. "Yours when you were a kid?" He wound it and the lullaby played.

"I bought it when I was a kid, yes." She held out her hand. "May I have it, please?"

He handed it to her. "You and Cal got the fences mended, huh?"

She put the music box into the drawer with the other things and firmly closed it. She felt sad and adrift when she should be congratulating herself on having made the best decision. This tiny corner of her life, which had been fashioned to fit quietly into her past, had burst into the forefront in these past weeks. She'd constructed a rosy scenario for a reunion with her daughter. Nothing nebulous about that. Yet, there was a dark side—a disastrous meeting with Jennifer that would subject Eden to her daughter's resentment, accusations, hatred. Now, thank God, she'd avoided any possibility of that.

"Eden?"

"Huh? Oh, no, that wasn't Cal. It was my father."

"He okay? Kinda late for just a chat."

"You're here," she said, her irritation at his boldness returning. "The late hour didn't cramp you any."

"Jesus, you're as prickly as a porcupine."

"Because I have company I didn't invite and who is lounging on my bed like he plans to stay awhile."

"Hey, lighten up," Nick said, as if nothing she said would offend him. "I haven't grabbed you, tried to kiss you or even made any unrestrained appetite moves on you. No bites or licks or even a quickie taste. In fact, I haven't even asked to see your drawerful of crotchless panties."

She compressed her lips to prevent the smile.

He brushed his finger along the edge of her nightgown. "Come on, babe, smile for me. I promise not to tell anyone if we actually laugh and enjoy each other. You know, the way we used to."

"Oh, Nickie . . ." The name she'd called him so many times in college slipped out as easily as the puff of breath that followed. She ducked her head and the towel drooped. She tried to grab it, but he pulled it off. She didn't need a mirror to know her hair looked as if it had been wrestling with the beaters on an electric mixer.

She lifted her chin. "Don't you dare make any insulting comments."

"Such as that you look too ugly to lure into bed? Weird because we're as close to being in bed as we are to admitting we want to be," he said expansively. "Then again, I've always been partial to you, no matter how you look. Besides, I won't have to worry about messing up your hair."

She wasn't going to charmed, cajoled or seduced. She was not. It would be crazy and stupid.

"You're no prize yourself, you know. Thirteen years of feeling sorry for yourself and bumming around the country doing God knows what with God knows who . . ."

"Wicked stuff and lots of wild women." His grin was so mischievous that Eden couldn't resist delving in though she knew she was opening doors she might not be able to close.

"Like what?"

"The wicked stuff? You really want to know, or are we making small talk?"

"I want to know."

"Did coke, got slashed with a knife when a guy caught me in bed with his wife, sold my skates for a bottle of booze, got arrested for stealing from a guy who owed me money and wouldn't pay. Before I came home, I woke up with a woman I didn't remember in a motel I couldn't name in a state I didn't recall traveling to. I had the hangover from hell, and my body felt as if I had been twisted and smashed like garbage in a crusher." He ticked off those lost years in an even, flat tone.

"It's a wonder you're alive," Eden said, amazed at the wreckage he'd made of thirteen years. Deeply imbedded in the curt summary were all the grim details of failure. And the seeds of renewal. After all, he had come home.

"What, no finger-wagging? No shock and outrage? No stepping back like I'm splattered with bird shit?"

"I never believed you were away on some missionary endeavor."

"Apparently Cal did."

"I don't understand."

"He asked me what I'd done, and I told him, just as I told you." He looked at the ceiling. "I got caught up in a rare unguarded moment when I thought he really cared. Not one of my smarter conclusions. Cal's show of caring for me is all bullshit. First thing out of his mouth after we got past the big brother, lecture-coming look was had I been tested for AIDS." He gave her a direct look. "I was last year and then again before I came home. I'm clean."

"Given your recklessness, that wasn't an unreasonable question," she said, defending Cal.

"I wasn't reckless. That implies I didn't know what I was doing. I knew exactly what I was doing and set out to do it better than most. It was suicide by the pleasure route. Why stick a gun in my mouth or leap off a bridge when I could die just as easily doing drugs, getting drunk and screwing my brains out?"

Eden shuddered as if she'd had a horrific peek into the graveyard of failed dreams. "But you didn't die. Obviously you didn't want to."

"Let's put it this way. I didn't give a shit one way or the other."

"I don't believe that."

"Believe it. You weren't there. It was bad."

"But you pulled yourself out. You're home, you're sober—I noticed you didn't drink at the party. Drugs?"

"No drugs," he said emphatically.

"You're working with the kids and—"

"Acting like a grown-up?"

"Yes."

"It's a miracle," he said as if he was presenting the high moment of the past few months.

"Don't be so flip, Nick. Most would have never survived."

He shrugged. "Please. Let's skip all the applause and cheery outlooks." He rolled off the bed, went to her dressing table and got her comb and brush. He then came over and sat down beside her. Without asking, he positioned her and began to work the comb through her snarled hair.

She was seated so that her bottom was nestled against his thigh. She was as aware of that pressure as the combing motion and of his other hand smoothing her hair.

He worked the snarls out gently, rubbing at her scalp whenever he pulled. She was relaxing, the upheaval of the evening retreating.

In a soft voice she asked, "So why did Eddie think you had influence with me?"

"He knows we used to be lovers."

She swung around so fast that the comb yanked at a stubborn snarl. "Ouch!" Nick soothed the spot. "You told him that?"

"Didn't have to. He already knew. It's hardly a secret."

"I didn't even live here then."

"People like tidbits about other people's lives and they're even more curious now that you're sleeping with my brother." He ran his fingers through her hair, checking for snarls. "That's too good to pass up."

"It's a totally different situation. You and I were kids. Cal and I are adults. I mean, my God, what does our dating in college have to do with anything?"

"Let me put it this way. If it doesn't have to do with anything, why are you remembering what it was like? Why is there so much tension between us? And why are we both itching to find out if it will be as good as it was before?"

Eden flinched.

Nick stopped combing. "Hit a sore spot?"

She moved away, taking the comb and brush from him, and walked to her dressing table. Laying the items down, she fiddled with the bottles and jars.

Would it be as pleasurable as before? Better? Was the tension self-imposed, or was it as real as his presence and her allowing him to be here? She wasn't a fool, nor would she have allowed any other man except Cal this accessibility to her. Her past intimacies with Nick had roared to the forefront of her thoughts since that night at the rink. And instead of their making a natural retreat, they'd become entrenched, so that she now made excuses for their presence rather than pushing them away.

Instead of moving forward in her relationship with Cal, she was mired in her memories of Nick. Of course, Nick hadn't helped by these unexpected appearances. Having him lying beside her on her bed, combing her hair, doing heart-to-hearts like an old lover catching up on the years of separation was as enticing as it was inappropriate.

From where he was still seated on the bed, he asked, "So what are you going to do to Eddie?"

Eden didn't return to the bed. Instead, she sat down on her dressing-table stool, knees together, hands clasped loosely. "Do to him? Like in punish? I'm not. But he has a responsibility to Karen and the baby he helped to create. At the very least, he should acknowledge that responsibility and be supportive of whatever decision she makes."

"Seems a little biased, doesn't it? I mean, he's ordered to be responsible but then he's supposed to support her decision whatever it is. What if Eddie disagrees?"

"Eddie disagrees? About what? He hasn't exactly been her knight in shining armor. He's been cold to her and treated her as if he never knew her. If Karen hadn't finally told me that he's the father, he'd be free and clear."

"But he's not free and clear. He's a kid looking at fatherhood when he hasn't figured out how to keep his jeans zipped. He's scared of his old man and he's terrified his hockey career will be in the tank."

"At the risk of sounding authoritative and unsympathetic, I will say that he should have thought about all of that before they had sex."

"Karen should have, too."

"I completely agree. She thought she was in love and she was a fool to think so. But all of this is irrelevant. The pregnancy is reality and it's not going away."

She stood, about to tell him they'd discussed

all they needed to discuss, that she'd get the red sweater and he could leave, when he asked, "Is that what happened for you. You thought you were in love with Todd?"

The jolt of hearing Jennifer's father's name coming from Nick brought her head up sharply. "Yes. But even more stupidly, I thought he loved me." She watched him curiously. "I'd forgotten I'd told you about all of that."

"One night at a keg party. You weren't totally sober. It was the only time you mentioned it."

"And you remembered all this time?"

"Come on. That's hardly a story I'm likely to forget. I believe you said you hoped the parents would die and then you would get your baby back."

"I was very weird back then."

"Actually, I thought it made you very human and honest."

"It's a wonder I didn't scare you off." She frowned. "Did you ask me a lot of questions?"

"Nope." Then he shrugged and stretched out once again on the bed. "Let's keep this in perspective. I was twenty-one and terminally horny. If I'd asked questions, you might have gotten all blubbery and depressed. And all it would have accomplished was making it less likely we'd have sex that night."

"That wasn't the only reason. You didn't want to know all that much about me, remember? We made that deal—good times, great sex, lots of fun and no expectations. I wanted it that way just as you did."

"Nickie and the princess," he said wistfully. "Jesus, it was a lifetime ago." He took a deep breath. "Are you seeing yourself in Karen?"

"Not directly. I didn't play the victim as Karen has done. I went over to Todd's house and confronted him and his parents. First I was called a tramp and a liar, then offered money to abort and then told that if I tried to mess up Todd's life, I'd regret it. I left in tears. My idealism was as broken as my heart."

"Goddamn bastards," he muttered.

"Pops said the same thing. He wanted to demand they take responsibility, but I wanted no part of them. I've never seen or heard from Todd or his family again."

Nick swung his legs off the bed and crossed to where she was seated. He guided her to her feet and into his arms. In a natural motion, her arms slipped around him, and they stood for a few silent moments.

With his mouth against her ear, he whispered, "I've never forgotten how good it was to be inside you."

His words floated past her as rhythmically as a familiar song. He then slid one hand into her hair. His thumb worked behind her ear, numbing her objections, making her feel as though she was drifting into a trance. It would be so simple to ignore the clamor of confused emotions within her.

She rubbed her lips together, her hands balling into fists of rejection poised to prevent him going any farther. His thumb caressing, his eyes delving through her thoughts, his body resting so easily against hers.

How easy it would be to just let go, to find out once and for all what would be reborn from this jumble of awareness and just plain desire for Nick. This was similar to her decision about Jennifer. As long as she kept it all in suspended animation she could chew it, argue for it and rail against it.

She wanted Nick. She loved Cal. Or had she in some bizarre way confused the two emotions and the two brothers?

"Eddie is why you came. Not this," she murmured in a delicate whisper, but not pushing him away.

"You're why I came. You're always why I come."

"Nickie, I don't want to want this."

"I know, babe. That's what makes you so intriguing."

His mouth settled over hers, his hand sliding down her back and urging her against him.

She should stop this. She should.

She really should . . .

Chapter 13

NICK EXPECTED EDEN TO STOP HIM, BUT SHE allowed him to tug her nightgown up and skim his fingers along her skin. Touching her legs, her hips and hearing only a breathy sigh allowed him further liberties. Her breasts pressed against him and she swayed a little, rubbing her nipples across his shirt. Despite her nightgown and his clothes, Nick felt them tighten.

He dipped his head and took one in his mouth and then the other, wetting the flannel, biting lightly, reveling in her hiss of desire. His own body hardened. And suddenly the emotional distance he'd kept for the past thirteen years vanished.

Because this was Eden. He wasn't thinking of Cal or payback. Small buzzing voices about honor and dishonesty and relinquishing the past to the cobwebs of history stung his mind like irritated bees. The resurrection of his conscience at this particular moment was not welcome.

He kissed her again, his tongue curling around hers in a lapping sexual foray. Lust drenched him, drowning out any thought of retreat. Backing up to the bed, he eased them both down so that she lay next to him. He touched her knees, her thighs, slipping his hand higher, bolder—finding her. Heat blistered through him.

When he realized his hand cupped cotton panties with a very real crotch—cotton, not silk or satin or flimsy nylon—Nick nearly lost it. The starkness of innocence fused closely to his own guile and smothered him in reproach. He squeezed his eyes closed, slipped his hand under the elastic and found her wet. His misgivings collapsed.

She brought one knee up, effectively giving him even more room to roam unchecked. Encouraging him, she opened his leather belt, freed the brass button from its closure, scraped her nails lightly along his balls before folding her hand around his cock as if she'd found the perfect size.

Something broke through his erotic fog and Nick found himself pushing her hand away. He stared down at her. Suddenly this was too easy. Not misgivings this time, but suspicions. He'd expected resistance. Total capitulation and unbridled eagerness didn't grow out of opposition. No way.

She lay on her back, one arm flung up beside her head, her hand open and relaxed. The other hand had found its way inside the placket opening of his shirt. Her eyes were closed, her mouth moist, open enough to show him she wanted more than he'd given her.

Nick took a shaky breath. He hadn't come here for this—or had he? His promise to Eddie was the reason—or was it? Proving to Cal he could get Eden back in his bed had been altered and modified and had taken as many twists and turns as the number of days since Bobby had knocked her down at the rink. Honor, goddammit, kept peeking and waving like it wanted to be his moral compass, his new best pal, his reward for good behavior. And he'd given in—at least for a little while. But here, now, with her wet, sainthood didn't interest him.

He wanted her, she wanted him. This was not complicated.

He tugged her panties down, his hand once more sliding between her legs, his forefinger scooping deep between the soft, swollen folds.

She arched up, head turning, her mouth seeking his. "You're playing with me," she whispered, her own hand sliding down his chest, across his belly, to slide under his briefs. "I can play, too."

She cupped him, fingers shy as if she needed to proceed cautiously. She smoothed and pulled like a virgin stumbling blindly through an erotic forest. She wasn't skilled like the redhead in Cincinnati or choreographed like the dancer in Atlanta. But she excited him immensely, recreating youthful randy energy he thought long ago lost and dead. He sucked in his breath and pushed his finger deeper, his thumb rubbing her arousal higher.

She gasped, her hand gripped around him so that he thought he'd explode. Again her fingers stroked until his belly turned into an inferno. He was on the verge of coming against her hand and about to pull away when suddenly she let go of him. She bucked her body back and scrambled off the bed as if he'd scalded her.

Nick saw stars. Was she having second thoughts? Then her moving away from the bed cued his darker instinct. This was all a goddamn act.

He raised his head, bracing his upper body on his forearms, breathing hard, his insides twisting and cutting like uncoiled bobwire. "What in the hell are you doing?"

She took a few more steps back from the bed's edge, tugging her panties back in place, flannel settling around her ankles in a flowery swirl. Arms at her sides, fingers flexing and then stilling, she studied him as though she'd arrived at some momentous conclusion. One he was sure, she thought him too doltish to figure out.

"I'm going to give you what you want," she said.

He stared hard. "Not standing way over there you aren't."

Something was up beside his cock, yet his wariness wasn't nearly as troublesome as the thought that he'd stupidly stepped into some diabolical game. Eden and Cal had argued—Nick figured that from Cal refusing to talk about her at the bar and Paul rolling his eyes and whispering, "Be glad you missed it. It's a wonder they didn't peel the paint from the walls." Eden had all but confirmed it a short time ago.

Was she now using him to get back at Cal? Had she somehow pricked through to his conscience—as fragile as it was—with her version of revenge? Was she doing anything different from what he'd done in baiting Cal by saying he could get her into bed?

"I made a decision about you and me," she said staunchly, as if any argument he might present would be useless. "I've made a lot of them in the past few hours, so one more should clean my life of all those hanging, untied threads."

"Ah, this about going to bed with me to find out if you're gripped by nostalgia or the real thing." He liked the idea, but not for any philosophical journey. Wanting sex with her, as far as Nick was concerned, wasn't theory, it was a hot fact. "I've been called weird things but never a hanging untied thread. What are the other threads you've so neatly tied up and put away? Dare I hope one of them was dumping Cal?"

She peered at him as though he'd said the unthinkable. "Actually, this will be best for all three of us."

"Spare me any fair-play-for-Cal scenarios." Nick pushed himself up against the headboard, shoved a hand through his hair and crossed his ankles. "He's not even here, and I'm forced to include him. Christ."

"I'm in love with Cal," she said, as if this was a defense too lofty to question.

"So you keep telling me. Is this to remind me or remind yourself?"

"You're being a smart-ass, Nick."

"So the smart-ass wants to know why you're looking to get climaxed by me when my big brother is the love of your life."

She glared in frustration. "I don't know, dammit."

"Naughty lust with bad boy Nick or boring true love with the worthy and wonderful Cal—

the choice seems pretty clear to me."

"Put that way, you lose."

"But I'm here making you wet, babe. Cal isn't."

She sighed, an indecisive sigh, and Nick knew with a kind of sweet relief that he'd won the round.

Eden said, "Maybe it's some silly nostalgic itch for the old days. Maybe it's even something emotionally unhealthy, a need to prove I can still excite you. Maybe it is just lust."

"Hey, maybe you love me," he said, surprising himself by the words, then bracing himself for laughter or one of her "in your dreams" quips.

"Of course I love you."

Nick blinked, wariness returning. "Yeah, right."

She paced the small area beside the bed as though she'd inadvertently trapped herself. "I've loved you since college, but that's not the issue," she said, dismissing her own words like a rumor long ago disproved.

But he wanted to hear them. Loved him since college? Why had he never known? And why in hell was she sleeping with Cal if she loved him?

Then, as if she read his mind, she said, "You're restless and you'd walk out on me as easily as you did once before. I know better than to let you back into my heart and I won't do that, Nick. I locked up my feelings for you and put them away a long time ago, because there was no future for them."

Questions stacked up in his mind, the main one being when was it that she'd decided she loved him. Was it in college, when sex was like the daily ration of food? After his injury, when he awakened and found her weeping beside his bed? She was the only one who had cried for him. Had it been on their last night together, when she'd tried to hold onto him, fighting the truth of his own decision to end their relationship? Or had she decided it was love long after he was out of her life? And why? He'd never asked her to love him, never said he loved her. How could he have missed this? Was he that thick? That calloused? That afraid?

"You told Cal about these feelings?" Nick asked, not liking the idea that she might have discussed him with his brother.

She slowly shook her head. "He wouldn't understand."

"Finally my brother and I agree on one thing. Already this is more complicated than it should be."

"Lust is always simple," she said, as if resigned or pleased.

"That it is. I want you. You want me. So far, neither one of us has satisfied that."

"Then it's time. Once and for all." Before he could sort out her meaning, she had pulled the nightgown up and over her head, then pushed her fingers through her hair, reminding him of a nymph on a hot summer day.

She wore only those panties—prim and white and virginal. Her breasts were fuller than he remembered, her body slender, although not the gazelle slimness of her college days. The faded stretch marks of her pregnancy weren't as visible as they once were, but Nick saw them. To his amazement, his fingers tingled with the memory of touching them, of telling her one rainy afternoon after they'd made love that the marks made her even more beautiful.

Assurance now washed off her. She stood in front of him, beguiling him into believing she was his for the taking, despite her relationship with his brother, despite his less than honorable thoughts about taking her to bed to prove his own superiority to Cal, despite having no clue where this all went afterward. But then that was her problem rather than his. Feeding his belly fire was a helluva lot more satisfying than finding his conscience.

She tipped her head to the side. Her voice was sultry, husky. "Come on, Nick, take off your clothes."

A warning scurried through his mind about who controlled whom, about who got seduced, about how much he'd forced the sexual tension into action. If this was any woman but Eden, he'd ignore his hesitation, but she was a different woman today. Playful seduction games in college were just games, but these moves on both their parts had more serious implications. Maybe it was just lust, but maybe not. A new wariness was born. He wanted her as he'd never wanted any other woman, and that gave him pause. "I don't think so."

Eden nodded as if her own thoughts paralleled his. "Still need some convincing, huh?" Then she rolled the panties down, stepped out of them and tossed them aside.

"Ah, Jesus," Nick groaned.

Hand planted on hip, she struck a confident

pose and gave him a smoldering look. "Bring any condoms?"

Shit. "No."

"Used them all up on Julie, huh? Never mind. You're in luck. I keep a ready supply." She lifted the lid from a covered dish with violets painted on a lavender background, took out a handful of condoms, walked to the bed and dropped them one at a time beside him.

He stared at them as if they were poison. "Not my brand."

She touched herself, a skimming motion that lasted less time than it took to offer a lazy smile. "Too bad."

"Look, slow down. Why are you doing this? You're flashing and flipping about like you've got multiple personalities."

"Maybe I have. Maybe I don't know myself any better than you do. Maybe I'm just moving on instinct, learning as I go. Perhaps I'm hoping that after tonight I'll have some great moment of clarity about me. About you."

Nick was more than confused. He was mystified. He had a bad feeling about all of this. That moment of clarity about him could mean she'd reject him instead of his brother. But then so what? He wasn't lovesick or obsessed or compelled to make some long-term promise. Yet for reasons that baffled him, he, too, longed for his own moment of clarity.

At his silence, she swept up a handful of the condom packets and dropped them back into the dish.

"Dammit, wait a minute." He grabbed the last packet before she did.

"I don't want to wait a minute or a second. I don't want time to ruminate, consider or reconsider. Either yes or no."

In lightning movements, he came off the bed, grabbed her and yanked her forward. For just a few seconds she looked surprised, as if she'd expected him to march out as he had that afternoon when he'd kissed her.

His jeans were open, but otherwise he was indeed still dressed. He disliked sex with his clothes on, but when she slid her hands inside his jeans, inside his briefs and over his bare butt, he lost it. He tumbled her onto the bed, freed himself and rolled on top of her.

"You're burning, babe . . . burning me up. . . ."

Her eyes were wide, reflecting desire so obvious a blind man could have seen. Her breasts were crushed against the cotton of his shirt, her legs were open and she was very wet.

He wrestled a condom on. He hated the goddamn things. Using them was like eating ice cream with a face mask on. He slid inside her, and despite the rubber, he relished the slick smoothness, which was as sweet as a kiss at a homecoming. He thrust deep, watching her, wanting her to sigh, to breathe her pleasure deeply, to show him that she wanted him with an unmeasured eagerness.

Instead, she said, "I'm not going to come."

"Yeah, you are, right now. It's gonna be your moment of clarity." He touched her, moving higher and deeper. But she froze, and he swore he felt her body wither beneath him. He stopped and rose enough to look into her eyes. "Christ, you're serious."

"I want to be on top," she said flatly. "I started this, I made the decision to do this with you and I want to be on top."

This Eden had come a long way from the college coed who couldn't get enough of him. This was her party with her rules—maybe not straightforward and logical, as she usually was, but he wasn't going to object. His presence wasn't for a command performance in seductive techniques; he was there to let her find her way—an instructive piece of truth that punched through his ego with the subtlety of a wrecking ball.

Nick complied, rolling onto his back, then lifting her astride him, amusement in his eyes. "You're a helluva lot of trouble, you know that?"

She perched like a princess, her smile more devilish than coy. "You could go home and call Julie."

"After what you've put me through? Not a chance. I'll probably swear off sex for a month."

"Poor Nickie."

"Shut up. Come down here and kiss me."

She leaned forward, her mouth covering his, tongues mutually searching and discovering, her body wriggling so that he felt more of her than his overloaded hormones could take. He gripped her hips, rocking her, shutting his eyes and pushing himself up into the most secret part of her. Tension built into an erotic high. And in a suspended moment of climactic perfection, he felt her come. Instantly he followed.

She lay spent across him.

He lay replete beneath her.

He gathered her close, finding a surcease that astounded him by its satisfaction. This coupling had been different, an oath of lavish absolutes that stirred an awakening spirit in his soul.

But if he had any hope of a cuddle-and-nuzzle chat about satisfaction and rediscovery, or that an encore was about to be requested, he was disappointed.

She rolled off him. Standing beside the bed, she stepped into her panties and pulled them up, then dragged her nightgown over her head. She kept her back to him, saying nothing. Going to a closet hook, she took a fuzzy pink robe, pulled it on, tied the ties as if it was a makeshift chastity belt and shoved her feet into furry slippers.

"Don't forget earmuffs and mittens," he muttered, mystified again by her actions.

She never looked at him or answered. She simply walked out of the room.

Nick lay sprawled where she'd left him, condom and cock shriveled and sticky, feeling that he'd been used, abused and abandoned. He eased off the bed and made his way to the bathroom, where he cleaned up, tucked in his shirt and zipped his jeans. He opened Eden's medicine cabinet, looking for aspirin for the headache he knew was coming, and saw birth control pills.

"Cal gets the benefit of the pills, and I get the rubbers. Not cool, babe. Not cool at all." He opened an aspirin bottle and downed three tablets, then turned on the water and drank from the faucet.

He peered into the mirror and saw the truth. His ghost of a conscience had been busily mucking out the cobwebs while he'd been sprawled a few feet away on his fantasy tour. She really did love Cal, and he was just the bad boy who raked up a few bacchanalian memories. Judging by her overdressed departure, her pleasure in those memories and in him had been one big bust.

Jesus.

Time to reassess, run away, or get blistering drunk.

Meanwhile, in the kitchen, Eden turned on the light over the stove, then opened the refrigerator and took out a carton of milk. She poured a large glass of milk, took a package of Double Stuffed Oreos from the cupboard and sat down at the small table. Killer wandered in and sat beside her, head cocked, whining softly.

"Chocolate's not good for you," she said, twisting the first cookie apart and licking the cream filling. He whined again, then gave her a woof whisper that she'd taught him when he was a puppy.

She gave him a cookie. "Just one. Now go lie down."

He did, looking bereft. She concentrated on the second cookie and sipped from the glass, relishing all her old Chicago memories of Oreos and icy milk—comfort food, sympathy food, food to set her world right when it was spinning disastrously out of control. Milk and Oreos after her mother died, after Todd rejected her, after she gave her baby away.

After . . . after . . . after . . .

After Nick.

She hated him. She loved him. She wanted him and she didn't, but more than anything, she feared the feelings she'd found deep within herself during their lovemaking.

Behind her she heard him approach, then stop. Seconds thumped away at the silence. She didn't move, praying he'd leave.

"Eden?"

She set the glass down and then the half-eaten cookie. Still without turning, without any desire to look at him, she guessed he wanted and expected an explanation. She had none she wanted him to hear. "I put the red sweater by the front door."

"Fine." A squeak from the floor told her he'd moved. "Look, I know I'm supposed to be saying something here. What happened—not all of it, but some—I know it was a little wild and unexpected and . . . Well, it should have been different than it was."

"Apologies aren't necessary." Eden heard the robotic tone of her voice and made no attempt to soften it. "I have to work tomorrow and I'd like to go to bed, so the sooner you're gone, the sooner I can do that."

He came fully into the kitchen, circled the table to face her and placed his palms flat on the wooden surface, leaning down to say, "Okay, it wasn't romance and violins, but it wasn't catastrophic."

Her head was lowered, eyes counting the broken pieces of cookie, then studying his splayed hands. Different from Cal's, rougher, nails clipped rather than cut and buffed; hands that deftly held a hockey stick, worked a stick shift; fingers that knew her body like a sculptor knows his clay. She swallowed hard and still refused to look up at him—she couldn't, not now, not tonight.

She pushed her chair back, stood, and took the carton of milk back to the refrigerator. Giving him wide berth, she started toward the living room. "I'll lock the door behind you."

"Wait a minute." In a few strides, he reached her, taking her arm and stopping her. "Did you hear what I said?"

She shrank away from him. "Do you want to take the sweater with you? If not, I can leave it on the front steps for you tomorrow."

"Forget the goddamned sweater!"

He shoved a hand through his hair, and she caught the desperation in his action and in his eyes. His body was tense and tight. That she knew his emotional edginess without touching him indicated just how much in tune with him she was, an instinct she didn't invite or want.

"You want an apology, Eden? You want me to grovel and beg? Just say so. You want to swear and scream at me? Then do that, but for crissake, do something besides act like a zombie."

When she simply stared at him, he sagged back against the doorjamb. She had the perfect opportunity to assure him he'd done nothing she hadn't encouraged, hadn't wanted, hadn't desired again and again and again, but she couldn't do it. She felt numb and exposed like a dark void that had no bottom. Her mind, her heart, her soul—they'd all circled around the truth she now feared. She had neither the energy nor the will to probe all the reasons why. The thought terrified her. Not tonight. Not now. Maybe not ever. She wanted to be alone. She wanted to sleep. She wanted to forget.

"You got what you wanted. I want you to leave."

"I got what I wanted?" he asked, as if finally she'd given him an opening. "What about what you wanted? You were doing the multiple personality gig from prim to seductive. You're acting like I forced you."

Thoughts tangled and swirled. If anything, she'd forced the issue, she'd tossed out logic and good sense and simply gone with her raging emotions. "No. You didn't force me. You made me come. Better than Cal. Is that what you need to hear?"

"What the hell kind of question is that?"

"One you need to answer within yourself."

"Christ. What is with you women that you have to probe every action like a deep ulterior meaning directed it? We fucked—"

She slapped him.

The sound of hand to flesh echoed in the stillness. The force of the blow turned his head sideways. He stood still, cheek exposed, seeking no retaliation. His breath came in a rush. Eden looked at her still-raised hand, the palm stinging, tingling with the feel of flesh and bone. He was right, but she hated him for putting it into those words.

Neither moved.

Poor Nick, she thought. He looked traumatized, he looked desperate and fearful and as unsure of himself as she'd ever seen him. That vulnerability in him drew her and she shuddered, yet she rejected the clawing need to take him in her arms. She stayed rigid, hands fisted full of the fuzzy fabric of her robe. A dark streak in her wanted to hit and scream and demand that he give her back her peace of mind.

Nick took a deep breath, the imprint of her hand dark on his cheek. "Eden, I'm at a loss here as to what to say or to do, but I need to know that you're going be okay. In the bedroom, you were spunky and sassy and even a little brittle, but at least you showed me something. Now you're like you were when you left the restaurant—distant and cold and detached, as if something inside you has died."

"Something has," she said softly, her voice hollow. She was far away, listening but not hearing; an impenetrable wall had risen to shield her. It wasn't what had died inside that pained her as much as what had come alive.

Moments later, she stood at the front door, the red sweater in one hand and the door latch in the other.

Nick swore, dragging his jacket on but not zipping it. She was starting to open the door when his hand held it closed.

"I don't like leaving you like this."

"I'm all right." Then for a fleeting second, she brightened, if only to get him out of the door faster. "Really, I'm okay."

"I'll call you in the morning before you go to work."

She nodded, thrust the red sweater at him, urged him out, then closed and locked the door, tension draining down and puddling at her feet. Leaning back against the wood, she slid down to the carpet, bringing her knees up to her chin and wrapping her arms about herself in a self-made cocoon.

Killer wandered over, tail down. He made a mewling sound of sympathy before he lay down next to her. She rubbed him behind his ears. "How did I get in such a mess, Pupper? Is it too late to start over? To want tomorrow to be the first day of my life?"

She curled down on the carpet, tears stinging her eyes. She yearned for her mother or her Aunt Josette or even the steadiness of a good friend such as Mary.

Killer stared at her, muzzle between his front paws, brown eyes soulful, patient.

"You know, don't you? You know I just made the worst mistake of my life."

The ringing phone awakened Eden.

Startled, she jerked upright. "Aaagh," she cried, when her body objected. Immediately she folded up on the floor again. She blinked, eyes coming into focus with gritty reluctance.

She'd slept all night on the floor. No wonder she was stiff and sore. Then details emerged through her fuzziness. Nick. Sex with Nick. Hating him. Loving him. Slapping him. Sending him away with an old red sweater for his dog.

Three rings.

She ground her fists into her bleary eyes, trying to remember where the phone was, hoping it would quit ringing before she found it. In that moment, she couldn't have identified her own ninety-pound dog in a lineup of beauty-groomed poodles. She tried to get up and every muscle screamed. Her head pounded, and the inside of her mouth tasted sour, like a crusty old milk carton.

Five rings.

Killer paced, wanting out. She got to her feet, staggering, grabbing for the door handle. Her back protested painfully.

Six rings.

"Shut up, goddammit, I'm coming." She barely recognized her own voice.

She staggered to the phone, using the furniture as a baby does in its first attempts to walk. She banged her hip on a corner of the desk, swore fluently and finally reached the phone at the eighth ring.

"H-hello?"

"It's Nick. Weren't you up?"

"No. What time is it?"

"Six-fifteen." When she didn't answer, he said, "I told you I'd call."

"You did? Oh, yes." The details of the previous night—all the details—exploded like cannon shot in her mind.

"Eden? You want me to come over and drive you to work?"

"Work?" She blinked first at the desk clock and then at her desk calendar. She shook her head, then realized he couldn't hear that. "No, I can drive. I have to go." And she hung up without waiting for him to respond. The phone immediately rang again. She picked it up, then put it down, then took it off the hook.

She made her way to the kitchen. The chair was still where she'd pushed it back to stand and get away from him. Her half-filled milk glass sat amidst cookie crumbs. The bag of open Oreos was on the floor and it was empty.

She looked at Killer. "I better not come home and find you've puked all over the house."

He burped.

She eased down, picked up the bag and put it in the trash. There were no crumbs; the floor had been licked clean.

He whined at the door and she let him out. She put on coffee, used the bathroom and by the time the dog was ready to come in, the coffee was ready. She poured a huge mug, added cream and four sugars. Caffeine and sugar—today she needed both. Sipping and enjoying the first satisfying thing that had come her way since she had awakened, she made her way to her bedroom.

The bed was rumpled, the room holding the smelling trace of sex. The imprint of Nick's head remained on one of the pillows. The torn condom packet perched on the floor, mocking her. She closed her eyes, wishing a fairy godmother would wave a wand and take it all away.

"Never around when you need them," she muttered, surveying the room as if an orgy of gargantuan proportions had left its residue. She set the mug down, took off her robe, nightgown, panties and slippers. She hung up the robe, shoved the slippers into the closet and closed the door. The nightgown and panties were tossed onto the bed along with the torn condom packet. Then she pulled the sheets, blankets and quilt from the mattress and tossed the pillows on top. She wrapped the entire bundle into a huge ball.

Walking naked to the kitchen, she pulled a green garbage bag from a roll. Back in the bedroom, she stuffed the bedding into the bag, tied the corners into a knot, dragged it into the living room, so she wouldn't forget to put it outside for the trash man.

After another swallow of coffee, she felt immensely better and went to take her shower.

Forty-five minutes later, she felt stalwart and in command of herself once again. She dressed, choosing satin underwear and her cherry-red wool suit, which set off her brunette hair with stunning intensity.

From the violet-decorated china container, she took the unopened condom packets and put them in the waste can. She should have dumped them after she'd gone on the pill. Cal had brought them that first time, assuring her that he didn't expect her to take care of the birth control. She'd been impressed by his forward and chivalrous thinking, and shuddered now at the thought of his ever knowing that Nick had used one with her.

It was the first time since she'd returned to the bedroom that she'd allowed herself to think directly about Nick. And even now, she picked her way through the tumble of thoughts as if she were walking across ice in spike heels.

Eden refused to consider any excuses for

wanting to have sex with Nick, nor did she intend to try and create one. Weeks of skirting the sensual drumbeat had done little to quiet the fantasy. In all honesty, she believed it had been just a matter of time. Playing it out hadn't been meticulously planned, but the pieces had been ripe for picking and placement.

She sat down at her dresser to finish her makeup and brush her hair. Staring at her reflection, she saw a cool honesty that carefully concealed a deep rattling knowledge that she was no longer the same woman.

"Making love with Nick when you know it only hurts everyone—my God," she muttered to her reflection. At least she could get some rags of comfort from the fact that she hadn't deliberately picked the fight with Cal. In a perverse way, she now wanted neither one of them.

She spritzed her hair, added earrings and took a last look at her bare mattress. Just like a criminal who has disposed of the evidence. So be it. She'd remake the bed when she got home. By then the smell of him and their lovemaking would be gone.

Chapter 14

CAL WAS UNEASY.

By midafternoon late the following week, he still hadn't spoken with or seen Eden.

Of course, this was just a snarl of unfortunate coincidences, or so he told himself. Yet their disagreement at The Windmill lay on his conscience.

He stopped by the high school, but she'd already left. Then he went to her house. But after waiting in her driveway for twenty-five minutes—more than ample time for her to get home—he concluded she had errands or was shopping. Using his cellular phone, he called his mother.

"I've spoken with her," Mary said. "We made plans for lunch, but no, I don't know where she is."

"We seem to be missing each other."

"How odd. It's hard to miss someone in Lonsdale."

Or she's avoiding me. A possibility he didn't want to think about.

"Have you tried the rink?" his mother asked.

"Why would she be there unless there was a game?"

"Nick may have seen her."

Why hadn't he thought of that? Probably because he didn't want to visualize Nick in any context regarding Eden. "Thanks. I'll stop over there."

Cal took a left at the next intersection and headed toward the ice rink.

That first morning after their argument over whether she should tell the Tuckers about giving Jennifer up for adoption, he had tried to call Eden on his way to Green Airport. Her line was busy. He was frustrated, because he had handled the situation at The Windmill awkwardly. His promise before Nick's party of not broaching the subject of Jennifer again hadn't included stopping Eden from hanging her past out for the comfort of Suzanne Tucker.

He liked the Tuckers and sympathized with them, but beyond that he didn't give a rat's ass. His concern was Eden, their argument and trying to find out why in hell he couldn't get in touch with her.

Again he'd gotten a busy signal at the airport moments before he boarded a business commuter to New York. It had been a trip he couldn't cancel. The yearly three-day seminar in Manhattan on retail strategies for small businesses was a permanent fixture on his late-winter calender.

Cal had attended the meetings with his father since his graduation from Brown. They were a must-do for any East Coast executive who wanted the inside track on fattening the bottom line. In addition, there were one-on-one contacts with corporate lobbyists from Washington, willing to share insight on bills favorable to retail business.

The perks were substantial, the nightly entertainment sophisticated, and Cal usually came home fired up with new retailing ideas for Scanlons and potential loopholes for the accountant.

This year, he was on the roster of speakers, a plum given to only the most consistent attendees. It meant heavy advertising for Scanlons in *The New York Times,* exposure for himself as a small-business owner, and if his presentation was well received, he'd be put on the A list of speakers for future events.

His father had attended year after year and never been invited to speak. Jack Scanlon had concluded that he had been ignored because the speakers committee was comprised of hard-assed elitists, who assumed New England was a synonym for Boston.

Cal had a slightly different perspective. While his father had good retail and financial sense, he'd never rolled with the social punches. After hours was when conversations weren't guarded, when inside secrets spilled along with the free-flowing Scotch, and when, as one story went, a deal was sealed between a lobbyist and a businessman because both got hard-ons over a natural blond stripper with big tits.

He'd related the blond stripper story to Eden shortly after they'd become intimate. She'd accused him—teasing, of course—of being the businessman.

"I never did believe those junkets were only

for you guys to exercise your Cross pens," she said breezily.

"I only looked. I didn't touch."

"It's a good thing I trust you or I'd be very leery of letting you go next year."

"Jealous, are you?" He loved it. Loved having her wanting him so much.

"And possessive."

Even better. Expecting at least a moderate amount of feminist outrage, Cal had been impressed by her candid response. Eden understood that men watching and wanting a stripper was as instinctive and as common as popcorn at the movies. He had reassured her, however. "I promise to say no to any T and A propositions."

Now Cal scowled at his vivid recall of that conversation, and yet the details of the debacle at The Windmill boiled down to one issue—Eden doing a tell-all to the Tuckers. It totally escaped him why she'd had this need to confess her mistake like some talk show guest. Was he missing something here? What had happened to her usual good sense?

Discretion was an attribute Jack Scanlon insisted upon in business dealings and in family matters. It was one of the rules Nick chose to ignore.

Cal had learned well from his father. Prudence combined with shrewdness worked to better his business acumen as well as brighten his light as the older sibling. Cal set the example, and if that meant Nick had to muddle around in second place, so be it. He'd had his chance to be a hero in hockey and blown it. His brother's failure proved his father's point. Nick hadn't followed the traditional family path, and the result had been disastrous.

Now Cal turned into the ice rink parking lot. Nick's Explorer was there, as was a rusted van and an old Chevy with a cracked windshield. Eden's dark-blue Honda was not.

"Damn," Cal muttered, hitting his fisted hand on the steering wheel. "This is getting ridiculous. Where in hell is she?"

He shoved the gearshift into Park, got out of his car and shivered when a blast of cold wind hit him. He pulled his collar up and tromped through the previous night's six inches of snow. His frustration had passed simmer and was bubbling into a high boil.

He'd made more than enough attempts to contact Eden and not just that first morning. He'd sent flowers to her at school with a poignant note of apology. She had called Scanlons, but Cal had been on his way to New York—a point he'd made in the note, but she either hadn't read it or didn't care. John Daws, his store manager, had taken the call and relayed the message: "The flowers are lovely. Thank Cal for me when he calls."

Thank Cal for me? Like he was some pesky suitor? Like she couldn't make the effort to thank him herself? Like she was clueless as to how worried he was that he'd upset her? Her response irritated and frustrated him. She could have said something to John about the note, something that would have meant something to him but wouldn't have meant anything to John.

Cal tried to call again from his New York hotel room and learned she was in a student/parent meeting. He'd come damn close to insisting she come to the phone, but decided that would just open up a whole new issue—his being selfish about a personal call when she was working. So he'd left a message where he could be reached, but she never returned the call.

That irritation—no, it was fury, goddammit—fury that she'd ignored his best apologetic efforts. Not about to spend his spare time chasing her down, he went to a party the night following the second all-day meeting.

Cal winced now at the memory, vowing never again. His father would have been appalled, and Nick would have had a good laugh at the irony of the good brother inside a pimp's playhouse. Cal was remorseful, but more than that, he was terrified that what he couldn't remember might be more debasing than what he could.

However, the night had yielded far more than a satyr's orgy of delights; it won him lucrative information about a huge tax break coming up for a vote in the Senate the following week. By the time Cal returned to Lonsdale, he'd calculated Scanlons could save close to ten grand with the bill's passage. That in itself justified his presence in the prurient atmosphere.

Now, as he entered the rink, he said a silent prayer that all the miscues with Eden had been just that. God knows he didn't want to lose her over some disagreement that could be smoothed out if only he could talk to her.

The rink was nearly deserted, with only Nick and Poppy and a few kids on the ice. Cal shivered. How it could be colder inside than out amazed him.

Poppy was seated in a folding chair, hands folded on top of a silver metal cane. Nick leaned against one of the center support posts, his shoulders hunched forward, his head down, listening to what Poppy was saying.

They both glanced up, falling silent when Cal approached.

"Hey, Cal! You're lookin' good," Poppy said, his face relaxing into a congenial smile.

"Good to see you, Poppy."

"What's up?" Nick asked.

"I'm not interrupting, am I?"

" 'Course not," Poppy said, shaking Cal's hand. "Haven't seen much of you around here."

"Nick was always the rink rat, you know that."

"That he is, and it's sure good to have him back. The kids couldn't have it better if Gretzky himself was working with them."

Nick, Cal noted, said nothing. No self-deprecating remarks or modest protests against being said to be in good company with Gretzky. On the other hand, there was no beam of pride either. Just a neutral mask, as if what Poppy had said could stand or collapse.

Cal shifted uncomfortably. To Nick he said, "Could we talk privately a few minutes?"

Poppy started to get to his feet, using the cane for support.

"You stay here," Nick said. "Cal and I can walk over by the stands."

Poppy shook his head. "Nope. Gettin' cold anyway. Think I'll go on back to the office and warm up."

Nick stood close until Poppy was steady on

his feet and had got the cane in motion. "You go on and talk to your brother, Nickie. I can make it by myself." He slowly made his way toward the office less than twenty feet away. Nick didn't move, watching. Poppy got to the door and turned. "You know, you're worse than a friggin' warden." But his tone held a softened gruffness, and Cal guessed that Nick's concern was welcome.

"Lay off the doubles," Nick called.

"Yeah, yeah, I hear ya. I'll stick to triples." He pushed the door open with the cane and went inside.

Nick chuckled, then turned to Cal. "So what's the big secret?"

Nodding toward the closed office door, Cal asked, "When did he start using a cane?"

"Last week. He gets leg cramps and a few times he's fallen. Doc said it was aging joints. He was worried about Poppy breaking a hip, so he ordered the cane. Poppy still thinks he's thirty and using a cane is for cripples."

"Tough break," Cal said. "Poppy has always managed the rink like a traffic cop at a six-way intersection. Not being able to get around is going to make that difficult."

"But not impossible. I run interference. For the most part the place runs fine. Poppy does his job and everyone respects him for it."

"Who's paying you for your time?" Cal hadn't forgotten his promise to speak to the school board about Nick working full time at the rink, but as yet he hadn't done it.

If Nick recalled it, he didn't say. Watching two boys pass a puck back and forth and then one shoot it into the net, Nick said, "I'm ripping off the parents by charging big bucks to teach their kids. Didn't take long to figure out that pretending I once knew how to play hockey is more lucrative than I thought."

Cal rolled his eyes. "Why did I ask?" he muttered.

"A better question is, why are you here? If it's about the sports budget cut for next year not including Poppy—"

"Poppy getting pink-slipped? I don't know what you're talking about."

Nick looked slightly confused. "Let me get this straight. You're the chairman of the school committee and you don't know about the rumored cuts? I haven't heard anything but complaints all week."

Cal relaxed. "Cuts in the sports programs are routine rumors every year."

"If they're like most rumors, a few are true."

"And most aren't. Frankly, we haven't finished marking up the whole budget."

"You're ducking and weaving."

"I honestly can't give you a solid answer, Nick. Money is tight as usual, and the taxpayers are pretty well tapped out. Adjustments will probably be needed—"

"What about Poppy? Is he gonna get shafted?"

Cal could sense Nick digging in his heels.

"I hope that's not necessary. In fact, I'll do everything I can to make sure it doesn't happen."

"Not good enough. His whole life is here at the rink, Cal. If he has to leave, it will kill him."

"Look, I like Poppy, the kids do, he's done a good job, and the last thing the committee will want to do is let him go."

"Poppy stays. No matter what, he stays. You can find other places to cut."

"I'll make sure your opinion is heard by the committee."

"Why doesn't that reassure me?"

"Because you want a guarantee I can't give," Cal said, knowing his answer was lame and wishing he could indeed promise. "God knows there are enough areas where, in my opinion, severe belt-tightening is needed. But every area has its supporters and interest groups. I have no doubt the sports department will be one of the most vociferous. And Poppy would have a large and noisy contingent of objectors if his job was slated for the ax."

Nick seemed to absorb this while staring in the direction of Poppy's office. "You know he's been like a father to me. One of the few people besides Mom that I missed while I was gone."

Cal scowled. "Like a father? You had a father and a damn good one."

"No. You had a father and a damn good one—for you. I had the expert on those rigid Scanlon rules of family tradition. Instead of a father I saw a self-appointed arbiter of what was and what wasn't an accomplishment. It didn't take long to figure out that anything I did was worthless unless you did it first."

"You never understood Dad's intent," Cal said, deliberately sidestepping Nick's observation of their father's partiality. "He wanted his sons to be well bred and capable of taking over a family business that has stood for quality and good taste since 1889."

"You forgot the part about dressing Lonsdale men," Nick said dryly, then added, "And you sound like some ad agency."

Cal ignored him. "Most would give anything to have a successful business handed to them. I sure appreciated it."

Nick said nothing.

Cal continued. "Scanlons has kept Mom financially secure. Surely you wanted that for her."

"Cut the horseshit, Cal. You make her sound like some withering, hand-wringing widow. She busted her ass after the old man died and you were grieving over losing Betsy. I know, I was there. She worked to save Scanlons when it was in the tank with suppliers and unpaid bills. If she's secure today, it's because of what she did for herself."

Cal gave him a measured look. "She called you in to help."

"Don't remind me," he muttered.

Cal compressed his lips and shook his head, realizing with some sadness just how much Nick detested Scanlons. "You can't do it, can you? You can't even admit you helped. The rough, rebellious Nick darkening the door of Scanlons and actually pitching in and being part of the family business—Dad would have been proud, and you cringe whenever it's even mentioned."

"I didn't do it for Scanlons. I did it to prove to myself I could be something other than a screw-up."

"And then you just walked away." Cal shook his head. Years had passed, and it still escaped him how Nick could work as if his next meal depended on his effort, but then turn aside, toss away his success like so much trash, walk away and never look back.

"You're the oldest. You're the one the old man groomed for the business. I just made sure you kept your place as the number one son. And you have. Big time."

Cal shoved his hands into his pockets, the frigid guilt of truth cascading its way down his spine like a thousand ice chips. He knew that he'd been the screw-up, not Nick. His brother's resentment of him was probably deserved, but Cal wasn't ready to assume the mantle of responsibility for Nick's messy and lonely life.

Nick said, "I'm gonna go check on Poppy. Be right back." He cupped his hands and shouted to one of the boys on the ice, "Hey, Morralas, if you want a ride home, get your butt in gear."

His face drawn, Cal slumped down on the folding chair, his thoughts more than troubled by the conversation he hadn't come here to have. Thinking of himself in Nick's shadow bored through him like a line of termites.

His brother had consistently stepped out of the way so that Cal got the credit. It was a habit fixed when they were kids but illustrated most clearly when Nick abruptly quit Little League, claiming pulled muscles in his legs. He'd walked away from the prospect of breaking a school record for hits in one season. Cal had been on another team and played with mediocre skill. When Cal's team won the league's state title and the trophies were handed out, the family applause was for Cal—not because of Cal's skill but because he'd stayed with his team when Nick just quit. Yet deep down, Cal knew that the competition always became easier when Nick wasn't in the picture.

Then Nick began playing hockey, taking command of the ice with a natural grace and precision that couldn't be copied. Even when he drew crowds at practices, Nick never boasted about the coach's praise or the buzz he was causing within the division.

Not until their mother berated Cal and his father for not honoring Nick's accomplishments did Cal begin to see the lengths to which Nick had gone to stay in the shadows.

Cal's revelation, however, led to no shaft of conviction or willingness to give up his own place. He'd viewed Nick as a fool for being so cowed by the old man while continuing to live and act like some silent prodigal rebel. Then he lost it all—the college scholarship, his hockey career, his future—all in one forty-second moment on the ice. Cal's assessment was that once his hockey career ended, Nick simply gave up. His life became a choice between failing at home and failing where no one would know.

Even his threat to get Eden back, even that lay as dead as all those dreams of being the next Bobby Orr.

He got to his feet as Nick approached, pulling keys from his jacket pocket. "I'm gonna split. I left Bobby home and his eyes are probably turning yellow."

Cal fell in step with him. "I haven't even

asked what I came here to ask. About Eden."

Nick halted. "What about her?"

"Have you seen her?"

"I saw her the night we were all at The Windmill."

"I know that. I meant lately. In the past few days."

"No."

"Damn."

"Is she missing?"

"From my life, yes. I don't know what in hell is going on."

The two men resumed walking. Nick said, "Maybe she's got a new boyfriend."

"Like you?"

"Not me." He paused, and Cal thought he heard a bit of regret in his tone. "If I was, I'd make sure I knew where she was." He held the door open for the Morralas kid.

By the time Cal was back in his car and leaving the rink parking lot, he'd decided that all the miscues might indeed be coincidental, but Nick had a point. He should know where Eden was, or at the very least, know her schedule.

The last thing he wanted was for their relationship to be as indecisive as drawing up the school budget. He wanted more with Eden than he presently had. These few days without her proved that. He loved her and the time had come to move their relationship forward.

He picked up the cellular phone and tried calling her again.

When the answering machine came on, he sighed deeply and hung up.

Chapter 15

"JUST WHO IN HELL DO YOU THINK YOU ARE, upsetting my wife? Dolly came home from your meeting together cryin' like she'd been to three funerals in one day."

"Believe me, Mr. Metcalf, my only intention was to make sure the facts were clear."

"Facts! What facts? They're as phony as that piss-assed program of yours. You've decided my kid is guilty and I'm tellin' you he hasn't done a goddamned thing."

Eden felt a line of sweat break out along the back of her neck. "Guilt isn't the issue. He's not on trial."

"No? Then how come you're sashayin' over here like some lady lawyer hopin' to make yourself look good?"

Making herself look good? God, that would be a pleasant change. "I didn't sashay over here, Mr. Metcalf. Your wife suggested it."

"Over here" was the Metcalf house, a fifties-style ranch in a neighborhood with year-around Virgin Mary lawn ornaments and cracked sidewalks that no one had shoveled clear of snow. The interior was homey with braided rugs, maple furnishings, lamps with orange bases and American Revolution print shades. Lacy curtains woven in a diamond design draped the windows in an R shape. Tiebacks were fashioned from braided orange ribbon.

A preponderance of framed pictures of Eddie and two younger brothers and a sister had whatever table space wasn't filled with back issues of *Hockey Digest*, battered pucks and ceramic ducks. Three hockey sticks wrapped with tape stood in one corner of the room.

Ben Metcalf owned the room in the way a restless lion owns his cage. The touches of Dolly Metcalf's frugal personality indicated she'd mistakenly decorated before realizing that she could have shopped at a hockey equipment store instead of K-Mart.

Eden had come here after learning from Dolly that if she wanted to speak to Eddie's father, she'd have to come to the house. He worked two jobs and couldn't fit in a daytime appointment at the school. Dolly had proposed this in Eden's office while her eyes darted about as if Ben might barge in at any moment.

Privately Eden believed Ben had never wanted to fit in the appointment, and his combativeness from the get-go had only sealed that initial impression. He'd called the school, threatening to make Eden's "piss-assed" program the first one slashed from the school budget. He could get it done, he'd bellowed, as slick and quick as makin' a phone call to his mother-in-law. Delphine Maxwell, school board member and probably the most leery of Eden's efforts, was Eddie's grandmother.

Eden had been outraged by his threats and his boorishness. Nevertheless, she jumped exactly as he'd expected. She'd spent her drive to the Metcalf house trying to convince herself she wasn't caving in to pressure. Eddie and Karen and their baby were the issue.

Now, browbeating her into slinking away as she'd done at sixteen when Todd's parents called her a tramp was not going to happen . . . no way. If she'd learned anything from that experience, it was that there were two kinds of parental protection. One was protection of their children from the evils of the world—commendable and proper. The other was more insidious because it dealt with parents going to any lengths to protect their own investment and expectations. Ben Metcalf had hockey star plans for his son, and he was prepared to make sure those plans weren't interrupted. Also, Eden suspected Metcalf was reliving his own hockey days via his son.

Eddie, by his courage in owning up to his responsibility, had in Ben Metcalf's skewed view betrayed his father's expectations. Eddie's fortitude gave her hope, and she felt emboldened.

"Let's cut to the chase here, Mr. Metcalf. You don't give a damn that your son screwed Karen and got her pregnant. Your big beef is that Eddie talked before you could convince him to keep quiet. Your son might be scared and he might be feeling trapped, but he was man enough to face the truth, then step forward and admit it."

"Sure he admitted it," Metcalf fired back. "You got him so friggin' scared he'd tell you he still sleeps with a teddy bear if you asked him."

Eden resisted, but only for a moment. "And would he say yes?"

"Hell, no, you think he'd admit that willingly?"

"Probably not. But it does point up a sad juxtaposition."

"A what?"

"A parallel."

"Yeah? And what's that?"

"A boy with a teddy bear and a boy about to be a father."

"I don't get it."

Eden sighed. "No, I don't expect you do."

The afternoon darkness of February felt as if it had settled somewhere in her body. She was tired and weary and beginning to have serious second thoughts about her abilities. Being a guidance counselor who set up course schedules and directed students to the best college for their academic performance was less complicated than wading into waters infested by parents who wouldn't see their kids in any light but the one that made them shine.

She decided to try another angle. "Mr. Metcalf, what convinces you that Eddie isn't the father?"

"I know, lady. I buy the rubbers for him." Pacing now, he flung his hands in the air, a "get a clue" gesture as if his son's sexual activity was included on his credit card along with skates, sticks and knee pads. Then, with obsequious patience, he said, "On his fourteenth birthday, I bought him a box of condoms and told him that since I knew he'd have sex, then he'd better use a rubber. I didn't want no kid of mine knockin' up some girl and ruinin' his future."

"You're a real family values kind of guy," Eden muttered.

"I call it responsible."

"And self-centered. You don't seem to be concerned about the young woman and her choice of whether she even wants sex."

"Are you kiddin'? That Sims girl was goin' bonkers tryin' to get into my son's jeans."

" 'No' is a complete sentence, Mr. Metcalf. And I'd like to think that boys are as capable of saying it as girls." She paused and then added, "However, this is all moot now. Karen is pregnant—"

"She can get rid of it."

"She doesn't want to do that."

"That isn't Eddie's problem."

"You're telling me you'd rather he duck all responsibility and in the future be known as a dead-beat dad and go on to explain to the children he has in the future that he has another child he didn't want and therefore pretends doesn't exist."

Ben Metcalf stepped close to Eden. "It's not his kid. Not."

Eden settled her shoulder bag in place and took her car keys from her pocket. "Good night, Mr. Metcalf."

She was at the door when he said, "What are you going to do? You better not start spreading rumors around about my kid or I'll make sure you're an ex-guidance counselor."

Eden whirled around. "Don't you threaten me."

"You gonna run to that boyfriend of yours to save your job?"

"Is that what you think this is all about? My job? A program? This is about kids making babies when they're barely more than babies themselves. It's about making a decision about having sex not because of peer pressure, or libido overload, or God forbid believing this is true love."

"Very passionate, Ms. Parrish."

"You're damn right I'm passionate. I wouldn't be here if I wasn't. But you know something, Mr. Metcalf? You have an opportunity to be incredibly proud of your son for his forthrightness in this, but instead you're acting more like a whining, hysterical child. Obviously you've done a few things right in raising Eddie, because he's not hiding behind you and his mother. He's not the one in denial. You are."

He grabbed her arm and jerked her toward him. "I've worked too goddamned hard so my kid could have what I didn't. Ain't no one . . . Not you or that tramp is gonna screw it up."

Eden peered down at where his hand gripped her arm. "Let go of me, Mr. Metcalf."

"And what are you gonna do? Report me for harassment? Run and whine to your boyfriend about how I touched you?"

"I'm going to jam my keys right into your balls," she said sweetly. His expression darkened until he glanced down and saw that while she hadn't touched him, her hand was fisted around her key ring; one of the heavier keys gleamed poised and sharp. Color drained from his face.

"You wouldn't dare."

"I'm from Chicago. We dare just about anything."

He glared at her as if considering whether to push it.

Eden didn't move.

"Wait till I tell the school just what kind of broad they hired."

She shrugged. "I'll deny it."

"You can't do that. You're a teacher. You'd be lying."

"And you're a parent who's asking his son to lie. Please tell me why it's all right for you, but a grievous sin for me."

"Ah, shit! You set me up."

"And I'm still waiting for you to let go of my arm."

Without saying anything, he released her. She opened the door and walked outside. He slammed it behind her so hard that she shuddered.

This had not been a day of unending accomplishment, she thought grimly. She was at her car with the key in the lock when she caught sight of a shadow moving just off to her side. She whirled around.

"Nick! My God, you scared me to death. What are you doing here?"

"Took a kid home from the rink and saw your car." Eden glanced across the street, and sure enough there was his Explorer. How she could have walked out of the house and not seen it?

Nick asked, "What are you doing over here?"

"I came to see Ben Metcalf about his son."

Nick tipped his head to the side, studying her.

"You look a little wired. You okay?"

Suddenly she longed to lean into him, longed to have him lift her up and carry her away to someplace quiet and dark and private, where she could get soppy and feel sorry for herself. Nick could listen and nod and show appropriate outrage. He wouldn't judge or advise or question, he'd just be Nickie. Taking a raw breath, she threw away that assortment of feelings, deeming them too dicey to suggest. Goosebumps blossomed beneath her coat.

"Eden?"

"Besides being cold from being inside the house and not taking off my coat, I'm fine."

He didn't move away, but instead leaned his right hip against the Honda just beyond the door handle. Not close enough to be intimidating, but too close for Eden. That was the problem with Nick. Whether he was present or absent, he was always too close.

"Busy week?" he asked.

"Yes."

"Seen Cal?"

"No. And what's with all the small-talk questions?" She curled her fingers around the door handle, wanting to get inside and crank up the heat.

He moved only enough to shrug. "He's looking for you."

"I know."

"And you've deliberately avoided him?"

"As a matter of fact, I have. But I would think that would please you. You've certainly told me often enough how much he irritates you."

Nick looked off into the distance, the wind

plowing through his hair, his expression so placid that Eden wanted to shake him. Finally he said, "Yeah, well, that's true. But he is my brother and he looked pretty rattled a little while ago."

"So you're here to plead his case?"

"Nope. Just checking to see if he has a case."

"I was angry at him and now he's annoyed with me. I plan to call him as soon as I get home, and everything will be straightened out."

"Everything?"

Their expressions collided. For more breathtaking seconds than Eden wanted to admit to, a kaleidoscope of taste and touch memories of Nick nearly stole her composure.

She opened her car door and slid inside. "That issue is not up for discussion."

"Look, I don't want you to feel guilty . . ."

"Guilty?" She glanced up at his concerned expression, refusing to be lulled into a soft response. Her hands gripped the wheel. "You mean a guilty conscience because it's not proper for me to have sex with you when I'm in love with Cal?"

"I feel guilty and I'm not even crazy about my brother."

"How could you possibly feel guilty? You said you have no conscience."

"I seem to be getting one and believe me I don't like it much."

"Well, don't encourage it and I'm sure it will die happily. And let me ease your mind about me. None of what happened between us is as simple as Catholic guilt. I wish it was. Then I could go to confession, receive penance, say my

Hail Marys and Our Fathers and life would be all brand new."

He scowled, digging his hands deeper into his pockets. She almost felt sorry for him. He looked befuddled and unnerved, his old opinions and theories spinning every which way. "Okay, if it's not guilt, then what is it?"

"Terror, Nick. Terror." She pulled her door closed, started the engine and drove away, leaving him standing in the middle of the street, hands still jammed in his pockets.

Chapter 16

RIGHT AFTER FIRST PERIOD ON VALENTINE'S Day, Karen Sims pranced into Eden's office carrying a huge teddy bear and a two-pound lacy, heart-shaped, red box of chocolates. Her pregnancy had begun to thicken her waist, but was made less obvious to the casual observer by her oversized sweater. Her freckly face was flushed with a dewy pinkness, her reddish-blond hair held atop her head with a huge pearl-colored clamp. Her green eyes sparkled as though she'd discovered the perfect path to happiness.

Eden had been returning various student files to the cabinet. She didn't have an appointment with Karen, but then she had an open door policy. Karen's smile begged a response.

Eden grinned. "That teddy bear is almost as big as you are."

"I got him and the candy this morning. I wanted to come in and show you sooner, but I had English class." She paused like an actor dramatically relating a story. "I mean I got off the bus, and you know how everyone is always standing around. Well, there were kids and teachers and a couple of parents. And there he was."

"Who?"

"Wait, wait, I'm getting to that. Anyway, he was just waiting for me and holding these like he'd been my secret admirer, like he didn't care who knew it and like he absolutely couldn't hold back any longer." She sighed. "It was so romantic."

"Valentine's Day is the best time for romantic secret admirers."

"Oh, but he's more than that."

"He is, is he?" Eden said, wondering what had happened to Karen's "I'll love Eddie forever" speech that Eden had heard just last week. Pregnant by one guy and getting gifts from another; boyfriends were exchanged like ill-fitting suits after a hasty shopping spree. Cavalier attitudes and disposable emotions. Perhaps, Eden mused, she was the one severely out of touch. Todd had been an absolute slime, and yet it had taken her a very long time to get past loving him. Her relationship with Nick in college had been the final purge of Todd.

What goes around comes around. Now she was determined to purge Nick with Cal, except that her purification process wasn't working on too many levels. Maybe the secret was two pounds of chocolate and a fuzzy teddy bear.

The teenager fidgeted, a silly grin growing permanent on her mouth. Apparently she was waiting for Eden to say something more, so Eden added, "Well, I'm pleased you're so happy."

Karen rolled her eyes. "No! I mean, you're not

supposed to say that. Sure it's okay 'cuz I am happy, but you're supposed to ask who it is."

This was the drum roll, she assumed. "All right. Who is it?"

"Edddddie." With a *ta-dah* and a twirl, Karen presented his name. Then she held up the two gifts as if they were Olympic gold medals.

"Well, how about that," Eden said lamely.

Karen dropped into a chair and then wrapped her arms around the gifts as though they were a direct connection to Eddie's heart. "Isn't he just about the coolest guy in the whole world?"

"Very cool. And very generous," Eden said, forcing her mind to sort it out. Obviously she'd missed something. Eddie going from pond scum to beloved king in the space of a week was indeed cause for celebration. Or skepticism.

Since her visit to Ben Metcalf, Eden had been stymied as to what to do next. She'd talked and she'd advised, but she couldn't force Ben Metcalf to show some parental leadership and support his son. Had Ben seen the light and acted? Or had Eddie struck out on his own? Then again, gifts were a gesture, they weren't a sign of commitment. Todd had bought her a heart-shaped necklace one Christmas. Nick had once given her a music box and she'd been sucked into believing that held deep significance. Not because it did, but because she wanted it to.

Hoping her cynicism hadn't calcified, she said, "Eddie and you have been spending time together, I presume."

"Oh, yes."

"That's terrific."

"No, it's more than that. And I have you to

thank, and well, I wanted to tell you and show you . . . and . . ." Tears welled in her eyes and she pressed her face into the teddy's furry head. Sniffling, she blubbered some more, her words not too coherent. Eden handed her the tissue box. She blew and dabbed and talked. "Oh, Ms. Parrish, if you hadn't made me come back to school and made me see that this wasn't all my fault and that I could be a good person and still do lots of things right . . ."

Eden's throat burned and she swallowed furiously. This is what's it's all about. Growth and maturity, then a sudden burst of wisdom; one teenager willing to learn that problem-solving starts with an attitude that looks forward instead of being crushed by what, at the time, seem like catastrophic circumstances.

"I'm so pleased, Karen, but the credit goes to you for taking control of your life. I just nudged you along a little."

Karen's eyes were as shiny as new leaves in the spring sunshine. "We've made so many plans."

"That's wonderful," Eden said, fast running out of superlatives. "But tell me exactly how all this wonderfulness came about. Eddie's transformation in particular."

"It was so weird. I mean like he just showed up at my house two nights ago and said we had to straighten out a few things. At first I thought he was going to be a jerk, but he was so cool." Her face turned dreamy and distant.

Weird then cool. Eden waited. After a few seconds of silence, she asked, "What was Eddie so cool about?"

"Oh." She straightened as though she'd come out of a trance. "Well, he asked me a zillion questions about the baby. You know, like this was the first one in history. He wanted to know if it was safe to touch my tummy, and if it hurt having it inside me, and if I knew if it was a boy or a girl, and how did it breathe and what made it grow. I mean like he really wanted to know. And you would have been so proud of me, 'cuz I answered all his questions." She preened. " 'Course, I didn't know most of the answers until last week, when I got some books and read . . ." Incredibly she hadn't run out of breath. She leaned forward, looking at Eden seriously. "You know our baby is a miracle."

The statement was so innocent, so forthright, so like Eden had felt with Jennifer that it was all Eden could do to remain in her chair. She wanted to draw Karen into her arms and say she did know and that she and Karen had a bond because they both realized the profoundness of pregnancy.

"I read in this book about how the sperm—that came from Eddie—well, the sperm—tons of them—they compete with each other like they're in this race. And not just a few, but millions try to get to the egg—that's what I have. It's like my egg is waiting and saying, 'I'm not going to wait forever. You guys better decide.' I mean, they're all like runners doing the whole race uphill. Anyway, the egg resists. I wasn't sure just why it does this—maybe having millions coming at you is real scary. But anyway, finally, one sperm gets to the egg and then they connect and it's called an embryo. When that happens—and

I thought this was so cool—no other sperm are allowed. It's like two lovers who close the doors so that it's very private. Just the two of them alone and growing without anything trying to stop them. I mean it's like two people who know that they can do miracles if only the bad stuff doesn't get into their lives."

Eden couldn't speak. Her heart pounded, her eyes stung, her hands were clammy. "Oh, Karen," she finally managed.

"Did I get something wrong? I know it's more medical-sounding in the books, but Eddie didn't understand all those big words, so I made it simpler. Did I mess up?"

"No," Eden said, her voice husky. "Oh my God, no, you didn't mess up anything. I've never heard it presented so eloquently."

Karen sagged back and relaxed.

Eden took a tissue from the box and dabbed her eyes. "After you told all this to Eddie, what happened?"

"He said he didn't want me to go through it all alone and that he'd be with me and that—well, we can't get married, at least not for a while. He's got college, and he wants me to go to school, too."

Eden, her composure back, held up both hands. "Whoa, slow down. You and Eddie have obviously made plans. What about his parents? Your mom?"

"They're going to help."

"Eddie's father, too?"

"Well, I don't know yet. He's not being so cool."

"Ah." So much for Ben's turnaround.

"Eddie says his dad won't freak and jump off a bridge or cut his wrists."

"That's encouraging," Eden said wryly.

"I'm going to talk to Mr. Metcalf."

Eden was immediately wary. "Karen, Mr. Metcalf isn't going to be awed by all this as Eddie obviously is."

"Oh, I know. Eddie already told me some of the stuff his father said, but I'm okay. I have Eddie on my side and he wants me and the baby. That's all I ever wanted. If his father wants to hate me and his grandchild, that's his problem."

"Actually, with that attitude, this is probably the best time to visit Ben Metcalf. You seem immune to anything negative."

Karen's face clouded. "This afternoon we're going to tell Eddie's grandmother."

Delphine Maxwell. Eden didn't envy Karen and Eddie. Delphine would pull no punches. "Mrs. Maxwell has her own ideas, too."

"Eddie wants to tell her before she finds out from someone else." Karen shrugged, dismissing the planned visit as if it was a ride to Pete's Pizza. Shifting the teddy and the box of chocolates, she said, "I better go. I have a class in a few minutes."

Eden rounded the desk. "Just one question. You didn't tell me what prompted Eddie to come and talk to you."

"Oh, it was his coach."

"Buck Cranston?" Eden asked incredulously.

"No, the other one. He works at the rink with the kids. Isn't this teddy adorable? I'm going to save it for when our baby can play with it."

"Nick?"

"Huh?"

"Nick Scanlon sent Eddie to talk with you?"

"Yeah, it was him. He told Eddie it had to be more than talk. It had to be real. It had to be about responsibility and thinking about someone else's life, not just your own. But you know all that. It's the same things you've been talking about."

Karen swept out, stopping to giggle with some friends who oohed and ahed over the teddy and chocolates.

Eden sat down before her knees gave way. "Oh my God."

He saw her immediately.

Hockey practice was almost over when she walked into the rink, went over to speak to Poppy and then sat down in a chair beside him.

Nick signaled to the players to wind it up. They skated over to him while he praised their improved skills and commented on some stickhandling sloppiness that if not checked could easily blow a lead. "Watch the overconfidence. It will kill your winning streak faster than you can duck a flying puck."

They all trooped off to the locker room, ruffling Bobby's fur as they passed.

Nick remained where he was, watching, wondering. "Well, Bobby, what do you think? Eden's here. Am I in trouble again?"

Bobby whined, sniffing at Nick's jacket pocket.

"Okay, okay, I know I promised." He pulled out a biscuit and Bobby snagged it and immediately began crunching on it. "She doesn't come over here on some whim. I know she likes Poppy, but I doubt he's the reason."

Bobby chewed, swallowed and then licked up the crumbs.

"Does she look mad to you?"

The retriever lifted his head, nosing his pocket again. "Hey, buddy, I'm trying to have a conversation with you and all you want is biscuits."

Bobby woofed.

Nick gave him another one, but this time Bobby clenched it between his teeth, jumped down from the bench and headed out.

"You think I'm stalling, do you?" Nick called as he picked up his clipboard of notes.

Bobby ambled forward, biscuit riding between his teeth like a pirate's knife. He moved right toward Eden.

"You're right. I am," Nick muttered, wondering why his pulse was jumping like a jackhammer.

Before he got within ten feet of her, she was on her feet and walking toward him. Dressed in a gray storm coat and black boots, she looked formidable. His heart raced to catch up with his pulse.

"Hi," he said, anticipating some kind of disaster. Bobby, meanwhile, had lain down at Poppy's feet.

"Hi yourself," she replied, as if they met this way every afternoon. "I want to take you for a drink—no, strike that. You can have coffee. I'll have the drink."

"Am I gonna need a drink?"

"I might need two."

Nick scowled. She looked intense and determined rather than rattled and annoyed.

"What's going on?"

Instead of answering him, she walked back to Poppy. "Could you keep Bobby here with you for about an hour?"

"Sure."

"Thanks. Nick, come on."

He looked at Poppy, who raised his eyebrows, then gave a beats me shrug.

"She didn't say anything? Give you any clue?" Nick asked, as he watched her sail out of the rink.

"Nope. Wanted to know how I was feeling, and I asked her about school. That's about it."

"Weird."

"Better move it out. Looks to me like she might come back in with a rope and haul you out."

She was in her car, the engine running, and when he hesitated in the parking lot to zip up his jacket, she put down the window and called, "Are you coming?"

"I'd like to know what in hell is going on."

"You'll find out. Hurry up. I don't have a lot of time."

The lure of Eden and his own curiosity more than made his decision. In the car, he felt consumed by her. Her scent, her presence, the neatness of the car—so like Eden. In college she would get after him for all the junk he carried around in that old Buick.

"Am I in some kind of trouble with you?"

"Have you done something that you should be?"

He frowned. "The last time we were together—"

"This isn't about sex."

"I meant at Metcalf's house."

"That wasn't together."

"Oh." Was this a dumb conversation or what? "Look, Eden, obviously you're pissed about something. Let's screw the word games."

"I wasn't aware I was acting pissed. I've invited you out for coffee. You're the one who thinks you're in trouble."

"Why does it feel like you're a county prosecutor looking to beef up her conviction record, instead of something simple like you wanting to pounce on my body."

"Been there, done that." He heard the amusement in her voice; he'd said the same thing to her once about getting drunk. At least, he thought it was about that—hell, he couldn't remember.

Nick sighed, sagging back against the headrest, and closed his eyes. "I'm fresh out of questions and speculation."

She chuckled then. She'd had the last word. Nick smiled to himself. She endlessly fascinated him, which accounted for him being here like some poor sucker getting set up for one of her hosings.

She stopped the car at a restaurant outside town. The Beef and Brew Tavern was flat-roofed and brick-fronted with undersized windows. The building sprawled awkwardly as though the builder had changed his mind in midconstruction, sliced off a second story and stuck it to the first and called it a function room. The parking lot at four in the afternoon was nearly empty.

"Are we way out here so that Cal doesn't find out you lured me away?"

"Nope. We're here because they make the best screwdrivers." She got out, then before closing the door, she leaned down to say, "I truly don't have a lot of time, Nick. I'm meeting Cal for dinner at seven and I have to shower and dress."

He got out of the car and said across the hood, "I presume you two made up."

"We did."

"Then you should be taking him out for a drink."

"Did that and then we—"

"Never mind. Spare me the salacious details."

She simply grinned.

Nick scowled. A thin but sharp edge of anger sliced through him, but he'd promised himself he wouldn't taunt or bait her, he wouldn't hover with innuendos tripping off his tongue just to get her reaction. Nope, he'd promised himself he'd behave, and so far it had worked as long as he didn't have to see her. So why in hell was he here?

"Look, if you're planning on waving any syrupy happiness with Cal under my nose, forget it."

"This doesn't have anything to do with Cal." She came around, took his arm and guided him into the restaurant, bypassing the tables and heading into the bar, where empty tables were plentiful.

Eden took off her coat, revealing a very conservative navy jacket and skirt. A light-blue blouse with a V neckline enhanced a string of pearls ovaled at her throat. Just an inch lower, she had a small raised beauty mark, which he'd kissed countless times on his way to her nipples.

A waitress appeared. Nick could smell her mouthwash when she talked. "Ma'am?"

"A screwdriver with Finlandia."

Nick said, "Johnny Walker. Water on the side."

Eden looked at him for too many moments after the waitress left. He said nothing, deciding he didn't like being the only one unsure of what was going on. Silence wavered precariously between them. The drinks arrived.

Nick picked up his glass. "You're on, Eden. I'm listening."

She took a sip of her screwdriver, waiting a few seconds for the liquid to slide down her throat. "I owe you an apology and I wanted to thank you for what you've done," she said softly.

Nick held his own glass suspended and then put it down before he dropped it. Pushing it aside, he rested his arms on the table and leaned toward her so that barely six inches separated them. "No more coded bullshit. What's going on?"

Unfazed, she said, "The thanks is for talking to Eddie, and I wanted to apologize for accusing you of taking his side when there are no sides. I was wrong to think that my way was the only way. But what is so incredible is that Karen and Eddie and the baby—A problem I was beginning to believe wasn't solvable suddenly solved itself." Quickly she filled him in on what Karen had said. "And it's all thanks to you."

He simply stared at her, his brain trying desperately to catch up, his mouth slightly open in astonishment. "Is this some perverse joke?"

"No joke."

"Then why the long-running drama? Why didn't you just say all this at the rink? You've built it up like my ass was gonna be fried and you held the can of gasoline."

"I wanted to get your attention to tell you how grateful I was. Especially, I wanted you to pay attention to what I said, not just dismiss it as no big deal."

"Believe me, Eden. Paying close attention to you has not been a major effort. All I have to do is be conscious."

She visibly relaxed, sitting back, turning her glass on the cocktail napkin. "I think there was a compliment in that."

Nick wasn't relaxed. "Dammit, don't flirt."

"I wasn't."

"And don't widen your eyes like you don't know what I'm talking about."

"Oh, Nick."

He stared at her, waiting for the sexy softening, waiting for some shaky confession from her that yes, there was more between them than an appreciation drink. But her empathetic expression held fast. She felt sorry for him, not horny. She was on a whole different emotional level. She'd evolved beyond him, and he was stuck in neutral, applying all the old standards from their past. He'd wanted to believe—hell, he'd convinced himself—that some river of desire ran deep and full between them. A desire that she could never reveal to Cal because it was private and secret and all Nick's. What a crock.

Even his most lucid moments of goodwill and cooperation, even those had been barnacles that clung to a wreckage of self-deluding fantasies.

She hadn't been flirting or fanning any fire of interest in him. Nothing between them mattered, because there was nothing to matter.

She took another swallow of her drink, her eyes cast down. He fully expected her to stand and prepare to leave. Nick eyed his drink and drank the water instead. The piano player arrived, a woman dressed in glittery white like a Miss America on the winner's runway. She played a few warm-up bars then launched into an old Eagles hit, "Desperado."

Because he didn't know what else to say, he commented, "You're serious about the apology, aren't you?"

"Absolutely," she said, as if he'd discovered the right question. "I had to tell you, Nick, and I wanted it to be private, so if I cried or threw myself in your arms and kissed you out of my gratitude and enthusiasm, I wouldn't start a rumor in Lonsdale about us that would hurt Cal."

"Okay."

She frowned.

"We're not in Lonsdale." When her frown deepened, he said, "You can skip the tears, but throwing yourself in my arms and kissing me could start anytime."

She laughed, but she didn't move.

Nick glanced around. "But there's not enough room here, and straddling my lap could get embarrassing. Ah, I know just the place." He slid his chair back and the waitress hurried over. "We'll be back, so leave the drinks. Bring me some more water."

"Yes, sir."

He took Eden's arm and drew her up.

"Where are we going?"

"Where you can throw yourself in my arms and kiss me."

She looked at him suspiciously. "This is silly."

"Yep."

"And crazy."

"That, too."

"It was a figure of speech, a way to say—"

"Yeah, I know. How grateful you are." He steered her from the bar and through the main restaurant. He could feel the resistance in her body. "You telling me you're all talk and no action?"

"I'm telling you I wasn't being literal."

Nick halted by the dining room hostess. "We're interested in seeing the function room."

"Oh. Well, the manager isn't in yet."

"That's fine. We don't need a tour, we just want to check it out on a preliminary basis."

"All the Saturdays in June are booked, I can tell you that," she said sympathetically. "But I'm sure it's okay if you want to look around. The door is unlocked."

Nick gripped Eden's arm and moved her forward.

"This is ridiculous, Nick. She thinks we're going to get married."

"Yeah, a shocking concept even as a joke."

"I give up."

"It took long enough."

The function room was indeed empty. The dying afternoon sun fell through a bank of windows that faced a grove of trees. Tables were stacked along one wall and chairs were coupled beside them. A maroon and gold carpet muted the hollowness. Nick closed the door, but he didn't turn on the lights. Shadows and silence swallowed them.

"Okay," he said leaning back against the wall. "The recipient of all your gratitude is ready for you to throw yourself into his arms and kiss him."

Suddenly she laughed, as if just doing something goofy and silly was okay. And Nick saw in her eyes what he, too, was thinking. They'd done goofy, silly things in college and yeah they were now adults, but who'd pronounced that being a grown-up meant it had to be all serious and solemn?

"Do I get a running start from across the room?" she asked.

"Whatever."

She reached over and flipped on the lights, which threw them into blinding brightness. She backed up so that she was at least twenty-five feet away. She stepped out of the navy pumps and took off the jacket. "I feel like a gymnast ready to launch into a vault."

"If you take off the skirt, you can run better."

"I could take off the blouse, too."

"Okay."

She giggled and Nick thought his heart would soar right out of his chest.

"I don't think so."

"Can't blame a guy for trying. Want me to hum a few bars of 'Desperado' "?

She laughed again. Before he was fully convinced she would actually do it, she started to run, then suddenly stopped.

"Now what?"

"Your knee. I'll hurt you if I jump on you."

"It's gonna hurt worse if you don't."

"You're sure?"

"Do it. Come on."

Once again she backed up, waited as if she was counting to three and then took off.

Nick braced himself. He doubted that she weighed more than 115 pounds, but coming at him at a dead run . . . He prayed his knee wouldn't collapse. Then she was there, launching herself up, her arms flung about his neck, her legs lifting and anchoring around his waist.

The breath whooshed out of him, but he caught her, held her steady. He fell back against the wall and cupped his hands beneath her bottom to hold her against him. His knee creaked but held.

For a few moments, both were quiet, letting their breathing even out. Softly she said, "This reminds me of that picture you have of us in the Explorer."

"Yeah. And it reminds me of what came afterwards."

"Is that why you kept it?"

"No. I don't need any reminders of how good it was with you. I kept it because it's the only one I have of us together."

She turned her head, but he heard the shaky intake of breath.

"So? You've flung yourself in my arms. Where's the kiss?"

And without saying anything, she laid her mouth over his. Not tentative, but a bit cautious. Nick opened his mouth, but when she didn't respond, he pulled away.

"I taught you better than that."

"What you taught me we can't do."

He grinned.

She didn't grin back.

"Hey, lighten up. That was a joke. I'm waiting for one kiss in my mouth not a tongue trip down into my jeans."

She shook her head, and for a few staggering heartbeats Nick was sure he'd crossed the line between teasing her and making her angry. Truthfully, he didn't give a shit. He wanted the kiss and he had no intention of letting her go until he got it.

Amusement finally sparkled in her eyes.

"This is just for you, Nickie."

Then she kissed him, really kissed. Their heat would have burned asbestos. Nick kissed back, pulling her deeper and deeper, so that he joined their mouths like an erotic seal of promise of more.

His mind spiraled like a pinwheel in a brisk wind, and he gave himself wholly to the sensation of her body tight against his, her hands plowing through his hair and her mouth making him wish they could stand here all night. Or slide to the floor. Or find a way, any way, that this could go on and on and on.

Then she slid her hands away, her body pulling back, her mouth lifting. And he didn't protest.

Later, back at the table, she ordered coffee. Nick didn't, nor did he touch the drink, not even the water. The taste of her coated his mouth, and he wanted to savor it as long as he could.

She reached across the table, which seemed to have gotten three times bigger than when they'd arrived. Her hand closed around his wrist. "That was fun. Very Nickie. Like the old days."

"Yeah, nothing like those good old memories, is there?"

She glanced at her watch. "We better go."

"Cal awaits."

"And Bobby, too."

"Somehow, I think Cal gets the better deal." He signaled to the waitress for the bill. When she came, he said, "Give it to the lady. This is her party."

On the ride back, Nick asked a few questions about Karen and Eddie. He wasn't all that interested, but it was a safe conversation and required little from him by way of response.

"I think the two of them are going to be just fine," Eden said finally, turning into the rink parking lot.

"Great."

"And you will, too, Nick."

"I will too what?"

"Be fine."

"Yeah."

He got out of the car, closing the door without saying anything and walking away with shoulders hunched against the wind. At the rink door, he turned, but her car had already disappeared around the corner.

Holy shit. Had she really run across that function room and leapt into his arms? Had she really kissed him like it was the last good kiss she'd ever get?

Had she?

Yeah. Oh, yeah.

This is just for you, Nickie.

Chapter 17

"OH, CAL, I'M SORRY I'M LATE," EDEN APOLogized as he stood and held her chair. She felt rushed and a bit frazzled. "Killer took off in the park after a neighbor's cat, and I had to get in the car and go find him. Then just as I was about to go out the door, Suzanne Tucker's sister called." At Cal's scowl, she said, "The discussion at The Windmill about adoption?"

He nodded. "Suzanne's sister and the biological parents who have changed their minds."

"Yes. Anyway, she was so grateful for the opportunity to talk to me, I didn't have the heart to put her off."

He brushed a kiss across her mouth before retaking his own chair. "Did you encourage her with words of wisdom?"

"I told her about my own feelings for Jennifer. It wasn't a pep talk as much as reinforcing the realities and risks of adoption, which I'm sure she's aware of and doesn't want to think about. As unconscionable as it seems to her and her husband, the courts lately have shown sympathetic favor to the child's biological connections over the adoptive parents. She needs to be prepared for that. Or as prepared as one can be."

"You know, I feel a little sorry for them."

"I do, too."

"Those people who adopted Jennifer—I hope they realize how much you sacrificed for them."

And she had made the sacrifice again recently, she thought, her own recent decision still raw. Eden's eyes shimmered at the memory, and she reached into her purse for a tissue.

She'd told Cal about her talk with her father and her conclusion that she would not see Jennifer. To his credit, he'd listened, finally saying that he understood the difficulty of her choice. Eden had been prepared for a "thank God, you came to your senses" response; she'd watched him closely, expecting to see triumph in his eyes. Instead, he'd been wonderful and understanding without being syrupy.

On some level, the daughter she hadn't seen for eighteen years would forever hold sway over her heart. Cal was absolutely right. She had sacrificed.

Clearing her throat, she said softly, "Thank you for saying that, for understanding. It means a lot to me."

He squeezed her hand and neither spoke for a few seconds.

Cal fiddled with opening his napkin and straightening the silver. The restaurant was in the Roger Williams Hotel. It was one of Lonsdale's few upscale dining rooms that attracted out-of-towners. Known for its calamari and prime rib, the personal touches made it a favorite. Tonight the special touch was a red rose for every woman in honor of Valentine's Day.

Finally Cal said, "Actually, you weren't all that late. I just got here a few minutes ago. Thank God, Harold held our reservation." He signaled a waiter, who hurried over to take their drink order.

After the waiter left, Cal leaned forward and took her hand. "You're wearing red. Is this for Valentine's Day or because I like you in red."

"Both." Her raspberry faille dress had an empire bodice and a sweeping skirt. Eden had bought it especially for tonight.

"You're beautiful, darling, and I'm the envy of every man in the room."

"Why, thank you." They twined their fingers together.

"I love you, Eden."

"I love you, too."

Both stared at each other, their gazes pools of pleasure and possibilities for what the night would bring.

They straightened when their drinks arrived. Cal lifted his in a toast. Eden did likewise. "To us, my love," he murmured, intimately. "May our happiness increase a hundredfold."

"Yes," she whispered as they clinked their glasses.

Cal took a long swallow and sighed. "What a day. Carlos, one of the suppliers, sent me polyester jackets instead of silk." He shuddered. "I had to call, and then it took a while to locate him and then I listened to a long harangue about orders being mixed up by some glitch in his new computer software. It was particularly irritating, because Carlos knows I can't abide poly. Poor John. He opened the carton, and from his expression of horror I thought it was a dead body. Now that I think about it, poly jackets in Scanlons are almost as bad."

"You're such a purist, Cal," she said, grinning and taking note of his own gray wool-and-silk suit. "Most of the polyester today looks and feels like silk."

"Not to my customers."

"That's because you've educated them in what to look for."

"Actually," he said, in a low, conspiratorial voice, "it's a trick to spoil them so badly that they'll never shop anywhere but Scanlons."

"Such deception."

"Long may the buying public stay blessedly ignorant." He settled back, loosening his tie a bit and looking relaxed, secure and polished. "So tell me about your day."

She did, leaving out the trip to the Beer and Brew with Nick. Only because it would unnecessarily raise questions, and she didn't want to spend their time together talking—or worse, arguing—about Nick. This was Valentine's Day, and their dinner was to be intimate and special as lovers shared on this day. She and Cal hadn't done enough special things together since Nick came home; she intended to remedy that.

Cal raised an eyebrow when she got to the part about Delphine Maxwell.

"Eddie and Karen are going to talk to her?" he asked. "If her hair wasn't already gray, it would turn gray when she hears this."

"I told Karen it might be awkward."

"God, I hope the woman realizes how far these two kids have come just in the past few weeks. Karen back in school and Eddie taking responsibility—that's quite a coup for you, Eden."

She couldn't not say anything, even though she hated bringing up his name. "Nick talked to Eddie, so he deserves the credit."

"Well, good for Nick. He obviously met Eddie on a level that the kid understood. My brother has indeed found his niche at the rink as well as some unexpected benefits. Maybe all his rebellion and rootless wandering has had some positive results."

Eden was only half listening, more intrigued by two women a few tables away glancing at Cal numerous times and then whispering.

She leaned forward. "I think you have two female admirers behind you to your left."

Cal turned, gave them a cursory glance and turned back. "Don't know them. Besides, I'm already taken."

"I don't think that's going to deter one of them She's sliding her chair back and getting up. She's coming this way."

"Damn. Interruptions we don't need."

"Now, be nice, Cal. She might be the wife of your next best customer."

"You're supposed to be jealous."

"If she takes her clothes off and throws herself into your arms . . ."

"I don't think women do that anymore."

"Probably not."

Where are we going?

Where you can throw yourself in my arms and kiss me.

If you take off your skirt you can run better.

I could take off my blouse, too.
I taught you to kiss better than that.
What you taught me I can't do.
This is just for you, Nickie.

Eden blinked, the images flashing then flitting away as quickly as they'd come. She focused on the approaching woman.

She was about forty, with the delicate bones and tight tissue-paper skin that had been moisturized and made up by a facial expert. Her mouth was generously red, her dark hair was done in a blunt cut similar to Eden's, but because of her height and long neck, it presented a mushroom cap effect. Wearing a watered silk burgundy dress and a casually donned cashmere sweater, she nonetheless approached Cal warily, as if, despite her socially adept manner, she wasn't entirely sure of herself.

"Excuse me," she said with a finishing school lilt. "I know I'm interrupting but I thought I recognized you."

Cal stood, looking politely blank, waiting for a name or a connection.

"I'm Amanda Rittenhouse. Aren't you Cal Scanlon?"

Cal scowled. "Yes, I am. This is Eden Parrish." The two women exchanged polite smiles.

Amanda said to Cal, "You were married to Betsy Gordon?" Cal nodded, and Amanda looked relieved that she hadn't made a mistake. "Betsy and I were sorority sisters at Brown. I was at your wedding, although obviously you wouldn't remember. So many of the guests were Betsy's friends. I was in Europe when Betsy was killed. Drunk drivers cause far too many horrible tragedies, don't they? You two had barely begun your marriage."

"It was a very difficult time. For me and for Betsy's family. Betsy did have a lot of friends. We simply weren't together long enough for them to become mine, too."

"I understand completely." She looked at Eden, her apology obviously sincere. "But I saw you and I did want to offer my sympathy, even belatedly."

Cal nodded. "Thank you."

After she went back to her own table, Eden whispered, "I think she wanted you to ask her to join us."

"Not a chance."

"Did you really not remember her?"

"Actually, I did when she said her name. At the wedding reception, I danced with her, and she proceeded to whisper in my ear that she wasn't wearing panties."

Eden laughed. "My God, she looks as prim and polite as a virgin queen."

"I told Betsy about it later, and she said, 'Oh, that's just Amanda. She's one of those people that likes to destroy a guy's perception of her.' "

"Even if the guy has just married one of her friends?"

"Guess so."

"Gee, it's a good thing she's matured or she might have done what I said at first."

"Taking off her clothes and throwing herself into my arms? I'd have to dump her on the floor," he said with more amusement than seriousness. "Besides, I'm stuck on you." He picked up the menu. "Let's order dinner."

It was nearing nine o'clock when they finished eating. Cal ordered coffee after the waiter cleared away the dishes. The room was still fairly crowded with diners.

Sipping the hot liquid, then sitting back in a relaxed manner, he said, "This is one of the few times I regret that I quit smoking."

"Hmm." Eden cupped her chin in one palm, turning her coffee cup with the other hand. She'd eaten too much and was pleasantly sleepy.

"Too bad it's so cold. We could have gone out to the terrace."

"Yes."

"You're tired, aren't you?"

"I'm sorry." She straightened and blinked, trying to rid her eyes of their heaviness. "Good company and good food and just being relaxed. I think I better ask for some more coffee, so I don't fall asleep driving home."

"I'd hoped this might be a longer night than it looks like it will be."

Eden wasn't so weary that she missed his point. "I haven't been much of a girlfriend lately, have I?"

"The relationship has been a little light on sexual encounters."

"A sweet way to say I've been neglecting you."

"I have been patient, Eden."

"More than patient. There's just been so many things that—well—finding time for us has been hard. I promise to do better. Now that Eddie and Karen are headed in the right direction, I feel some of the load has been lifted."

"Good. And Nick seems to be out of the picture."

"Nick?" Suddenly she was wide-awake. "When was he ever in our picture? As you said before, he seems to be doing okay."

He visibly relaxed. Eden let out a breath as if she'd avoided a collision. Any time Nick's name came up, Eden felt as if the ground beneath their relationship was as reliable as quicksand.

"I'd hoped things would work out for him and Julie," Cal said, picking up the conversation again.

"I don't know anything about that."

"Nor does Julie, apparently. She was in the store the other day. She said he's avoided her phone calls and generally given her the brush-off."

"She can be a little pushy. Nick always liked to do the chasing rather than be chased."

"Your experience with him?" he asked casually.

Eden's defenses sprang to life, and she quickly arrested them. "My past experience, Cal. Past," she emphasized. "Don't read more into it than there is." But there was more. More than she knew how to handle. More than she could simply ignore. God, what was she doing even venturing into this conversation? Her hands were clammy, and she felt her personal relationships had become a high wire act over a sea of sharks.

Cal looked mollified, but Eden couldn't be sure anymore. Was he really mollified or did she just want him to be?

"Well, enough about Nick," he said dismissively. "One of these days, he'll probably find someone."

"I'm sure he will."

"Meanwhile there's you and me."

"Always." She relaxed again. Eden sipped her coffee as Cal reached under the table.

He placed a small heart-shaped box of chocolates in front of her. Lace outlined the heart and a cascade of red and pink ribbons flowed over the top.

"How sweet of you."

"Open it."

"Cal, I'm stuffed. Tomorrow I'll really enjoy them."

He leaned forward, his fingers brushing the lace where her hand was. "I was hoping to steal one of the chocolate-covered cherries."

She pushed the box toward him.

"It's your candy," he said, moving it back to her.

She lifted the lid and then stared in astonishment at the arrangement of candies. All dark chocolates that she loved, but they faded into nothing in contrast with the focal point: a pear-shaped diamond set in a ring of white gold.

Eden simply zoned out into a clueless stupor. Her numbed mind latched onto the desperate idea that whoever had originally packed the chocolates had lost her ring.

"Darling?"

Reality flooded her. "How could you do this?" she snapped. "No warning. My God, Cal."

Obviously crestfallen, he muttered, "That

wasn't quite the reaction I had in mind."

She covered her mouth, stunned by her outburst of anger, by the nausea climbing in her throat. Frantically she swallowed. When she felt it was safe to talk, she said flatly, "We agreed to wait until summer."

"Which is four months away." She heard the tight grit of control in his tone.

She was handling this horribly, but a place inside her rose up in protest at being blindsided. She knew she should be pleased, surprised and honored, but inside she was furious that he'd simply rushed ahead when he knew specifically that she'd wanted to wait.

Cal drained his coffee cup, saying, again with that tonal control, "I'm at a loss as to why there's some magic in waiting. We love each other. We've discussed marriage. I even went to the same jeweler. The ring is the one you picked out at Portobello in Newport."

"I didn't pick it out. I said I liked it," she said without any pretense of pleasure. "I also liked a dozen others. What woman wouldn't. They were all breathtaking." She glared at the ring now as if it was part of some plot against her. Which was ridiculous. And idiotic. And over the top. If she ever needed proof of the ragged volatility in her life, this reaction provided it.

"Maybe I should have brought the entire goddamn dozen and you could have picked out your favorite."

"That's not what I meant."

"No? Then what in hell did you mean? Or is this my fault for ignoring the exact meaning of what you said that day? Let me see if I remember it correctly." He paused, as if timing an entrance, then said, "Ah, yes, it was, 'Oh look, Cal, I'd love to have a ring like that.' "

"I don't remember exactly what I said," she lied and was amazed she didn't even care.

"But I do, because I wanted to get you the ring you wanted—not what I might have chosen, but what you chose."

She covered her face with her hands, wishing she could leap back to before she opened the box. Why hadn't she suspected? Valentine's Day. A special dinner. Romantic conversation and even talking about Nick hadn't caused a major ripple. That in itself should have been a signal. And that box of chocolates. Now that she recalled, it wasn't even sealed. She definitely deserved the Dumb Bunny of the Week award.

Calming herself, she lowered her hands and looked directly at Cal. "Please, let's not fight about this. I'm sorry I reacted so selfishly. I truly am. Obviously you planned all this and went to a lot of trouble and I'm spoiling it."

Then, as if she'd spoken magic, his tight demeanor relaxed. Leaning toward her, he took her left hand and rubbed his thumb on her ring finger. "Eden, I want to marry you. I want a commitment beyond an occasional dinner and making love when you can fit it into your schedule."

"I want that, too."

"Then let me put the ring on your finger and forget all this four months of waiting silliness." He lowered his head for a moment, his voice sad and disappointed. "I'd wanted this to be romantic and special. Instead I feel I'm locking you up like some poor creature who wants to be free."

Eden lifted the ring from the box, reached for his hand and placed it on his palm. "Slip it on my finger."

He looked as if he wanted to ask if she was absolutely sure, but was afraid.

He slid on the ring, holding his fingers over it as thought it was a secret seal.

His eyes met hers. "Will you marry me?"

St. Mark's Church had a huge sanctuary, and the open loft that extended over the last ten pews housed a pipe organ that dated back to the nineteenth century. Many of the parish Catholics believed that *O Santissimo* still flowed from the pipes if one carefully listened. The elaborate altar, sidelighted by stained glass, focused on a polished mahogany cross.

Eden genuflected and then hurried through a side door and down a flight of stairs that led to the church basement. Conversation and some laughter greeted her when she pushed open the crash-proof door.

The large room was filled with items stacked on long white-cloth-covered tables for the upcoming tag sale to benefit foreign missionaries. Everything from children's clothing to a white-elephant table, where an ugly lamp with purple pineapples bulging from its base was being examined by Mary Scanlon.

Eden smiled at the other women; all were wearing gray and white butcher aprons. She spoke to those she knew and hurried over to Mary.

Mary glanced up, smiled and said, "I was beginning to think you changed your mind."

"I was going to come earlier, but I knew you'd be busy." Truthfully, she'd wanted to cancel seconds after she'd called Mary that morning.

"What do you think?" Mary asked, holding up the lamp as if some beauty must exist in the ceramic shape. "Five dollars?"

Eden unzipped her blue and white ski jacket. "To pay someone to take it?"

Mary sighed. "You're right. It is ghastly. Probably a wedding gift from a cranky uncle." She wrote "$2" on a sticky tag and put it on the lamp.

Then she turned to Eden, a scowl settling across her features. "You look exhausted. You're pale and you have dark circles under your eyes."

"I used makeup, but I guess it didn't work."

Mary, always endearingly blunt, said, "Some sleep would be better."

"It's not just that." Although she hadn't slept well the past two nights, not since her dinner with Cal. In fact, running away had lapped at the edges of her mind, despite rule number four from the guidance counselor book of wisdom: abandoning a problem isn't a solution. God, who had come up with that stupid rule? Of course it was a solution. Running would get her out of this mess.

Finally, in a shaky voice, she said, "I'm stressed. Scared. Worried. Mary, I don't know what to do."

Mary studied her a few moments, making Eden feel Cal's mother could see her turmoiled conscience. "Since I know things are going well at school, and you've made your decision about Jennifer, then the distress must involve my sons." At Eden's stricken face, Mary nodded and took her hand. "Believe me, I have few illusions about either of them, although I love them both dearly. Whatever they've done to make you so unhappy can't be so bad that there is no solution. Come on. Father Murray is here, and I know he would be glad to listen—"

Eden shrank away. "I can't talk to Father."

"Of course you can. He's very understanding. I didn't mean making a confession. Just tell him what's bothering you and let him advise you."

"God, Mary, I can't." She took quick steps away from Mary's reach.

Obviously confused, Mary said, "But I thought that's why you were so insistent on coming here today."

"Not to see Father Murray. To see you. I need a friend, Mary, not a confessor." Eden's eyes were swimming and her mouth began to tremble. She struggled to control herself.

Mary reached for her hands, saying, "All right. Then we need some privacy." She took off her apron and laid it beside the ugly lamp. Then, taking Eden's arm as if she needed physical support, Mary called to Harriet, the woman in charge. "I'll be back in a little while."

Upstairs in the sanctuary, they chose a pew near the back and slid in. It was shadowed and far enough from the center aisle that unless someone was looking, they could easily be missed. For a few moments they sat side by side, the solitude broken only by Eden's uneven breathing.

In a soft voice Mary said, "Tell me what's troubling you."

Eden almost laughed. "Do we have all month?"

"We have all the time you need."

Eden held her purse in the center of her lap, her fingers wound through the shoulder strap. Now that she was here, her courage was fading. "You've been such a good friend to me and sometimes you've even been like a mother. When I first met you when Nick was hurt, I thought you were so strong and so supportive. You never rushed at Nick with what he should do now he couldn't play hockey. And you didn't sputter a lot of cliches about time easing disappointments and life taking new paths."

Mary listened, her patience obvious. Eden realized her own stalling tactics, but she felt her insides settle down.

"Nick needed time to deny and be angry," Mary said.

"Cal and Nick's dad asked questions and made suggestions—all of them good, but I just had the sense Nick needed someone to say that it wasn't weird if he felt like his life was as useless as his shattered knee."

Mary nodded. "A tragedy such as Nick experienced—not just the knee, but the effect that injury had on his future—he needed to find bottom. Or as Nick would call it, the underbelly of hell."

"And his father and Cal thought he should do a chin-up and get on with life?"

"Yes."

"Do you think their attitude is why it's taken Nick so long?"

Mary chuckled, shaking her head. "No. Nick did a lot of misery-basking, feeling sorry for himself for too long, but he had some valid reasons that go deeper than just a messed-up career."

"His resentment of Cal?"

"That was part of it."

The diverted conversation helped to calm Eden, and she realized that understanding more about Nick and Cal's relationship might show her a solution to her own dilemma.

"Nick never talked about his family much when we dated and even now, he says little unless it's to jab at Cal."

"And Cal jabs back."

"Yes, I guess he does, but it's different. Cal puts it all in the context of annoyance. Sort of Nick needs to get it together and grow up. While Nick's comments have a sarcastic bite, like taking any advice from Cal is an insult."

"You recall after Nick came home and started rehabilitation, that first time you came for a visit?"

Eden shuddered. After Nick had broken up with her, she had driven down to Lonsdale a few times to see him—as a friend, she'd told herself then, but she'd hoped he might reconsider their relationship. But that never happened. "He and his father were in a shouting match."

"I'd like to say that was rare, but it wasn't. Nick was so stubborn, so determined to keep his distance from anything Jack suggested. Jack was just as dogged in his attempt to make Nick like Cal. Nick accused his father of being happy that he'd gotten hurt just to shove it in his face that if he'd done as he was told and followed his brother's example, then the Scanlon family tradition would be intact. Jack called Nick a thankless bastard."

Listening, Eden began to understand the depth of Nick's anger at Cal. It had more to do with his father than it did with his brother. In the same vein, Eden realized a lot of her own unsettling feelings had more to do with her own indecisiveness than about either Nick or Cal.

Mary said, "But we're getting way off track here. You didn't come here to talk about the past."

"Maybe I did and I didn't know it. Tell me about Nick and Cal and their dad."

Mary took a deep breath. "Nick's injury was destructive to him emotionally because it took away the one area where he excelled. From the moment he knew Cal would never be a hockey player, the sport became an obsession for Nick. His dream was to be so extraordinary that his father would admit he was wrong."

"Wrong that Nick was wasting his time?"

"Nick hoped. But Jack clung to the belief that Nick was always wrong to disobey, because Jack thought he knew what was best for him."

"My God, that sounds like mental and emotional abuse."

Mary sighed, a sadness filtering her words. "Jack refused to see Nick in any light except the one Cal stood in. He tried for years to make Nick like Cal. He wanted his sons to follow him into the business. Cal was willing, like a bowl of soft clay given over to its creator. Nick, on the other hand, was like clay already formed as hard as steel. His independence and rebellion—Jack couldn't change that, and his insistence that Nick follow Cal's example put Nick in a real dilemma. He wanted to obey his father, but sports, where he was exceptional, held no interest for Jack. So Nick held himself back so that Cal would look good. In Nick's logic, if Cal did well in sports and his father approved, that would translate into Nick getting approval."

"Couldn't you do something?" Eden asked, appalled at the hold Jack had on his two sons.

"Believe me, I tried. I argued and shouted, used calmness and logic. Nothing worked. I even considered divorce."

Eden's eyes widened. She knew Mary felt strongly that there were too many divorces. "You must have been desperate."

"I came here and talked to the priest, Father Kelly at the time. Of course, he didn't see it the way I did. He viewed Jack as a strong role model, and how could I seriously be upset that he wanted his two sons to be successful? By the time I'd left, I began to wonder if I was the one with the problem."

"So what did you do?"

"I stayed."

Eden frowned. "Just like that? Something must have changed your mind."

Mary glanced away, staring at the Madonna and Child in one of the stained glass windows. "Jack told me if I divorced him, I'd never get custody of the boys. He knew too many judges, he had too much influence. It was odd, because it was like hearing all this from some stranger, not the man I'd loved for so long. I knew he was right. If I left, the boys would lose more than if I stayed."

"So you did what any mother would do. You sacrificed."

"As you did for Jennifer. You looked at the circumstances, and the future for your daughter, and made a decision."

"Aunt Josette convinced me. At sixteen, I had illusions about motherhood."

"Then your aunt was wise."

"Like you."

The two women were silent, the far-off sound of tag-sale sorting and an occasional door closing the only noises.

"You stayed, but I know you didn't just sit back like a wuss."

Mary chuckled. "No, I didn't. I encouraged Nick to do his best and be himself. Approval wasn't as important as being true to his own talents. He took some of that to heart when he started playing hockey . . ." Mary paused, lowering her head, shaking it as if gripped by sad memories.

"What?" Eden asked.

"One Sunday, after Mass, a number of people congratulated me on having such a talented son. I thought they were talking about Cal. But it was Nick. They spoke of the praise coming from his coach and how hordes of people were showing up at practices just to watch Nick skate. I was appalled that I didn't know, nor did Jack or Cal—or so they claimed—but the point was that

Nick never told anyone, because he believed no one cared, or worse, he'd get in trouble for being better than Cal. I was furious with both Jack and Cal, although Cal, to his credit, started going to Nick's games and at one time tried to tell Jack that Nick wasn't just a hockey player, he was NHL material."

"Did his father ever see that?"

"The hockey scholarship to BU impressed Jack. I honestly believed that finally things would turn around. Then Nick got hurt and in that instant it was all gone. Jack didn't help with his 'See, if you'd done as I told you and followed Cal' line of argument. Nick simply folded inward. He wanted nothing to do with his father or with his brother. It was like the more trouble he could get into, the better he liked it."

Mary sighed. "For a while he lived with the not-quite ex-wife of one of Jack's business associates and didn't care who knew it. At about that time Cal and Betsy were planning their wedding. So, here again, Cal was doing the Jack Scanlon proper thing, while Nick was being deliberately improper. The double resentment was sealed in cement.

"Jack died and then Cal lost Betsy, and suddenly Nick was the only one with any common sense. Scanlons was in financial trouble, and Nick came in and worked and reorganized—it was an amazing sight. Here was this rebel who hadn't even set foot in the store since he was about ten suddenly running it better than it had ever been run. Then Cal came back to work. Because he'd worked there for so long, Cal took a lot of credit he didn't deserve. Nick, as he'd done for so many years, stepped aside. But that time he did more—he walked away for five years."

Eden shook her head in amazement. "It explains so much."

"And I need to correct an impression I'm sure I've left about Cal. He didn't do anything that Nick wouldn't have done if their roles had been reversed."

"Taken advantage of his place, you mean."

"Exactly. And Cal has become a fine man. He knows Nick's resentment isn't just in Nick's mind. I think in his own way he's tried to make up for it. Nick, on the other hand, hasn't been as willing to let the past settle."

"And here I am in the middle."

Mary smiled. "It has made both of them more aware of each other than I think they want to be."

Eden sat still for a long time, too aware of the rawness in her throat, holding off what felt like weeks of unshed tears. Mary put her arm around her, saying nothing, and the simple gesture released Eden's tension and the tears came. Mary held her, letting her cry. Eden took tissues from her purse and blew her nose.

"Is being in the middle what you wanted to talk to me about?"

Eden showed her the engagement ring. "Cal asked me to marry him."

Mary brightened, then paled. "This is the problem, isn't it?"

"Oh, Mary, I feel so trapped. Cal knew I wanted to wait until summer before we did anything. I reacted very badly the other night and I know it hurt him."

"But you accepted the ring."

"I just didn't have the heart to refuse after being so bitchy."

"There's a but in there. Nick?"

She nodded. "It's such a mess and I don't know how it happened and I never wanted to wind up like this and now—God, I can't believe I'm going to tell you all this in front of the crucifix. God will be shocked and probably strike me dead."

"God isn't shockable, Eden. And after raising the two men who have so upset you, I'm not either."

"I love Cal, but I feel things for Nick . . ."

"And you want to make the right choice."

"The right choice is Cal. I know that. He's everything any woman would want. And I've hurt him terribly."

"And Nick is everything a woman shouldn't want."

"You're not being very helpful."

"You're not answering my question."

Eden looked away.

"Eden?"

"I had sex with Nick," she said baldly, "and I loved it. I hated him because I loved it. And I hated him because he made me question my feelings for Cal."

"And Cal giving you the ring is forcing a decision."

"One I don't want to make."

"But you must, Eden. You can't marry a man you don't love, and you can't allow your future to be so limited that you would choose a man because he's good in bed."

"It wasn't even romantic, Mary. And I was so furious with him and myself, I threw away everything we touched. Sheets, blankets, pillows, my clothes, even the quilt."

"It sounds to me as if a lot more was going on inside you then guilt or even anger. But that aside, both Nick and Cal are adults. A broken engagement is better than a divorce. And if Nick goes off on one of his rebellious snits because you've decided to marry Cal, then it's his problem."

Eden looked toward the altar, noting the colors of light streaming through the stained glass. "I wish I believed in spiritual signs."

Mary smiled. "Sometimes signs are more down to earth. Does Nick know about the engagement?"

"I haven't seen him, so I don't know."

"Perhaps you and Cal should tell him together."

Eden shuddered.

"Do you want me to do it?"

Eden laughed derisively. "All this presupposes Nick will even care."

"Oh, he'll care. The question is whether he'll care because his ego is punctured or because he cares for you."

Chapter 18

A LITTLE AFTER FOUR O'CLOCK TWO DAYS later, Eden whistled for Killer, snapped a leash on his collar and walked across her mushy front yard. The weather had warmed into a forty degree February thaw, but instead of the much-desired sunshine, clouds rolled across the sky threatening rain.

She crossed the street, took a shortcut through the park and down another block, halting about a hundred feet from Nick's duplex. The Explorer was parked at the curb.

Her heart worked as if she'd broken a running record; she tried to convince herself the fast rate had to do with keeping up with Killer's trot and not her own uneasiness.

She made her way down the uneven sidewalk, mentally reciting her motive for showing up at his door. Killer had been acting sluggish from lack of exercise and, with the warming temperatures, she'd decided to go to Nick's so that the two dogs could play. She grimaced. Her excuse sounded suspiciously contrived.

Irrationally she blamed Cal for her having to do any of this. It baffled her as to why he hadn't called Nick and crowed a little, perhaps throwing off a line like "You cruise, you lose." No. Unlike Cal. Too crass. Too Nick-sounding. Cal would be more graceful. Then again, given their past animosity, Cal should be congratulated for not rubbing it in.

However, Eden couldn't stand the waiting; she was jumpy.

If only she had some idea of what Nick's reaction would be.

Some perverse, melodramatic side of her wanted him to declare his everlasting love, convince her that he'd always loved her and then propose the ultimate lover-sacrifice and offer to kill himself if she married Cal.

"Which is as likely as me passing out from sunstroke right now," she muttered.

Killer sniffed around the bushes, watered them and then trotted up the apartment house steps.

"Here goes, Pupper." Taking a deep breath, she knocked.

Almost instantly, the door was flung open. "Cal, you forgot your gloves—" Nick's effusive grin shrank immediately when he saw who it was. "Eden. What are you doing here? Everything okay?"

Her entire body felt like a helium balloon that had been overinflated. "Uh, Killer and I were walking and, well, he and Bobby hadn't seen each other for a while so we, uh . . ."

"Came to visit," he finished for her. "A great idea. Bobby's out in the yard." Nick rubbed Killer's ears. "He's missed you, Pupper." He released the leash, handing it to Eden, and led

Killer to the back door. Eden trailed behind. A few seconds later, Killer raced out into a fenced area, where Bobby greeted him.

Nick turned back to her, and she took an unnecessary step to her left and hit her hip on a chair.

If he noticed her agitation, he didn't react. "Want some coffee? 'Fraid I don't have any Earl Grey."

"Coffee's fine."

She coiled the leash and put it and her shoulder bag on a chair. She wore her blue parka over black leggings and a white turtleneck sweater. Mittens covered her hands—and the ring.

The apartment was sparse, the furniture more functional than attractive. The most used piece was a Formica table, its dull black top spattered with gray chips that resembled old asphalt. Papers, a stack of hockey pucks and carry-out coffee containers were strewn around. A navy sweatshirt had been tossed over a tired recliner. On the kitchen counter stood a toaster, an opened package of bread and a bottle of liquor.

"The seal isn't broken," he said, as if reading her mind.

"I'm glad."

"Just glad? No probing questions like why a drunk would keep a sealed bottle of whiskey?"

"To test your resolve to stay sober?"

"Too obvious."

She hated guessing games.

"Want to try again?"

"No."

"Suit yourself." He switched the coffee maker to the warming setting and disposed of the grounds, saying nothing more about the bottle.

To keep from studying him, she focused on the mugs he took from the drain board, on the milk from the refrigerator, and his pouring the steaming liquid. But it was no use. If ever there was a bad time for him to look sexy and dangerous while he acted as if she was as intriguing as the toast crumbs on the counter, today was it.

He hadn't shaved. His dark hair was mussed and needed cutting. He wore socks but no shoes, faded, patched jeans with no belt and a wrinkled unbuttoned shirt that wasn't tucked in.

To her disgust, her stomach curled up as if temptation was a fist ready with a sucker punch. "I hope I'm not interrupting you," she said, when he placed her mug of coffee on the table. It suddenly occurred to her that she was going to have to remove the mittens to handle the coffee, and she wasn't ready to do that. Not yet.

"Actually I haven't been up too long. I was at the rink all night working on the Zamboni," he said, referring to the ice-resurfacing machine. "Came home about five A.M. and fell into bed. Guess I zonked out. Cal woke me about an hour ago, banging on the door. I wasn't too happy to see him until he gave me the great news." He smiled broadly at her.

Great news? Like her engagement to Cal? Well, she thought, so much for Mary's theories. No hurt ego here. No caring one way or the other. And so much for all her concern about telling him. Cal had been obviously gripped by guilt, had come over here and told his brother of the engagement.

"You certainly do look happy about it," she said, trying for blandness and coolness.

"You don't." He watched her over the rim of his mug as he sipped. One hip was propped against the counter edge, while Eden felt adrift in the middle of the floor.

"Don't what?"

"Don't look happy."

"I'm thrilled." If two words had ever sounded more sarcastic, more warped . . . *Get a grip here. You wanted no hassles, no fights, no feelings left trapped between the two of us, and now that it's all hunky-dory, you're angry.*

"Cal's news was what I was hoping—even praying—would happen."

The more he said, the more foolish she felt. "Well, I'm glad your prayers were answered," she said, reaching for the leash and her bag.

"So's Poppy."

"Poppy?" She frowned, glancing back at him.

"He didn't deserve to get pink-slipped as a nonessential. Not after all the time and work he's put in to make the rink run smoothly. Cal gets the credit for the job-save and my gratitude for keeping his promise and convincing the board. Plus, and this was a bonus I wasn't expecting, they didn't cut the sports budget. In fact, it got a small increase. Cal said the town council has to give final approval, but he assured me it would."

For a long, confusing moment she stared at him, leash dangling from one hand, shoulder bag en route to her shoulder. She'd misunderstood, leaped to the wrong conclusion. Nick didn't know about the engagement.

"You had no clue about the wrangle over the school budget?" he asked, catching her astonishment. "I can't believe that, Eden. Where have you been? Your department was one being considered for some tightening. Cal said it escaped only because of the strides you've made in the pregnancy awareness program. The Karen-Eddie thing cemented the proposal you presented as doable and not just theory. He said the Maxwell woman was very impressed."

"I haven't talked to Cal about this," she said vaguely. Why hadn't Cal said something the last time they spoke? Or had he and she'd given it little attention? Her she been that absorbed in personal matters? "Delphine has very definite ideas. Having her on my side is a plus."

"Yeah. He figured she would freak about Eddie being the father, but she was impressed by the maturity of the two kids and their taking responsibility."

"Wonderful."

He frowned. "You sure you're okay?"

She glanced down at her mittened hands. "Did you and Cal discuss anything else?"

"Just that I'll be coaching full-time. Buck wants to work with the younger kids, so I'll be doing the senior high school team."

"How exciting for you. I guess this means you'll be staying and living here in Lonsdale."

"Yeah. Have to find a better place to live, though. This was okay until I knew just what I wanted to do. Now I know. Cal mentioned some land for sale on the edge of Franklin Woods. Think I'm gonna take a look. Always wanted a log cabin, so if I can swing the land, it would be a perfect place to build one."

"It sounds as if you've made a lot of permanent plans."

"As permanent as is possible. Coming home was the smartest thing I could have done." He looked at her untouched mug of coffee. "For godsake, you can't drink coffee with mittens on."

And before she could back away, he pulled off the right mitten and then the left. She instinctively balled her hands. But Nick was tossing the mittens aside and refilling his own coffee mug, never noticing the ring. She scowled. His friendliness and good mood irritated her. She was miserable, and here he was basking in the happiness of fresh starts and new beginnings.

She picked up the mug and crossed the kitchen to glance out the window.

Just tell him. Get it over with and then try to make a gracious departure. "Nick, there's something—"

Behind her, he said, "Don't get me wrong if I say this . . ."

"What?"

"I'm glad you stopped by, but Cal could come back for his gloves."

She turned. "And be annoyed at finding me here?"

"Yeah."

"And that could mess up this new buddy-buddy relationship between you two?"

He winked, lowering his voice as if they had a secret. "Nah. This ain't even living dangerously. You've got all your clothes on."

Eden bristled. "I don't think that's very funny."

"Come on, lighten up. "You're too touchy."

"I'm not touchy," she snapped. "You were obviously making a reference to that night we had sex."

Nick tapped the heel of his hand against the side of his head as if trying to make sense of the conversation. "Are you looking for a fight or am I not awake yet? Now that I think about it, you've been weird since you got here. Why are you so uptight?"

Moisture stung her eyes and that appalled her. No way could she let herself cry. She swallowed hard. "I didn't know you and Cal were getting along so well."

"That's made you uptight? Come on, Eden. That doesn't make sense. Correct me if I'm wrong, but haven't you been the crusader for sibling love and forgiveness between us?"

"Considering the circumstances . . ."

Setting down his mug and frowning at her, he asked, "What circumstances? That I'm getting along with my brother?" He stepped close, his fingers playing along the open zipper track of her jacket. With the smallest move he could reach inside and cup her breast. "Hey, babe, it might not last. I could do something or he could say something and the truce will be history."

Eden didn't move and when he reached for her hand, she flinched. His fingers touched her palm and she instinctively pulled back. But he wasn't looking at her hand, he was looking into her eyes. She felt more than a bit panicky, about to blurt it out, when his thumb glided over her knuckles, grazing the ring. Then his body went perfectly still.

He glanced down and Eden closed her eyes.

"Son of a bitch . . ." He let go of her hand as if it had scalded him, turned aside and cursed again. He breathed deeply, a slight shudder evident across his shoulders.

"Nick, I'm sorry."

"For what?" He'd moved, so she couldn't see his face except in profile. The muscle at his jaw clenched. "For getting engaged?"

"No. That Cal didn't tell you."

"I'd rather you were sorry about the engagement. Hell, I'd rather you weren't engaged, period." He moved from her, walking to the counter.

Eden had no words to say. She'd been prepared for some furious reaction that she would then have to defuse. Not this calmness, this iron control. Then, to her horror, he lifted the liquor bottle, broke the seal and flipped the cap into the trash.

Panic filled her eyes.

He held it by the neck. His voice was even, his gaze riveted on her. "Guess this means we have to quit those sprints at the Beer and Brew. And no more conversations about my unrestrained appetites. Or unplanned sexual encounters when I give you every reason to hate me."

Eden pressed her lips together, holding her silence. Her eyes stung badly with unshed tears, not of disappointment, but of sadness for the man who in a very real way would always own a piece of her heart. Letting go this time was more wrenching and more confusing than the breakup of thirteen years ago. Then he'd walked away because he didn't want her. This time she was walking away by choice, and the hollowness within her felt as if it would never be filled.

She feared saying how she felt. It wasn't fair to Cal or to Nick for her to allow any emotion to show that might indicate she wasn't sure of her decision. She'd accepted Cal's ring and she would marry him. But this pain she felt with Nick . . .

She touched his arm. "I'm sorry you had to find out from me. I didn't think it was fair for you to hear it at the rink."

"Wouldn't have mattered. I'm used to losing more than I'm used to winning."

"Oh, Nickie."

He straightened, his eyes shuttered, revealing nothing. He held up the bottle. "Bought this as a bet with myself. If I got you back, then I'd dump it down the drain. If I didn't, then I'd drink it. Funny, I wasn't counting on an engagement. So looks like he won you after all. I'll have to congratulate him."

Eden stared. Suddenly his stoic acceptance and the cavalier use of her as a trophy was more rattling and upsetting than if he'd been furiously jealous. "Is that all this was about, Nick? One of you winning? You getting drunk if you didn't and staying sober if you did? Those times we were together were all some planned strategy of getting me back, as if I was some piece of property you owned?" That helium balloon feeling returned, and she could barely breathe. She counted ten heartbeats before she spoke. "I knew there was rivalry. I knew you and Cal were at odds because of me, but a win or lose wager . . . You never wanted me or cared about a good relationship with your brother. You only cared about Nick. About Nick getting what he deserves."

"I got what I deserved, didn't I? I lost. Everyone should be happy. Most of all Cal," he said evenly.

Eden wanted to believe his easy acceptance was all a lie, all bravado to save his pride, all control to hold his temper. It was too painful to think she meant so little to him.

But he wouldn't look at her. He just kept staring down at the open bottle dangling from his hand.

She wasn't about to contribute to his destruction, and it was crazy to push him, but the alternative of just walking out and leaving him like this . . . she simply couldn't.

Taking a breath, she walked closer to him. She tried to take the bottle, but his grip tightened. He stared at the ring. A vein throbbed in his neck, his eyes narrowed, and a sudden explosion of tension burst from him for the first time. "Goddamn him."

Then he pushed her away, turned and dumped the liquor down the drain, dropping the bottle into the sink.

Eden should have felt relieved, but in truth she was simply confused. He twisted and glared at her now, his gray eyes icy. "Why the hell did you say yes?"

She blinked at the starkness in his face. "Why did I say yes? Why do you think? I'm in love with him."

"Bullshit."

"It's not!" And abruptly she knew she had the furious reaction that she wanted. This was Nick. Not a soft acceptance of circumstances he didn't like, but anger and frustration. And for her, this was easier. She wouldn't cry or let him see just how much one choice had sliced away the other. In a countering tone, she asked, "And what would you know about love anyway? What would you know about stability and trust and caring?"

His gaze bored into hers so fiercely, so cutting, that she had to look away. "You left out responsibility and success and bringing honor to the Scanlon name. Christ, you sound like my old man and my brother."

She steadied herself and her voice; she wanted to match his careless attitude. "I've spent days worrying about what I should do. What a waste of my time that was. I should have told you right away and not given a damn how you would react, because obviously everything you ever had with me had nothing to do with caring about me. It had everything to do with your cock."

He swung around, pointing at her. "Wrong. It had to do with you. With proving to Cal that you were mine once and would be again. That what we had was a helluva lot better than anything he had, even on his best nights. It had to do with getting you back into my bed, and I did exactly that."

She grabbed the leash from the chair and went to the back door, pulling it open. His palm hit the wood panel above her head and slammed it shut. He flung the leash aside, grabbed her and swung her around to face him, then pushed her up against the door.

His body crowded hers, his hands flattened on the wood panels on either side of her head. She was locked in place.

He was so close she could hear his wrist pulse. His body hummed with heat. In a low tone, he asked, "Does he know we had sex? Does he know I used a rubber he bought? Does he know I can make you come even when you don't want to?" Then, as if his own words had turned on him like traitors, he seemed to dissolve against her.

Eden literally quit breathing while he burrowed against her like a wounded animal. He crushed her to him, his mouth pressed against her ear, whispering words rising from his very depths. "I didn't win you, Eden . . . I lost you. . . ." He breathed deeply, his mouth hot against her ear. "I-I don't want to get drunk, so here I am, babe, left with enough anger to keep on hurting you. Sweet Christ, I've done that—did it then and did it now—hurt your heart and poisoned your soul. . . ."

Eden slipped her arms around him, wanting to hold and soothe and comfort and realizing that she had been right. Nick in pain and filled with sorrow was much more of a threat to her than Nick angry. Tears glazed her eyes. "Nickie, this is all so awful, so hard. . . ."

Nick pulled back and stared down at her. The ice and the fire and fury were all gone. "I want to kiss you, babe. I want to sweep you up into my arms and make love to you. I want to . . ."

But his voice trailed off, while Eden felt poised on some precipice. Instead of turning the want into action, he kissed her forehead, her tears, then her slightly parted mouth, but before she could respond, he drew her away as if putting her in a place of safety. Picking up the leash, he opened the door and whistled. The two dogs came bounding inside.

No more painful words, no more meaningful looks, no more moments for her heart to soar and then weep. She pulled on her mittens, took the now-leashed Killer and went to the front door. Nick had his back turned. She wanted to say something, but what? Good-bye? See you at the next game? See you at my wedding?

There was nothing left to say. There was no reason to linger. It was time to go.

At home she got out her appointment book and thumbed through the pages to June.

The first Saturday in June would be perfect for the wedding.

Just twelve short weeks from now, she'd be Eden Parrish Scanlon.

"Why didn't Cal tell me? He was at my place for nearly an hour and he deliberately didn't say one goddamn word."

"I can't answer that question, Nick. You'll have to ask him," his mother said calmly from a kitchen chair she'd drawn up to the table covered with newspapers. She was polishing some sterling silver.

By contrast, Nick was ticked, irritated and wound up tighter than a hungry python. He had paced the length of his mother's kitchen four times in the two minutes since he'd arrived. Bobby lay by the door in a torpedo position, head down between his front paws, watching Nick move as if he'd seen it all before. Which he had.

Coming here and discussing this with his mother had never been his intention, but twenty-four hours after seeing Eden wearing that goddamn ring, he was still furious and he still hadn't been able to reach Cal.

"I'd like him to come out from wherever he's hiding. He's out when I go to Scanlons. He's out when I go to his house, or he's not answering the door. If he's so proud of all this, why is he doing a disappearing act like he stole her from me?"

"Perhaps he's waiting until you calm down."

"Because he knows he's fu—" At his mother's scowl, he quickly muttered, "He knows he's screwed. Big time."

"Or that he's doing precisely the right thing and doesn't want to rub it in your face."

"Nice try, Mom. But let's not hand out any trophies just yet." He took a plastic half-gallon of milk from the refrigerator and lifted it to his mouth, drinking deeply. He then wiped the top on his shirt and recapped it. "How long have you known?"

"That your manners are atrocious? Since you started that habit in sixth grade."

He grinned. "Look at all the glasses I saved you from washing. How long have you known about the engagement?"

"For a few days. Eden told me, but that's not what's important." She finished one piece and picked up another, smearing it with silver cream. "What is important is that you're overreacting, as if Eden was tricked by some particularly adept con man. This is your brother we're discussing, and their engagement isn't all that stunning. I might remind you, Cal and Eden were involved long before you came home."

He took one of the chairs, turned it around and straddled it, facing his mother. Her voice still hadn't risen above the cordial level. It was one of her consistencies he'd always admired. She could discuss any subject without breaking a sweat; her judgments were forthright, clear and logical. Nick knew she had no illusions about either of her sons. She called their behavior as she saw it and without apology or excuses.

"And you don't think Cal knew that would bug me?"

"I think your homecoming had him looking forward to doing exactly what you would have done if the situation had been reversed. Taking some egotistic pride in the fact that she was with him and not you."

"Well, at least you admit he's no goddamn saint."

"Nor are you."

"The difference is that I've known that for years. Cal is still flaunting his halo of first-born superiority."

"And you still resent it. Listen to yourself, Nick. You're holding on to anger and resentment over something that can't be changed."

"I didn't come home with any agenda against Cal."

"Of course you didn't. Yet I've witnessed that old resentment and anger return because of Eden. Between that and Cal's reasoning of protecting what he believes is now his—well, Eden is the one in the crossfire."

"Which stinks to hell all by itself," Nick said, having realized before Eden left his apartment that the picture of himself from her perspective wasn't admirable. Still, Cal was hardly a candidate for the Nobel Peace prize. "Of all the women in the state, why couldn't he find one who hadn't been involved with me? Doesn't that strike you as a bit coincidental?" Nick's frown grew deeper. "No, on second thought, not a coincidence. Calculated."

"Now, wait a minute. Cal and Eden have been seeing each other for almost a year. It's not like he took up with her the day you came home. Nor was she your girlfriend when you took off five years ago."

Nick threw his hands in the air. "Fine. Fine. Fine. That's all true, and maybe it wasn't calculated at first, but I know Cal. His superior attitude of she's mine and not yours wasn't accidental."

"Perhaps it was pride that his relationship with Eden was strong enough to survive you." Mary paused, finding a clean spot on her polish cloth. "I think the more serious question here is what all of this maneuvering has done to Eden."

"Cal should have told me. He shouldn't have put her—ah, Jesus!"

"What is it?"

But Nick's mind was racing. His brother hadn't put Eden into an awkward position because he had no clue it would have been that way. Eden had never said anything or done anything that would have alarmed Cal.

Despite all the swagger between brothers, Eden had managed to stay separate because she'd separated herself into two people. The Eden Nick had kissed, had flirted with and finally had sex with was not the same Eden Cal had asked to marry him.

For weeks she'd been straddling an emotional fence between her commitment to Cal and her disgust with herself for what had happened with Nick.

"Dare I ask if that's some enlightenment that's making you so thoughtful?" His mother peered at him, eyebrows raised hopefully.

"I don't know."

"Hmm." Mary held up a silver candy dish to the light. "This was a wedding gift from an aunt of your father's. I remember thinking it was a lovely but a totally useless gift. As a result I polished it about once a year and then put it away until it was time to polish it again. I can't help but wonder if that's what you've been doing since you got home."

Nick scowled. "What are you talking about?"

"Polishing up your relationship with Cal as needed, and now that things aren't going your way, you're going back to the old tarnished role of feeling sorry for yourself."

"If I was feeling sorry for myself, I'd be passed out drunk or damn close to it."

"Ah. But you're not drunk. You're here railing like you've been pushed out of the way undeservedly."

"She doesn't love Cal."

"She told you that?"

"No. She claims she does."

"Claims? You don't believe her?"

"I called it bullshit."

"Now, I'm sure that put a big smile on her face," Mary said adroitly.

Nick stood, shoving the chair back. "You, of all people, should understand how this pisses me off."

"And you, of all people, know that one doesn't get everything one wants all the time. That's what's at issue here, isn't it? You want Eden, and you're furious because your brother has her. Please note I didn't say you love her, simply that you want her. Women tend to know the difference, even if you men don't, which is precisely the dilemma Eden is in. She knows the difference."

"It's more than sex," Nick said in a low voice, not having a clue as to how he knew, but he did.

"Pardon me?"

Nick raised an eyebrow. "You heard me."

"Did you tell her that?"

"Are you serious? She wouldn't believe me. Hell, I'm not even sure what that means." His challenge to Cal that he could get her back into his bed, oddly enough, never had been connected to that one time at her house. Yet Nick knew he didn't have a prayer of a chance of convincing Eden. Not now.

"Falling in love is a messy process, Nick. Sex is just messy. I think Cal knows the difference."

"You're weighing in pretty heavy on Cal's

side in this. He's no shining example—"

Mary put the dish down with a hard thump. "Stop right there. That shining example stuff is old moss. I'm not your father and I never have viewed your behavior or your aspirations as models for Cal, nor is his life a model for you. However, Cal is a good man and he loves Eden. Asking her to marry him has been on his mind for months. Conflict exists because of you, Nick. Not Cal and Eden."

He shoved his hands through his hair and drew a deep breath. "Okay, I'm the bastard in this triangle. But I know this: She doesn't love Cal. So why in God's name would she want to marry a man she doesn't love?"

His mother screwed the cap onto the silver-polish bottle, slid her chair back and rose. She went to the sink, where she washed her hands.

"Mom?

She turned and dried her hands on a towel. "Eden has made her choice, Nick. You must be a gentleman and accept that choice. I know you're an honorable man. And even with your shortcomings, I don't think you'd hurt Eden by being in her face about the past. Let it go. Let her go and get on with your life."

"But why—?"

"Enough questions. You must put Eden's happiness ahead of your own need to not let your brother win if you really care for her, and I think you do. So I suggest that instead of ranting at your brother, you extend your hand, congratulate him and tell him how lucky he is to have Eden."

Later in the Explorer, with Bobby perched on

the seat beside him, Nick drove toward his apartment.

"Well, it's over, Bobby."

Bobby whined.

"Somehow, shrugging and saying 'So be it' isn't making me feel real swell." He turned the corner and slammed on the brakes when a dog who looked a lot like Killer raced across the road after an orange cat.

Bobby woofed, his nose smearing the windshield. His tail started wagging, and Nick pulled over and stopped. He opened the door and whistled. The dog stopped, turned, head tipped as if wondering who had caught him.

"Killer? Hey, Pupper, is that you?"

He bounded for Nick, who ruffled his fur when he leaped up into the sports vehicle. The two animals lumbered into the back, sitting rump to rump, muzzle to muzzle, like a couple of show dogs perched on the winner's platform.

"I bet Eden doesn't know you're carousing in the neighborhood. How did you escape? Did you make a hole under the backyard fence?" Nick grinned at the panting dog. "Well, let's get you home. I owe a major apology to your mistress. Saving you from the claws of that cat might at least get me in the door."

At Eden's house, when Nick found the front door slightly open, the possibility of something being wrong leaped to life inside him. Killer bounded through, as did Bobby. Nick walked in behind them, glancing around for Eden, feeling intrusive and yet a bit uneasy at the heavy silence.

"Eden?"

The two dogs headed for the water dish in the kitchen and Nick made his way toward her bedroom. The door wasn't closed, and yet he still slowed his pace and approached cautiously. The quiet of the house slipped away at the bedroom door. He heard her talking in a soft voice. He stopped at the doorway, struck by how familiar it all seemed. She sat on the edge of her bed with her back to him in almost the same place as when he'd come in that night to wait for her to get off the phone with her father.

"Please . . . y-you must listen to me. . . ."

Nick started to step away, not wanting to listen, but then he heard more than words. He heard terror.

"Please, please, don't do this. It's all settled and . . . I made the decision. Please. Don't cry. I know you're angry and disappointed. Wait. Don't hang up!"

He stood rooted. He watched as she pressed the receiver against herself as if unwilling to release the dead connection. She lowered her head, hunching forward, rocking slightly. She looked small, alone and scared.

Nick entered the room, rounding the bed and not until he was within inches of her did she look up.

Her eyes swam with tears and he'd never seen her so pale.

"Oh, Jesus, Nickie. I don't know what to do."

Immediately he gathered her against him. Her body trembled and she leaned on him as though he was a bulwark between her and devastation. He rubbed his hands across her shoulders, the tension a lair of knots. "What happened? I heard a little bit of the phone call."

"I already made the decision. It was the right one. I know it was. It had truly been all settled, and now—"

"What decision, babe? What had been settled?"

"About Jennifer."

Nick frowned, his hands continuing to rub her shoulders. "Jennifer who? Not that Courtney Love look-alike with the red razor nails?"

She shook her head, mouth trembling.

Realization came. "Oh, Christ. Not your daughter?"

She didn't need to answer, and he sat down on the bed when she tugged at him. "Hold me, Nickie. Just for a few minutes."

He never hesitated, amazed at how quickly and solidly she burrowed in, like a small animal that needed to be warm and safe. Nick lifted her onto his lap, holding her, rocking her, waiting until her tension relaxed.

Finally he said, "Tell me about Jennifer."

It was many seconds before she spoke. "She wants to come here. She wants to meet me."

"I don't see the problem."

She blinked. "You don't?" Then she shuddered, as if realizing the reason for his simple reaction. "Of course. You don't know about all that has happened. I told Cal and your mother, not you."

"You don't want her to come?"

"I don't. I c-can't. I made the decision twice not to interfere in her life, when I gave her up and a few weeks ago with my dad." She went on to explain about the Maynards calling her father and presenting Jennifer's request to see her "real" mother, and her own ultimate decision to refuse. "I'm not her real mother, Nick. I haven't been since the day I put her in Laura Maynard's arms. I had this all worked out, and both the Maynards were relieved when I decided to refuse to meet Jennifer."

"I gather Jennifer sees this differently."

"Oh, Nick, she was crying and hysterical and threatening to run away and asking me why I hate her so much." She looked up at Nick, her eyes filled with pain. "I don't hate her. I—No! I can't even think about that."

"You love her, Eden. My God, there's nothing wrong with that. If you didn't love her you wouldn't be this upset."

"She can't come here. She can't." She reached over and opened the night table drawer. "See all these things? This is what I have of Jennifer. They're all here—booties, a journal, the music box I bought her—all here, hidden away like a private diary, but this is my past with her. If she comes here, then I'm starting a future with her, and I can't do that."

"Understandable, but that doesn't close the door. You need to find another solution. You've worked with enough teenagers to know how volatile their emotions are. You'd never forgive yourself if Jennifer ran away because of this."

"Oh God!"

"What about you going to see her?"

Eden blinked, as if the concept was so outrageous she must have heard him wrong. "Go to see her?"

"That way you control the meeting and when it's over, you can leave. You won't have all the memories of her here in your house, but you will have some new ones in your heart."

She stared at him a long time. "When did you get so wise?"

"Credit my mother. She's the brilliant one. On occasion, some of the stuff she tells me penetrates my not-too-willing brain." He reached around her and handed her the phone. "Call her back, Eden. Tell her you're coming to see her."

Eden took the phone and punched out the number.

Chapter 19

TRAFFIC TO GREEN AIRPORT IN WARWICK moved with the usual early-morning congestion. Eden had intended to drive herself and leave her car in the security lot, but Cal insisted on taking her.

"You haven't said more than three words since we left Lonsdale," Cal said.

"Just a lot on my mind."

"I think this is a wrong decision." He held up his hand as if to ward off her disagreement. "I know you don't agree and I promised myself I wouldn't argue. But having said that—"

"Cal, please," she said wearily. "I've decided and I'm going and there's nothing more to be said."

"I'm worried about you, sweetheart, how this is going to affect you. You could be setting yourself up for a disaster."

She was tired of being second-guessed. "Give me an example of this disaster you keep harping on."

"I don't know! How could I? I've never been in your kind of situation."

"No, you haven't. And that's precisely why

you have no right to pontificate dire warnings or conclude I'm incapable of handling the consequences of this trip. If there are any."

The set of his jaw indicated she hadn't altered his opinion, but he also must have realized he was getting nowhere. Then again, what did he expect? That she'd suddenly say, "You're right, let's go home, I sure don't want to set myself up for disaster"?

Eden turned and watched the passing scenery without really seeing it. As Nick had urged her, she'd called Jennifer back and laid out what she was going to do: come to Chicago, meet with her and give the two of them time together to talk. Although Eden had no idea what she was going to say. Unlike meeting parents or students, when she had some preparation by virtue of position, experience and objectivity, meeting a daughter after sixteen years was a shaky and terrifying experience.

This visit wasn't the culmination of years of searching. Nor did she have grand plans for an ongoing mother-daughter relationship. Cal's disaster scenario was premised on her being a victim, but her real concern, even more worrisome, occurred to her this morning while she was packing.

What if once she saw and spent time with Jennifer, she couldn't leave? Couldn't let go and walk away a second time? And what if this trip became the first of many visits? Did she want that? Deep down in her soul, did she secretly want Jennifer back?

Oh God, she thought, *perhaps Cal was right*.

Cal said, "I'm making the mistake by not going with you."

"It's better this way." She patted his leg, softening her next words. "You'd still be trying to talk me out of it when I'm face to face with her."

He nodded. "I hate to admit it, but you're right."

And there the topic was left. Exactly where it had always been. In that moment Eden recognized that Cal's unbending stance had more to do with his distaste for mucking about with past decisions than with Jennifer specifically. Clearly he had a point in having a forward-looking attitude, in embracing the ability to move on while expecting the past to provide experience and insight for the future. Obviously this was Cal's reasoning when it came to Nick, yet when it concerned Eden's response to Jennifer, Cal had taken a much harder line. Jennifer was a finished issue. Leave the door closed. Don't think about revisiting it any more than you'd consider trying to find Jennifer's father. Don't, don't, don't had become Cal's mantra.

He parked in the short-term lot, then carried her bag into the terminal. While in Chicago, she planned to stay two extra days and visit with her dad and Aunt Josette. When she had called and told them her decision, her father wasn't as surprised as she'd expected. "Smart move, you coming here. That makes you the poker player with the best hand." Likening a visit with Jennifer to a poker hand confused her, but at least there would be no lecture.

She didn't check her bag, opting instead to carry it and avoid waiting in Chicago. Security restrictions didn't allow anyone but ticketed passengers at the boarding gates, so she and Cal had coffee at the Dunkin' Donuts stand and talked briefly about other things.

Finally Eden glanced at her watch. "I better go."

She stood, and Cal drew her into his arms. "I'll see you in a few days."

"Yes."

He stared into her eyes, as though he was hoping she'd change her mind and see this issue his way. To reassure him she understood his uneasiness, she kissed him, then said, "It will all be worked out. I promise."

"I love you and I don't want to see you hurt."

"I know." She kissed him again and then walked away.

Fifteen minutes later, she boarded the nonstop flight to Chicago and made her way down the aisle to her seat. She got her bag in the overhead rack, settled in, buckled her seat belt and gazed out the window, watching the ground crew.

When the passenger for the other seat shoved his bag into the overhead rack and Eden turned, her eyes widened into huge pools of astonishment.

"Nick! What are you doing here?"

He frowned seriously. "Isn't this flight going to Chicago?"

She grinned. She couldn't help it. "You know it is."

He checked his ticket stub. "Well, I'll be damned, you're right. And what do you know, this is my seat."

"Just a coincidence, I'm sure," she said lightly.

"Hell, no." He settled into the seat, found the belt ends and snapped them together. "Actually, I had to oil my rusted charm to get Dianna over at Sea Breeze Travel to see things my way."

"Hmm, now let me think," Eden said, tapping her finger on her chin. "Did you sleep with her before or after she wrote up the ticket?"

"Nope. Gave up sex with strangers. Too risky. Besides, I gave her something better."

"I didn't know there was anything better," Eden quipped, the words spilling out so easily, so unfiltered, that for a few seconds she wondered if she'd spoken them or just thought about them.

"She doesn't have your insight, babe."

Let it alone, she warned herself, but she couldn't. "I shouldn't have said that. And certainly not after giving you such a rough time about having a jock mentality with unrestrained appetites."

He shrugged. "Hey, what's one or two bad habits between friends."

Silence drifted like scents of yesterday. Their past relationship with all its volatility and the most recent scene at his apartment, followed by his gentle insistence on her visiting Jennifer—all held threads of the unexpected.

"So who has Bobby?"

"One of the kids on the team. How 'bout Killer?"

"I boarded him at the Puppy Palace. He's been there before and doesn't mind. Actually, I almost called you."

"Good thing you didn't. I would have had to think fast to keep this a surprise."

"Things have a way of working out, don't they," she said, abruptly relaxing and taking his unexpected arrival as a good sign; it seemed natural and comforting.

Nick hiked his eyebrows up and down, then leaned toward her in a conspiratorial manner. "What convinced Dianna over at Sea Breeze was a forty percent discount on some silk jacket she wanted from Scanlons for her boyfriend."

"Forty percent! My God, does Cal know?"

"Nope."

"He'll be furious."

"Yep."

"He won't do it."

"Yeah, he will. I'm still an owner, despite my unScanlon-like behavior. Believe me, if Cal has a choice between getting stuck for one jacket or having me working there full-time, he'll take the loss and be grateful."

This ease with Nick, his determination to come and his actually being here were surreal, and at the same time so soothing that Eden felt as if she'd stumbled into some crazy wonderland. There was no tension, no bite or bitterness, no second-guessing—there was just Nick, outrageous and funny, and she was gliding with him like a dancer who knows her routine flawlessly.

"You didn't have to come with me."

"And miss an opportunity to snatch you away to my den of iniquity and turn you into my sex slave?"

She folded her arms and eyed him seriously, but her amusement won out. "Been there, done that."

"Damn. And here I thought I was original."

She let her head fall back on the seat and she laughed. Deeply and happily. For the first time since Jennifer's phone call, she felt the tension release and flow away.

The flight attendants did their spiel as the plane taxied into position for takeoff. As it started down the runway, engines at full throttle, Nick slipped his hand in hers and, to her amazement, it was clammy.

She glanced over at him. His eyes were closed, his mouth set in a grim line, his other hand gripping the armrest.

"Nick, you're afraid to fly."

"Only when I'm in a plane."

She found that piece of news both insightful and genuinely noble. He'd come despite his fears.

Finally, when they were airborne and level and beverages were being served, Nick relaxed. His expression, however, was serious as he sipped his coffee. "Actually I'm trying to get back in your good graces again after acting like such an ass over the engagement."

Eden hadn't expected an apology. Those singular moments of revealing his deeply felt remorse were more than enough.

"Hey, you're supposed to say you'll at least think about forgiving me."

"I already forgave you," she said softly. "I even moved you onto my very small list of most cherished friends when you told me I should go see Jennifer. But you hardly needed to come to Chicago with me."

"There's another reason. You shouldn't be going alone." He paused. "Especially after you say good-bye to her, you should have someone with you."

Eden's heart turned over at his unselfish gesture that went farther than words and became action. A tiny thought nagged that she should want Cal telling her this, Cal sitting here, and the significance of it being Nick and not Cal wasn't lost on her.

Eden slipped her hand in Nick's and felt his fingers wind with hers. "At this very moment I think you're the most wonderful, the most incredible man I've ever known and I love you for being who you are."

Nick grinned. "I can live with that."

They landed at O'Hare and within a half an hour they were in a rental car that Nick insisted upon and headed away from the airport.

The Maynards lived in Park Ridge, a suburb of Chicago. The closer they got, the more Eden could feel her tension level rise. Nick found the street and drove past the sprawling ranch three times before stopping in front.

Eden didn't move. "God, now that I'm here, I'm not sure I should be."

"She's just as scared."

"You're coming with me?"

"No. I'll go get some coffee, buy the *Sun-Times* and catch up on what the Black Hawks are doing." He leaned across the seat and tipped her chin up. "Smile, babe. This is good and right and what your heart is telling you to do. That's all you need to think about."

"Oh, Nickie, I hope so."

He kissed her then. Not long, not particularly

intimate, but a poignant seal to his words.

She opened the door and got out, turning to him, but before she could ask, he said, "I'll be here when you're finished."

Not until she was walking up the walk and he was driving away did it strike her that he always knew what she needed before she did.

Nick had just driven around the corner and out of sight when Eden noted a front-window curtain move. *No turning back now,* she thought, and took a deep breath as she walked up the front steps. Before she could ring the bell, the door flew open, and there just a few feet away, stood her daughter.

Eden was awed beyond words. At seventeen, Jennifer Maynard could have been Eden at the same age. Long cinnamon-colored hair, parted in the middle and tucked behind her ears, the same wide blue eyes that revealed apprehension and soaring expectancy at the same time. Eden saw minor resemblances to Todd Wynnstock, but Jennifer definitely favored her. She appeared incredibly grown-up and poised in dark wool slacks and a turtleneck sweater. Around her neck was a clutter of gold chains.

"You really came. You really did," Jennifer said in a wispy voice that sounded unsteady and amazed.

Eden wanted to hug her, to hold her, to tell her how beautiful she was. Instead she said, "I'm very glad that I changed my mind about seeing you." Eden stepped inside, too unprepared and too overwhelmed.

Jennifer's smile just didn't quit. "This is so

cool. You're so pretty and our hair is the same color, and we're the same height and I bet there's a zillion things—"

"Honey, why not let Eden catch her breath before you bombard her." Laura Maynard had appeared from another room, as if she'd been waiting for her cue. Wearing slacks and a sweater-vest over a cotton blouse, she was a bit heavier than Eden remembered. She hadn't lost her engaging smile or the nervous habit of twisting her ring that Eden had noted when they first met.

"You have a lovely home," Eden said, paying little attention to anything or anyone except Jennifer.

"David will be here. He went to get some soda. Jenny loves 7-Up, and she and her girlfriend went through a dozen cans when Alison slept over. You know how teenagers are—Oh dear, I shouldn't have said that." She suddenly looked terrified as if Eden might lose all composure and flee the house.

"Actually, I work with teenagers," Eden began, then instead of adding to that, she said, "I understand your awkwardness. I feel it, too. It's better if we just admit it rather than turning it into the elephant in the room that no one wants to acknowledge."

"Kids my age?" Jennifer asked, with a touch of something Eden couldn't quite define. Jealousy? Resentment?

"Some, and some younger. The high school has expanded their guidance program to assist parents and the kids with other issues beyond college and career placement."

She watched Eden, her eyes wide. "Do they like you?"

Eden chuckled. "On their best days, I think so. We have disagreements, but—"

"Do you ever think about me when you see them?" She'd tipped her head slightly, her fingers playing with the gold chains around her neck. Eden suddenly felt trapped. It was a loaded question. No matter how she answered, she would be sending Jennifer dangerous signals.

Laura, to Eden's relief, intervened. "Jenny, let's not bombard Eden with questions the first five minutes after she gets here." Laura came farther into the room, her hands rubbing down the front of her slacks. "Let me take your coat and purse. Or is that called a tote?"

"A tote. I'll keep this with me."

Jennifer looked at the bag like she was gauging the contents by the size. Laura hung up her coat.

Turning back, she chattered on, while Jennifer stared, her smile coming suddenly and then when she thought Eden wasn't noticing, her expression was more curious. Eden felt more on display than when she spoke to an assembly of parents, and twice as jittery. Nick would tell her to take a breath, trust her instincts and believe this was the absolutely right thing to do.

Still nervously talking, Laura Maynard said, "I've planned lunch, and you'll want to catch up on all that Jenny has done, and—oh yes, of course, you're welcome to stay the night."

"Thank you for the offer, Laura," Eden said quickly, wanting to head off any such notions, "but I've made other arrangements." It sounded cold and blunt, but she wanted it clear this was a short visit, not a weekend trip.

"Hello, Eden," David Maynard said from the archway between the living room and the dining area. His dark hair was gray at the temples, his face stern and a bit worried.

Eden stepped forward and offered her hand. "It's good to see you again, David."

"Well, you certainly have grown and ma—" His gaze darted to Jennifer and back to Eden. He cleared his throat. "You've changed, just like all of us." He walked to Jennifer and slipped an arm around her, as if to indicate their solidarity. "Can I be honest here?"

"Oh, Daddy, you're gonna spoil everything," Jennifer pleaded, her face paling. She pulled away, giving him a stern look.

David pressed his mouth tight. "She doesn't want me to be as truthful with you as I have been with them. Actually, I've been opposed to this meeting from the first suggestion and I was angry when I heard that Jenny had called you herself. A choice between her running away and you coming here—well, it was hardly a choice. I'm not sure anything of importance will be accomplished beyond Jenny having some romantic view of her past."

"Daddy! How can you say that? She's not some sloppy trash. She's beautiful and sophisticated. I mean, she had a baby at sixteen and she's not poor or living in some horrible place."

"Jennifer," Eden said, deliberately not using the nickname Jenny if for no other reason than to keep herself out of the we're-all-a-family scene, "I think your father's concern is broader than what happened to me."

"Are you a success because you gave me away?"

"Jenny, for heaven's sake," Laura said, obviously distressed.

Eden decided not to dance around this. With a bit of her guidance counselor tone, she said, "If you define success by loving what I do and wanting to do the best I can, then yes."

"So if you'd kept me, then it would have been harder."

"Jennifer, I didn't exchange you for a career. It wasn't a choice for me, but one for you."

"But—"

Laura stepped forward, taking Jennifer's arm and directing her to the kitchen. "I think Eden has had enough questions on an empty stomach."

Jennifer left reluctantly, and Laura said, "I'm sorry."

"Don't be. She's curious and full of questions."

David nodded, his eyes troubled.

Eden felt as if Laura had placed her in the all-wise guru category. David viewed her with a resignation that reminded her of Cal. He didn't like it, but he was stuck and hoping that if he was patient enough, it would just all go away.

Eden felt awkward and uneasy, like an intruder suddenly thrust into a family unit that had been complete without her. She had a sense that David had been much more vocal with Laura and Jennifer about his objections.

David shoved a hand through his hair. "Look,

it's probably better if I don't hang around. Jenny is determined to pepper you with questions, and I'm not sure I want to hear them all."

Eden nodded. "Let me reassure you that I'm not here with any underlying motives."

"I wish I could say the same for Jenny." He glanced toward the kitchen, and Eden swore she saw his eyes glisten. "She's been like a stranger the past few days since your phone call."

Laura slipped a supportive arm around his waist. "He's very protective of her and Jenny thinks he treats her like a baby. Since you called, she has built you up into some romantic ideal who was forced to give her up. To be honest, I think she hoped you'd be a more tragic figure, who has suffered greatly and has never gotten over losing her. She wants you to have great regrets."

"I'd be lying if I didn't admit to regrets."

David looked stark and suddenly worried.

Laura hugged him tighter. "Of course you would. You loved her. I think it's wonderful that you have gotten on with your life, knowing your decision, although painful, was best for Jenny."

Abruptly Eden wanted to retrieve her coat and flee.

How much less stressful for the worried David. And for Laura, the peacemaker, who wanted to understand but at the same time would probably have preferred that Eden had never come.

And Jennifer. Caught between the parents she loves and this stranger who gave her life.

David kissed Laura, then went out through the kitchen, and in a few minutes Eden heard an outside door close. Laura managed a weak smile as she gestured Eden toward the kitchen. Jennifer was standing at the window, her back turned. She swung around at their footsteps, her eyes glistening.

"Oh, Jenny . . ."

Eden crossed to her, taking her hand and leading her to a chair. She lightly touched her hair, memorizing the silk texture.

"Jennifer, I want you to stop crying."

She lifted her head. "I hate him for what he said to you."

Eden sat down at the table. "He loves you and he's afraid."

"He's never afraid! Guys that I date are all scared of him. Once he stormed into a party I was at. There must have been forty kids there and he didn't care. He dragged me home like I was a little kid."

"The house was raided fifteen minutes later by the police looking for drugs," Laura said.

Eden nodded. "Your father must have known."

"He's a cop," Jennifer said, a glimmer of pride in her eyes that she was too innocent to hide.

"He didn't want you getting arrested."

"It wasn't a big deal. They let most of the kids go."

"Would you have rather been hauled to the precinct and then have your dad called?"

Jennifer paled. "Oh God, I would have been mortified. I mean, he's always expected so much of me."

"Maybe it's more that he's always been so

proud of you and that an arrest would have hurt you later."

"Eden's right, Jenny. You know how worried he gets about drugs and drinking." Laura looked at Eden. "She is one of the brightest students in her class and getting arrested would disappoint a lot of teachers."

"Teachers who have high expectations for their students are the best kind," Eden said.

"Are you that kind of teacher?"

"Yes. And if you were one of my students, I would expect great things."

"You would?"

"Absolutely."

With an apparent area of agreement firmly in place, Laura said, "Why don't we have something to eat, and then the two of you can have a private talk."

Eden squeezed Jennifer's hand in a gesture of agreement.

Lunch had obviously been carefully planned, with Jennifer presenting a chocolate dessert she'd made herself. Eden raved and Laura told how Jennifer had been helping in the kitchen since she was eight years old. Dishes were cleared away, and finally Jennifer and Eden returned to the living room.

"Would you like to see my room?" Jennifer asked.

"Yes, I'd like that."

The moment Eden stepped into the room, she guessed a lot of straightening had been done. A double bed with a quilt of pink roses over a lacy dust ruffle dominated the room. The dressing table held tubes, jars and bottles, the mirror was stuck with photos and mementos. A desk with a computer sat in the corner with disks scattered about, what appeared to be edited pages and a number of copies of the school newspaper. A Chicago Black Hawks banner had been tacked to the wall.

"Are you a hockey fan?"

"My new boyfriend is."

Eden nodded. "Lots of school stuff. You're a senior this year. What about college?"

"I'm going to Columbia in Chicago. I want to major in journalism. I've worked on my school newspaper and do a monthly interview piece on one of the kids who has done something cool. Like help clean up the environment or adopt a 'grandparent' in a nursing home. That kind of stuff."

"What a wonderful idea! Was it yours?"

She nodded. "It's supposed to show how kids do good stuff not just drugs and sex." Then, without taking a breath, Jennifer asked, "Why did you give me away?"

So much for easing into all of this, Eden thought grimly. She sat down on the bed and Jennifer sat beside her. "Because I wanted you to have the best, and that meant two adult parents who would love you and raise you into a well-adjusted young woman."

"Didn't you love me enough to do all that?"

"Oh, Jennifer, I adored you." Eden knew the heartfelt words fell short. How could she describe tearing her heart to shreds? The regrets. Her fury at Todd and his parents for their rejection. The loss that was as real as if her baby had died. "You were the most beautiful baby I'd ever seen, and giving you away was the hardest and the most profound decision I've ever made. I was sixteen and still in school. Your father—and I'm going to be truthful here, no excuses, okay?"

Jennifer's eyes were as big as half-dollars. "Did he rape you?" she whispered, the question rife with horror.

"No," Eden said emphatically. "He was my boyfriend and I thought we loved each other. When I learned I was pregnant, I went to him, but he didn't want anything to do with me. I didn't want to believe him, because I thought I loved him, believed he loved me. Looking back now, I know it was infatuation with a popular guy and a curiosity about sex. Not the best combination. I was ill-equipped to raise you and give you what you needed the most—stability and the chance to grow up and become the fine person you are."

"He didn't want me? He never tried to find out what happened to me?" The tears glistened, and Eden hated Todd Wynnstock all over again.

"Honey, he was a jerk and a coward. Nothing like David Maynard—he's a real father. You were angry at him earlier, but his worry about me coming here is because he's afraid he might lose you. And men, well, sometimes they aren't as tactful as we women want them to be."

"He promised he wouldn't say anything."

"I know. But it's okay. I was impressed by his honesty, his obvious love and protection of you."

"You were?"

"You're very fortunate to have such good parents."

"Yeah, I guess. Dad does kind of smother me," she admitted. "Most of the time, it's okay."

Frankly Eden was grateful for David's 'smothering' just as he should be grateful that Eden hadn't changed her mind. Oddly her reasoning wasn't that Jennifer belonged here, but that her own decision at sixteen—shaky and angst-filled and terrifying as it was—had been absolutely right. Looking at the mature young woman in front of her convinced her of that.

"But you never tried to find me," Jennifer said wistfully.

"I knew who had adopted you. I insisted on meeting Laura and David because I couldn't hand you to people I'd never seen. But from the beginning it was my intent to let your adoption be the closure."

"Weren't you ever curious?"

"Oh, sweetheart, of course I was. Not a day has gone by that I haven't thought of you. Yet jumping in and out of your life as if I had some moral right to you would have been hell on your parents. You would have been torn up and felt forced to make choices a child shouldn't be burdened with. I wanted you to be a little girl growing up into a young woman, not a child unsure of where she belonged or who loved her the most."

Jennifer stood and paced the room, her hands jammed in her slacks pockets. Eden watched, feeling the tenuous closure. There was little more to be said. She lifted the tote from the floor, about to open it.

"I want to be with you." Jennifer looked at her directly, her eyes holding that finality Eden had seen in Karen Sims's eyes weeks ago when she told Eden she was quitting school.

This was what she'd dreaded, she realized suddenly. Not her own inability to leave, but Jennifer taking it a step farther by grasping onto this visit as a beginning of a life with her birth mother. This made David's fear and worry even more poignant and more understandable. He feared losing Jennifer because she wanted to go with Eden, not because of Eden forcing the issue.

Being logical and smart was much less draining with her students than with her daughter. "I don't think that will work."

"Yes, it will! You work with kids my age, so you don't want me. Is that it? But I don't know anything about you and I want to."

Eden felt a protective shield close around her heart. She couldn't allow this. She simply couldn't. Now, wanting to wind this up, she shifted the subject. "I'm going to be married in a few months." She showed Jennifer the ring.

"To the guy who brought you here?"

"No. He's a friend I've known since college. In fact he coaches hockey and—"

"What's the guy you're going to marry like?"

"He runs a family business and he's the school committee chairman. His mother and I are good friends."

"Are you going to have babies?"

"Perhaps."

"I could come and help."

"No."

"But you're my mother."

"No!"

Jennifer swung around, her hair flying. "Why? You did what you wanted. Your plans for me all worked out so that you wouldn't feel guilty about giving me away. Now all I want is to be part of your life."

Eden had to find a way to reconcile this. Otherwise the Maynards would be frantic, as she would be in their place. Jennifer was too caught up in the drama of having found her real mother and believing it was cool to start an ongoing relationship. Why had she ever believed she could walk in and then just walk out? *Oh, Nick, I wish you were here with me.*

She needed some time, but she also realized that to thwart all of Jennifer's efforts wasn't wise. It could risk Eden becoming larger than life, an irresistible image Jennifer could then continue to magnify into an obsession that became her life. Eden didn't want that. "How about a compromise?"

"Like what?" Jennifer asked warily.

"You finish high school and get your journalism degree. Give yourself time to think about what's the right thing to do for you and for your parents. By then you'll be moving into a career, perhaps a serious relationship and you can more objectively decide how I fit in your life. For my part, I'll make sure your parents know where I am and how to contact me."

"But that's years from now."

"Not so many. In the meantime, you'll get smarter and we'll have lots to talk about."

"You won't change your mind. I mean like disappear or something."

"I promise."

Jennifer didn't say anything, and before she could present another argument for running off to be with her, Eden reached into the tote. "I brought you some things that are very special to me. I think you should have them."

Jennifer drew closer.

Eden lifted a pair of yellow booties, which Jennifer touched as if they were spun glass. "You bought these for me, didn't you?"

"About two months before you were born. But there's something else." Then she lifted the music box that she'd wound up and played at least two dozen times since that first phone call from her father.

"It's beautiful," Jennifer said, taking it and setting it on her lap. "Does it play?"

"The key is at the side."

Jennifer wound it and they both sat listening to the tinny version of Brahms's "Lullaby." When it finished, she wound it again, and this time when it finished both of them had tears in their eyes.

"Is it okay to tell you that I'm glad you were my mother?"

"Oh, Jennifer, it's more than okay. It's the most wonderful thing you could have said."

She stared down at the music box. "If you give me this, will you forget me?"

"No, sweetheart, I could never forget you."

"And you mean it that I can come and see you after college?"

"If you still want to."

And then Jennifer was in her arms and they were hugging and gripping and squeezing as if making up for sixteen years in sixteen seconds.

Leaving, Eden realized a little while later, was even more emotional than her arrival. Laura hugged Eden after Jennifer told her mother of the compromise. Then Jennifer went off to find her father. He came back, still looking a bit concerned.

"Jennifer says you're leaving."

"Yes."

"On the level with this compromise deal?"

"You have my word."

"She means more to Laura and me than anything I could name."

"I know. Thank you for being such wonderful parents."

Eden hugged Jennifer once again. The years fell away, and for a few seconds she was lost in regret that she'd missed so much of her daughter's life. But she was also filled with pride that her instinct at sixteen to think first of what was best for her baby had indeed been nurturing and mothering at its most unselfish.

Before she burst into tears, she said her goodbyes, hurried down the steps and across the yard. Nick was slumped down in the seat and sat up instantly, leaning over to open the door.

"Thank God, you're here."

"I came back an hour after I dropped you off. I didn't want you to be finished and have no one here. How did it go?"

"Wonderful and terrible. I can't talk. Not yet." Her eyes stung, her throat was raw and hot, her heart as fragile as a handful of unstrung pearls. "You know what I'd like?"

"For someone to hold you together."

"How did you know?"

"Because you look like I have when I'm about to fly into a million pieces."

"Not fly. Break. And I think I already have."

Chapter 20

"THE LADY WILL HAVE A SCREWDRIVER. I'LL have a cheeseburger with fries and coffee. Eden, you want something to eat?"

She gave him a blank look. "Pardon?"

"Bring her a cheeseburger, too."

The restaurant was a bar and grill a few miles from Park Ridge. Nick had taken a table away from the jukebox pumping out rap music.

She sat with her arms on the table, her head was lowered. She had said little since he drove away from the Maynards. Nick had honored her silence.

Her drink arrived along with his coffee. She lifted it, drinking a quarter of it at the first gulp.

She looked at him, saying. "I'm so glad you came with me."

"Me, too."

"I feel wonderful and sad, euphoric and depressed."

"Sounds normal."

Then in a burst, she talked. All of it. From her first impression of Jennifer, to David Maynard's worry, to their private talk in Jennifer's bedroom, to the compromise and finally the music box. In the midst, the cheeseburgers and fries arrived. Nick ate and listened. Eden nibbled and talked. By the time the food was consumed, the dishes cleared and more coffee served, Eden had wound down.

Finally he asked, "What do you think Jennifer will do?"

"I guess it depends on how much the next four years change and mature her." She sighed, obviously more relaxed now that the visit was behind her.

"Does it matter to you what her decision is?"

"Yes."

"You'd like her to contact you?"

"Yes." Her face lit with excitement.

He nodded. "A bit of a change, isn't it?"

"The difference between thinking about meeting her and actually doing it. The compromise was for my benefit as well as hers, although I doubt she sensed that. But when she said, 'I want to be with you,' she had that I'll-do-this-and-you-can't-stop-me look. The compromise surprised her, I think. She expected me to try to reason her out of her decision, which wouldn't have worked. When my dad and aunt first suggested I give Jennifer up, I was horrified. Give my baby to strangers? No way. Aunt Josette wisely didn't argue, but began to present me with the realities of a child raising a child. It's more of finding the answer in the problem rather than barking out orders and rules."

"All the work you've done with teenagers obviously gave you some crucial insight."

"Whatever goes around comes around has some validity. My own decision about Jennifer was one of the reasons I went into guidance counseling."

"Ironic that you then wind up counseling her."

"Yes, it is. Funny how all you've learned kicks in when you need it most. But I have to admit that I wasn't as sure of myself as with the kids at school. Emotional involvement makes the implications at least feel more momentous."

Nick turned his coffee mug, continuing to draw her out. "You probably knew she wouldn't agree to never seeing you again."

She nodded. "At that point she was vehement, so I knew I had to present something. I had visions of her turning up on my doorstep next week. Followed by a worried David and a weeping Laura." She lifted the mug of coffee the waitress brought for her. "Leaving was hard. I felt as if I was giving her up all over again."

"In a way you probably did."

She leaned back and let out a deep breath. "I'm tired. Thanks for listening, for letting me unwind. Most of all, thanks for not questioning my decision."

Unlike what he had done with her relationship with Cal. And unlike with the engagement. With those he hadn't felt as generous or as understanding, just a bit less dishonorable than usual. What hesitation he had demonstrated was attributable to his conscience that was hell-bent on rearing its head. Eden's hands cradled the mug of coffee, and Nick couldn't help noting the ring.

In that instant she glanced up. He made no attempt to hide the resolve plainly visible in his expression. Behind it was desire and regret and his own choice to step back. Whatever there had been between them was finished. She wanted Cal. He didn't like it, but with honor came scruples.

"If things were different for us," Eden began, as if needing to say something.

"Yeah. But they aren't."

"You know what I'd do if I could do anything I wanted?"

"Eden, don't."

"I'd do as I did with Jennifer. I'd compromise and take both of you."

"Forget it. Not in a heartbeat. I don't share."

But she went on in an almost clinical, precise way that was totally opposite to her range of emotions about Jennifer. "Something is off-kilter inside me, Nick. I'm going to marry one man and I want to go to bed with another. That makes me not a very nice woman."

"What do you want from me? Agreement? Sympathy? Some insightful answer I don't have?" Nick raised his hand and signaled for the check.

"This scares you, doesn't it?"

"Yes." *Leave it, babe. I might not be a total bastard, but I'm no saint.*

She watched him, perhaps expecting some amplification of his fear, but when the silence lengthened, she glanced away. Finishing her coffee, she dabbed her mouth with a napkin. "Are you staying overnight?"

"No. I've got an 8:10 flight. There's time to drop you at your father's."

The check arrived. Nick read it and gave the

waiter a large bill, waving him away, not wanting change.

Back in the car, Nick told himself to not raise the issue again, but some inner demon of self-flagellation pricked at him. He turned to Eden. "Why did you ask? Did you think I had something else in mind for tonight?"

"I didn't want you to push me."

"Because you wouldn't say no?"

She glanced down at the ring and then balled up her hands.

She hadn't really answered his question, which left a gap large enough for him to ply her with seducing persuasion and probably succeed. What galled him was that the opportunity lay like a free nugget of gold, his for the taking. Added to that, however, was her pointed assault on his motives. He'd done damn little around Eden in the past few weeks that would have won him any awards for high moral character. That is until this trip. Maybe he'd asked for her suspicion, but it still ticked him off.

He started the car and headed toward Kennedy Expressway. Minutes later, unable to drop the issue, he asked, "You think that's what this trip with you was all about, don't you? You took that den of iniquity crap on the plane seriously? You believe I came with you so that after I'd been a swell understanding friend, I could collect my reward in bed?"

When she still said nothing, Nick's thread of restraint snapped. "Don't clam up on me, Eden. That's exactly what you thought, didn't you?"

"Look, if I've misjudged you, I'm sorry, but it did cross my mind."

"Jesus, I can't win, can I? I admit that most of the time I've been with you my motives have been less than exemplary, but this time—Oh, hell, never mind. It doesn't matter."

"It does matter," she said fiercely, looking suddenly stricken. "I've made you angry and ruined all this, haven't I?"

"I ruined everything between us a long time ago," he said wearily, abruptly, and wanting to be anywhere but here with her. "This episode was just an attempt to work on my limited good intentions when it comes to you. Getting you out of my sight and out of my mind is better for both of us."

She started to speak, and he touched his forefinger to her mouth. "Leave it here, Eden. Just let it go."

Her father was watching from the window when Nick pulled up in front of the white and green house. He got out of the car, took her bag from the backseat and walked up to the door with her.

She'd withdrawn, as if trying to summon up some final response, but there was none. He wondered why there wasn't something crucial to say. Strange that he was walking away from her for the second time, and like the first, the finale settled nothing. Thirteen years ago, he had wanted her out of his life because she deserved better, but they had been together that final night.

With this second parting, there was no intimate interlude between frustrated lovers snatching their fill to prepare for the coming famine in their respective lives.

Sure he wanted her. Hell, he always wanted her, but this time . . . He shook off the direction of his thoughts.

She reached up and brushed her mouth across his cheek. "Thanks again for today."

He backed away. "Sure."

He had little else to say, no capacity left to struggle against emotions he couldn't handle, didn't deserve and at that instant, deeply resented for their stamina. All he wanted was to get away. He glanced at his watch. "It's getting late. I need to get to the airport and turn the car in."

She nodded and he was glad the outdoor lights didn't illuminate her face.

"See you in a few days," she said.

"Good-bye, Eden."

He walked quickly back to the car, and she watched him drive away, the ramifications of his words and subsequent action very clear. They'd argued for the last time. They'd traded barbs and banter for the last time.

This good-bye was final.

She glanced at her finger and the diamond's glitter, its mere presence signaling another finality, another decision—one she'd made reluctantly with Cal, one made so as to not hurt a man she cared deeply about. But caring deeply and loving eternally were vastly different. The finality of Nick's good-bye stripped away any pretense of his ego, his selfishness and even his payback to Cal. He had changed. He had refused to take advantage of a perfect opportunity, even though Nick was a master at creating any kind of opportunity when he wanted something—namely her.

She should be pleased by his new direction, his new view of her, his willingness to simply step aside with no hard feelings. This is what she wanted, wasn't it? Hadn't she told him to grow up? Hadn't she been appalled by his resentment of Cal? Now that Nick had removed himself, instead of being relieved she realized she was empty and sad and a bit desperate.

Her father pulled open the door. "You gonna stand out here alone all night, applecheeks?"

"Oh, Pops, it's so good to see you." She was in his arms, and then folded in an even longer hug from her Aunt Josette. The sight of her aunt's clutter of ceramic dust-collectors, the scent of cinnamon rolls and her father's occasional cigar brought back fond memories. It was good to be home.

No, not a bit desperate, Eden thought a half an hour later. *Very desperate.* She was in her old bedroom, with its ecru lace curtains and maple double bed, after telling her father and her aunt she'd see them in the morning. Listening to her father praise her for the Jennifer decision and then her aunt saying she'd made a difficult choice once but had been rewarded with happiness for both her daughter and herself hit Eden like a beam of truth. Choices that lead to happiness was what they were saying.

That was where she'd made her mistake. She'd spent too much emotion on the choices. Then, to her astonishment, all those scattered pieces of her heart that she'd been trying relentlessly to force together for Cal unexpectedly became a flawless whole. Eden considered Nick's good-bye, irritated with herself because she'd stood like a tongue-tied simpleton and watched him walk away instead of trying to stop him.

She'd fought this for weeks. But now, with a clarity that stunned her by its completeness, she knew it was no longer a choice of one brother over the other; it was the resolution in her heart, a settled decision within herself that in its simplicity couldn't be more apparent. She stared at her hand and with a new resolve, she slipped off the engagement ring.

Could she reach him in time? And if so, would he agree? And most of all, was she crazy or desperate or both?

She made the phone call and she waited, pacing as far as the cord would reach, and sent up numerous prayers that he hadn't changed his flight to an earlier one. She had him paged a second time and she waited. Three minutes, four minutes. Finally after what seemed like forever, he was on the line.

"Eden, what's wrong?"

Her heart lifted at least three feet. "Nick, I want you to come back and get me."

"My flight leaves in fifteen minutes. What's the problem? Something happen with your dad?"

"No. He and my aunt are great. I want you. I want to be with you." She held the phone as if it were an intimate connection to him. "Nick, please. Don't ask questions and don't say no."

"Christ, Eden, this is crazy. Tomorrow . . ."

"Don't. No tomorrow. This is tonight, for us. Just for us."

Silence punctuated by background noise in the terminal made her pulse race. "Nick, are you there? You didn't hang up, did you?"

"No, but I should. Eden, are you sure? I haven't got enough honor to walk away once I see you again."

"I'm sure. Please hurry."

He arrived fairly quickly, and Eden, after a hasty explanation to her father and her aunt, which really explained nothing, was out the door and in the car with her heart clamoring at high speed.

Moments later, Nick pulled away and then abruptly stopped after he'd turned the corner. He tugged Eden into his arms, his mouth settling on hers like a man dying of thirst. Eden's hunger, now that she'd allowed it free rein, poured through her. For the first time since January, when Nick had come home, she felt a freedom to feel without questioning, without wondering, without fearing her heart.

He drew back, taking note of her ringless finger. That could mean not having Cal between them via the engagement or it could mean just for tonight. Or it could mean she called Cal and broke it off. Not a chance—she wouldn't do that long distance. *Don't ask,* he warned himself. Tonight was about them. She wanted it and so did he. He banished all thoughts of his brother. No questions was her request, and that was fine with him. Tomorrow was a thousand miles away. "Where do you want to go?"

"To bed."

He grinned. "That's my kind of answer."

The hotel was near the airport. Eden paid no attention to its name, its lobby or the Chicago skyline captured in the prints framed on the walls of the room Nick had taken. It was decorated in cream and toast with a gold spread on the king-size bed.

"Not very romantic," Nick murmured, pulling the covers back and watching her unbutton her blouse.

"It's romantic because we're here," she whispered.

And with the sleekness of a gazelle, she had her blouse off, her skirt down and tossed aside, so that she stood in panty hose and bra, while Nick felt his mouth go dry. She reached for the elastic and he stopped her. First he took off the bra, kissing each nipple and handling her breasts as if he were touching them for the first time. With the gentlest of motions he peeled down the hose, touching his mouth to her tummy, the sweetness between her thighs and dropping one kiss on each knee. Eden gasped, running her fingers through his hair.

"Oh, Nickie . . ." She drew him against her, thinking that nothing she had ever felt was so good and so right. They stayed that way, her body bowed over his, holding him in place until his arms wrapped around her legs.

When he lifted her up, she yelped with laughter rather than surprise. "What are you doing?" she asked, giggling.

"Giving you a chance to look before you touch." He dumped her on her back on the bed and went to work on his own clothes. She lay sprawled, her grin nonstop, totally at ease under his gaze while he disposed of his clothes. "So what's it gonna be," he asked. "Me or you on top or are we gonna have a wrestling match?" His eyes danced with amusement.

She smiled with a coyness that he adored. "We haven't wrestled since college."

"And I always pin you," he said, with that touch of mischievous aplomb she'd always adored.

"Not this time," she said gaily when he reached for her. She was quick, rolling from him, then grabbing his thigh so that he lost his balance and sprawled across the bed with a loud *oof*! Eden immediately straddled his back.

"I'm the winner," she declared, giving him a playful poke in the ribs.

He lay still for a few seconds while Eden savored her victory. Then suddenly he bucked, tossing her up and flipping her so that she was beneath him.

She stared at him, trying to look pouty. "Not fair."

He grinned. "I never play fair with you. You're too sneaky."

"Me!" she squealed. "I certainly am not."

He leaned down and nuzzled her neck. "Sneaky and nasty and too quick for your own good." He kissed her open mouth before she could protest. "But I wouldn't change you."

Eden grinned. "Yes, you would. You told me once you like pliant, obedient women who know how to fry over-easy eggs without breaking the yoke."

Nick shook his head. "Nope, I'll take the lady

wrestler who leaps into my arms over unbroken egg yokes anytime."

They searched and savored each other with their eyes while the silence slipped around them, hovering as if waiting for more frolic or something more serious.

Nick was starting to roll to the side when she grabbed him, drawing him back, whispering, urging him to cover her, to lie with her.

"This is better than any of my fantasies," he said, before he kissed her mouth, her cheeks, her eyes, whispering words of longing and cherishment. She took short breaths, her hand sliding between their bodies, where she took hold of him, sending even stronger shots of rapture through him.

Joining their bodies brought a new level of devouring arousal. Nick hard and pulsing, Eden wet and soft. She wrapped her legs around his hips, amazed at how complete and right she felt. Hope and forevers rushed through her. Nick began to move, his body taut, his eyes hot, as he watched the flush come on her cheeks.

He lifted himself up a bit while she resisted him pulling away; she finally won and tugged him down. The burning between their bodies made their skin slick. Eden moved, lifting her hips, dragging him deeper into her, locking him to her with smoldering intimacy.

Nick thought the top of his head would explode. He wanted to hold back, to clutch the moment, to keep Eden in this suspended pleasure for eternity.

"Nickie, please . . . make us come together."

Nick squeezed his eyes shut, a grimace straining on his mouth. Her body enfolded his with a mesmerizing grip. He plunged deeper, finding her most secret core, finding himself enveloped. Finally and completely he'd come home.

"Oh, yes, like that," she cried softly. "Like that . . ."

Eden arched up, her body reaching for his, her heart in tandem with his to find their mutual pleasure. Nick felt the sensation rush and roar toward a repletion he'd never had with any other woman. So many years lost, so many nights alone, and with the stupidity only he'd been capable of demonstrating, he'd used her to get his brother for reasons so asinine, they made him cringe with despair.

"Don't, Nick. Don't cling to all the regrets of yesterday."

He halted on the precipice of his climax, the words roaring, climbing and finally daring to be heard.

"I love you, Eden, I love you."

She drew him to her, tears glistening in her eyes, her arms holding him, taking him, feeling their satisfaction reach its release—so savage, so sweet, and so complete.

The night became a feast of delicious sensations, sleep finally coming for Eden a few hours before dawn. At about seven, she awakened, her body pleasantly sore. She reached for Nick and found the sheets cool to the touch. His scent was there, and she buried her face in the pillow. The room was quiet, the bathroom door ajar. He was gone.

On the night table was a note. "I thought I'd found the miracle after I climbed out of hell and came home. Then there was you. Nothing else for me will ever be the same again."

She folded the note, holding it tight in her hand. He'd said he loved her and yet he hadn't stayed for morning-after explanations. She was glad; she wanted to treasure the night, cherish its moments. He'd asked no questions, made no demands, extracted no decision from her. *So unlike the old Nickie,* she thought with a smile. She hadn't been wrong about her own feelings, but there was still her engagement to be settled.

Now the reality of Cal had to faced.

Three days later, she flew back to Rhode Island and walked into Cal's arms at the airport.

His embrace was fierce and long. "Good to have you back, sweetheart. I missed you."

"How is everyone?" she asked, feeling as if she'd been away for three months.

"Mom said the church made a fortune on the rummage sale and she told me to tell you the purple pineapple lamp was one of the first things sold. I presume you know what she's talking about."

"Yes."

"Five senior girls have formed a 'willing to wait' group and they've committed themselves to not having sex before marriage. Sounds ambitious but laudable. Word from the parents I've talked with gives you and your awareness program a lot of the credit."

"That's great."

"Let me see, what else? Oh, yeah. Kids won their hockey game last night. Nick has really set a fire under the players."

"He expects the best and he's getting it."

Hometown happenings, she thought, finding comfort and warmth in Cal's chatter. Goals and dreams and solvable problems. Life now was clear and inevitable like opening her eyes after being too long in the dark.

They got into Cal's car, and in a few minutes they were on the interstate. Eden couldn't wait any longer. "Aren't you going to ask about Jennifer?"

"You'll tell me when you're ready."

"I expected you to have a lot of questions. You were so worried about me encountering disaster."

If Cal heard the slight bite in her tone, he ignored it. "Is it all straightened out?"

Eden looked at him. "You mean, is the door finally closed forever?"

He glanced over at her. "I guess I was an alarmist, wasn't I?"

She appreciated his admission. "Yes, you were."

"I don't want to argue with you, sweetheart. If you want to talk about this, fine. If you want to argue, then let's wait a few days. You just got home."

"You're right." Eden leaned back in the seat and closed her eyes. Tomorrow or the next day or next week. It didn't matter, for time couldn't displace those now-fixed pieces of her heart.

The miles sped by, and the heat and darkness made her sleepy.

A few miles from Lonsdale, Cal said, "I'm not angry about it, you know."

Eden forced her eyes open. "Not angry? About what?"

"Nick told me he went to Chicago with you."

Eden waited for tension to knot in her stomach, for some inner scramble in search for an excuse, but neither happened. She was as calm on the inside as she appeared on the outside.

"He thought I should have someone with me."

"Didn't I tell you that?"

"You offered to come and I said no. Nick just came."

She expected him to ask if there was a difference, but instead he grumbled good-naturedly, "And stuck me with some dame named Dianna who wanted a forty percent discount on a silk jacket. Not a closeout or end of season item. A spring one, for godsake."

"So did you give it to her?"

He chuckled. "Yeah, I gave it to her. Seems her boyfriend's father was a customer of Scanlons years ago when Dad was alive. Made a bundle in the stock market and is building a house outside town. He wants to invest in a Rhode Island business, namely, Scanlons. Asked me to consider putting in a women's line. I talked to Mom and Nick about it and they didn't object. Of course, I'll have to expand the floor space, but I think the time has come."

"How wonderful for you," Eden said, genuinely pleased. "Did Nick know about this benefactor?"

"I'm not sure, but I think so. When I asked him, he just shrugged and said he never pays much attention to names. But whether he knew or not, he gets all the credit for this. A few of those forty percent discounts to the right people, and Scanlons will be a success story going into the next century."

"I'm so glad, Cal. And even more so that you and Nick have gotten past all your old problems."

"I wouldn't go that far. You can't fix years in a few weeks, but I think we've both acknowledged we're both getting too old to hold grudges and it's time to move on."

Again she closed her eyes. For her, too. It was time to move on.

Chapter 21

THE FOLLOWING AFTERNOON, EDEN WAS seated in Cal's living room when he arrived home from Scanlons. She'd come from school and let herself in with her key.

"Sweetheart, I didn't know you were coming over," Cal said, taking off his coat and tossing it on the couch. He poured Scotch into a tumbler, took a sip and said, "Let me order some dinner. That Italian place we like has started doing deliveries." But when he looked closely at her, his expression changed to concern. "Are you all right?"

"No, I'm not all right," Eden said, not wanting to drag any of this out any longer than necessary. "I have to tell you something and I don't know how to do it without hurting you."

He put his glass aside. "Look, let's have some dinner first and relax a bit. It's just past five. We have all evening to talk. I know I put you off about discussing Jennifer, but if you want to do it tonight, we can."

"It's not about Jennifer." She told him about her compromise with Jennifer and some of the details of the visit with the Maynards, emphasizing that she was settled and happy with the decision.

"Well, college and getting her career started will take a few years, and who knows what can happen after that," Cal said, loosening his tie. He sat down beside her, one hand resting on her knee. "We could go into the den and build a fire." His mouth twitched into a grin at his own double entendre.

Eden didn't move, nor did she visibly respond. "This isn't easy for me."

"I can see that," he said grimly. "Okay, it's not about Jennifer, so that leaves only one other person. Nick."

Her hesitation spoke volumes.

"Christ, I should have known." Cal got to his feet, picked up his glass and walked a few steps before turning around. "He made a move on you in Chicago and seduced you into going to bed with him, didn't he? Damn him!"

Eden felt her heart hammering in her ears. She could say no and be technically right, but she couldn't do that. There was too much at stake. In a low voice, she said, "I made the move on Nick, Cal. I seduced him into making love."

For a full minute he stared. "I don't believe you. Did he tell you to say that to cover his ass?"

"You don't believe that about your brother. You may have your differences, but neither of you would use me like that."

He swallowed the rest of his drink, put the glass down a little too hard and began to pace the room. She could see his fury and his disappointment. "You had a weak moment. All those old memories and whatever. Now you feel badly and you're asking me to forgive you."

Be blunt and precise. Get it out and don't leave any doubts.

"I can't marry you."

He looked as if he'd been blindsided. He recovered instantly ready to believe she'd spoken too hastily. Sitting down, he hovered by her solicitously. "Don't be ridiculous, Eden. Not marry me—my God! Look, you're probably still resonating from your trip and the emotional backlash of Jennifer. In addition, you're feeling guilty about what happened with Nick. That's understandable. We'll have a nice relaxing dinner—"

"Dammit, Cal, you're not listening to me!" She jackknifed off the couch, impatient to get things settled. "Don't find excuses or patronize me as if I don't know what I'm doing."

Cal flattened himself back on the couch cushions like she'd turned into some wild-eyed she-cat. "Take it easy. Okay, okay, I'm listening."

She relaxed a bit. "I didn't want it to be like this. I wanted it to be civilized and adult and with no misunderstandings."

"Look, we can work it out. Why don't you go back to the beginning."

She was already shaking her head. "There is no beginning. I've known it for a long, long time and I never should have let things get as far as they did with you."

She sat down again, her fingers smoothing her skirt.

Cal sat beside her, taking her hands. "Is this because I sprang the engagement on you? We can wait if you want."

"Please don't make this any harder, Cal." She drew her hands away. "I didn't go to bed with Nick because I was horny. I'm in love with him. I can't marry you, because I don't love you."

He looked at her a long, long time. "You don't love me? Just like that? Nick comes home, and suddenly my future with you is destroyed. And where is the prick anyway? If he's so goddamned determined to take you away from me, why isn't he over here like a man?"

"Nick has no idea I'm here."

"Yeah, right. He's the beginning of all of this. He hated that you were with me, that I had one of his old girlfriends. The moment I heard he'd come back, I knew his old jock mentality would have him prowling around you like some wolf on the make."

"Stop it! Stop it! You're reducing all of this to just sex."

"Exactly. And from where I'm sitting, that's what it is."

"I'm in love with him!" The five words pierced the clutter of rhetoric, and Eden, hearing her own conviction tumble out so forcefully, was stunned. Then she took up her purse and reached inside for the ring; she placed it on the coffee table.

Cal said nothing, staring at it, then at her, searching her face as if any minute she'd grin and say this was all a joke. But when the smile didn't come, the words weren't changed or denied, she knew he believed her.

"How long have you known?"

"For a while. I tried to ignore it, but there have been too many—oh, Cal, I don't know what to call them. Inner signals, signs, connections from the past, reaffirmations since he returned." She pressed her hands onto her lap. "In a way it felt like my life was on hold until he came back. Then it started moving again, and no matter how many times I tried to tell myself I was imagining things, deep in my heart, I was facing the real me for the first time."

"And you haven't told Nick any of this?" he asked, as if he might still be able to save them.

"No. I had to talk to you first. It wasn't a choice between brothers, but a recognition of myself and who I am and what I want. That's what made coming to you and being honest so hard. I've known for a long time and I didn't want to face it because it would hurt you. It would be wrong and cruel to marry you when the feelings I have for you are gratitude, respect and friendship."

"Love can grow from those feelings," he said softly, but it was clear he understood there was no going back.

"In many ways I do love you, but it's not the deep, abiding, forever-after kind of love that should be there."

He stood, walking to the window and looking out on the starry night. "And for Nick you have this deep, abiding love?"

"Yes."

He turned, and she was reminded of how handsome and sophisticated he was. Right for some fortunate woman. Just not right for her.

Cal said, "I told Nick once that I wouldn't let him break your heart again. It appears it never mended from the last time, and now he's the one who's put it all together. I suspect on some level I've known since your less than enthusiastic reaction to the engagement. That's probably the reason I didn't shout it from the rooftops. I expected you to break it." In a resigned and weary tone, he added, "That feeling hardly boded an auspicious future."

She went to him. "You'll have a future, Cal. You're too respected and too well liked to be alone for long."

He didn't look too reassured, but she knew Cal well. Perhaps he'd brood for a few days, feel sorry for himself, but then he'd move on. Once word was out that he and Eden were no longer dating, the women would flock to him. Cal wouldn't be able to resist all that attention.

"And what about you, Eden? Are you planning to leave your job?"

"Of course not." She paused. Although their personal and professional lives shouldn't affect each other, Eden was realistic. This could be awkward for Cal. "Would you like my resignation?"

"Are you crazy? Delphine would have my head. She thinks you're running the best guidance department in Lonsdale's history. By the way, I do, too."

Eden slipped her arms around him and he reciprocated.

"Thank you for understanding," she said softly.

"Let's not go that far," he muttered. "I'm still pissed at Nick."

But Eden felt the settling of relief. She closed her eyes, recalling words she'd said to Mary in the church sanctuary. I wish there was some sign. Nick had said he loved her. For a night. For a while. Or for a lifetime. With her engagement to Cal broken, she'd soon know the answer.

The following morning, a brisk wind whipped at the few brave snowdrops on the sheltered side of Nick's duplex, but winter had lost its steel grip. The sun hovered behind struggling cumulus clouds, playing a game of catch me if you can with those trying to find some warmth in the errant sunbeams.

Today Nick intended to go see Eden. He knew she'd been home for a few days, because he'd driven by her house and seen her car. He wasn't particularly pleased by the turn of events in Chicago. He loved Eden and although that revelation was momentous and wonderful to him, he wasn't sure what to do with it. When it was just sex, it was easy. Love, he realized, was a whole new arena and frankly it scared the hell out of him. Thank God, the rest of his life wasn't in the same turmoil.

The Lonsdale Wolves were headed for the playoffs, the land he'd looked at in Franklin Woods was affordable, he had the plans for a log cabin with the accoutrements to make it more homey than rugged and his brother and he had never gotten along better.

And once he saw Eden . . . He intended to be very clear. She couldn't marry Cal. Not now.

He was about to put on his jacket when there was a knock on the door.

Nick pulled it open. "Cal? I didn't know you

were—" But he didn't get the sentence finished. Cal, with fury in his eyes, fists moving faster than the surprised Nick could get out of the way, wound up and punched him in the gut. Nick sucked in his breath and doubled over in pain. Cal shoved him back and slammed the door.

Wheezing and gasping for air, Nick counted to three and then rushed at Cal head first. Punching his brother in return finished nothing, for Cal clutched him, and the two men hit the floor with a thud.

"What the hell is wrong with you?" Nick snapped, protecting his gut from another punch.

"It what's wrong with you! You and Eden. Our engagement is broken thanks to you, you son of a bitch, and that pisses me off!"

The two men, still on the floor, glared at each other, breath coming hard. "It's over between you two?" he asked, wondering if this was a joke or some trick.

"Yeah, she told me what happened in Chicago."

"She told you?" Nick was stunned. He wouldn't have told his brother or anyone under any circumstances. "Why in God's name did she do that?"

"So I wouldn't kill you. She's in love with you, although it escapes me how she could want you when she has me." Cal scowled, staring at his brother.

Nick glared back. "Yeah, I can see how that would be a hurdle for you to get past."

"You're goddamn right." Cal leaned over and took a fistful of Nick's shirt. "So here's the word, little brother. If you hurt her or walk out on her or ever break her heart, that gut-punch will be just the beginning."

Nick was about to shove Cal away when the still-open door moved slightly.

"Well, this is quite a sight." They both swung around to where Eden stood, arms crossed, Killer and Bobby standing on either side of her. "Don't you think you two are a little old for fistfights?"

In sync, they both said no.

Nick got to his feet, as did Cal. They both brushed at their clothes.

Cal warned Nick, "Remember my words, little brother." Then, satisfied he'd made Nick understand he was serious, he offered his hand.

Nick held up his and backed away. "No, thanks. I don't want to end up on the floor again."

Eden said, "Shake your brother's hand, Nick."

Nick raised his eyebrows when Eden walked forward, took his hand and pulled him toward Cal. "Do it."

Nick complied, asking Cal, "Is she always this bossy?"

"Always." The handshake complete, Cal said, "I should say the best man won, but he obviously didn't."

"And I was the one accused of having a big ego," Nick muttered.

"Let's leave it at the right man won," Cal conceded.

Nick looked at Eden, who was grinning, and Cal, who looked as forthright as Nick believed possible. "Well, I'll be damned."

Then in a gesture the two brothers hadn't made in years, they clasped each other tightly for a short but profound moment.

Cal passed by Eden, and she caught his hand. "Did anyone ever tell you how wonderful you are."

"Yeah, you did." He kissed her forehead, then cleared his throat and added with a false sternness, "Don't forget you have a report to deliver to the school committee on Tuesday night. I know I'm wonderful, but I'm also unforgiving about late reports."

"I'll be there."

Cal was gone. Nick and Eden faced each other.

Nick scowled, closing in on her. "You could have called me and told me what happened."

A small smile twitched around her mouth. "And miss seeing you and your brother tangling like a couple of kids?"

"Just what I needed," he grumbled. "A woman who doesn't care if I have a week-long stomachache."

"Poor Nick. Fighting over true love is a tough job."

He took her by the shoulders, his hands sliding down to her hands and then to her hips, tugging her close to him. "Is it true that you're really in love with me?"

She put her arms around his neck. "How about if I give you proof?"

He cupped her bottom and lifted her against him. "I'm up for anything you want to try."

She grinned. "How about a walk in the park instead?"

"The park? Instead of me and you?" He looked genuinely disappointed. "Not my idea of stimulating."

"I promise you'll like the park," she said, kissing him before she handed him his jacket. He shrugged into it, grumbling about dumb-ass ideas when a nice warm bed would make him much happier.

The dogs trotted out in front of them and Eden slipped her hand in Nick's as they walked to Barrington Park. It wasn't until Eden came to a stop by the tree that Nick understood.

Then, while Eden watched, he stepped a bit closer to her and raised his hand to the place where he'd carved the heart and the initials. "It's been here a long time, scarred over, permanent, the lines not as sharp, weathered and old, but I remember when I carved it, I wanted it to be here forever."

"Perhaps it's a sign that stayed until we were together again." She took his hand and drew him around the trunk and showed him a freshly carved heart, this one with her initials above his.

"My God."

"One afternoon I saw you and Bobby here by this tree and I couldn't figure out what you were looking at, so after you left, I came over and saw the heart. Then I carved my own when I got home from Chicago."

He cupped her chin. "After I told you I loved you."

"Yes. I needed to hear you say it."

"And what if I hadn't?"

"Then I would have known you didn't love me, that it really was just rivalry with Cal. I would have known that the heart you carved was for yesterday and had nothing to do with today or tomorrow."

"Or forever."

"Yes."

She touched his arm. And then he turned and pulled her into his embrace, his heart bursting, a new kind of joy streaming around them. After a long kiss, he took her hand, whistled for the dogs and crossed the street to her house.

Inside, in the bedroom, their eagerness glistened into impatient kisses and touches, bodies swaying with a delicate primal energy. Clothes fell away as they tumbled across the bed, joining their bodies.

Nick raised up, looking deep into her eyes. "The last time I was here with you, we were here together and it—"

"Was wonderful and terrifying because I knew I loved you and it scared me."

"That first time should have been romance and roses and candles and love."

"It should have been as it was, Nickie."

He searched her face. "What did I ever do to deserve you?"

"You were just you. That's all I ever wanted."

"I came home to put myself back together and found the missing years when I found you."

Her fingers touched his mouth, his cheeks, brushing his chin as if she'd discovered a long-lost map. "I love you," she whispered.

Their bodies joined and lifted, then drifted down into fulfillment.

Bobby and Killer wandered in, standing side by side, tails wagging.

"I think we have company," Nick whispered.

"I think Bobby knew from the beginning," Eden said, reaching for her red hat and tossing it to him.

Bobby caught it, dropped it, woofed twice and grinned.